Charles Lamb

The Essays of Elia and Eliana

Charles Lamb

The Essays of Elia and Eliana

ISBN/EAN: 9783742820662

Manufactured in Europe, USA, Canada, Australia, Japa

Cover: Foto ©Andreas Hilbeck / pixelio.de

Manufactured and distributed by brebook publishing software
(www.brebook.com)

Charles Lamb

The Essays of Elia and Eliana

COLLECTION

OF

BRITISH AUTHORS

TAUCHNITZ EDITION.

VOL. 1038.

THE ESSAYS OF ELIA AND ELIANA
BY
CHARLES LAMB.
IN ONE VOLUME.

LEIPZIG: BERNHARD TAUCHNITZ.

PARIS: C. REINWALD, 15, RUE DES SAINTS PÈRES.

COLLECTION

OF

BRITISH AUTHORS

TAUCHNITZ EDITION.

VOL. 1038.

THE ESSAYS OF ELIA AND ELIANA
BY
CHARLES LAMB.

IN ONE VOLUME.

THE ESSAYS

OF

ELIA AND ELIANA

BY

CHARLES LAMB.

LEIPZIG

BERNHARD TAUCHNITZ

1869.

CONTENTS.

THE LAST ESSAYS OF ELIA.

CONTENTS.

ELIANA.

TO ELIA.

Elia, thy reveries and vision'd themes
    To Care's low heart a luscious pleasure prove
Wild as the mystery of delightful dreams,
    Soft as the anguish of remember'd love;
Like records of past days their memory dances,
    Mid the cool feelings manhood's reason brings,
As the unearthly visions of romances
    Peopled with sweet and uncreated things;—
And yet thy themes thy gentle worth enhances!
    Then wake again thy wild harp's tenderest strings;
Sing on, sweet bard; let fairy loves again
    Smile in thy dreams with angel extacies;
Bright o'er our souls will break the heavenly strain
    Through the dull gloom of earth's realities.

TO ELIA.

Delightful author! unto whom I owe
    Moments and moods of fancy and of feeling,
    Afresh to grateful memory now appealing,
Fain would I "bless thee ere I let thee go!"
From month to month has the exhaustless flow
    Of thy original mind, its worth revealing
    With quaintest humour and deep pathos healing
The world's rude wounds, reviv'd life's early glow;
And mixt with this, at times, to earnest thought,
    Glimpses of truth, most simple and sublime,
By thy imagination have been brought
    Over my spirit. From the olden time
Of authorship thy patent should be dated,
And thou with Marvell, Browne, and Burton mated.

BERNARD BARTON.

THE ESSAYS OF ELIA.

THE SOUTH-SEA HOUSE.

READER, in thy passage from the Bank—where thou hast been receiving thy half-yearly dividends (supposing thou art a lean annuitant like myself)—to the Flower Pot, to secure a place for Dalston, or Shacklewell, or some other thy suburban retreat northerly—didst thou never observe a melancholy-looking, handsome, brick and stone edifice, to the left, where Threadneedle Street abuts upon Bishopsgate? I dare say thou hast often admired its magnificent portals ever gaping wide, and disclosing to view a grave court, with cloisters and pillars, with few or no traces of goers-in or comers-out—a desolation something like Balclutha's.[*]

This was once a house of trade—a centre of busy interests. The throng of merchants was here—the quick pulse of gain—and here some forms of business are still kept up, though the soul be long since fled. Here are still to be seen stately porticos; imposing staircases, offices roomy as the state apartments in palaces—deserted, or thinly peopled with a few straggling clerks; the still more sacred interiors of court and committee rooms, with venerable faces of beadles, door-keepers—directors seated in form on solemn days (to proclaim a dead dividend) at long worm-eaten tables, that have been mahogany, with tarnished gilt-leather coverings, supporting massy silver inkstands long since dry;—the oaken wainscots hung with pictures of deceased governors and sub-governors, of Queen Anne, and the two first monarchs of the Brunswick dynasty;—huge charts, which subsequent discoveries have antiquated;—dusty maps of Mexico, dim as dreams, and soundings of the Bay of Panama! The long passages hung with buckets, appended, in idle row, to walls, whose substance might defy any, short of the last, conflagration:—with vast ranges of cellarage under all, where dollars and pieces of eight once lay, an "unsunned heap," for Mammon to have solaced his solitary heart withal—long since dissipated, or

[*] I passed by the walls of Balclutha, and they were desolate. — OSSIAN.

scattered into air at the blast of the breaking of that famous Bubble.——

Such is the SOUTH-SEA HOUSE. At least such it was forty years ago, when I knew it—a magnificent relic! What alterations may have been made in it since, I have had no opportunities of verifying. Time, I take for granted, has not freshened it. No wind has resuscitated the face of the sleeping waters. A thicker crust by this time stagnates upon it. The moths, that were then battening upon its obsolete ledgers and day-books, have rested from their depredations, but other light generations have succeeded, making fine fretwork among their single and double entries. Layers of dust have accumulated (a superfœtation of dirt!) upon the old layers, that seldom used to be disturbed, save by some curious finger, now and then, inquisitive to explore the mode of book-keeping in Queen Anne's reign; or, with less hallowed curiosity, seeking to unveil some of the mysteries of that tremendous HOAX, whose extent the petty peculators of our day look back upon with the same expression of incredulous admiration and hopeless ambition of rivalry as would become the puny face of modern conspiracy contemplating the Titan size of Vaux's superhuman plot.

Peace to the manes of the Bubble! Silence and destitution are upon thy walls, proud house, for a memorial!

Situated, as thou art, in the very heart of stirring and living commerce—amid the fret and fever of speculation—with the Bank, and the 'Change, and the India House about thee, in the heyday of present prosperity, with their important faces, as it were, insulting thee, their *poor neighbour out of business*—to the idle and merely contemplative—to such as me, old house! there is a charm in thy quiet:—a cessation—a coolness from business—an indolence almost cloistral—which is delightful! With what reverence have I paced thy great bare rooms and courts at eventide! They spoke of the past:—the shade of some dead accountant, with visionary pen in ear, would flit by me, stiff as in life. Living accounts and accountants puzzle me. I have no skill in figuring. But thy great dead tomes, which scarce three degenerate clerks of the present day could lift from their enshrining shelves—with their old fantastic flourishes and decorative rubric interlacings—their sums in triple columniations, set down with formal superfluity of ciphers—with pious sentences at the beginning, without which our religious ancestors never ventured to open a book of business, or bill of lading—the costly vellum covers of some of them almost persuading us that we are got into some *better library*—are very agreeable and edifying spectacles I can look upon these defunct dragons with complacency. Thy heavy odd-shaped ivory-handled penknives (our ancestors had everything on a larger scale than we have hearts for) are as good as anything from Herculaneum. The pounce-boxes of our days have gone retrograde.

The very clerks which I remember in the South-Sea House —I speak of forty years back— had an air very different from those in the public offices that I have had to do with since. They partook of the genius of the place!

They were mostly (for the establishment did not admit of superfluous salaries) bachelors. Generally (for they had not much to do) persons of a curious and speculative turn of mind. Old-fashioned, for a reason mentioned before; humourists, for they were of all descriptions; and, not having been brought together in early life (which has a tendency to assimilate the members of corporate bodies to each other), but, for the most part, placed in this house in ripe or middle age, they necessarily carried into it their separate habits and oddities, unqualified, if I may so speak, as into a common stock. Hence they formed a sort of Noah's ark. Odd fishes. A lay-monastery. Domestic retainers in a great house, kept more for show than use. Yet pleasant fellows, full of chat—and not a few among them had arrived at considerable proficiency on the German flute.

The cashier at that time was one Evans, a Cambro-Briton. He had something of the choleric complexion of his countrymen stamped on his visage, but was a worthy, sensible man at bottom. He wore his hair, to the last, powdered and frizzed out, in the fashion which I remember to have seen in caricatures of what were termed, in my young days, *Maccaronies*. He was the last of that race of beaux. Melancholy as a gib-cat over his counter all the forenoon, I think I see him making up his cash (as they call it) with tremulous fingers, as if he feared every one about him was a defaulter; in his hypochondry, ready to imagine himself one; haunted, at least, with the idea of the possibility of his becoming one: his tristful visage clearing up a little over his roast neck of veal at Anderton's at two (where his picture still hangs, taken a little before his death by desire of the master of the coffee-house, which he had frequented for the last five-and-twenty years), but not attaining the meridian of its animation till evening brought on the hour of tea and visiting. The simultaneous sound of his well-known rap at the door with the stroke of the clock announcing six, was a topic of never-failing mirth in the families which this dear old bachelor gladdened with his presence. Then was his *forte*, his glorified hour! How would he chirp and expand over a muffin! How would he dilate into secret history! His countryman, Pennant himself, in particular, could not be more elo-, quent than he in relation to old and new London—the site of old theatres, churches, streets gone to decay—where Rosamond's pond stood—the Mulberry-gardens—and the Conduit in Cheap—with many a pleasant anecdote, derived from paternal tradition, of those grotesque figures which Hogarth has immortalized in his picture of *Noon*—the worthy descendants of those heroic confessors, who, flying to this country from the wrath of Louis the Fourteenth and his dragoons, kept alive the flame of pure religion in the sheltering obscurities of Hog Lane and the vicinity of the Seven Dials!

Deputy, under Evans, was Thomas Tame. He had the air and stoop of a nobleman. You would have taken him for one, had you met him in one of the passages leading to Westminster Hall. By stoop, I mean that gentle bending of the body forwards, which, in great men, must be supposed to be the effect of an habitual condescending attention to the applications of their inferiors. While he held you in converse, you felt strained to the height in the colloquy. The conference over, you were at leisure to smile at the comparative insignificance of the pretensions which had just awed you. His intellect was of the shallowest order. It did not reach to a saw or a proverb. His mind was in its original state of white paper. A sucking babe might have posed him. What was it then? Was he rich? Alas, no! Thomas Tame was very poor. Both he and his wife looked outwardly gentlefolks, when I fear all was not well at all times within. She had a neat meagre person, which it was evident she had not sinned in over-pampering; but in its veins was noble blood. She traced her descent, by some labyrinth of relationship, which I never thoroughly understood,—much less can explain with any heraldic certainty at this time of day,—to the illustrious but unfortunate house of Derwentwater. This was the secret of Thomas's stoop. This was the thought —the sentiment—the bright solitary star of your lives,—ye mild and happy pair,—which cheered you in the night of intellect, and in the obscurity of your station! This was to you instead of riches, instead of rank, instead of glittering attainments: and it was worth them all together. You insulted none with it; but, while you wore it as a piece of defensive armour only, no insult likewise could reach you through it. *Decus et solamen.*

Of quite another stamp was the then accountant, John Tipp. He neither pretended to high blood, nor in good truth cared one fig about the matter. He "thought an accountant the greatest character in the world, and himself the greatest accountant in it." Yet John was not without his hobby. The fiddle relieved his vacant hours. He sang, certainly, with other notes than to the Orphean lyre. He did, indeed, scream and scrape most abominably. His fine suite of official rooms in Threadneedle Street, which, without anything very substantial appended to them, were enough to enlarge a man's notions of himself that lived in them (I know not who is the occupier of them now*), resounded fortnightly to the notes of a concert of "sweet breasts," as our ancestors would have called them, culled from club-rooms, and orchestras—chorus singers—first and second violoncellos—double basses—and clarionets—who ate his cold mutton and drank his punch and praised his ear. He sat like Lord Midas among them. But at the desk Tipp was quite another sort of creature. Thence all ideas, that were purely ornamental, were banished. You could not speak of anything romantic without rebuke. Politics were excluded. A newspaper was thought too refined and abstracted. The whole duty of man consisted in writing off dividend warrants. The striking of the annual balance in the company's books (which, perhaps, differed from the balance of last year in the sum of 25*l.* 1*s.* 6*d.*) occupied his days and nights for a month previous. Not that Tipp was blind to the deadness

[* I have since been informed, that the present tenant of them is a Mr. Lamb, a gentleman who is happy in the possession of some choice pictures, and among them a rare portrait of Milton, which I mean to do myself the pleasure of going to see, and at the same time to refresh my memory with the sight of old scenes. Mr. Lamb has the character of a right courteous and communicative collector.]

of *things* (as they called them in the city) in his beloved house, or did not sigh for a return of the old stirring days when South-Sea hopes were young (he was indeed equal to the wielding of any the most intricate accounts of the most flourishing company in these or those days); but to a genuine accountant the difference of proceeds is as nothing. The fractional farthing is as dear to his heart as the thousands which stand before it. He is the true actor, who, whether his part be a prince or a peasant, must act it with like intensity. With Tipp form was everything. His life was formal. His actions seemed ruled with a ruler. His pen was not less erring than his heart. He made the best executor in the world: he was plagued with incessant executorships accordingly, which excited his spleen and soothed his vanity in equal ratios. He would swear (for Tipp swore) at the little orphans, whose rights he would guard with a tenacity like the grasp of the dying hand that commended their interests to his protection. With all this there was about him a sort of timidity (his few enemies used to give it a worse name)—a something which, in reverence to the dead, we will place, if you please, a little on this side of the heroic. Nature certainly had been pleased to endow John Tipp with a sufficient measure of the principle of self-preservation. There is a cowardice which we do not despise, because it has nothing base or treacherous in its elements; it betrays itself, not you: it is mere temperament; the absence of the romantic and the enterprising; it sees a lion in the way, and will not, with Fortinbras, "greatly find quarrel in a straw," when some supposed honour is at stake. Tipp never mounted the box of a stage-coach in his life; or leaned against the rails of a balcony; or walked upon the ridge of a parapet; or looked down a precipice; or let off a gun; or went upon a water-party; or would willingly let you go if he could have helped it: neither was it recorded of him, that for lucre, or for intimidation, he ever forsook friend or principle.

Whom next shall we summon from the dusty dead, in whom common qualities become uncommon? Can I forget thee, Henry Man, the wit, the polished man of letters, the *author*, of the South-Sea House? who never enteredst thy office in a morning or quittedst it in mid-day (what didst *thou* in an office?) without some quirk that left a sting! Thy gibes and thy jokes are now extinct, or survive but in two forgotten volumes, which I had the good fortune to rescue from a stall in Barbican, not three days ago, and found thee terse, fresh, epigrammatic, as alive. Thy wit is a little gone by in these fastidious days—thy topics are staled by the "new-born gauds" of the time:—but great thou used to be in Public Ledgers, and in Chronicles, upon Chatham, and Shelburne, and Rockingham, and Howe, and Burgoyne, and Clinton, and the war which ended in the tearing from Great Britain her rebellious colonies,—and Keppel, and Wilkes, and Sawbridge, and Bull, and Dunning, and Pratt, and Richmond—and such small politics.——

A little less facetious, and a great deal more obstreperous, was fine rattling, rattleheaded Plumer. He was descended,—not in a right line, reader (for his lineal pretensions, like his personal, favoured a little of the sinister bend)—from the Plumers of Hertfordshire. So tradition gave him out; and certain family features not a little sanctioned the opinion. Certainly old Walter Plumer (his reputed author) had been a rake in his days, and visited much in Italy, and had seen the world. He was uncle, bachelor-uncle, to the fine old whig still living, who has represented the county in so many successive parliaments, and has a fine old mansion near Ware. Walter flourished in George the Second's days, and was the same who was summoned before the House of Commons about a business of franks, with the old Duchess of Marlborough. You may read of it in Johnson's Life of Cave. · Cave came off cleverly in that business. It is certain our Plumer did nothing to discountenance the rumour. He rather seemed pleased whenever it was, with all gentleness, insinuated. But besides his family pretensions, Plumer was an engaging fellow and sang gloriously.——

Not so sweetly sang Plumer as thou sangest, mild, childlike, pastoral M——; a flute's breathing less divinely whispering than thy Arcadian melodies, when, in tones worthy of Arden, thou didst chant that song sung by Amiens to the banished duke, which proclaims the winter wind more lenient than for a man to be ungrateful. Thy sire was old surly M——, the unapproachable churchwarden of Bishopsgate. He knew not what he did, when he begat thee, like spring, gentle offspring of blustering winter:—only unfortunate in thy ending, which should have been mild, conciliatory, swan-like.——

Much remains to sing. Many fantastic shapes rise up, but they must be mine in private:—already I have fooled the reader to the top of his bent;—else could I omit that strange creature Woollett, who existed in trying the question, and *bought litigations!*—and still stranger, inimitable, solemn Hepworth, from whose gravity Newton might have deduced the law of gravitation. How profoundly would he nib a pen—with what deliberation would he wet a wafer!——

But it is time to close—night's wheels are rattling fast over me—it is proper to have done with this solemn mockery.

Reader, what if I have been playing with thee all this while—peradventure the very *names*, which I have summoned up before thee, are fantastic—insubstantial —like Henry Pimpernel, and old John Naps of Greece:—

Be satisfied that something answering to them has had a being. Their importance is from the past.

OXFORD IN THE VACATION.

CASTING a preparatory glance at the bottom of this article—as the very connoisseur in prints, with cursory eye (which, while it reads, seems as though it read not), never fails to consult the *quis sculpsit* in the corner, before he pronounces some rare piece to be a Vivares, or a Woollett—methinks I hear you exclaim, Reader, *Who is Elia?*

Because in my last I tried to divert thee with some half-forgotten humours of some old clerks defunct, in an old house of business, long since gone to decay, doubtless you have already set me down in your mind as one of the selfsame college—a votary of the desk—a notched and cropt scrivener—one that sucks his sustenance, as certain sick people are said to do, through a quill.

Well, I do agnise something of the sort. I confess that it is my humour, my fancy—in the forepart of the day, when the mind of your man of letters requires some relaxation (and none better than such as at first sight seems most abhorrent from his beloved studies)—to while away some good hours of my time in the contemplation of indigos, cottons, raw silks, piece-goods, flowered or otherwise. In the first place • • • • • • • • and then it sends you home with such increased appetite to your books • • • • • not to say, that your outside sheets, and waste wrappers of foolscap, do receive into them, most kindly and naturally, the impression of sonnets, epigrams, *essays*—so that the very parings of a counting-house are, in some sort, the settings up of an author. The enfranchised quill, that has plodded all the morning among the cart-rucks of figures and ciphers, frisks and curvets so at its ease over the flowery carpet-ground of a midnight dissertation.—It feels its promotion. • • • • So that you see, upon the whole, the literary dignity of *Elia* is very little, if at all, compromised in the condescension.

Not that, in my anxious detail of the many commodities incidental to the life of a public office, I would be thought blind to certain flaws, which a cunning carper might be able to pick in this Joseph's vest. And here I must have leave, in the fulness of my soul, to regret the abolition, and doing-away-with altogether, of those consolatory interstices, and sprinklings of freedom, through the four seasons,—the *red-letter days*, now become, to all intents and purposes, *dead-letter days*. There was Paul, and Stephen, and Barnabas—

Andrew and John, men famous in old times

—we were used to keep all their days holy, as long back as when I was at school at Christ's. I remember their effigies, by the same token, in the old Basket Prayer Book. There hung Peter in his uneasy posture—holy Bartlemy in the troublesome act of flaying, after the famous Marsyas by Spagnoletti.—I honoured them all, and could almost have wept the defalcation of Iscariot—so much did we love to keep holy memories sacred:—only methought I a little grudged at the coalition of the *better Jude* with Simon—clubbing (as it were) their sanctities together, to make up one poor gaudy-day between them—as an economy unworthy of the dispensation.

These were bright visitations in a scholar's and a clerk's life— "far off their coming shone."—I was as good as an almanac in those days. I could have told you such a saint's-day falls out next week, or the week after. Peradventure the Epiphany, by some periodical infelicity, would, once in six years, merge in a Sabbath. Now am I little better than one of the profane. Let me not be thought to arraign the wisdom of my civil superiors, who have judged the further observation of these holy tides to be papistical, superstitious. Only in a custom of such long standing, methinks, if their Holinesses the Bishops had, in decency, been first sounded— but I am wading out of my depths. I am not the man to decide the limits of civil and ecclesiastical authority—I am plain Elia—no

Selden, nor Archbishop Usher—though at present in the thick of their books, here in the heart of learning, under the shadow of the mighty Bodley.

I can here play the gentleman, enact the student. To such a one as myself, who has been defrauded in his young years of the sweet food of academic institution, nowhere is so pleasant, to while away a few idle weeks at, as one or other of the Universities. Their vacation, too, at this time of the year, falls in so pat with *ours*. Here I can take my walks unmolested, and fancy myself of what degree or standing I please. I seem admitted *ad eundem*. I fetch up past opportunities. I can rise at the chapel-bell, and dream that it rings for *me*. In moods of humility I can be a Sizar, or a Servitor. When the peacock vein rises, I strut a Gentleman Commoner. In graver moments, I proceed Master of Arts. Indeed I do not think I am much unlike that respectable character. I have seen your dim-eyed vergers, and bed-makers in spectacles, drop a bow or a curtsy, as I pass, wisely mistaking me for something of the sort. I go about in black, which favours the notion. Only in Christ Church reverend quadrangle I can be content to pass for nothing short of a Seraphic Doctor.

The walks at these times are so much one's own,—the tall trees of Christ's, the groves of Magdalen! The halls deserted, and with open doors, inviting one to slip in unperceived, and pay a devoir to some Founder, or noble or royal Benefactress (that should have been ours) whose portrait seems to smile upon their over-looked beadsman, and to adopt me for their own. Then, to take a peep in by the way at the butteries, and sculleries, redolent of antique hospitality: the immense caves of kitchens, kitchen fire-places, cordial recesses; ovens whose first pies were baked four centuries ago; and spits which have cooked for Chaucer! Not the meanest minister among the dishes but is hallowed to me through his imagination, and the Cook goes forth a Manciple.

Antiquity! thou wondrous charm, what art thou? that, being nothing, art everything! When thou *wert*, thou wert not antiquity—then thou wert nothing, but hadst a remoter *antiquity*, as thou calledst it, to look back to with blind veneration; thou thyself being to thyself flat, jejune, *modern*! What mystery lurks in this retroversion? or what half Januses* are we, that cannot look forward with the same idolatry with which we for ever revert! The mighty future is as nothing, being everything! the past is everything, being nothing!

What were thy *dark ages*? Surely the sun rose as brightly then as now, and man got him to his work in the morning? Why is it we can never hear mention of them without an accompanying feeling, as though a palpable ob-

* Januses of one face.—
SIR THOMAS BROWNE.

scure had dimmed the face of things, and that our ancestors wandered to and fro groping!

Above all thy rarities, old Oxenford, what do most arride and solace me, are thy repositories of mouldering learning, thy shelves——

What a place to be in is an old library! It seems as though all the souls of all the writers, that have bequeathed their labours to these Bodleians, were reposing here, as in some dormitory, or middle state. I do not want to handle, to profane the leaves, their winding-sheets. I could as soon dislodge a shade. I seem to inhale learning, walking amid their foliage; and the odour of their old moth-scented coverings is fragrant as the first bloom of those sciential apples which grew amid the happy orchard.

Still less have I curiosity to disturb the elder repose of MSS. Those *variæ lectiones*, so tempting to the more erudite palates, do but disturb and unsettle my faith. I am no Herculanean raker. The credit of the three witnesses might have slept unimpeached for me. I leave these curiosities to Porson, and to G. D.—whom, by the way, I found busy as a moth over some rotten archive, rummaged out of some seldom-explored press, in a nook at Oriel. With long poring, he is grown almost into a book. He stood as passive as one by the side of the old shelves. I longed to new-coat him in russia, and assign him his place. He might have mustered for a tall Scapula.

D. is assiduous in his visits to these seats of learning. No inconsiderable portion of his moderate fortune, I apprehend, is consumed in journeys between them and Clifford's Inn—where, like a dove on the asp's nest, he has long taken up his unconscious abode, amid an incongruous assembly of attorneys, attorneys' clerks, apparitors, promoters, vermin of the law, among whom he sits, "in calm and sinless peace." The fangs of the law pierce him not—the winds of litigation blow over his humble chambers—the hard sheriff's officer moves his hat as he passes—legal nor illegal discourtesy touches him—none thinks of offering violence or injustice to him—you would as soon "strike an abstract idea."

D. has been engaged, he tells me, through a course of laborious years, in an investigation into all curious matter connected with the two Universities; and has lately lit upon a MS. collection of charters, relative to C——, by which he hopes to settle some disputed points—particularly that long controversy between them as to priority of foundation. The ardour with which he engages in these liberal pursuits, I am afraid, has not met with all the encouragement it deserved, either here or at C——. Your caputs, and heads of colleges, care less than anybody else about these questions.— Contented to suck the milky fountains of their Alma Maters, without inquiring into the venerable gentlewomen's years, they rather hold such curiosities to be impertinent—unreverend. They have their good glebe lands *in manu*, and care not much to rake into the title-deeds. I gather at least so much from other sources, for D. is not a man to complain.

D. started like an unbroke heifer, when I interrupted him. *A priori* it was not very probable that we should have met in Oriel. But D. would have done the same, had I accosted him on the sudden in his own walks in Clifford's Inn, or in the Temple. In addition to a provoking short-sightedness (the effect of late studies and watchings at the midnight oil) D. is the most absent of men. He made a call the other morning at our friend M.'s in Bedford Square; and, finding nobody at home, was ushered into the hall, where, asking for pen and ink, with great exactitude of purpose he enters me his name in the book—which ordinarily lies about in such places, to record the failures of the untimely or unfortunate visitor—and takes his leave with many ceremonies, and professions of regret. Some two or three hours after, his walking destinies returned him into the same neighbourhood again, and again the quiet image of the fireside circle at M.'s—Mrs. M. presiding at it like a Queen Lar, with pretty A. S. at her side—striking irresistibly on his fancy, he makes another call (forgetting that they were "certainly not to return from the country before that day week") and disappointed a second time,

inquires for pen and paper as before: again the book is brought, and in the line just above that in which he is about to print his second name (his re-script)—his first name (scarce dry) looks out upon him like another Sosia, or as if a man should suddenly encounter his own duplicate!—The effect may be conceived. D. made many a good resolution against any such lapses in future. I hope he will not keep them too rigorously.

For with G. D.—to be absent from the body, is sometimes (not to speak it profanely) to be present with the Lord. At the very time when, personally encountering thee, he passes on with no recognition——or, being stopped, starts like a thing surprised—at that moment, reader, he is on Mount Tabor—or Parnassus - or co-sphered with Plato—or, with Harrington, framing "immortal common-wealths"—devising some plan of amelioration to thy country, or thy species——peradventure meditating some individual kindness or courtesy, to be done to *thee thyself*, the returning consciousness of which made him to start so guiltily at thy obtruded personal presence.

[D. commenced life, after a course of hard study in the house of "pure Emanuel," as usher to a knavish fanatic schoolmaster at * * *, at a salary of eight pounds per annum, with board and lodging. Of this poor stipend, he never received above half in all the laborious years he served this man. He tells a pleasant anecdote, that when poverty, staring out at his ragged knees, has sometimes compelled him, against the modesty of his nature, to hint at arrears, Dr. * * * would take no immediate notice, but after supper, when the school was called together to even-song, he would never fail to introduce some instructive homily against riches, and the corruption of the heart occasioned through the desire of them—ending with "Lord, keep 'Thy servants, above all things, from the heinous sin of avarice. Having food and raiment, let us therewithal be content. Give me Hagar's wish"—and the like—which, to the little auditory, sounded like a doctrine full of Christian prudence and simplicity, but to poor D. was a receipt in full for that quarter's demand at least.

And D. has been under-working for himself ever since;—drudging at low rates for unappreciating booksellers,—wasting his fine erudition in silent corrections of the classics, and in those unostentatious but solid services to learning which commonly fall to the lot of laborious scholars, who have not the heart to sell themselves to the best advantage. He has published poems, which do not sell, because their character is unobtrusive, like his own, and because he has been too much absorbed in ancient literature to know what the popular mark in poetry is, even if he could have hit it. And, therefore, his verses are properly, what he terms them, *crotchets*; voluntaries; odes to liberty and spring; effusions; little tributes and offerings, left behind him upon tables and window-seats at parting from friends' houses; and from all the inns of hospitality, where he has been courteously (or but tolerably) received in his pilgrimage. If his muse of kindness halt a little behind the strong lines in fashion in this excitement-loving age, his prose is the best of the sort in the world, and exhibits a faithful transcript of his own healthy, natural mind, and cheerful, innocent tone of conversation.]

D. is delightful anywhere, but he is at the best in such places as these. He cares not much for Bath. He is out of his element at Buxton, at Scarborough, or Harrowgate. The Cam and the Isis are to him "better than all the waters of Damascus." On the Muses' hill he is happy, and good, as one of the Shepherds on the Delectable Mountains; and when he goes about with you to show you the halls and colleges, you think you have with you the Interpreter at the House Beautiful.

———

CHRIST'S HOSPITAL

FIVE AND THIRTY YEARS AGO.

In Mr. Lamb's "Works," published a year or two since, I find a magnificent eulogy on my old school,* such as it was, or now appears to him to have been, be-

* Recollections of Christ's Hospital.

tween the years 1782 and 1789. It happens, very oddly, that my own standing at Christ's was nearly corresponding with his; and, with all gratitude to him for his enthusiasm for the cloisters, I think he has contrived to bring together whatever can be said in praise of them, dropping all the other side of the argument most ingeniously.

I remember L. at school; and can well recollect that he had some peculiar advantages, which I and others of his schoolfellows had not. His friends lived in town, and were near at hand; and he had the privilege of going to see them, almost as often as he wished, through some invidious distinction, which was denied to us. The present worthy subtreasurer to the Inner Temple can explain how that happened. He had his tea and hot rolls in a morning, while we were battening upon our quarter of a penny loaf—our *crug*—moistened with attenuated small beer, in wooden piggins, smacking of the pitched leathern jack it was poured from. Our Monday's milk porritch, blue and tasteless, and the pease soup of Saturday, coarse and choking, were enriched for him with a slice of "extraordinary bread and butter," from the hot-loaf of the Temple. The Wednesday's mess of millet, somewhat less repugnant (we had three banyan to four meat days in the week)—was endeared to his palate with a lump of double-refined, and a smack of ginger (to make it go down the more glibly) or the fragrant cinnamon. In lieu of our *half-pickled* Sundays, or *quite fresh* boiled beef on Thursdays (strong as *caro equina*), with detestable marigolds floating in the pail to poison the broth—our scanty mutton scrags on Fridays—and rather more savoury, but grudging, portions of the same flesh, rotten-roasted or rare, on the Tuesdays (the only dish which excited our appetites, and disappointed our stomachs, in almost equal proportion)—he had his hot plate of roast veal, or the more tempting griskin (exotics unknown to our palates), cooked in the paternal kitchen (a great thing), and brought him daily by his maid or aunt! I remember the good old relative (in whom love forbade pride) squatting down upon some odd stone in a by-nook of the cloisters, disclosing the viands (of higher regale than those cates which the ravens ministered to the Tishbite); and the contending passions of L. at the unfolding. There was love for the bringer; shame for the thing brought, and the manner of its bringing; sympathy for those who were too many to share in it; and, at top of all, hunger (eldest, strongest of the passions!) predominant, breaking down the stony fences of shame, and awkwardness, and a troubling overconsciousness.

I was a poor friendless boy. My parents, and those who should care for me, were far away. Those few acquaintances of theirs, which they could reckon upon being kind to me in the great city, after a little forced notice, which they had the grace to take of me on my first arrival in town, soon grew tired of my holiday visits. They seemed to them to recur too often, though I thought them few enough; and, one after another, they all failed me, and I felt myself alone among six hundred playmates.

O the cruelty of separating a poor lad from his early homestead! The yearnings which I used to have towards it in those unfledged years! How, in my dreams, would my native town (far in the west) come back, with its church, and trees, and faces! How I would wake weeping, and in the anguish of my heart exclaim upon sweet Calne in Wiltshire!

To this late hour of my life, I trace impressions left by the recollection of those friendless holidays. The long warm days of summer never return but they bring with them a gloom from the haunting memory of those *whole-day-leaves*, when, by some strange arrangement, we were turned out, for the live-long day, upon our own hands, whether we had friends to go to, or none. I remember those bathing-excursions to the New River, which L. recalls with such relish, better, I think, than he can—for he was a home-seeking lad, and did not much care for such water-pastimes:—How merrily we would sally forth into the fields; and strip under the first warmth of the sun; and wanton like young dace in the streams; getting us appetites for noon, which those of us that were penniless (our scanty morning crust long since exhausted) had not the means of allaying—while the cattle, and the birds, and the fishes, were at feed about us, and we had nothing to satisfy our cravings—the very beauty of the day, and the exercise of the pastime, and the sense of liberty, setting a keener edge upon them! —How faint and languid, finally, we would return, towards nightfall, to our desired morsel, half-rejoicing, half-reluctant, that the hours of our uneasy liberty had expired!

It was worse in the days of winter, to go prowling about the streets objectless—shivering at cold windows of print shops, to extract a little amusement; or haply, as a last resort, in the hopes of a little novelty, to pay a fifty-times repeated visit (where our individual faces should be as well known to the warden as those of his own charges) to the Lions in the Tower—to whose levée, by courtesy immemorial, we had a prescriptive title to admission.

L.'s governor (so we called the patron who presented us to the foundation) lived in a manner under his paternal roof. Any complaint which he had to make was sure of being attended to. This was understood at Christ's, and was an effectual screen to him against the severity of masters, or worse tyranny of the monitors. The oppressions of these young brutes are heart-sickening to call to recollection. I have been called out of my bed, and *waked for the purpose*, in the coldest winter nights—and this not once, but night after night—in my shirt, to receive the discipline of a leathern thong, with eleven other sufferers, because it pleased my callow overseer, when there has been any talking heard after we were gone to bed, to make the six last beds in the dormitory, where the youngest children of us slept, answerable for an offence they neither dared to commit, nor had the power to hinder.—The same execrable tyranny drove the younger part of us from the fires, when our feet were perishing with snow; and, under the cruelest penalties, forbade the indulgence of a drink of water, when we lay in sleepless summer nights, fevered with the season, and the day's sports.

There was one H——, who, I learned in after days, was seen expiating some maturer offence in the hulks. (Do I flatter myself in fancying that this might be the planter of that name, who suffered—at Nevis, I think, or St. Kitts,—some few years since? My friend Tobin was the benevolent instrument of bringing him to the gallows.) This petty Nero actually branded a boy, who had offended him, with a red-hot iron; and nearly starved forty of us, with exacting contributions, to the one half of our bread, to pamper a young ass, which, incredible as it may seem, with the connivance of the nurse's daughter (a young flame of his) he had contrived to smuggle in, and keep upon the leads of the *ward*, as they called our dormitories. This game went on for better than a week, till the foolish beast, not able to fare well but he must cry roast meat—happier than Caligula's minion, could he have kept his own counsel—but, foolisher, alas! than any of his species in the fables—waxing fat, and kicking, in the fulness of bread, one unlucky minute would needs proclaim his good fortune to the world below; and, laying out his simple throat, blew such a ram's horn blast, as (toppling down the walls of his own Jericho) set concealment any longer at defiance. The client was dismissed, with certain attentions, to Smithfield; but I never understood that the patron underwent any censure on the occasion. This was in the stewardship of L.'s admired Perry.

Under the same *facile* administration, can L. have forgotten the cool impunity with which the nurses used to carry away openly, in open platters, for their own tables, one out of two of every hot joint, which the careful matron had been seeing scrupulously weighed out for our dinners? These things were daily practised in that magnificent apartment, which L. (grown connoisseur since, we presume) praises so highly for the grand paintings "by Verrio and others," with which it is "hung round and adorned." But the sight of sleek well-fed blue-coat boys in pictures was, at that time, I believe, little consolatory to him, or us, the living ones, who saw the better part of our provisions carried away before our faces by harpies; and ourselves reduced (with the Trojan in the hall of Dido)

To feed our mind with idle portraiture.

L. has recorded the repugnance of the school to *gags*, or the fat of fresh beef boiled; and sets it down to some superstition. But these unctuous morsels are never grateful to young palates (children are universally fat-haters), and in strong, coarse, boiled meats, *unsalted*, are detestable. A *gay-eater* in our time was equivalent to a *goule*, and held in equal detestation. —— suffered under the imputation:

> . . . . 'Twas said
> He ate strange flesh.

He was observed, after dinner, carefully to gather up the remnants left at his table (not many, nor very choice fragments, you may credit me)—and, in an especial manner, these disreputable morsels, which he would convey away, and secretly stow in the settle that stood at his bedside. None saw when he ate them. It was rumoured that he privately devoured them in the night. He was watched, but no traces of such midnight practices were discoverable. Some reported, that, on leave-days, he had been seen to carry out of the bounds a large blue check handkerchief, full of something. This then must be the accursed thing. Conjecture next was at work to imagine how he could dispose of it. Some said he sold it to the beggars. This belief generally prevailed. He went about moping. None spake to him. No one would play with him. He was excommunicated; put out of the pale of the school. He was too powerful a boy to be beaten, but he underwent every mode of that negative punishment, which is more grievous than many stripes. Still he persevered. At length he was observed by two of his schoolfellows, who were determined to get at the secret, and had traced him one leave-day for the purpose, to enter a large worn-out building, such as there exist specimens of in Chancery Lane, which are let out to various scales of pauperism, with open door, and a common staircase. After him they silently slunk in, and followed by stealth up four flights, and saw him tap at a poor wicket, which was opened by an aged woman, meanly clad. Suspicion was now ripened into certainty. The informers had secured their victim. They had him in their toils. Accusation was formally preferred, and retribution most signal was looked for. Mr. Hathaway, the then steward (for this happened a little after my time), with that patient sagacity which tempered all his conduct, determined to investigate the matter, before he proceeded to sentence. The result was, that the supposed mendicants, the receivers or purchasers of the mysterious scraps, turned out to be the parents of ——, an honest couple come to decay,—whom this seasonable supply had, in all probability, saved from mendicancy; and that this young stork, at the expense of his own good name, had all this while been only feeding the old birds! —The governors on this occasion, much to their honour, voted a present relief to the family of ——, and presented him with a silver medal. The lesson which the steward read upon RASH JUDGMENT, on the occasion of publicly delivering the medal to ——, I believe, would not be lost upon his auditory.—I had left school then, but I well remember ——. He was a tall, shambling youth, with a cast in his eye, not at all calculated to conciliate hostile prejudices. I have since seen him carrying a baker's basket. I think I heard he did not do quite so well by himself as he had done by the old folks.

I was a hypochondriac lad; and the sight of a boy in fetters, upon the day of my first putting on the blue clothes, was not exactly fitted to assuage the natural terrors of initiation. I was of tender years, barely turned of seven; and had only read of such things in books, or seen them but in dreams. I was told he had *run away*. This was the punishment for the first offence.—As a novice I was soon after taken to see the dungeons. These were little, square, Bedlam cells, where a boy could just lie at his length upon straw and a blanket—a mattress, I think, was afterwards substituted—with a peep of light, let in askance, from a prison-orifice at top, barely enough to read by. Here the poor boy was locked in by himself all day, without sight of any but the porter who brought him his bread and water—who *might not speak to him;*—or of the beadle, who came twice a week to call him out to receive his periodical chastisement, which was almost welcome, because it separated him for a brief interval from solitude:—and here he was shut up by himself *of nights*, out of the reach of any sound, to suffer whatever horrors the weak nerves, and superstition incident to his time of life, might subject him to.* This was the penalty for the second offence. Wouldst thou like, reader, to see what became of him in the next degree?

The culprit, who had been a third time an offender, and whose expulsion was at this time deemed irreversible, was brought forth, as at some solemn *auto da fé*, arrayed in uncouth and most

* One or two instances of lunacy, or attempted suicide, accordingly, at length convinced the governors of the impolicy of this part of the sentence, and the midnight torture to the spirits was dispensed with.—This fancy of dungeons for children was a sprout of Howard's brain; for which (saving the reverence due to Holy Paul) methinks I could willingly spit upon his statue.

appalling attire—all trace of his late "watchet-weeds" carefully effaced, he was exposed in a jacket, resembling those which London lamplighters formerly delighted in, with a cap of the same. The effect of this divestiture was such as the ingenious devisers of it could have anticipated. With his pale and frighted features, it was as if some of those disfigurements in Dante had seized upon him. In this disguisement he was brought into the hall (*L.'s favourite state-room*), where awaited him the whole number of his schoolfellows, whose joint lessons and sports he was thenceforth to share no more; the awful presence of the steward, to be seen for the last time; of the executioner beadle, clad in his state robe for the occasion; and of two faces more, of direr import, because never but in these extremities visible. These were governors; two of whom, by choice, or charter, were always accustomed to officiate at these *Ultima Supplicia;* not to mitigate (so at least we understood it), but to enforce the uttermost stripe. Old Bamber Gascoigne, and Peter Aubert, I remember, were colleagues on one occasion, when the beadle turning rather pale, a glass of brandy was ordered to prepare him for the mysteries. The scourging was, after the old Roman fashion, long and stately. The lictor accompanied the criminal quite round the hall. We were generally too faint with attending to the previous disgusting circum-

stances to make accurate report with our eyes of the degree of corporal suffering inflicted. Report, of course, gave out the back knotty and livid. After scourging, he was made over, in his *San Benito*, to his friends, if he had any (but commonly such poor runagates were friendless), or to his parish officer, who, to enhance the effect of the scene, had his station allotted to him on the outside of the hall gate.

These solemn pageantries were not played off so often as to spoil the general mirth of the community. We had plenty of exercise and recreation *after* school hours; and, for myself, I must confess, that I was never happier than *in* them. The Upper and the Lower Grammar Schools were held in the same room; and an imaginary line only divided their bounds. Their character was as different as that of the inhabitants on the two sides of the Pyrenees. The Rev. James Boyer was the Upper Master; but the Rev. Matthew Feilde presided over that portion of the apartment, of which I had the good fortune to be a member. We lived a life as careless as birds. We talked and did just what we pleased, and nobody molested us. We carried an accidence, or a grammar, for form; but, for any trouble it gave us, we might take two years in getting through the verbs deponent, and another two in forgetting all that we had learned about them. There was now and then the formality of saying a lesson, but if you had not learned it, a brush across the shoulders (just enough to disturb a fly) was the sole remonstrance. Feilde never used the rod; and in truth he wielded the cane with no great good will—holding it "like a dancer." It looked in his hands rather like an emblem than an instrument of authority; and an emblem, too, he was ashamed of. He was a good easy man, that did not care to ruffle his own peace, nor perhaps set any great consideration upon the value of juvenile time. He came among us, now and then, but often staid away whole days from us; and when he came, it made no difference to us—he had his private room to retire to, the short time he staid, to be out of the sound of our noise. Our mirth and uproar went on. We had classics of our own, without being beholden to "insolent Greece or haughty Rome," that passed current among us—Peter Wilkins—the Adventures of the Hon. Captain Robert Boyle—the Fortunate Blue-coat Boy—and the like. Or we cultivated a turn for mechanic and scientific operations; making little sun-dials of paper; or weaving those ingenious parentheses, called *cat-cradles;* or making dry peas to dance upon the end of a tin pipe; or studying the art military over that laudable game "French and English," and a hundred other such devices to pass away the time—mixing the useful with the agreeable—as would have made the souls of Rousseau and John Locke chuckle to have seen us.

Matthew Feilde belonged to that class of modest divines who affect to mix in equal proportion the *gentleman,* the *scholar,* and the *Christian;* but, I know not how, the first ingredient is generally found to be the predominating dose in the composition. He was engaged in gay parties, or with his courtly bow at some episcopal levée, when he should have been attending upon us. He had for many years the classical charge of a hundred children, during the four or five first years of their education; and his very highest form seldom proceeded further than two or three of the introductory fables of Phædrus. How things were suffered to go on thus, I cannot guess. Boyer, who was the proper person to have remedied these abuses, always affected, perhaps felt, a delicacy in interfering in a province not strictly his own. I have not been without my suspicions, that he was not altogether displeased at the contrast we presented to his end of the school. We were a sort of Helots to his young Spartans. He would sometimes, with ironic deference, send to borrow a rod of the Under Master, and then, with Sardonic grin, observe to one of his upper boys, "how neat and fresh the twigs looked." While his pale students were battering their brains over Xenophon and Plato, with a silence as deep as that enjoined by the Samite, we were enjoying ourselves at our ease in our little Goshen. We saw a little into the secrets of his discipline, and the prospect did but the more reconcile us to our lot. His thunders rolled innocuous for us; his storms came near, but never touched us; contrary to Gideon's miracle, while all around were drenched, our fleece was dry.* His boys turned out the better scholars; we, I suspect, have the advantage in temper. His pupils cannot speak of him without something of terror allaying their gratitude; the remembrance of Feilde comes back with all the soothing images of indolence, and summer slumbers, and work like play, and innocent idleness, and Elysian exemptions, and life itself a "playing holiday."

Though sufficiently removed from the jurisdiction of Boyer, we were near enough (as I have said) to understand a little of his system. We occasionally heard sounds of the *Ululantes*, and caught glances of Tartarus. B. was a rabid pedant. His English style was crampt to barbarism. His Easter anthems (for his duty obliged him to those periodical flights) were grating as **scrannel** pipes.**—He would laugh—ay, and heartily— but then it must be at Flaccus's quibble about *Rex*——or at the *tristis severitas in vultu*, or *inspicere in patinas*, of Terence—thin jests, which at their first broaching could hardly have had *vis* enough to move a Roman muscle.—He had two wigs, both pedantic, but of different omen. The one serene, smiling, fresh powdered, betokening a mild day. The other, an old discoloured, unkempt, angry caxon, denoting frequent and bloody execution. Woe to the school, when he made his morning appearance in his *passy*, or *passionate wig*. No comet expounded surer.—J. B. had a heavy hand. I have known him double his knotty fist at a poor trembling child (the maternal milk hardly dry upon its lips) with a "Sirrah, do you presume to set your wits at me?"—Nothing was more common than to see him make a headlong entry into the school-room, from his inner recess, or library, and, with turbulent eye, singling out a lad, roar out, "Od's my life, sirrah" (his favourite adjuration), "I have a great mind to whip you,"—then, with as sudden a retracting impulse, fling back into his lair—and, after a cooling lapse of some minutes (during which all but the culprit had totally forgotten the context) drive headlong out again, piecing out his imperfect sense, as if it had

* Cowley.

** In this and everything B. was the antipodes of his coadjutor. While the former was digging his brains for crude anthems, worth a pig-nut, F. would be recreating his gentlemanly fancy in the more flowery walks of the Muses. A little dramatic effusion of his, under the name of Vertumnus and Pomona, is not yet forgotten by the chroniclers of that sort of literature. It was accepted by Garrick, but the town did not give it their sanction.—B. used to say of it, in a way of half-compliment, half-irony that it was too classical for representation.

been some Devil's Litany, with the expletory yell—"*and I will too.*"—In his gentler moods, when the *rabidus furor* was assuaged, he had resort to an ingenious method, peculiar, for what I have heard, to himself, of whipping the boy, and reading the Debates, at the same time; a paragraph and a lash between; which in those times, when parliamentary oratory was most at a height and flourishing in these realms, was not calculated to impress the patient with a veneration for the diffuser graces of rhetoric.

Once, and but once, the uplifted rod was known to fall ineffectual from his hand—when droll squinting W—— having been caught putting the inside of the master's desk to a use for which the architect had clearly not designed it, to justify himself, with great simplicity averred, that *he did not know that the thing had been forewarned.* This exquisite irrecognition of any law antecedent to the *oral* or *declaratory*, struck so irresistibly upon the fancy of all who heard it (the pedagogue himself not excepted) that remission was unavoidable.

L. has given credit to B.'s great merits as an instructor. Coleridge, in his literary life, has pronounced a more intelligible and ample encomium on them. The author of the Country Spectator doubts not to compare him with the ablest teachers of antiquity. Perhaps we cannot dismiss him better than with the pious ejaculation of C.—when he heard that his old master was on his death-bed: "Poor J. B.!—may all his faults be forgiven; and may he be wafted to bliss by little cherub boys, all head and wings, with no *bottoms* to reproach his sublunary infirmities."

Under him were many good and sound scholars bred.—First Grecian of my time was Lancelot Pepys Stevens, kindest of boys and men, since Co-grammarmaster (and inseparable companion) with Dr. T——e. What an edifying spectacle did this brace of friends present to those who remembered the anti-socialities of their predecessors!—You never met the one by chance in the street without a wonder, which was quickly dissipated by the almost immediate subappearance of the other. Generally arm-in-arm, these kindly coadjutors lightened for each other the toilsome duties of their profession, and when, in advanced age, one found it convenient to retire, the other was not long in discovering that it suited him to lay down the fasces also. Oh, it is pleasant, as it is rare, to find the same arm linked in yours at forty, which at thirteen helped it to turn over the *Cicero De Amicitiâ*, or some tale of Antique Friendship, which the young heart even then was burning to anticipate!—Co-Grecian with S. was Th——, who has since executed with ability various diplomatic functions at the Northern courts. Th—— was a tall, dark, saturnine youth, sparing of speech, with raven locks.—

Thomas Fanshaw Middleton followed him (now Bishop of Calcutta), a scholar and a gentleman in his teens. He has the reputation of an excellent critic; and is author (besides the Country Spectator) of a Treatise on the Greek Article, against Sharpe.—M. is said to bear his mitre high in India, where the *regni novitas* (I dare say) sufficiently justifies the bearing. A humility quite as primitive as that of Jewel or Hooker might not be exactly fitted to impress the minds of those Anglo-Asiatic diocesans with a reverence for home institutions, and the church which those fathers watered. The manners of M. at school, though firm, were mild and unassuming.—Next to M. (if not senior to him) was Richards, author of the Aboriginal Britons, the most spirited of the Oxford Prize Poems; a pale, studious Grecian.—Then followed poor S——, ill-fated M——! of these the Muse is silent.

Finding some of Edward's race
Unhappy, pass their annals by.

Come back into memory, like as thou wert in the day-spring of thy fancies, with hope like a fiery column before thee—the dark pillar not yet turned—Samuel Taylor Coleridge—Logician, Metaphysician, Bard!—How have I seen the casual passer through the Cloisters stand still, intranced with admiration (while he weighed the disproportion between the *speech* and the *garb* of the young Mirandula), to hear thee unfold, in thy deep and sweet intonations, the mysteries of Jamblichus, or Plotinus (for even in those years thou waxedst not pale at such philosophic draughts) or reciting Homer in his Greek, or Pindar ——while the walls of the old Grey Friars re-echoed to the accents of the *inspired charity-boy!* —Many were the "wit-combats" (to dally awhile with the words of old Fuller), between him and C. V. Le G——, "which two I behold like a Spanish great galleon, and an English man of war: Master Coleridge, like the former, was built far higher in learning, solid, but slow in his performances. C. V. L., with the English man of war, lesser in bulk, but lighter in sailing, could turn with all times, tack about, and take advantage of all winds, by the quickness of his wit and invention."

Nor shalt thou, their compeer, be quickly forgotten, Allen, with the cordial smile, and still more cordial laugh, with which thou wert wont to make the old Cloisters shake, in thy cognition of some poignant jest of theirs; or the anticipation of some more material, and, peradventure practical one, of thine own. Extinct are those smiles, with that beautiful countenance, with which (for thou wert the *Nireus formosus* of the school), in the days of thy maturer waggery, thou didst disarm the wrath of infuriated town-damsel, who, incensed by provoking pinch, turning tigress-like round, suddenly converted by thy angel-look, exchanged the half-formed terrible "*bl*——," for a gentler greeting—"*bless thy handsome face!*"

Next follow two, who ought to be now alive, and the friends of Elia—the junior Le G—— and F——; who impelled, the former by a roving temper, the latter by too quick a sense of neglect—ill capable of enduring the slights poor Sizars are sometimes subject to in our seats of learning—exchanged their Alma Mater for the camp; perishing, one by climate, and one on the plains of Salamanca:—Le G——, sanguine, volatile, sweet-natured; F——, dogged, faithful, anticipative of insult, warm-hearted, with something of the old Roman height about him.

Fine, frank-hearted Fr——, the present master of Hertford, with Marmaduke T——, mildest of Missionaries—and both my good friends still—close the catalogue of Grecians in my time.

———

THE TWO RACES OF MEN.

THE human species, according to the best theory I can form of it, is composed of two distinct races, *the men who borrow, and the men who lend*. To these two original diversities may be reduced all those impertinent classifications of Gothic and Celtic tribes, white men, black men, red men. All the dwellers upon earth, "Parthians, and Medes, and Elamites," flock hither, and do naturally fall in with one or other of these primary distinctions. The infinite superiority of the former, which I choose to designate as the *great race*, is discernible in their figure, port, and a certain instinctive sovereignty. The latter are born degraded. "He shall serve his brethren." There is something in the air of one of this cast, lean and suspicious; contrasting with the open, trusting, generous manners of the other.

Observe who have been the greatest borrowers of all ages—Alcibiades—Falstaff—Sir Richard Steele—our late imcomparable Brinsley—what a family likeness in all four!

What a careless, even deportment hath your borrower! what rosy gills! what a beautiful reliance on Providence doth he manifest,—taking no more thought than lilies! What contempt for money,—accounting it (yours and mine especially) no better than dross! What a liberal confounding of those pedantic distinctions of *meum* and *tuum*! or rather, what a noble simplification of language (beyond Tooke), resolving these supposed opposites into one clear, intelligible pronoun adjective!—What near approaches doth he make to the primitive *community*,—to the extent of one half of the principle at least!

He is the true taxer who "calleth all the world up to be taxed;" and the distance is as vast between him and *one of us*, as subsisted between the Augustan Majesty and the poorest obolary Jew that paid it tribute-pittance at Jerusalem!—His exactions, too, have such a cheerful, voluntary air! So far removed from your sour parochial or state-gatherers, —those ink-horn varlets, who carry their want of welcome in their faces! He cometh to you with a smile, and troubleth you with no receipt; confining himself to no set season. Every day is his Candlemas, or his Feast of Holy Michael. He applieth the *lene tormentum* of a pleasant look to your purse,—which to that gentle warmth expands her silken leaves, as naturally as the cloak of the traveller, for which sun and wind contended! He is the true Propontic which never ebbeth! The sea which taketh handsomely at each man's hand. In vain the victim, whom he delighteth to honour, struggles with destiny; he is in the net. Lend therefore cheerfully, O man ordained to lend—that thou lose not in the end, with thy worldly penny, the reversion promised. Combine not preposterously in thine own person the penalties of Lazarus and of Dives!—but, when thou seest the proper authority coming, meet it smilingly, as it were half-way. Come, a handsome sacrifice! See how light *he* makes of it! Strain not courtesies with a noble enemy.

Reflections like the foregoing were forced upon my mind by the death of my old friend, Ralph Bigod, Esq., who parted this life on Wednesday evening; dying, as he had lived, without much trouble. He boasted himself a descendant from mighty ancestors of that name, who heretofore held ducal dignities in this realm. In his actions and sentiments he belied not the stock to which he pretended. Early in life he found himself invested with ample revenues; which, with that noble disinterestedness which I have noticed as inherent in men of the *great race*, he took almost immediate measures entirely to dissipate and bring to nothing: for there is something revolting in the idea of a king holding a private purse; and the thoughts of Bigod were all regal. Thus furnished, by the very act of disfurnishment; getting rid of the cumbersome luggage of riches, more apt (as one sings)

To slacken virtue, and abate her edge,
Than prompt her to do aught may merit
 praise,

he set forth, like some Alexander, upon his great enterprise, "borrowing and to borrow!"

In his periegesis, or triumphant progress throughout this island, it has been calculated that he laid a tythe part of the inhabitants under contribution. I reject this estimate as greatly exaggerated: —but having had the honour of accompanying my friend, divers times, in his perambulations about this vast city, I own I was greatly struck at first with the prodigious number of faces we met, who claimed a sort of respectful acquaintance with us. He was one day so obliging as to explain the phenomenon. It seems, these were his tributaries; feeders of his exchequer; gentlemen, his good friends (as he was pleased to express himself), to whom he had occasionally been beholden for a loan. Their multitudes did no way disconcert him. He rather took a pride in numbering them; and, with Comus, seemed pleased to be "stocked with so fair a herd."

With such sources, it was a wonder how he contrived to keep his treasury always empty. He did it by force of an aphorism, which he had often in his mouth, that "money kept longer than three days stinks." So he made use of it while it was fresh. A good part he drank away (for he was an excellent toss-pot), some he gave away, the rest he threw away, literally tossing and hurling it violently from him—as boys do burrs, or as if it had been infectious,—into ponds, or ditches, or deep holes, inscrutable cavities of the earth;—or he would bury it (where he would never seek it again) by a river's side under some bank, which (he would facetiously observe) paid no interest—but out away from him it must go peremptorily, as Hagar's offspring into the wilderness, while it was sweet. He never missed it. The streams were perennial which fed his fisc. When new supplies became necessary, the first person that had the felicity to fall in with him, friend or stranger, was sure to contribute to the deficiency. For Bigod had an *undeniable* way

with him. He had a cheerful, open exterior, a quick jovial eye, a bald forehead, just touched with grey (*cana fides*). He anticipated no excuse, and found none. And, waiving for a while my theory as to the *great race*, I would put it to the most untheorising reader, who may at times have disposable coin in his pocket, whether it is not more repugnant to the kindliness of his nature to refuse such a one as I am describing, than to say *no* to a poor petitionary rogue (your bastard borrower), who, by his mumping visnomy, tells you that he expects nothing better; and, therefore, whose preconceived notions and expectations you do in reality so much less shock in the refusal.

When I think of this man; his fiery glow of heart; his swell of feeling; how magnificent, how *ideal* he was; how great at the midnight hour; and when I compare with him the companions with whom I have associated since, I grudge the saving of a few idle ducats, and think that I am fallen into the society of *lenders*, and *little* men.

To one like Elia, whose treasures are rather cased in leather covers than closed in iron coffers, there is a class of alienators more formidable than that which I have touched upon; I mean your *borrowers of books*—those mutilators of collections, spoilers of the symmetry of shelves, and creators of odd volumes. There is Comberbatch, matchless in his depredations!

That foul gap in the bottom shelf facing you, like a great eye-tooth knocked out—(you are now with me in my little back study in Bloomsbury, reader!)—with the huge Switzer-like tomes on each side (like the Guildhall giants, in their reformed posture, guardant of nothing) once held the tallest of my folios, *Opera Bonaventuræ*, choice and massy divinity, to which its two supporters (school divinity also, but of a lesser calibre,—Bellarmine, and Holy Thomas), showed but as dwarfs,—itself an Ascapart!—*that* Comberbatch abstracted upon the faith of a theory he holds, which is more easy, I confess, for me to suffer by than to refute, namely, that "the title to property in a book (my Bonaventure, for instance), is in exact ratio to the claimant's powers of understanding and appreciating the same." Should he go on acting upon this theory, which of our shelves is safe?

The slight vacuum in the left-hand case—two shelves from the ceiling—scarcely distinguishable but by the quick eye of a loser—was whilom the commodious resting-place of Brown on Urn Burial. C. will hardly allege that he knows more about that treatise than I do, who introduced it to him, and was indeed the first (of the moderns) to discover its beauties—but so have I known a foolish lover to praise his mistress in the presence of a rival more qualified to carry her off than himself.—Just below, Dodsley's dramas want their fourth volume, where Vittoria Corombona is! The remainder nine are as distasteful as Priam's refuse sons, when the Fates *borrowed* Hector. Here stood the Anatomy of Melancholy, in sober state.—There loitered the Complete Angler; quiet as in life, by some stream side. In yonder nook, John Buncle, a widower-volume, with "eyes closed," mourns his ravished mate.

One justice I must do my friend, that if he sometimes, like the sea, sweeps away a treasure, at another time, sea-like, he throws up as rich an equivalent to match it. I have a small under-collection of this nature (my friend's gatherings in his various calls), picked up, he has forgotten at what odd places, and deposited with as little memory at mine. I take in these orphans, the twice-deserted. These proselytes of the gate are welcome as the true Hebrews. They stand in conjunction; natives, and naturalised. The latter seem as little disposed to inquire out their true lineage, as I am.—I charge no warehouse-room for these deodands, nor shall ever put myself to the ungentlemanly trouble of advertising a sale of them to pay expenses.

To lose a volume to C. carries some sense and meaning in it. You are sure that he will make one hearty meal on your viands, if he can give no account of the platter after it. But what moved thee, wayward, spiteful K., to be so importunate to carry off with thee, in spite of tears and adjurations to thee to forbear, the Letters of that princely woman, the thrice noble Margaret Newcastle—knowing at the time, and knowing that I knew also, thou most assuredly wouldst never turn over one leaf of the illustrious folio:—what but the mere spirit of contradiction, and childish love of getting the better of thy friend? —Then, worst cut of all! to transport it with thee to the Gallican land—

Unworthy land to harbour such a sweetness,
A virtue in which all ennobling thoughts dwell,
Pure thoughts, kind thoughts, high thoughts, her sex's wonder!

——hadst thou not thy playbooks, and books of jests and fancies, about thee, to keep thee merry, even as thou keepest all companies with thy quips and mirthful tales? Child of the Greenroom, it was unkindly done of thee. Thy wife, too, that part-French, better part-Englishwoman!—that *she* could fix upon no other treatise to bear away, in kindly token of remembering us, than the works of Fulke Greville Lord Brook—of which no Frenchman, nor woman of France, Italy, or England, was ever by nature constituted to comprehend a tittle! *Was there not Zimmerman on Solitude?*

Reader, if haply thou art blessed with a moderate collection, be shy of showing it; or if thy heart overfloweth to lend them, lend thy books; but let it be to such a one as S. T. C.—he will return them (generally anticipating the time appointed) with usury; enriched with annotations, tripling their value. I have had experience. Many are these precious MSS. of his—(in *matter* oftentimes, and almost in *quantity* not unfrequently, vying with the originals) in no very clerkly hand—legible in my Daniel; in old Burton; in Sir Thomas Browne; and those abstruser cogitations of the Greville, now, alas! wandering in Pagan lands.—I counsel thee, shut not thy heart, nor thy library, against S. T. C.

———

NEW YEAR'S EVE.

EVERY man hath two birth-days: two days at least, in every year, which set him upon revolving the lapse of time, as it affects his moral duration. The one is that which in an especial manner he termeth *his*. In the gradual desuetude of old observances, this custom of solemnizing our proper birth-day hath nearly passed away, or is left to children, who reflect nothing at all about the matter, nor understand anything in it beyond cake and orange. But the birth of a New Year is of an interest too wide to be pretermitted by king or cobbler. No one ever regarded the First of January with indifference. It is that from which all date their time, and count upon what is left. It is the nativity of our common Adam.

Of all sound of all bells—(bells,

the music nighest bordering upon heaven)—most solemn and touching is the peal which rings out the Old Year. I never hear it without a gathering-up of my mind to a concentration of all the images that have been diffused over the past twelvemonth; all I have done or suffered, performed or neglected, in that regretted time. I begin to know its worth, as when a person dies. It takes a personal colour; nor was it a poetical flight in a contemporary, when he exclaimed

I saw the skirts of the departing Year.

It is no more than what in sober sadness every one of us seems to be conscious of, in that awful leave-taking. I am sure I felt it, and all felt it with me, last night; though some of my companions affected rather to manifest an exhilaration at the birth of the coming year, than any very tender regrets for the decease of its predecessor. But I am none of those who—

Welcome the coming, speed the parting guest.

I am naturally, beforehand, shy of novelties; new books, new faces, new years,—from some mental twist which makes it difficult in me to face the prospective. I have almost ceased to hope; and am sanguine only in the prospects of other (former) years. I plunge into foregone visions and conclusions. I encounter pell-mell with past disappointments. I am armour-proof against old dis-couragements. I forgive, or overcome in fancy, old adversaries. I play over again *for love*, as the gamesters phrase it, games for which I once paid so dear. I would scarce now have any of those untoward accidents and events of my life reversed. I would no more alter them than the incidents of some well-contrived novel. Methinks, it is better that I should have pined away seven of my goldenest years, when I was thrall to the fair hair, and fairer eyes, of Alice W—n, than that so passionate a love adventure should be lost. It was better that our family should have missed that legacy, which old Dorrell cheated us of, than that I should have at this moment two thousand pounds *in banco*, and be without the idea of that specious old rogue.

In a degree beneath manhood, it is my infirmity to look back upon those early days. Do I advance a paradox when I say, that, skipping over the intervention of forty years, a man may have leave to love *himself*, without the imputation of self-love?

If I know aught of myself, no one whose mind is introspective —and mine is painfully so—can have a less respect for his present identity than I have for the man Elia. I know him to be light, and vain, and humoursome; a notorious * * *; addicted to * * * *; averse from counsel, neither taking it, nor offering it;—* * * besides; a stammering buffoon; what you will; lay it on, and spare not; I subscribe to it all, and much more, than thou canst be willing to lay at his door—but for the child Elia—that "other me," there, in the background—I must take leave to cherish the remembrance of that young master—with as little reference, I protest, to his stupid changeling of five-and-forty, as if it had been a child of some other house, and not of my parents. I can cry over its patient small-pox at five, and rougher medicaments. I can lay its poor fevered head upon the sick pillow at Christ's, and wake with it in surprise at the gentle posture of maternal tenderness hanging over it, that unknown had watched its sleep. I know how it shrank from any the least colour of falsehood. —God help thee, Elia, how art thou changed!—Thou art sophisticated.—I know how honest, how courageous (for a weakling) it was —how religious, how imaginative, how hopeful! From what have I not fallen, if the child I remember was indeed myself,—and not some dissembling guardian, presenting a false identity, to give the rule to my unpractised steps, and regulate the tone of my moral being!

That I am fond of indulging, beyond a hope of sympathy, in such retrospection, may be the symptom of some sickly idiosyncrasy. Or is it owing to another cause: simply, that being without wife or family, I have not learned to project myself enough out of myself; and having no offspring of my own to dally with, I turn back upon memory, and adopt my own early idea, as my heir and favourite? If these speculations seem fantastical to thee, reader (a busy man, perchance), if I tread out of the way of thy sympathy, and am singularly conceited only, I retire, impenetrable to ridicule, under the phantom cloud of Elia.

The elders, with whom I was brought up, were of a character not likely to let slip the sacred observance of any old institution; and the ringing out of the Old Year was kept by them with circumstances of peculiar ceremony. —In those days the sound of those midnight chimes, though it seemed to raise hilarity in all around me, never failed to bring a train of pensive imagery into my fancy. Yet I then scarce conceived what it meant, or thought of it as a reckoning that concerned me. Not childhood alone, but the young man till thirty, never feels practically that he is mortal. He knows it indeed, and, if need were, he could preach a homily on the fragility of life; but he brings it not home to himself, any more than in a hot June we can appropriate to our imagination the freezing days of December. But now, shall I confess a truth?— I feel these audits but too powerfully. I begin to count the probabilities of my duration, and to grudge at the expenditure of moments and shortest periods, like misers' farthings. In proportion as the years both lessen and shorten, I set more count upon their periods, and would fain lay my ineffectual finger upon the spoke of the great wheel. I am not content to pass away "like a weaver's shuttle." Those metaphors solace me not, nor sweeten the unpalatable draught of mortality. I care not to be carried with the tide, that smoothly bears human life to eternity; and reluct at the inevitable course of destiny. I am in love with this green earth; the face of town and country; the unspeakable rural solitudes and the sweet security of streets. I would set up my tabernacle here. I am content to stand still at the age to which I am arrived; I, and my friends: to be no younger, no richer, no handsomer. I do not want to be weaned by age; or drop, like mellow fruit, as they say, into the grave.—Any alteration, on this earth of mine, in diet or in lodging, puzzles and discomposes me. My household-gods plant a terrible fixed foot, and are not rooted up without blood. They do not willingly seek Lavinian shores. A new state of being staggers me.

Sun, and sky, and breeze, and solitary walks, and summer holidays, and the greenness of fields, and the delicious juices of meats and fishes, and society, and the cheerful glass, and candle-light, and fireside conversations, and innocent vanities, and jests, and *irony itself*—do these things go out with life?

Can a ghost laugh, or shake his gaunt sides, when you are pleasant with him?

And you, my midnight darlings, my Folios; must I part with the intense delight of having you (huge armfuls) in my embraces? Must knowledge come to me, if it come at all, by some awkward experiment of intuition, and no longer by this familiar process of reading?

Shall I enjoy friendships there, wanting the smiling indications which point me to them here,— the recognisable face—the "sweet assurance of a look?"—

In winter this intolerable disinclination to dying—to give it its mildest name—does more especially haunt and beset me. In a genial August noon, beneath a sweltering sky, death is almost problematic. At those times do such poor snakes as myself enjoy an immortality. Then we expand and burgeon. Then we are as strong again, as valiant again, as wise again, and a great deal taller. The blast that nips and shrinks me, puts me in thoughts of death. All things allied to the insubstantial, wait upon that master feeling; cold, numbness, dreams, perplexity; moonlight itself, with its shadowy and spectral appearances,—that cold ghost of the sun, or Phœbus' sickly sister, like that innutritious one denounced in the Canticles:—I am none of her minions—I hold with the Persian.

Whatsoever thwarts, or puts me out of my way, brings death unto my mind. All partial evils, like humours, run into that capital plague-sore.—I have heard some profess an indifference to life. Such hail the end of their existence as a port of refuge; and speak of the grave as of some soft arms, in which they may slumber as on a pillow. Some have wooed death——but out upon thee, I say, thou foul, ugly phantom! I detest, abhor, execrate, and (with Friar John) give thee to six score thousand devils, as in no instance to be excused or tolerated, but shunned as an universal viper; to be branded, proscribed, and spoken evil of! In no way can I be brought to digest thee, thou thin, melancholy *Privation*, or more frightful and confounding *Positive*!

Those antidotes, prescribed against the fear of thee, are altogether frigid and insulting, like thyself. For what satisfaction hath a man, that he shall "lie down with kings and emperors in death," who in his lifetime never greatly coveted the society of such bed-fellows?—or, forsooth, that "so shall the fairest face appear?"—why, to comfort me, must Alice W—n be a goblin? More than all, I conceive disgust at those impertinent and misbecoming familiarities, inscribed upon your ordinary tombstones. Every dead man must take upon himself to be lecturing me with his odious truism, that "Such as he now is I must shortly be." Not so shortly, friend, perhaps, as thou imaginest. In the meantime I am alive. I move about. I am worth twenty of thee. Know thy betters! Thy New Years' days are past. I sur-

vive, a jolly candidate for 1821. Another cup of wine—and while that turncoat bell, that just now mournfully chanted the obsequies of 1820 departed, with changed notes lustily rings in a successor, let us attune to its peal the song made on a like occasion, by hearty, cheerful Mr. Cotton.

THE NEW YEAR.

Hark, the cock crows, and yon bright
 star
Tells us, the day himself's not far;
And see where, breaking from the night,
He gilds the western hills with light.
With him old Janus doth appear,
Peeping into the future year,
With such a look as seems to say
The prospect is not good that way.
Thus do we rise ill sights to see,
And 'gainst ourselves to prophesy;
When the prophetic fear of things
A more tormenting mischief brings,
More full of soul-tormenting gall
Than direst mischiefs can befall.
But stay! but stay! methinks my sight,
Better informed by clearer light,
Discerns sereneness in that brow
That all contracted seemed but now.
His revers'd face may show distaste,
And frown upon the ills are past;
But that which this way looks is clear,
And smiles upon the New-born Year.
He looks too from a place so high,
The year lies open to his eye;
And all the moments open are
To the exact discoverer.
Yet more and more he smiles upon
The happy revolution.
Why should we then suspect or fear
The influences of a year,
So smiles upon us the first morn,
And speaks us good so soon as born?
Plague on't! the last was ill enough,
This cannot but make better proof;
Or, at the worst, as we brush'd through
The last, why so we may this too;
And then the next in reason shou'd
Be superexcellently good:
For the worst ills (we daily see)
Have no more perpetuity
Than the best fortunes that do fall;
Which also bring us wherewithal

Longer their being to support,
Than those do of the other sort:
And who has one good year in three,
And yet repines at destiny,
Appears ungrateful in the case,
And merits not the good he has.
Then let us welcome the New Guest
With lusty brimmers of the best:
Mirth always should Good Fortune meet,
And renders e'en Disaster sweet:
And though the Princess turn her back,
Let us but line ourselves with sack,
We better shall by far hold out,
Till the next year she face about.

How say you, reader—do not these verses smack of the rough-magnanimity of the old English vein? Do they not fortify like a cordial; enlarging the heart, and productive of sweet blood, and generous spirits, in the concoction? Where be those puling fears of death, just now expressed or affected?—Passed like a cloud—absorbed in the purging sunlight of clear poetry—clean washed away by a wave of genuine Helicon, your only Spa for these hypochondrics. And now another cup of the generous! and a merry New Year, and many of them to you all, my masters!

MRS. BATTLE'S OPINIONS ON WHIST.

"A clean fire, a clean hearth,* and the rigour of the game." This was the celebrated *wish* of old Sarah Battle (now with God), who, next to her devotions, loved a good game of whist. She was none of your lukewarm gamesters, your half-and-half players, who have no objection to take a hand, if you want one to make up a rubber; who affirm that they have no pleasure in winning; that they like to win one game and lose another; that they can while away an hour very agreeably at a card-table, but are indifferent whether they play or no; and will desire an adversary, who has slipped a wrong card, to take it up and play another.** These insufferable triflers are the curse of a table. One of these flies will spoil a whole pot. Of such it may be said that they do not play at cards, but only play at playing at them.

Sarah Battle was none of that breed. She detested them, as I do, from her heart and soul, and would not, save upon a striking emergency, willingly seat herself at the same table with them. She loved a thorough-paced partner, a determined enemy. She took, and gave, no concessions. She hated favours. She never made a revoke, nor ever passed it over in her adversary without exacting the utmost forfeiture. She fought a good fight: cut and thrust. She held not her good sword (her cards) "like a dancer." She sate bolt upright; and neither showed you her cards, nor desired to see yours. All people have their blind side—their superstitions; and I have heard her declare, under the

[* This was before the introduction of rugs, reader. You must remember the intolerable crash of the unswept cinders botwixt your foot and the marble.]

[** As if a sportsman should tell you he liked to kill a fox one day and lose him the next.]

roae, that Hearts was her favourite suit.

I never in my life—and I knew Sarah Battle many of the best years of it—saw her take out her snuff-box when it was her turn to play; or snuff a candle in the middle of a game; or ring for a servant, till it was fairly over. She never introduced, or connived at, miscellaneous conversation during its process. As she emphatically observed, cards were cards; and if I ever saw unmingled distaste in her fine last-century countenance, it was at the airs of a young gentleman of a literary turn, who had been with difficulty persuaded to take a hand; and who, in his excess of candour, declared, that he thought there was no harm in unbending the mind now and then, after serious studies, in recreations of that kind! She could not bear to have her noble occupation, to which she wound up her faculties, considered in that light. It was her business, her duty, the thing she came into the world to do,—and she did it. She unbent her mind afterwards—over a book.

Pope was her favourite author: his Rape of the Lock her favourite work. She once did me the favour to play over with me (with the cards) his celebrated game of Ombre in that poem; and to explain to me how far it agreed with, and in what points it would be found to differ from, tradrille. Her illustrations were apposite and poignant; and I had the pleasure of sending the substance of them to Mr. Bowles; but I suppose they came too late to be inserted among his ingenious notes upon that author.

Quadrille, she has often told me, was her first love; but whist had engaged her maturer esteem. The former, she said, was showy and specious, and likely to allure young persons. The uncertainty and quick shifting of partners—a thing which the constancy of whist abhors; the dazzling supremacy and regal investiture of Spadille—absurd, as she justly observed, in the pure aristocracy of whist, where his crown and garter give him no proper power above his brother-nobility of the Aces;—the giddy vanity, so taking to the inexperienced, of playing alone; above all, the overpowering attractions of a *Sans Prendre Vole*,—to the triumph of which there is certainly nothing parallel or approaching, in the contingencies of whist;—all these, she would say, make quadrille a game of captivation to the young and enthusiastic. But whist was the *solider* game: that was her word. It was a long meal; not like quadrille, a feast of snatches. One or two rubbers might co-extend in duration with an evening. They gave time to form rooted friendships, to cultivate steady enmities. She despised the chance-started, capricious, and everfluctuating alliances of the other. The skirmishes of quadrille, she would say, reminded her of the petty ephemeral embroilments of the little Italian states, depicted by Machiavel: perpetually changing postures and connexions; bitter foes to-day, sugared darlings to-morrow; kissing and scratching in a breath;—but the wars of whist were comparable to the long, steady, deep-rooted, rational antipathies of the great French and English nations.

A grave simplicity was what she chiefly admired in her favourite game. There was nothing silly in it, like the nob in cribbage —nothing superfluous. No *flushes* —that most irrational of all pleas that a reasonable being can set up:—that any one should claim four by virtue of holding cards of the same mark and colour, without reference to the playing of the game, or the individual worth or pretensions of the cards themselves! She held this to be a solecism; as pitiful an ambition at cards as alliteration is in authorship. She despised superficiality, and looked deeper than the colours of things.—Suits were soldiers, she would say, and must have an uniformity of array to distinguish them: but what should we say to a foolish squire, who should claim a merit from dressing up his tenantry in red jackets, that never were to be marshalled —never to take the field?—She even wished that whist were more simple than it is; and, in my mind, would have stripped it of some appendages, which, in the state of human frailty, may be venially, and even commendably, allowed of. She saw no reason for the deciding of the trump by the turn of the card. Why not one suit always trumps?—Why two colours, when the mark of the suit would have sufficiently distinguished them without it?'

"But the eye, my dear madam, is agreeably refreshed with the variety. Man is not a creature of pure reason—he must have his senses delightfully appealed to. We see it in Roman Cotholic countries, where the music and the paintings draw in many to worship, whom your quaker spirit of unsensualising would have kept out.—You yourself have a pretty collection of paintings—but confess to me, whether, walking in your gallery at Sandham, among those clear Vandykes, or among the Paul Potters in the ante-room, you ever felt your bosom glow with an elegant delight, at all comparable to *that* you have it in your power to experience most evenings over a well-arranged assortment of the court-cards?—the pretty antic habits, like heralds in a procession—the gay triumph-assuring scarlets—the contrasting deadly-killing sables—the 'hoary majesty of spades'—Pam in all his glory!—

"All these might be dispensed with; and with their naked names upon the drab pasteboard, the game might go on very well, pictureless. But the *beauty* of cards would be extinguished for ever. Stripped of all that is imaginative in them, they must degenerate into mere gambling. Imagine a dull deal board, or drum head, to spread them on, instead of that nice verdant carpet (next to nature's), fittest arena for those courtly combatants to play their gallant jousts and turneys in!—Exchange those delicately-turned ivory markers—(work of Chinese artist, unconscious of their symbol,—or as profanely slighting their true application as the arrantest Ephesian journey-man that turned out those little shrines for the goddess)—exchange them for little bits of leather (our ancestors' money, or chalk and a slate!")—

The old lady, with a smile, confessed the soundness of my logic; and to her approbation of my arguments on her favourite topic that evening, I have always fancied myself indebted for the legacy of a curious cribbage-board, made of the finest Sienna marble, which her maternal uncle (old Walter Plumer, whom I have elsewhere celebrated), brought with him from Florence:—this, and a trifle of five hundred pounds, came to me at her death.

The former bequest (which I do not least value), I have kept with religious care; though she herself, to confess a truth, was never greatly taken with cribbage. It was an essentially vulgar game, I have heard her say,—disputing with her uncle, who was very partial to it. She could never heartily bring her mouth to pronounce "*Go*"—or "*That's a go.*" She called it an ungrammatical game. The pegging teased her. I once knew her to forfeit a rubber (a five-dollar stake) because she would not take advantage of the turn-up knave, which would have given it her, but which she must have claimed by the disgraceful tenure of declaring "*two for his heels.*" There is something extremely genteel in this sort of self-denial. Sarah Battle was a gentlewoman born.

Piquet she held the best game at the cards for two persons, though she would ridicule the pedantry of the terms—such as pique—repique—the capot—they savoured (she thought) of affectation. But games for two, or even three, she never greatly cared for. She loved the quadrate, or square. She would argue thus:—Cards are warfare: the ends are gain, with glory. But cards are war, in disguise of a sport: when single adversaries encounter, the ends proposed are too palpable. By themselves, it is too close a fight; with spectators, it is not much bettered. No looker-on can be interested, except for a bet, and then it is a mere affair of money; he cares not for your luck *sympathetically*, or for your play.—Three are still worse; a mere naked war of every man against every man, as in cribbage, without league or alliance; or a rotation of petty and contradictory interests, a succession of heartless leagues, and not much more hearty infractions of them, as in tradrille.—But in square games (*she meant whist*), all that is possible to be attained in card-playing is accomplished. There are the incentives of profit with honour, common to every species—though the *latter* can be but very imperfectly enjoyed in those other games, where the spectator is only feebly a participator. But the parties in whist are spectators and principals too. They are a theatre to themselves, and a looker-on is not wanted. He is rather worse than nothing, and an impertinence. Whist abhors neutrality, or interests beyond its sphere. You glory in some surprising stroke of skill or fortune, not because a cold—or even an interested—bystander witnesses it, but because your *partner* sympathises in the contingency. You win for two. You triumph for two. Two are exalted. Two again are mortified; which divides their disgrace, as the conjunction doubles (by taking off the invidiousness) your glories. Two losing to two are better reconciled, than one to one in that close butchery. The hostile feeling is weakened by multiplying the channels. War becomes a civil game. By such reasonings as these the old lady was accustomed to defend her favourite pastime.

No inducement could ever prevail upon her to play at any game, where chance entered into the composition, *for nothing*. Chance, she would argue—and here again, admire the subtlety of her conclusion;—chance is nothing, but where something else depends upon it. It is obvious that cannot be *glory*. What rational cause of exultation could it give to a man to turn up size ace a hundred times together by himself? or be-

fore spectators, where no stake was depending?—Make a lottery of a hundred thousand tickets with but one fortunate number—and what possible principle of our nature, except stupid wonderment, could it gratify to gain that number as many times successively without a prize? Therefore she disliked the mixture of chance in backgammon, where it was not played for money. She called it foolish, and those people idiots, who were taken with a lucky hit under such circumstances. Games of pure skill were as little to her fancy. Played for a stake, they were a mere system of over-reaching. Played for glory, they were a mere setting of one man's wit, —his memory, or combination-faculty rather—against another's; like a mock-engagement at a review, bloodless and profitless. She could not conceive a *game* wanting the spritely infusion of chance, the handsome excuses of good fortune. Two people playing at chess in a corner of a room, whilst whist was stirring in the centre, would inspire her with insufferable horror and ennui. Those well-cut similitudes of Castles and Knights, the *imagery* of the board, she would argue, (and I think in this case justly) were entirely misplaced and senseless. Those hard-head contests can in no instance ally with the fancy. They reject form and colour. A pencil and dry slate (she used to say) were the proper arena for such combatants.

To those puny objectors against

cards, as nurturing the bad passions, she would retort, that man is a gaming animal. He must be always trying to get the better in something or other:—that this passion can scarcely be more safely expended than upon a game at cards: that cards are a temporary illusion; in truth, a mere drama; for we do but *play* at being mightily concerned, where a few idle shillings are at stake, yet, during the illusion, we *are* as mightily concerned as those whose stake is crowns and kingdoms. They are a sort of dream-fighting; much ado; great battling, and little bloodshed; mighty means for disproportioned ends: quite as diverting, and a great deal more innoxious, than many of those more serious *games* of life, which men play without esteeming them to be such.

With great deference to the old lady's judgment in these matters, I think I have experienced some moments in my life, when playing at cards *for nothing* has even been agreeable. When I am in sickness, or not in the best spirits, I sometimes call for the cards, and play a game at piquet *for love* with my cousin Bridget—Bridget Elia.

I grant there is something sneaking in it; but with a toothache, or a sprained ankle,—when you are subdued and humble,—you are glad to put up with an inferior spring of action.

There is such a thing in nature, I am convinced, as *sick whist*.

I grant it is not the highest style of man—I deprecate the manes of Sarah Battle—she lives not, alas! to whom I should apologise.

At such times, those *terms* which my old friend objected to, come in as something admissible.—I love to get a tierce or a quatorze, though they mean nothing. I am subdued to an inferior interest. Those shadows of winning amuse me.

That last game I had with my sweet cousin (I capotted her)—(dare I tell thee, how foolish I am?)—I wished it might have lasted for ever, though we gained nothing, and lost nothing, though it was a mere shade of play: I would be content to go on in that idle folly for ever. The pipkin should be ever boiling, that was to prepare the gentle lenitive to my foot, which Bridget was doomed to apply after the game was over: and, as I do not much relish appliances, there it should ever bubble. Bridget and I should be ever playing.

A CHAPTER ON EARS.

I have no ear.—

Mistake me not, reader—nor imagine that I am by nature destitute of those exterior twin appendages, hanging ornaments, and (architecturally speaking) handsome volutes to the human capital. Better my mother had never borne me.—I am, I think, rather delicately than copiously provided with those conduits; and I feel no disposition to envy the mule for his plenty, or the mole for her exactness, in those ingenious labyrinthine inlets—those indispensable side-intelligencers.

Neither have I incurred, or done anything to incur, with Defoe, that hideous disfigurement, which constrained him to draw upon assurance — to feel "quite unabashed,"* and at ease upon that article. I was never, I thank my stars, in the pillory; nor, if I read them aright, is it within the compass of my destiny, that I ever should be.

When therefore I say that I have no ear, you will understand me to mean—*for music.* To say that this heart never melted at the concord of sweet sounds, would be a foul self-libel. "*Water parted from the sea*" never fails to move it strangely. So does "*In infancy.*" But they were used to be sung at her harpsichord (the old-fashioned instrument in vogue in those days) by a gentlewoman—the gentlest, sure, that ever merited the appellation—the sweetest—why should I hesitate to name Mrs. S——, once the blooming Fanny Weatheral of the Temple—who had power to thrill the soul of Elia, small imp as he was, even in his long coats; and to make him glow, tremble, and blush with a passion, that not faintly indicated the dayspring of that absorbing sentiment which was afterwards destined to overwhelm and subdue his nature quite for Alice W——n.

* ["Earless on high stood, unabashed, Defoe."—*Dunciad.*]

I even think that *sentimentally* I am disposed to harmony. But *organically* I am incapable of a tune. I have been practising "*God save the King*" all my life; whistling and humming of it over to myself in solitary corners; and am not yet arrived, they tell me, within many quavers of it. Yet hath the loyalty of Elia never been impeached.

I am not without suspicion, that I have an undeveloped faculty of music within me. For thrumming, in my mild way, on my friend A.'s piano, the other morning, while he was engaged in an adjoining parlour,—on his return he was pleased to say, "*he thought it could not be the maid!*" On his first surprise at hearing the keys touched in somewhat an airy and masterful way, not dreaming of me, his suspicions had lighted on *Jenny.* But a grace, snatched from a superior refinement, soon convinced him that some being—technically perhaps deficient, but higher informed from a principle common to all the fine arts—had swayed the keys to a mood which Jenny, with all her (less cultivated) enthusiasm, could never have elicited from them. I mention this as a proof of my friend's penetration, and not with any view of disparaging Jenny.

Scientifically I could never be made to understand (yet have I taken some pains) what a note in music is; or how one note should differ from another. Much less in voices can I distinguish a soprano from a tenor. Only sometimes the thorough-bass I contrive to guess at, from its being super-eminently harsh and disagreeable. I tremble, however, for my mis-application of the simplest terms of *that* which I disclaim. While I profess my ignorance, I scarce know what to *say* I am ignorant of. I hate, perhaps, by mis-nomers. *Sostenuto* and *adagio* stand in the like relation of ob-scurity to me; and *Sol, Fa, Mi, Re*, is as conjuring as *Baralipton*.

It is hard to stand alone in an age like this,—(constituted to the quick and critical perception of all harmonious combinations, I verily believe, beyond all preced-ing ages, since Jubal stumbled upon the gamut,) to remain, as it were, singly unimpressible to the magic influences of an art, which is said to have such an especial stroke at soothing, elevating, and refining the passions.—Yet, rather than break the candid current of my confessions, I must avow to you that I have received a great deal more pain than pleasure from this so cried-up faculty.

I am constitutionally suscept-ible of noises. A carpenter's hammer, in a warm summer noon, will fret me into more than mid-summer madness. But those un-connected, unset sounds, are no-thing to the measured malice of music. The ear is passive to those single strokes; willingly en-during stripes while it hath no task to con. To music it cannot be passive. It will strive—mine at least will—spite of its inapti-tude, to thrid the maze; like an unskilled eye painfully poring upon hieroglyphics. I have sat through an Italian Opera, till, for sheer pain, and inexplicable an-guish, I have rushed out into the noisiest places of the crowded streets, to solace myself with sounds, which I was not obliged to follow, and get rid of the dis-tracting torment of endless, fruit-less, barren attention! I take re-fuge in the unpretending assem-blage of honest common-life sounds;—and the purgatory of the Enraged Musician becomes my paradise.

I have sat at an Oratorio (that profanation of the purposes of the cheerful playhouse) watching the faces of the auditory in the pit (what a contrast to Hogarth's Laughing Audience!) immove-able, or effecting some faint emo-tion—till (as some have said, that our occupations in the next world will be but a shadow of what de-lighted us in this) I have imagined myself in some cold Theatre in Hades, where some of the *forms* of the earthly one should be kept up, with none of the *enjoyment;* or like that

——Party in a parlour
All silent, and all DAMNED.

Above all, those insufferable concertos, and pieces of music, as they are called, do plague and embitter my apprehension.— Words are something; but to be exposed to an endless battery of mere sounds; to be long a dying; to lie stretched upon a rack of roses; to keep up languor by unintermitted effort; to pile honey upon sugar, and sugar upon honey, to an interminable tedious sweetness; to fill up sound with feeling, and strain ideas to keep pace with it; to gaze on empty frames, and be forced to make the pictures for yourself; to read a book, *all stops*, and be obliged to supply the verbal matter; to invent extempore tragedies to answer to the vague gestures of an inexplicable rambling mime—these are faint shadows of what I have undergone from a series of the ablest-executed pieces of this empty *instrumental music*.

I deny not, that in the opening of a concert, I have experienced something vastly lulling and agreeable:—afterwards followeth the languor and the oppression.—Like that disappointing book in Patmos; or, like the comings on of melancholy, described by Burton, doth music make her first insinuating approaches: — "Most pleasant it is to such as are melancholy given, to walk alone in some solitary grove, betwixt wood and water, by some brook side, and to meditate upon some delightsome and pleasant subject, which shall affect him most, *amabilis insania*, and *mentis gratissimus error*. A most incomparable delight to build castles in the air, to go smiling to themselves, acting an infinite variety of parts, which they suppose, and strongly imagine, they act, or that they see done.—So delightsome these toys at first, they could spend whole days and nights without sleep,

even whole years in such contemplations, and fantastical meditations, which are like so many dreams, and will hardly be drawn from them—winding and unwinding themselves as so many clocks, and still pleasing their humours, until at the last the SCENE TURNS UPON A SUDDEN, and they being now habituated to such meditations and solitary places, can endure no company, can think of nothing but harsh and distasteful subjects. Fear, sorrow, suspicion, *subrusticus pudor*, discontent, cares, and weariness of life, surprise them on a sudden, and they can think of nothing else: continually suspecting, no sooner are their eyes open, but this infernal plague of melancholy seizeth on them, and terrifies their souls, representing some dismal object to their minds; which now, by no means, no labour, no persuasions, they can avoid, they cannot be rid of, they cannot resist."

Something like this "SCENE TURNING" I have experienced at the evening parties, at the house of my good Catholic friend Nov——; who, by the aid of a capital organ, himself the most finished of players, converts his drawing-room into a chapel, his week days into Sundays, and these latter into minor heavens.[*]

When my friend commences upon one of those solemn anthems, which peradventure struck upon my heedless ear, rambling in the

[*] I have been there, and still would go
'Tis like a little heaven below.—
            DR. WATTS.

side aisles of the dim Abbey, some five-and-thirty years since, waking a new sense, and putting a soul of old religion into my young apprehension—(whether it be *that*, in which the Psalmist, weary of the persecutions of bad men, wisheth to himself dove's wings —or *that other*, which, with a like measure of sobriety and pathos, inquireth by what means the young man shall best cleanse his mind)—a holy calm pervadeth me. —I am for the time

———rapt above earth,
And possess joys not promised at my birth.

But when this master of the spell, not content to have laid a soul prostrate, goes on, in his power, to inflict more bliss than lies in her capacity to receive— impatient to overcome her "earthly" with his "heavenly,"—still pouring in, for protracted hours, fresh waves and fresh from the sea of sound, or from that inexhausted *German* ocean, above which, in triumphant progress, dolphin-seated, ride those Arions *Haydn* and *Mozart*, with their attendant Tritons, *Bach*, *Beethoven*, and a countless tribe, whom to attempt to reckon up would but plunge me again in the deeps,—I stagger under the weight of harmony, reeling to and fro at my wits' end;—clouds, as of frankincense, oppress me—priests, altars, censers, dazzle before me—the genius of *his* religion hath me in her toils—a shadowy triple tiara invests the brow of my friend, late so naked, so ingenuous—he is Pope,—and by him sits, like as in the anomaly of dreams, a she-Pope too,—tri-coroneted like himself!—I am converted, and yet a Protestant;—at once *malleus hereticorum*, and myself grand heresiarch: or three heresies centre in my person:— I am Marcion, Ebion, and Cerinthus—Gog and Magog—what not?—till the coming in of the friendly supper-tray dissipates the figment, and a draught of true Lutheran beer (in which chiefly my friend shows himself no bigot) at once reconciles me to the rationalities of a purer faith; and restores to me the genuine unterrifying aspects of my pleasant-countenanced host and hostess.

ALL FOOLS' DAY.

The compliments of the season to my worthy masters, and a merry first of April to us all!

Many happy returns of this day to you—and you—and *you*, Sir—nay, never frown, man, nor put a long face upon the matter. Do not we know one another? what need of ceremony among friends? we have all a touch of *that same*— you understand me—a speck of the motley. Beshrew the man who on such a day as this, the *general festival*, should affect to stand aloof. I am none of those sneakers. I am free of the corporation, and care not who know it. He that meets me in the forest to-day, shall meet with no wiseacre, I can tell him. *Stultus sum.* Translate me that, and take the meaning of it to yourself for your pains. What! man, we have four quarters of the globe on our side, at the least computation.

Fill us a cup of that sparkling gooseberry—we will drink no wise, melancholy, politic port on this day—and let us troll the catch of Amiens—*duc ad me—duc ad me* —how goes it?

Here shall he see
Gross fools as he.

Now would I give a trifle to know, historically and authentically, who was the greatest fool that ever lived. I would certainly give him in a bumper. Marry, of the present breed, I think I could without much difficulty name you the party.

Remove your cap a little further, if you please: it hides my bauble. And now each man bestride his hobby, and dust away his bells to what tune he pleases. I will give you, for my part,

——— The crazy old church clock,
And the bewildered chimes.

Good master Empedocles,* you are welcome. It is long since you went a salamander-gathering down Ætna. Worse than samphire-picking by some odds. 'Tis a mercy your worship did not singe your mustachios.

Ha! Cleombrotus!** and what

[* ——— He who, to be deem'd
A god, leap'd fondly into Etna
flames—]

[** ——— He who, to enjoy
Plato's Elysium, leap'd into the
sea—]

salads in faith did you light upon at the bottom of the Mediterranean? You were founder, I take it, of the disinterested sect of the Calenturists.

Gebir, my old free-mason, and prince of plasterers at Babel,* bring in your trowel, most Ancient Grand! You have claim to a seat here at my right hand, as patron of the stammerers. You left your work, if I remember Herodotus correctly, at eight hundred million toises, or thereabout, above the level of the sea. Bless us, what a long bell you must have pulled, to call your top workmen to their nuncheon on the low grounds of Shinar. Or did you send up your garlic and onions by a rocket? I am a rogue if I am not ashamed to show you our Monument on Fish-street Hill, after your altitudes. Yet we think it somewhat.

What, the magnanimous Alexander in tears?—cry, baby, put its finger in its eye, it shall have another globe, round as an orange, pretty moppet!

Mister Adams——' odso, I honour your coat—pray do us the favour to read to us that sermon, which you lent to Mistress Slipslop—the twenty and second in your portmanteau there—on Female Incontinence—the same—it will come in most irrelevantly and impertinently seasonable to the time of day.

Good Master Raymund Lully,

[* The builders next of Babel on the
plain
Of Sennaar—]

you look wise. Pray correct that error.——

Duns, spare your definitions. I must fine you a bumper, or a paradox. We will have nothing said or done syllogistically this day. Remove those logical forms, waiter, that no gentleman break the tender shins of his apprehension stumbling across them.

Master Stephen, you are late. —Ha! Cokes, it is you?—Aguecheek, my dear knight, let me pay my devoir to you.—Master Shallow, your worship's poor servant to command.—Master Silence, I will use few words with you.—Slender, it shall go hard if I edge not you in somewhere— You six will engross all the poor wit of the company to-day.—I know it, I know it.

Ha! honest R——, my fine old Librarian of Ludgate, time out of mind, art thou here again? Bless my doublet, it is not over-new, threadbare as thy stories:—what dost thou flitting about the world at this rate?—Thy customers are extinct, defunct, bed-rid, have ceased to read long ago.—Thou goest still among them, seeing if, peradventure, thou canst hawk a volume or two.—Good Granville S——, thy last patron, is flown.

King Pandion, he is dead,
All thy friends are lapt in lead.—

Nevertheless, noble R——, come in, and take your seat here, between Armado and Quisada; for in true courtesy, in gravity, in fantastic smiling to thyself, in courteous smiling upon others, in the goodly ornature of well-apparelled speech, and the commendation of wise sentences, thou art nothing inferior to those accomplished Dons of Spain. The spirit of chivalry forsake me for ever, when I forget thy singing the song of Macheath, which declares that he might be *happy with either*, situated between those two ancient spinsters—when I forget the inimitable formal love which thou didst make, turning now to the one, and now to the other, with that Malvolian smile—as if Cervantes, not Gay, had written it for his hero; and as if thousands of periods must revolve, before the mirror of courtesy could have given his invidious preference between a pair of so goodly-propertied and meritorious-equal damsels. • • • •

To descend from these altitudes, and not to protract our Fools' Banquet beyond its appropriate day,—for I fear the second of April is not many hours' distant —in sober verity I will confess a truth to thee, reader. I love a *Fool*—as naturally, as if I were of kith and kin to him. When a child, with child-like apprehensions, that dived not below the surface of the matter, I read those *Parables*—not guessing at the involved wisdom—I had more yearnings towards that simple architect, that built his house upon the sand, than I entertained for his more cautious neighbour: I grudged at the hard censure pronounced upon the quiet soul that kept his talent; and—prizing their simplicity be-

4*

yond the more provident, and, to my apprehension, somewhat *unfeminine* wariness of their competitors—I felt a kindliness, that almost amounted to a *tendre*, for those five thoughtless virgins.—I have never made an acquaintance since, that lasted: or a friendship, that answered; with any that had not some tincture of the absurd in their characters. I venerate an honest obliquity of understanding. The more laughable blunders a man shall commit in your company, the more tests he giveth you, that he will not betray or overreach you. I love the safety which a palpable hallucination warrants; the security, which a word out of reason ratifies. And take my word for this, reader, and say a fool told it you, if you please, that he who hath not a dram of folly in his mixture, hath pounds of much worse matter in his composition. It is observed, that "the foolisher the fowl or fish, —woodcocks, —dotterels—cods'-heads, &c., the finer the flesh thereof," and what are commonly the world's received fools but such whereof the world is not worthy? and what have been some of the kindliest patterns of our species, but so many darlings of absurdity, minions of the goddess, and her white boys?—Reader, if you wrest my words beyond their fair construction, it is you, and not I, that are the *April Fool*.

——

A QUAKERS' MEETING.

Still-born Silence! thou that art
Flood-gate of the deeper heart!
Offspring of a heavenly kind!
Frost o' the mouth, and thaw o' the mind!
Secrecy's confidant, and he
Who makes religion mystery!
Admiration's speaking'st tongue!
Leave, thy desert shades among,
Reverend hermit's hallow'd cells,
Where retired devotion dwells!
With thy enthusiasms come,
Seize our tongues, and strike us dumb!*

READER, would'st thou know what true peace and quiet mean; would'st thou find a refuge from the noises and clamours of the multitude; would'st thou enjoy at once solitude and society; would'st thou possess the depth of thine own spirit in stillness, without be'ng shut out from the consolatory faces of thy species; would'st thou be alone and yet accompanied; solitary, yet not desolate; singular, yet not without some to keep thee in countenance; a unit in aggregate; a simple in composite.—come with me into a Quakers' Meeting.

Dost thou love silence deep as that "before the winds were made?" go not out into the wilderness, descend not into the profundities of the earth; shut not up thy casements; nor pour wax into the little cells of thy ears, with little-faith'd self-mistrusting Ulysses.—Retire with me into a Quakers' Meeting.

For a man to refrain even from good words, and to hold his peace, it is commendable; but for a multitude it is great mastery.

* From "Poems of all sorts," by Richard Fleckno, 1653.

What is the stillness of the desert compared with this place? what the uncommunicating muteness of fishes?—here the goddess reigns and revels.—"Boreas, and Cesias, and Argestes loud," do not with their interconfounding uproars more augment the brawl—nor the waves of the blown Baltic with their clubbed sounds —than their opposite (Silence her sacred self) is multiplied and rendered more intense by numbers, and by sympathy. She too hath her deeps, that call unto deeps. Negation itself hath a positive more and less; and closed eyes would seem to obscure the great obscurity of midnight.

There are wounds which an imperfect solitude cannot heal. By imperfect I mean that which a man enjoyeth by himself. The perfect is that which he can sometimes attain in crowds, but nowhere so absolutely as in a Quakers' Meeting.—Those first hermits did certainly understand this principle, when they retired into Egyptian solitudes, not singly, but in shoals, to enjoy one another's want of conversation. The Carthusian is bound to his brethren by this agreeing spirit of incommunicativeness. In secular occasions, what so pleasant as to be reading a book through a long winter evening, with a friend sitting by—say, a wife—he, or she, too, (if that be probable), reading another without interruption, or oral communication?—can there be no sympathy without the gabble of words?—away with this inhuman, shy, single, shade-and-cavern-haunting solitariness. Give me, Master Zimmerman, a sympathetic solitude.

To pace alone in the cloisters or side aisles of some cathedral, time-stricken;

> Or under hanging mountains,
> Or by the fall of fountains;

is but a vulgar luxury compared with that which those enjoy who come together for the purposes of more complete, abstracted solitude. This is the loneliness "to be felt."—The Abbey Church of Westminster hath nothing so solemn, so spirit-soothing, as the naked walls and benches of a Quakers' Meeting. Here are no tombs, no inscriptions.

> ———— Sands, ignoble things,
> Dropt from the ruined sides of kings—

but here is something which throws Antiquity herself into the fore-ground—SILENCE—eldest of things—language of old Night— primitive discourser—to which the insolent decays of mouldering grandeur have but arrived by a violent, and, as we may say, unnatural progression.

> How reverend is the view of these hushed heads,
> Looking tranquillity!

Nothing-plotting, nought-caballing, unmischievous synod! convocation without intrigue! parliament without debate! what a lesson dost thou read to council, and to consistory!—if my pen treat of you lightly—as haply it will wander—yet my spirit hath gravely felt the wisdom of your custom, when, sitting among you in deepest peace, which some out-welling tears would rather confirm than disturb, I have reverted to the times of your beginnings, and the sowings of the seed by Fox and Dewesbury.—I have witness-ed that which brought before my eyes your heroic tranquillity, in-flexible to the rude jests and serious violences of the insolent soldiery, republican or royalist, sent to molest you—for ye sate betwixt the fires of two persecu-tions, the outcast and off-scouring of church and presbytery.—I have seen the reeling sea-ruffian, who had wandered into your receptacle with the avowed intention of dis-turbing your quiet, from the very spirit of the place receive in a moment a new heart, and pre-sently sit among ye as a lamb amidst lambs. And I remember Penn before his accusers, and Fox in the bail dock, where he was lifted up in spirit, as he tells us, and "the Judge and the Jury became as dead men under his feet."

Reader, if you are not ac-quainted with it, I would recom-mend to you, above all church-narratives, to read Sewel's History of the Quakers. It is in folio, and is the abstract of the journals of Fox and the primitive Friends. It is far more edifying and affecting than anything you will read of Wesley and his colleagues. Here is nothing to stagger you, nothing to make you mistrust, no suspi-cion of alloy, no drop or dreg of the worldly or ambitious spirit. You will here read the true story of that much-injured, ridiculed man (who perhaps hath been a byword in your mouth)—James Naylor: what dreadful sufferings, with what patience, he endured, even to the boring through of his tongue with red-hot irons, without a murmur; and with what strength of mind, when the delusion he had fallen into, which they stigmatised for blasphemy, had given way to clearer thoughts, he could re-nounce his error, in a strain of the beautifullest humility, yet keep his first grounds, and be a Quaker still!—so different from the practice of your common con-verts from enthusiasm, who, when they apostatize, *apostatize all*, and think they can never get far enough from the society of their former errors, even to the renun-ciation of some saving truths, with which they had been mingled, not implicated.

Get the writings of John Wool-man by heart; and love the early Quakers.

How far the followers of these good men in our days have kept to the primitive spirit, or in what proportion they have substituted formality for it, the Judge of Spi-rits can alone determine. I have seen faces in their assemblies upon which the dove sate visibly brooding. Others, again, I have watched, when my thoughts should have been better engaged, in which I could possibly detect no-thing but a blank inanity. But quiet was in all, and the disposition to unanimity, and the absence of the fierce controversial workings.—If the spiritual pretensions of the Quakers have abated, at least they make few pretences. Hypocrites they certainly are not, in their preaching. It is seldom, indeed, that you shall see one get up amongst them to hold forth. Only now and then a trembling female, generally *ancient*, voice is heard—you cannot guess from what part of the meeting it proceeds—with a low, buzzing, musical sound, laying out a few words which "she thought might suit the condition of some present," with a quaking diffidence, which leaves no possibility of supposing that anything of female vanity was mixed up, where the tones were so full of tenderness, and a restraining modesty.—The men, for what I have observed, speak seldomer.

Once only, and it was some years ago, I witnessed a sample of the old Foxian orgasm. It was a man of giant stature, who, as Wordsworth phrases it, might have danced "from head to foot equipt in iron mail." His frame was of iron, too. But *he* was malleable. I saw him shake all over with the spirit—I dare not say of delusion. The strivings of the outer man were unutterable—he seemed not to speak, but to be spoken from. I saw the strong man bowed down, and his knees to fail—his joints all seemed loosening—it was a figure to set off against Paul preaching—the words he uttered were few, and sound—he was evidently resisting his will—keeping down his own word-wisdom with more mighty effort than the world's orators strain for theirs. "He had been a WIT in his youth," he told us, with expressions of a sober remorse. And it was not till long after the impression had begun to wear away that I was enabled, with something like a smile, to recall the striking incongruity of the confession—understanding the term in its worldly acceptation—with the frame and physiognomy of the person before me. His brow would have scared away the Levities—the Jocos Risus-que—faster than the Loves fled the face of Dis at Enna.—By *wit*, even in his youth, I will be sworn he understood something far within the limits of an allowable liberty.

More frequently the Meeting is broken up without a word having been spoken. But the mind has been fed. You go away with a sermon not made with hands. You have been in the milder caverns of Trophonius; or as in some den, where that fiercest and savagest of all wild creatures, the TONGUE, that unruly member, has strangely lain tied up and captive. You have bathed with stillness.—O, when the spirit is sore fretted, even tired to sickness of the janglings and nonsense-noises of the world, what a balm and a solace it is to go and seat yourself for a quiet half-hour upon some undisputed corner of a bench, among the gentle Quakers!

Their garb and stillness conjoined, present a uniformity, tranquil and herd-like—as in the pasture—"forty feeding like one."—

The very garments of a Quaker seem incapable of receiving a soil; and cleanliness in them to be something more than the absence of its contrary. Every Quakeress is a lily; and when they come up in bands to their Whitsunconferences, whitening the easterly streets of the metropolis, from all parts of the United Kingdom, they show like troops of the Shining Ones.

THE OLD AND THE NEW SCHOOLMASTER.

My reading has been lamentably desultory and immethodical. Odd, out of the way, old English plays, and treatises, have supplied me with most of my notions, and ways of feeling. In every thing that relates to *science*, I am a whole Encyclopædia behind the rest of the world. I should have scarcely cut a figure among the franklins, or country gentlemen, in king John's days. I know less geography than a schoolboy of six weeks' standing. To me a map of old Ortelius is as authentic as Arrowsmith. I do not know whereabout Africa merges into Asia; whether Ethiopia lie in one or other of those great divisions; nor can form the remotest conjecture of the position of New South Wales, or Van Diemen's Land. Yet do I hold a correspondence with a very dear friend in the first-named of these two Terræ In-cognitæ. I have no astronomy. I do not know where to look for the Bear, or Charles's Wain; the place of any star; or the name of any of them at sight. I guess at Venus only by her brightness—and if the sun on some portentous morn were to make his first appearance in the West, I verily believe, that, while all the world were gasping in apprehension about me, I alone should stand unterrified, from sheer incuriosity and want of observation. Of history and chronology I possess some vague points, such as one cannot help picking up in the course of miscellaneous study; but I never deliberately sat down to a chronicle, even of my own country. I have most dim apprehensions of the four great monarchies; and sometimes the Assyrian, sometimes the Persian, floats as *first* in my fancy. I make the widest conjectures concerning Egypt, and her shepherd kings. My friend *M.*, with great painstaking, got me to think I understood the first proposition in Euclid, but gave me over in despair at the second. I am entirely unacquainted with the modern languages; and, like a better man than myself, have "small Latin and less Greek." I am a stranger to the shapes and texture of the commonest trees, herbs, flowers—not from the circumstance of my being town-born—for I should have brought the same inobservant spirit into the world with me, had I first seen it "on Devon's leafy shores,"—and am no less at a loss among purely town objects, tools, engines, mechanic processes. —Not that I affect ignorance— but my head has not many mansions, nor spacious; and I have been obliged to fill it with such cabinet curiosities as it can hold without aching. I sometimes wonder how I have passed my probation with so little discredit in the world, as I have done, upon so meagre a stock. But the fact is, a man may do very well with a very little knowledge, and scarce be found out, in mixed company; everybody is so much more ready to produce his own, than to call for a display of your acquisitions. But in a *tête-à-tête* there is no shuffling. The truth will out. There is nothing which I dread so much, as the being left alone for a quarter of an hour with a sensible, well-informed man, that does not know me. I lately got into a dilemma of this sort.—

In one of my daily jaunts between Bishopsgate and Shacklewell, the coach stopped to take up a staid-looking gentleman, about the wrong side of thirty, who was giving his parting directions (while the steps were adjusting), in a tone of mild authority, to a tall youth, who seemed to be neither his clerk, his son, nor his servant, but something partaking of all three. The youth was dismissed, and we drove on. As we were the sole passengers, he naturally enough addressed his conversation to me; and we discussed the merits of the fare; the civility and punctuality of the driver; the circumstance of an opposition coach having been lately set up, with the probabilities of its success—to all which I was enabled to return pretty satisfactory answers, having been drilled into this kind of etiquette by some years' daily practice of riding to and fro in the stage aforesaid— when he suddenly alarmed me by a startling question, whether I had seen the show of prize cattle that morning in Smithfield? Now, as I had not seen it, and do not greatly care for such sort of exhibitions, I was obliged to return a cold negative. He seemed a little mortified, as well as astonished, at my declaration, as (it appeared) he was just come fresh from the sight, and doubtless had hoped to compare notes on the subject. However, he assured me that I had lost a fine treat, as it far exceeded the show of last year. We were now approaching Norton Falgate, when the sight of some shop-goods *ticketed* freshened him up into a dissertation upon the cheapness of cottons this spring. I was now a little in heart, as the nature of my morning avocations had brought me into some sort of familiarity with the raw material; and I was surprised to find how eloquent I was becoming on the state of the India market; when, presently, he dashed my incipient vanity to the earth at once, by inquiring whether I had ever made any calculation as to the value of the rental of all the retail shops in London. Had he asked of me what song the Syrens sang, or what name

Achilles assumed when he hid himself among women, I might, with Sir Thomas Browne, have hazarded a "wide solution."* My companion saw my embarrassment, and, the almshouses beyond Shoreditch just coming in view, with great good-nature and dexterity shifted his conversation to the subject of public charities; which led to the comparative merits of provision for the poor in past and present times, with observations on the old monastic institutions, and charitable orders; but, finding me rather dimly impressed with some glimmering notions from old poetic associations, than strongly fortified with any speculations reducible to calculation on the subject, he gave the matter up; and, the country beginning to open more and more upon us, as we approached the turnpike at Kingsland (the destined termination of his journey), he put a home thrust upon me, in the most unfortunate position he could have chosen, by advancing some queries relative to the North Pole Expedition. While I was muttering out something about the Panorama of those strange regions (which I had actually seen), by way of parrying the question, the coach stopping relieved me from any further apprehensions. My companion getting out, left me in the comfortable possession of my ignorance; and I heard him, as he went off, putting questions to an outside

* Urn Burial.

passenger, who had alighted with him, regarding an epidemic disorder that had been rife about Dalston, and which my friend assured him had gone through five or six schools in that neighbourhood. The truth now flashed upon me, that my companion was a schoolmaster; and that the youth, whom he had parted from at our first acquaintance, must have been one of the bigger boys, or the usher.—He was evidently a kind-hearted man, who did not seem so much desirous of provoking discussion by the questions which he put, as of obtaining information at any rate. It did not appear that he took any interest, either, in such kind of inquiries, for their own sake; but that he was in some way bound to seek for knowledge. A greenish-coloured coat, which he had on, forbade me to surmise that he was a clergyman. The adventure gave birth to some reflections on the difference between persons of his profession in past and present times.

Rest to the souls of those fine old Pedagogues; the breed, long since extinct, of the Lilys, and the Linacres: who believing that all learning was contained in the languages which they taught, and despising every other acquirement as superficial and useless, came to their task as to a sport! Passing from infancy to age, they dreamed away all their days as in a grammar-school. Revolving in a perpetual cycle of declensions, conjugations, syntaxes, and prosodies; renewing constantly the occupations which had charmed their studious childhood; rehearsing continually the part of the past; life must have slipped from them at last like one day. They were always in their first garden, reaping harvests of their golden time, among their *Flori* and their *Spici-legia;* in Arcadia still, but kings; the ferule of their sway not much harsher, but of like dignity with that mild sceptre attributed to king Basileus; the Greek and Latin, their stately Pamela and their Philoclea; with the occasional duncery of some untoward tyro, serving for a refreshing interlude of a Mopsa, or a clown Damœtas!

With what a savour doth the Preface to Colet's, or (as it is sometimes called) Paul's Accidence, set forth! "To exhort every man to the learning of grammar, that intendeth to attain the understanding of the tongues, wherein is contained a great treasury of wisdom and knowledge, it would seem but vain and lost labour; for so much as it is known, that nothing can surely be ended, whose beginning is either feeble or faulty; and no building be perfect whereas the foundation and groundwork is ready to fall, and unable to uphold the burden of the frame." How well doth this stately preamble (comparable to those which Milton commendeth as "having been the usage to prefix to some solemn law, then first promulgated by Solon or Lycurgus") correspond with and illustrate that pious zeal for conformity, expressed in a succeeding clause, which would fence about grammar-rules with the severity of faith-articles!—"as for the diversity of grammars, it is well profitably taken away by the King's Majestics wisdom, who foreseeing the inconvenience, and favourably providing the remedie, caused one kind of grammar by sundry learned men to be diligently drawn, and so to be set out, only everywhere to be taught for the use of learners, and for the hurt in changing of school-maisters." What a *gusto* in that which follows: "wherein it is profitable that he (the pupil) can orderly decline his noun and his verb." *His* noun!

The fine dream is fading away fast; and the least concern of a teacher in the present day is to inculcate grammar-rules.

The modern schoolmaster is expected to know a little of everything, because his pupil is required not to be entirely ignorant of anything. He must be superficially, if I may so say, omniscient. He is to know something of pneumatics; of chemistry; of whatever is curious or proper to excite the attention of the youthful mind; an insight into mechanics is desirable, with a touch of statistics; the quality of soils, &c., botany, the constitution of his country, *cum multis aliis.* You may get a notion of some part of his expected duties by consulting the famous Tractate on Education, addressed to Mr. Hartlib.

All these things—these, or tho

desire of them—he is expected to instil, not by set lessons from professors, which he may charge in the bill, but at school intervals, as he walks the streets, or saunters through green fields (those natural instructors), with his pupils. The least part of what is expected from him is to be done in school-hours. He must insinuate knowledge at the *mollia tempora fandi.* He must seize every occasion—the season of the year—the time of the day—a passing cloud—a rainbow—a waggon of hay—a regiment of soldiers going by—to inculcate something useful. He can receive no pleasure from a casual glimpse of Nature, but must catch at it as an object of instruction. He must interpret beauty into the picturesque. He cannot relish a beggar-man, or a gipsy, for thinking of the suitable improvement. Nothing comes to him, not spoiled by the sophisticating medium of moral uses. The Universe—that Great Book, as it has been called—is to him, indeed, to all intents and purposes, a book out of which he is doomed to read tedious homilies to distasting schoolboys.—Vacations themselves are none to him, he is only rather worse off than before; for commonly he has some intrusive upper-boy fastened upon him at such times; some cadet of a great family; some neglected lump of nobility, or gentry; that he must drag after him to the play, to the Panorama, to Mr. Bartley's Orrery, to the Panopticon, or into the country, to a friend's house, or his favourite watering-place. Wherever he goes this uneasy shadow attends him. A boy is at his board, and in his path, and in all his movements. He is boy-rid, sick of perpetual boy.

Boys are capital fellows in their own way, among their mates; but they are unwholesome companions for grown people. The restraint is felt no less on the one side than on the other.—Even a child, that "plaything for an hour," tires *always.* The noises of children, playing their own fancies—as I now hearken to them, by fits, sporting on the green before my window, while I am engaged in these grave speculations at my neat suburban retreat at Shacklewell—by distance made more sweet—inexpressibly take from the labour of my task. It is like writing to music. They seem to modulate my periods. They ought at least to do so—for in the voice of that tender age there is a kind of poetry, far unlike the harsh prose-accents of man's conversation.—I should but spoil their sport, and diminish my own sympathy for them, by mingling in their pastime.

I would not be domesticated all my days with a person of very superior capacity to my own—not, if I know myself at all, from any considerations of jealousy or self-comparison, for the occasional communion with such minds has constituted the fortune and felicity of my life—but the habit of too constant intercourse with splrits above you, instead of raising you, keeps you down. Too frequent doses of original thinking from others restrain what lesser portion of that faculty you may possess of your own. You get entangled in another man's mind, even as you lose yourself in another man's grounds. You are walking with a tall varlet, whose strides out-pace yours to lassitude. The constant operation of such potent agency would reduce me, I am convinced, to imbecility. You may derive thoughts from others; your way of thinking, the mould in which your thoughts are cast, must be your own. Intellect may be imparted, but not each man's intellectual frame.—

As little as I should wish to be always thus dragged upward, as little (or rather still less) is it desirable to be stunted downwards by your associates. The trumpet does not more than stun you by its loudness, than a whisper teases you by its provoking inaudibility.

Why are we never quite at our ease in the presence of a schoolmaster?—because we are conscious that he is not quite at his ease in ours. He is awkward, and out of place in the society of his equals. He comes like Gulliver from among his little people, and he cannot fit the stature of his understanding to yours. He cannot meet you on the square. He wants a point given him, like an indifferent whist-player. He is so used to teaching, that he wants to be teaching you. One of these professors, upon my complaining that these little sketches of mine were anything but methodical, and that I was unable to make them otherwise, kindly offered to instruct me in the method by which young gentlemen in *his* seminary were taught to compose English themes. The jests of a schoolmaster are coarse, or thin. They do not *tell* out of school. He is under the restraint of a formal or didactive hypocrisy in company, as a clergyman is under a moral one. He can no more let his intellect loose in society than the other can his inclinations. He is forlorn among his coevals; his juniors cannot be his friends.

"I take blame to myself," said a sensible man of this profession, writing to a friend respecting a youth who had quitted his school abruptly, "that your nephew was not more attached to me. But persons in my situation are more to be pitied than can well be imagined. We are surrounded by young, and, consequently, ardently affectionate hearts, but *we* can never hope to share an atom of their affections. The relation of master and scholar forbids this. *How pleasing this must be to you, how I envy your feelings!* my friends will sometimes say to me, when they see young men whom I have educated, return after some years' absence from school, their eyes shining with pleasure, while they shake hands with their old master, bringing a present of game to me, or a toy to my wife, and thanking me in the warmest terms for my care of their education. A holiday is begged for the boys; the house is a scene of happiness; I, only, am sad at heart.—This fine-spirited and warm-hearted youth, who fancies he repays his master with gratitude for the care of his boyish years—this young man—in the eight long years I watched over him with a parent's anxiety, never could repay me with one look of genuine feeling. He was proud, when I praised; he was submissive, when I reproved him; but he did never *love* me—and what he now mistakes for gratitude and kindness for me, is but the pleasant sensation which all persons feel at revisiting the scenes of their boyish hopes and fears; and the seeing on equal terms the man they were accustomed to look up to with reverence. My wife, too," this interesting correspondent goes on to say, "my once darling Anna, is the wife of a schoolmaster.— When I married her—knowing that the wife of a schoolmaster ought to be a busy notable creature, and fearing that my gentle Anna would ill supply the loss of my dear bustling mother, just then dead, who never sat still, was in every part of the house in a moment, and whom I was obliged sometimes to threaten to fasten down in a chair, to save her from fatiguing herself to death—I expressed my fears that I was bringing her into a way of life unsuitable to her; and she, who loved me tenderly, promised for my sake to exert herself to perform the duties of her new situation. She promised, and she kept her word. What wonders will not woman's love perform?— My house is managed with a propriety and decorum unknown in other schools; my boys are well fed, look healthy, and have every proper accommodation; and all this performed with a careful economy, that never descends to meanness. But I have lost my gentle *helpless* Anna! When we sit down to enjoy an hour of repose after the fatigue of the day, I am compelled to listen to what have been her useful (and they are really useful) employments through the day, and what she proposes for her to-morrow's task. Her heart and her features are changed by the duties of her situation. To the boys, she never appears other than the *master's wife*, and she looks up to me as the *boy's master;* to whom all show of love and affection would be highly improper, and unbecoming the dignity of her situation and mine. Yet *this* my gratitude forbids me to hint to her. For my sake she submitted to be this altered creature, and can I reproach her for it?"—For the communication of this letter I am indebted to my cousin Bridget.

———

IMPERFECT SYMPATHIES.

I am of a constitution so general, that it consorts and sympathiseth with all things; I have no antipathy, or rather idiosyncrasy in anything. Those natural repugnancies do not touch me, nor do I behold with prejudice the French, Italian, Spaniard, or Dutch.—*Religio Medici.*

THAT the author of the Religio Medici mounted upon the airy stilts of abstraction, conversant about notional and conjectural essences; in whose categories of Being the possible took the upper hand of the actual; should have overlooked the impertinent individualities of such poor concretions as mankind, is not much to be admired. It is rather to be wondered at, that in the genus of animals he should have condescended to distinguish that species at all. For myself—earth-bound and fettered to the scene of my activities,—

Standing on earth, not rapt above the sky,

I confess that I do feel the differences of mankind, national or individual, to an unhealthy excess. I can look with no indifferent eye upon things or persons. Whatever is, is to me a matter of taste or distaste; or when once it becomes indifferent it begins to be disrelishing. I am, in plainer words, a bundle of prejudices—made up of likings and dislikings—the veriest thrall to sympathies, apathies, antipathies. In a certain sense, I hope it may be said of me that I am a lover of my species. I can feel for all indifferently, but I cannot feel towards all equally. The more purely-English word that expresses sympathy, will better explain my meaning. I can be a friend to a worthy man, who upon another account cannot be my mate or *fellow.* I cannot *like* all people alike.*

I have been trying all my life to like Scotchmen, and am obliged to desist from the experiment in despair. They cannot like me—and in truth, I never knew one of that nation who attempted to do it. There is something more plain and ingenuous in their mode of proceeding. We know one another at first sight. There is an

* I would be understood as confining myself to the subject of *imperfect sympathies.* To nations or classes of men there can be no direct antipathy. There may be individuals born and constellated so opposite to another individual nature, that the same sphere cannot hold them. I have met with my moral antipodes, and can believe the story of two persons meeting (who never saw one another before in their lives) and instantly fighting.

—— We by proof find there should be
'Twixt man and man such an antipathy,
That though he can show no just reason
    why
For any former wrong or injury,
Can neither find a blemish in his fame,
Nor aught in face or feature justly blame,
Can challenge or accuse him of no evil,
Yet notwithstanding hates him as a devil.

The lines are from old Heywood's "Hierarchie of Angels," and he subjoins a curious story in confirmation, of a Spaniard who attempted to assassinate a king Ferdinand of Spain, and being put to the rack could give no other reason for the deed but an inveterate antipathy which he had taken to the first sight of the king.
—— The cause which to that act compell'd him
Was, he ne'er loved him since he first behold him.

order of imperfect intellects (under which mine must be content to rank) which in its constitution is essentially anti-Caledonian. The owners of the sort of faculties I allude to, have minds rather suggestive than comprehensive. They have no pretences to much clearness or precision in their ideas, or in their manner of expressing them. Their intellectual wardrobe (to confess fairly) has few whole pieces in it. They are content with fragments and scattered pieces of Truth. She presents no full front to them—a feature or side-face at the most. Hints and glimpses, germs and crude essays at a system, is the utmost they pretend to. They beat up a little game peradventure—and leave it to knottier heads, more robust constitutions, to run it down. The light that lights them is not steady and polar, but mutable and shifting: waxing, and again waning. Their conversation is accordingly. They will throw out a random word in or out of season, and be content to let it pass for what it is worth. They cannot speak always as if they were upon their oath—but must be understood, speaking or writing, with some abatement. They seldom wait to mature a proposition, but e'en bring it to market in the green ear. They delight to impart their defective discoveries as they arise, without waiting for their development. They are no systematizers, and would but err more by attempting it. Their minds, as I said before, are suggestive merely. The brain of a true Caledonian (if I am not mistaken) is constituted upon quite a different plan. His Minerva is born in panoply. You are never admitted to see his ideas in their growth—if, indeed, they do grow, and are not rather put together upon principles of clock-work. You never catch his mind in an undress. He never hints or suggests anything, but unlades his stock of ideas in perfect order and completeness. He brings his total wealth into company, and gravely unpacks it. His riches are always about him. He never stoops to catch a glittering something in your presence to share it with you, before he quite knows whether it be true touch or not. You cannot cry *halves* to anything that he finds. He does not find, but bring. You never witness his first apprehension of a thing. His understanding is always at its meridian—you never see the first dawn, the early streaks.—He has no falterings of self-suspicion. Surmises, guesses, misgivings, half-intuitions, semi-consciousnesses, partial illuminations, dim instincts, embryo conceptions, have no place in his brain or vocabulary. The twilight of dubiety never falls upon him. Is he orthodox—he has no doubts. Is he an infidel—he has none either. Between the affirmative and the negative there is no border-land with him. You cannot hover with him upon the confines of truth, or wander in the maze of a probable argument. He always keeps the path. You cannot make excursions with him—for he sets you right. His taste never fluctuates. His morality never abates. He cannot compromise, or understand middle actions. There can be but a right and a wrong. His conversation is as a book. His affirmations have the sanctity of an oath. You must speak upon the square with him. He stops a metaphor like a suspected person in an enemy's country. "A healthy book!"—said one of his countrymen to me, who had ventured to give that appellation to John Buncle,—"Did I catch rightly what you said? I have heard of a man in health, and of a healthy state of body, but I do not see how that epithet can be properly applied to a book." Above all, you must beware of indirect expressions before a Caledonian. Clap an extinguisher upon your irony, if you are unhappily blest with a vein of it. Remember you are upon your oath. I have a print of a graceful figure after Leonardo da Vinci, which I was showing off to Mr. * * * * After he had examined it minutely, I ventured to ask him how he liked MY BEAUTY (a foolish name it goes by among my friends)—when he very gravely assured me, that "he had considerable respect for my character and talents" (so he was pleased to say), "but had not given himself much thought about the degree of my personal pretensions." The misconception staggered me, but did not seem much to disconcert him.—Persons of this nation are particularly fond of affirming a truth—which nobody doubts. They do not so properly affirm, as annunciate it. They do indeed appear to have such a love of truth (as if, like virtue, it were valuable for itself) that all truth becomes equally valuable, whether the proposition that contains it be new or old, disputed, or such as is impossible to become a subject of disputation. I was present not long since at a party of North Britons, where a son of Burns was expected; and happened to drop a silly expression (in my South British way), that I wished it were the father instead of the son— when four of them started up at once to inform me, that "that was impossible, because he was dead." An impracticable wish, it seems, was more than they could conceive. Swift has hit off this part of their character, namely their love of truth, in his biting way, but with an illiberality that necessarily confines the passage to the margin.* The tediousness of these people is certainly provoking. I wonder if they ever tire one another!—In my early life I had a

* There are some people who think they sufficiently acquit themselves, and entertain their company, with relating facts of no consequence, not at all out of the road of such common incidents as happen every day; and this I have observed more frequently among the Scots than any other nation, who are very careful not to omit the minutest circumstances of time or place; which kind of discourse, if it were not a little relieved by the uncouth terms and phrases, as well as accent and gesture, peculiar to that country, would be hardly tolerable. —*Hints towards an Essay on Conversation.*

passionate fondness for the poetry of Burns. I have sometimes foolishly hoped to ingratiate myself with his countrymen by expressing it. But I have always found that a true Scot resents your admiration of his compatriot even more than he would your contempt of him. The latter he imputes to your "imperfect acquaintance with many of the words which he uses;" and the same objection makes it a presumption in you to suppose that you can admire him.—Thomson they seem to have forgotten. Smollett they have neither forgotten nor forgiven, for his delineation of Rory and his companion, upon their first introduction to our metropolis.—Speak of Smollett as a great genius, and they will retort upon you Hume's History compared with *his* Continuation of it. What if the historian had continued Humphrey Clinker?

I have, in the abstract, no disrespect for the Jews. They are a piece of stubborn antiquity, compared with which Stonehenge is in its nonage. They date beyond the pyramids. But I should not care to be in habits of familiar intercourse with any of that nation. I confess that I have not the nerves to enter their synagogues. Old prejudices cling about me. I cannot shake off the story of Hugh of Lincoln. Centuries of injury, contempt, and hate, on the one side, —of cloaked revenge, dissimulation, and hate, on the other, between our and their fathers, must and ought to affect the blood of the children. I cannot believe it can run clear and kindly yet; or that a few words, such as candour, liberality, the light of the nineteenth century, can close up the breaches of so deadly a disunion. A Hebrew is nowhere congenial to me. He is least distasteful on 'Change—for the mercantile spirit levels all distinctions, as all are beauties in the dark. I boldly confess that I do not relish the approximation of Jew and Christian, which has become so fashionable. The reciprocal endearments have, to me, something hypocritical and unnatural in them. I do not like to see the Church and Synagogue kissing and congeeing in awkward postures of an affected civility. If *they* are converted, why do they not come over to us altogether? Why keep up a form of separation, when the life of it is fled? If they can sit with us at table, why do they keck at our cookery? I do not understand these half convertites. Jews christianizing—Christians judaizing—puzzle me. I like fish or flesh. A moderate Jew is a more confounding piece of anomaly than a wet Quaker. The spirit of the synagogue is essentially *separative*. B—— would have been more in keeping if he had abided by the faith of his forefathers. There is a fine scorn in his face, which nature meant to be of——Christians.—The Hebrew spirit is strong in him, in spite of his proselytism. He cannot conquer the Shibboleth. How it breaks out, when he sings, "The Children of Israel passed through the Red Sea!" The auditors, for the moment, are as Egyptians to him, and he rides over our necks in triumph. There is no mistaking him. B—— has a strong expression of sense in his countenance, and it is confirmed by his singing. The foundation of his vocal excellence is sense. He sings with understanding, as Kemble delivered dialogue. He would sing the Commandments, and give an appropriate character to each prohibition. His nation, in general, have not over-sensible countenances. How should they? —but you seldom see a silly expression among them.—Gain, and the pursuit of gain, sharpen a man's visage. I never heard of an idiot being born among them. —Some admire the Jewish female-physiognomy. I admire it—but with trembling. Jael had those full dark inscrutable eyes.

In the Negro countenance you will often meet with strong traits of benignity. I have felt yearnings of tenderness towards some of these faces—or rather masks—that have looked out kindly upon one in casual encounters in the streets and highways. I love what Fuller beautifully calls—these "images of God cut in ebony." But I should not like to associate with them, to share my meals and my good nights with them—because they are black.

I love Quaker ways, and Quaker worship. I venerate the Quaker principles. It does me good for the rest of the day when I meet any of their people in my path.

When I am ruffled or disturbed by any occurrence, the sight, or quiet voice of a Quaker, acts upon me as a ventilator, lightening the air, and taking off a load from the bosom. But I cannot like the Quakers (as Desdemona would say) "to live with them." I am all over sophisticated—with humours, fancies, craving hourly sympathy. I must have books, pictures, theatres, chit-chat, scandal, jokes, ambiguities, and a thousand whim-whams, which their simpler taste can do without. I should starve at their primitive banquet. My appetites are too high for the salads which (according to Evelyn) Eve dressed for the angel; my gusto too excited

To sit a guest with Daniel at his pulse.

The indirect answers which Quakers are often found to return to a question put to them may be explained, I think, without the vulgar assumption, that they are more given to evasion and equivocating than other people. They naturally look to their words more carefully, and are more cautious of committing themselves. They have a peculiar character to keep up on this head. They stand in a manner upon their veracity. A Quaker is by law exempted from taking an oath. The custom of resorting to an oath in extreme cases, sanctified as it is by all religious antiquity, is apt (it must be confessed) to introduce into the laxer sort of minds the notion of two kinds of truth—the one applicable to the solemn affairs of justice, and the other to the common proceedings of daily intercourse. As truth bound upon the conscience by an oath can be but truth, so in the common affirmations of the shop and the market-place a latitude is expected, and conceded upon questions wanting this solemn covenant. Something less than truth satisfies. It is common to hear a person say, "You do not expect me to speak as if I were upon my oath." Hence a great deal of incorrectness and inadvertency, short of falsehood, creeps into ordinary conversation; and a kind of secondary or laic-truth is tolerated, where clergy-truth—oath-truth, by the nature of the circumstances, is not required. A Quaker knows none of this distinction. His simple affirmation being received upon the most sacred occasions, without any further test, stamps a value upon the words which he is to use upon the most indifferent topics of life. He looks to them, naturally, with more severity. You can have of him no more than his word. He knows, if he is caught tripping in a casual expression, he forfeits, for himself at least, his claim to the invidious exemption. He knows that his syllables are weighed—and how far a consciousness of this particular watchfulness, exerted against a person, has a tendency to produce indirect answers, and a diverting of the question by honest means, might be illustrated, and the practice justified by a more sacred example than is proper to be adduced upon this occasion. The admirable presence of mind, which is notorious in Quakers upon all contingencies, might be traced to this imposed self-watchfulness—if it did not seem rather an humble and secular scion of that old stock of religious constancy, which never bent or faltered, in the Primitive Friends, or gave way to the winds of persecution, to the violence of judge or accuser, under trials and racking examinations. "You will never be the wiser, if I sit here answering your questions till midnight," said one of those upright Justicers to Penn, who had been putting law-cases with a puzzling subtlety. "Thereafter as the answers may be," retorted the Quaker. The astonishing composure of this people is sometimes ludicrously displayed in lighter instances.—I was travelling in a stage-coach with three male Quakers, buttoned up in the straitest nonconformity of their sect. We stopped to bait at Andover, where a meal, partly tea apparatus, partly supper, was set before us. My friends confined themselves to the tea-table. I in my way took supper. When the landlady brought in the bill, the eldest of my companions discovered that she had charged for both meals. This was resisted. Mine hostess was very clamorous and positive. Some mild arguments were used on the part of the Quakers, for which the heated mind of the good lady seemed by no means a fit recipient. The guard came with his usual peremptory notice. The Quakers pulled out their money and formally tendered it—so much for tea—I, in humble imitation, tendering mine—for the supper which I had taken. She would not relax in her demand. So they all three quietly put up their silver, as did myself, and marched out of the room, the eldest and gravest going first, with myself closing up the rear, who thought I could not do better than follow the example of such grave and warrantable personages. We got in. The steps went up. The coach drove off. The murmurs of mine hostess, not very indistinctly or ambiguously pronounced, became after a time inaudible—and now my conscience, which the whimsical scene had for a while suspended, beginning to give some twitches, I waited, in the hope that some justification would be offered by these serious persons for the seeming injustice of their conduct. To my great surprise not a syllable was dropped on the subject. They sat as mute as at a meeting. At length the eldest of them broke silence, by inquiring of his next neighbour, " Hast thee heard how indigos go at the India House?" and the question operated as soporific on my moral feeling as far as Exeter.

———

WITCHES, AND OTHER NIGHT FEARS.

WE are too hasty when we set down our ancestors in the gross for fools, for the monstrous inconsistencies (as they seem to us) involved in their creed of witchcraft. In the relations of this visible world we find them to have been as rational, and shrewd to detect an historic anomaly, as ourselves. But when once the invisible world was supposed to be open, and the lawless agency of bad spirits assumed, what measures of probability, of decency, of fitness, or proportion—of that which distinguishes the likely from the palpable absurd—could they have to guide them in the rejection or admission of any particular testimony?—That maidens pined away, wasting inwardly as their waxen images consumed before a fire—that corn was lodged, and cattle lamed—that whirlwinds uptore in diabolic revelry the oaks of the forest—or that spits and kettles only danced a fearful-innocent vagary about some rustic's kitchen when no wind was stirring—were all equally probable where no law of agency was understood. That the prince of the powers of darkness, passing by the flower and pomp of the earth, should lay preposterous siege to the weak fantasy of indigent eld—has neither likelihood nor unlikelihood *à priori* to us, who have no measure to guess at his policy, or standard to estimate what rate those anile souls may fetch in the devil's market. Nor, when the wicked are expressly symbolised by a goat, was it to be wondered at so much, that *he* should come sometimes in that body, and assert his metaphor.— That the intercourse was opened at all between both worlds was perhaps the mistake—but that once assumed, I see no reason for disbelieving one attested story of this nature more than another on the score of absurdity. There is no law to judge of the lawless, or canon by which a dream may be criticised.

I have sometimes thought that I could not have existed in the days of received witchcraft; that I could not have slept in a village where one of those reputed hags dwelt. Our ancestors were bolder or more obtuse. Amidst the universal belief that these wretches were in league with the author of all evil, holding hell tributary to their muttering, no simple justice of the peace seems to have scrupled issuing, or silly Headborough serving, a warrant upon them—as if they should subpœna Satan!—Prospero in his boat, with his books and wand about him, suffers himself to be conveyed away at the mercy of his enemies to an unknown island. He might have raised a storm or two, we think, on the passage. His acquiescence is in exact analogy to the non-resistance of witches to the constituted powers. —What stops the Fiend in Spenser from tearing Guyon to pieces—or who had made it a condition of his prey that Guyon must take assay of the glorious bait—we have no guess. We do not know the laws of that country.

From my childhood I was extremely inquisitive about witches and witch-stories. My maid, and more legendary aunt, supplied me with good store. But I shall mention the accident which directed my curiosity originally into this channel. In my father's book-closet the history of the Bible by Stackhouse occupied a distinguished station. The pictures with which it abounds—one of the ark, in particular, and another of Solomon's temple, delineated with all the fidelity of ocular admeasurement, as if the artist had been upon the spot— attracted my childish attention. There was a picture, too, of the Witch raising up Samuel, which I wish that I had never seen. We shall come to that hereafter. Stackhouse is in two huge tomes; and there was a pleasure in removing folios of that magnitude, which, with infinite straining, was as much as I could manage, from the situation which they occupied upon an upper shelf. I have not met with the work from that time to this, but I remember it consisted of Old Testament stories, orderly set down, with the *objection* appended to each story, and the *solution* of the objection regularly tacked to that. The *objection* was a summary of whatever difficulties had been opposed to the credibility of the history by the shrewdness of ancient or modern infidelity, drawn up with an almost complimentary excess of candour. The *solution* was brief, modest, and satisfactory. The bane and antidote were both before you. To doubts so put, and so quashed, there seemed to be an end for ever. The dragon lay dead, for the foot of the veriest babe to trample on. But —like as was rather feared than realized from that slain monster in Spenser—from the womb of those crushed errors young dragonets would creep, exceeding the prowess of so tender a Saint George as myself to vanquish. The habit of expecting objections to every passage set me upon starting more objections, for the glory of finding a solution of my own for them. I became staggered and perplexed, a sceptic in long-coats. The pretty Bible stories which I had read, or heard read in church, lost their purity and sincerity of impression, and were turned into so many historic or chronologic theses to be defended against whatever impugners. I was not to disbelieve them, but— the next thing to that—I was to be quite sure that some one or other would or had disbelieved them. Next to making a child an infidel is the letting him know that there are infidels at all. Credulity is the man's weakness, but the child's strength. O, how ugly sound scriptural doubts from the mouth of a babe and a suckling!—I should have lost myself in these mazes, and have pined away, I think, with such unfit sus-

tenance as these husks afforded, but for a fortunate piece of ill-fortune which about this time befell me. Turning over the picture of the ark with too much haste, I unhappily made a breach in its ingenious fabric—driving my inconsiderate fingers right through the two larger quadrupeds, the elephant and the camel, that stare (as well they might) out of the two last windows next the steerage in that unique piece of naval architecture. Stackhouse was henceforth locked up, and became an interdicted treasure. With the book, the *objections* and *solutions* gradually cleared out of my head, and have seldom returned since in any force to trouble me. But there was one impression which I had imbibed from Stackhouse which no lock or bar could shut out, and which was destined to try my childish nerves rather more seriously.—That detestable picture!

I was dreadfully alive to nervous terrors. The night-time, solitude, and the dark, were my hell. The sufferings I endured in this nature would justify the expression. I never laid my head on my pillow, I suppose, from the fourth to the seventh or eighth year of my life—so far as memory serves in things so long ago —without an assurance, which realized its own prophecy, of seeing some frightful spectre. Be old Stackhouse then acquitted in part, if I say, that to his picture of the Witch raising up Samuel —(O that old man covered with a mantle!)—I owe—not my midnight terrors, the hell of my infancy—but the shape and manner of their visitation. It was he who dressed up for me a hag that nightly sate upon my pillow—a sure bedfellow, when my aunt or my maid was far from me. All day long, while the book was permitted me, I dreamed waking over his delineation, and at night (if I may use so bold an expression) awoke into sleep, and found the vision true. I durst not, even in the day-light, once enter the chamber where I slept, without my face turned to the window, aversely from the bed where my witch-ridden pillow was. Parents do not know what they do when they leave tender babes alone to go to sleep in the dark. The feeling about for a friendly arm—the hoping for a familiar voice—when they wake screaming—and find none to soothe them—what a terrible shaking it is to their poor nerves! The keeping them up till midnight, through candle-light and the unwholesome hours, as they are called,—would, I am satisfied, in a medical point of view, prove the better caution.—That detestable picture, as I have said, gave the fashion to my dreams—if dreams they were—for the scene of them was invariably the room in which I lay. Had I never met with the picture, the fears would have come self-pictured in some shape or other—

Headless bear, black man, or ape—

but, as it was, my imaginations took that form.—It is not book, or picture, or the stories of foolish servants, which create these terrors in children. They can at most but give them a direction. Dear little T. H., who of all children has been brought up with the most scrupulous exclusion of every taint of superstition—who was never allowed to hear of goblin or apparition, or scarcely to be told of bad men, or read or hear of any distressing story—finds all this world of fear, from which he has been so rigidly excluded *ab extra*, in his own "thick-coming fancies;" and from his little midnight pillow, this nurse-child of optimism will start at shapes, unborrowed of tradition, in sweats to which the reveries of the cell-damned murderer are tranquillity.

Gorgons, and Hydras, and Chimæras dire—stories of Celæno and the Harpies—may reproduce themselves in the brain of superstition—but they were there before. They are transcripts, types—the archetypes are in us, and eternal. How else should the recital of that, which we know in a waking sense to be false, come to affect us at all?—or

  —— Names, whose sense we see not,
  Fray us with things that be not?

Is it that we naturally conceive terror from such objects, considered in their capacity of being able to inflict upon us bodily injury?—O, least of all! These terrors are of older standing. They date beyond body—or, without the body, they would have been the same. All the cruel, tormenting, defined devils in Dante—tearing, mangling, choking, stifling, scorching demons—are they one half so fearful to the spirit of a man, as the simple idea of a spirit unembodied following him—

Like one that on a lonesome road
Doth walk in fear and dread,
And having once turn'd round, walks on
And turns no more his head;
Because he knows a frightful fiend
Doth close behind him tread. *

That the kind of fear here treated of is purely spiritual—that it is strong in proportion as it is objectless upon earth—that it predominates in the period of sinless infancy—are difficulties, the solution of which might afford some probable insight into our ante-mundane condition, and a peep at least into the shadowland of pre-existence.

My night-fancies have long ceased to be afflictive. I confess an occasional nightmare; but I do not, as in early youth, keep a stud of them. Fiendish faces, with the extinguished taper, will come and look at me; but I know them for mockeries, even while I cannot elude their presence, and I fight and grapple with them. For the credit of my imagination, I am almost ashamed to say how tame and prosaic my dreams are grown. They are never romantic, seldom even rural. They are of architecture and of buildings—cities abroad, which I have never seen and hardly have hoped to see. I have traversed, for the seeming length of a natural day, Rome, Amsterdam, Paris, Lisbon—their churches, palaces, squares, market-places, shops, suburbs, ruins, with an inexpressible sense of delight—a map-like distinctness of trace, and a day-light vividness of vision, that was all but being awake.—I have formerly travelled among the Westmoreland fells—my highest Alps,—but they are objects too mighty for the grasp of my dreaming recognition; and I have again and again awoke with ineffectual struggles of the inner eye, to make out a shape, in any way whatever, of Helvellyn. Methought I was in that country, but the mountains were gone. The poverty of my dreams mortifies me. There is Coleridge, at his will can conjure up icy domes, and pleasure-houses for Kubla Khan, and Abyssinian maids, and songs of Abara, and caverns,

Where Alph, the sacred river, runs,

to solace his night solitudes—when I cannot muster a fiddle. Barry Cornwall has his tritons and his nereids gamboling before him in nocturnal visions, and proclaiming sons born to Neptune—when my stretch of imaginative activity can hardly, in the night season, raise up the ghost of a fish-wife. To set my failures in somewhat a mortifying light—it

* Mr. Coleridge's Ancient Mariner.

was after reading the noble Dream of this poet, that my fancy ran strong upon these marine spectra; and the poor plastic power; such as it is, within me set to work to humour my folly in a sort of dream that very night. Methought I was upon the ocean billows at some sea nuptials, riding and mounted high, with the customary train sounding their conchs before me, (I myself, you may be sure, the *leading god*,) and jollily we went careering over the main, till just where Ino Leucothea should have greeted me (I think it was Ino) with a white embrace, the billows gradually subsiding, fell from a sea roughness to a sea calm, and thence to a river motion, and that river (as happens in the familiarization of dreams) was no other than the gentle Thames, which landed me in the wafture of a placid wave or two, alone, safe and inglorious, somewhere at the foot of Lambeth palace.

The degree of the soul's creativeness in sleep might furnish no whimsical criterion of the quantum of poetical faculty resident in the same soul waking. An old gentleman, a friend of mine, and a humorist, used to carry this notion so far, that when he saw any stripling of his acquaintance ambitious of becoming a poet, his first question would be,—"Young man, what sort of dreams have you?" I have so much faith in my old friend's theory, that when I feel that idle vein returning upon me, I presently subside into my proper element of prose, re-membering those eluding nereids, and that inauspicious inland landing.

———

VALENTINE'S DAY.

Hail to thy returning festival, old Bishop Valentine! Great is thy name in the rubric, thou venerable Archflamen of Hymen! Immortal Go-between; who and what manner of person art thou? Art thou but a *name*, typifying the restless principle which impels poor humans to seek perfection in union? or wert thou indeed a mortal prelate, with thy tippet and thy rochet, thy apron on, and decent lawn sleeves? Mysterious personage! Like unto thee, assuredly, there is no other mitred father in the calendar; not Jerome, nor Ambrose, nor Cyril; nor the consigner of undipt infants to eternal torments, Austin, whom all mothers hate; nor he who hated all mothers, Origen; nor Bishop Bull, nor Archbishop Parker, nor Whitgift. Thou comest attended with thousands and ten thousands of little Loves, and the air is

Brush'd with the hiss of rustling wings.

Singing Cupids are thy choristers and thy precentors; and instead of the crosier, the mystical arrow is borne before thee.

In other words, this is the day on which those charming little missives, ycleped Valentines, cross and intercross each other at every street and turning. The weary and all forspent twopenny postman sinks beneath a load of delicate embarrassments, not his own. It is scarcely credible to what extent this ephemeral courtship is carried on in this loving town, to the great enrichment of porters, and detriment of knockers and bell-wires. In these little visual interpretations, no emblem is so common as the *heart*,—that little three-cornered exponent of all our hopes and fears,—the bestuck and bleeding heart; it is twisted and tortured into more allegories and affectations than an opera-hat. What authority we have in history or mythology for placing the headquarters and metropolis of god Cupid in this anatomical seat rather than in any other, is not very clear; but we have got it, and it will serve as well as any other. Else we might easily imagine, upon some other system which might have prevailed for anything which our pathology knows to the contrary, a lover addressing his mistress, in perfect simplicity of feeling, "Madam, my *liver* and fortune are entirely at your disposal;" or putting a delicate question, "Amanda, have you a *midriff* to bestow?" But custom has settled these things, and awarded the seat of sentiment to the aforesaid triangle, while its less fortunate neighbours wait at animal and anatomical distance.

Not many sounds in life, and I include all urban and all rural sounds, exceed in interest a *knock* at the door. It "gives a very echo to the throne where hope is seated." But its issues seldom answer to this oracle within. It is so seldom that just the person we want to see comes. But of all the clamorous visitations the welcomest in expectation is the sound that ushers in, or seems to usher in, a Valentine. As the raven himself was hoarse that announced the fatal entrance of Duncan, so the knock of the postman on this day is light, airy, confident, and befitting one that bringeth good tidings. It is less mechanical than on other days; you will say, "That is not the post, I am sure." Visions of Love, of Cupids, of Hymens!—delightful eternal commonplaces, which "having been will always be;" which no schoolboy nor school-man can write away; having your irreversible throne in the fancy and affections—what are your transports, when the happy maiden, opening with careful finger, careful not to break the emblematic seal, bursts upon the sight of some well-designed allegory, some type, some youthful fancy, not without verses—

Lovers all,
A madrigal,

or some such devise, not over-abundant in sense—young Love disclaims it,—and not quite silly—something between wind and water, a chorus where the sheep might almost join the shepherd, as they did, or as I apprehend they did, in Arcadia.

All Valentines are not foolish; and I shall not easily forget thine, my kind friend (if 1 may have leave to call you so) E. B——. E. B. lived opposite a young maiden whom he had often seen, unseen, from his parlour window in C——e Street. She was all joyousness and innocence, and just of an age to enjoy receiving a Valentine, and just of a temper to bear the disappointment of missing one with good humour. E. B. is an artist of no common powers; in the fancy parts of designing, perhaps inferior to none; his name is known at the bottom of many a well-executed vignette in the way of his profession, but no further; for E. B. is modest, and the world meets nobody half way. E. B. meditated how he could repay this young maiden for many a favour which she had done him unknown; for when a kindly face greets us, though but passing by, and never knows us again, nor we it, we should feel it as an obligation: and E. B. did. This good artist set himself at work to please the damsel. It was just before Valentine's day three years since. He wrought, unseen and unsuspected, a wondrous work. We need not say it was on the finest gilt paper with borders—full, not of common hearts and heartless allegory, but all the prettiest stories of love from Ovid, and older poets than Ovid (for E. B. is a scholar). There was Pyramus and Thisbe, and be sure Dido was not forgot. nor Hero and Leander, and swans more than sang in Cayster, with mottoes and fanciful devices, such as beseemed—a work, in short, of magic. Iuis dipt the woof. This on Valentine's eve he commended to the all-swallowing indiscriminate orifice (O ignoble trust!) of the common post; but the humble medium did its duty, and from his watchful stand, the next morning he saw the cheerful messenger knock, and by-and-by the precious charge delivered. He saw, unseen, the happy girl unfold the Valentine, dance about, clap her hands, as one after one the pretty emblems unfolded themselves. She danced about, not with light love, or foolish expectations, for she had no lover; or, if she had, none she knew that could have created those bright images which delighted her. It was more like some fairy present; a God-send, as our familiarly pious ancestors termed a benefit received where the benefactor was unknown. It would do her no harm. It would do her good for ever after. It is good to love the unknown. I only give this as a specimen of E. B. and his modest way of doing a concealed kindness.

Good morrow to my Valentine, sings poor Ophelia; and no better wish, but with better auspices, we wish to all faithful lovers, who are not too wise to despise old legends, but are content to rank themselves humble diocesans of old Bishop Valentine and his true church.

———

MY RELATIONS.

I am arrived at that point of life at which a man may account it a blessing, as it is a singularity, if he have either of his parents surviving. I have not that felicity —and sometimes think feelingly of a passage in "Browne's Christian Morals," where he speaks of a man that hath lived sixty or seventy years in the world. "In such a compass of time," he says, "a man may have a close apprehension what it is to be forgotten, when he hath lived to find none who could remember his father, or scarcely the friends of his youth, and may sensibly see with what a face in no long time Oblivion will look upon himself."

I had an aunt, a dear and good one. She was one whom single blessedness had soured to the world. She often used to say, that I was the only thing in it which she loved; and, when she thought I was quitting it, she grieved over me with mother's tears. A partiality quite so exclusive my reason cannot altogether approve. She was from morning till night poring over good books and devotional exercises. Her favourite volumes were, "Thomas à Kempis," in Stanhope's translation; and a Roman Catholic Prayer Book, with the *matins* and *complines* regularly set down—terms which I was at that time too young to understand. She persisted in reading them, although admonished daily concerning their Papistical tendency; and went to church every Sabbath, as a good Protestant should do. These were the only books she studied; though, I think at one period of her life, she told me, she had read with great satisfaction the "Adventures of an Unfortunate Young Nobleman." Finding the door of the chapel in Essex Street open one day—it was in the infancy of that heresy—she went in, liked the sermon, and the manner of worship, and frequented it at intervals for some time after. She came not for doctrinal points, and never missed them. With some little asperities in her constitution, which I have above hinted at, she was a steadfast, friendly being, and a fine *old Christian*. She was a woman of strong sense, and a shrewd mind—extraordinary at a *repartee;* one of the few occasions of her breaking silence —else she did not much value wit. The only secular employment I remember to have seen her engaged in, was the splitting of French beans, and dropping them into a china basin of fair water. The odour of those tender vegetables to this day comes back upon my senses, redolent of soothing recollections. Certainly it is the most delicate of culinary operations.

Male aunts, as somebody calls them, I had none—to remember. By the uncle's side I may be said to have been born an orphan. Brother, or sister, I never had any —to know them. A sister, I think, that should have been Elizabeth died in both our infancies. What a comfort, or what a care, may I not have missed in her!—But I have cousins sprinkled about in Hertfordshire—besides *two*, with whom I have been all my life in habits of the closest intimacy, and whom I may term cousins *par excellence*. These are James and Bridget Elia. They are older than myself by twelve, and ten, years; and neither of them seems disposed, in matters of advice and guidance, to waive any of the prerogatives which primogeniture confers. May they continue still in the same mind; and when they shall be seventy-five, and seventy-three, years old (I cannot spare them sooner), persist in treating me in my grand climacteric precisely as a stripling, or younger brother!

James is an inexplicable cousin. Nature hath her unities, which not every critic can penetrate; or, if we feel, we cannot explain them. The pen of Yorick, and of none since his, could have drawn J. E. entire—those fine Shandean lights and shades, which make up his story. I must limp after in my poor antithetical manner, as the fates have given me grace and talent. J. E. then —to the eye of a common observer at least—seemeth made up of contradictory principles. The genuine child of impulse, the frigid philosopher of prudence—the phlegm of my cousin's doctrine, is invariably at war with his temperament, which is high sanguine. With always some fire-new project in his brain, J. E. is the systematic opponent of innovation, and crier down of everything that has not stood the test of age and experiment. With a hundred fine notions chasing one another hourly in his fancy, he is startled at the least approach to the romantic in others; and, determined by his own sense in everything, commends *you* to the guidance of common sense on all occasions.—With a touch of the eccentric in all which he does or says, he is only anxious that *you* should not commit yourself by doing anything absurd or singular. On my once letting slip at table, that I was not fond of a certain popular dish, he begged me at any rate not to *say* so—for the world would think me mad. He disguises a passionate fondness for works of high art (whereof he hath amassed a choice collection), under the pretext of buying only to sell again—that his enthusiasm may give no encouragement to yours. Yet, if it were so, why does that piece of tender, pastoral Domenichino hang still by his wall?—is the ball of his sight much more dear to him?—or what picture-dealer can talk like him?

Whereas mankind in general are observed to warp their speculative conclusions to the bent of their individual humours, *his* theories are sure to be in diametrical opposition to his constitution. He is courageous as Charles of Sweden, upon instinct; chary of his person upon principle, as a travelling Quaker. He has been preaching up to me, all my life, the doctrine of bowing to the great—the necessity of forms, and manner, to a man's getting on in the world. He himself never aims at either, that I can discover,—and has a spirit that would stand upright in the presence of the Cham of Tartary. It is pleasant to hear him discourse of patience—extolling it as the truest wisdom—and to see him during the last seven minutes that his dinner is getting ready. Nature never ran up in her haste a more restless piece of workmanship than when she moulded this impetuous cousin —and Art never turned out a more elaborate orator than he can display himself to be, upon his favourite topic of the advantages of quiet and contentedness in the state, whatever it be, that we are placed in. He is triumphant on this theme, when he has you safe in one of those short stages that ply for the western road, in a very obstructing manner, at the foot of John Murray's street—where you get in when it is empty, and are expected to wait till the vehicle hath completed her just freight—a trying three quarters of an hour to some people. He wonders at your fidgetiness,— "where could we be better than we are, *thus sitting, thus consulting?*"—"prefers, for his part, a state of rest to locomotion,"—with an eye all the while upon the coachman,—till at length, waxing out of all patience, at *your want of it,* he breaks out into a pathetic remonstrance at the fellow for de-

taining us so long over the time which he had professed, and declares peremptorily, that "the gentleman in the coach is determined to get out, if he does not drive on that instant."

Very quick at inventing an argument, or detecting a sophistry, he is incapable of attending *you* in any chain of arguing. Indeed, he makes wild work with logic; and seems to jump at most admirable conclusions by some process not at all akin to it. Consonantly enough to this, he hath been heard to deny, upon certain occasions, that there exists such a faculty at all in man as *reason;* and wondereth how man came first to have a conceit of it—enforcing his negation with all the might of *reasoning* he is master of. He has some speculative notions against laughter, and will maintain that laughing is not natural to *him*—when peradventure the next moment his lungs shall crow like chanticleer. He says some of the best things in the world, and declareth that wit is his aversion. It was he who said, upon seeing the Eton boys at play in their grounds—*What a pity to think that these fine ingenuous lads in a few years will all be changed into frivolous Members of Parliament!*

His youth was fiery, glowing, tempestuous—and in age he discovereth no symptom of cooling. This is that which I admire in him. I hate people who meet Time half way. I am for no compromise with that inevitable spoiler. While he lives, J. E. will take his swing.—It does me good, as I walk towards the street of my daily avocation, on some fine May morning, to meet him marching in a quite opposite direction, with a jolly handsome presence, and shining sanguine face, that indicates some purchase in his eye—a Claude- or a Hobbima—for much of his enviable leisure is consumed at Christie's and Phillips's—or where not, to pick up pictures, and such gauds. On these occasions he mostly stoppeth me, to read a short lecture on the advantage a person like me possesses above himself, in having his time occupied with business which he *must* do—assureth me that he often feels it hang-heavy on his hands—wishes he had fewer holidays- and goes off—Westward Ho!—chanting a tune, to Pall Mall—perfectly convinced that he has convinced me——while I proceed in my opposite direction tuneless.

It is pleasant, again, to see this Professor of Indifference doing the honours of his new purchase, when he has fairly housed it. You must view it in every light, till *he* has found the best—placing it at this distance, and at that, but always suiting the focus of your sight to his own. You must spy at it through your fingers, to catch the aërial perspective—though you assure him that to you the landscape shows much more agreeable without that artifice. Woe be to the luckless wight who does not only not respond to his rapture, but who should drop an un-

seasonable intimation of preferring one of his anterior bargains to the present!—The last is always his best hit—his "Cynthia of the minute."—Alas! how many a mild Madonna have I known to *come in*—a Raphael!—keep its ascendancy for a few brief moons—then, after certain intermedial degradations, from the front drawing-room to the back gallery, thence to the dark parlour,—adopted in turn by each of the Carracci, under successive lowering ascriptions of filiation, mildly breaking its fall—consigned to the oblivious lumber-room, *go out* at last a Lucca Giordano, or plain Carlo Maratti!—which things when I beheld—musing upon the chances and mutabilities of fate below hath made me to reflect upon the altered condition of great personages, or that woeful Queen of Richard the Second—

————set forth in pomp,
She came adorned hither like sweet
    May:
Sent back like Hallowmass or shortest
    day.

With great love for *you*. J. E. hath but a limited sympathy with what you feel or do. He lives in a world of his own, and makes slender guesses at what passes in your mind. He never pierces the marrow of your habits. He will tell an old-established play-goer, that Mr. Such-a-one, of So-and-so (naming one of the theatres), is a very lively comedian—as a piece of news! He advertised me but the other day of some pleasant green lanes which he had found out for me, *knowing me to be a great walker*, in my own immediate vicinity—who have haunted the identical spot any time these twenty years!—He has not much respect for that class of feelings which goes by the name of sentimental. He applies the definition of real evil to bodily sufferings exclusively—and rejecteth all others as imaginary. He is affected by the sight, or the bare supposition, of a creature in pain, to a degree which I have never witnessed out of womankind. A constitutional acuteness to this class of sufferings may in part account for this. The animal tribe in particular he taketh under his especial protection. A broken-winded or spurgalled horse is sure to find an advocate in him. An over-loaded ass is his client for ever. He is the apostle to the brute kind—the never-failing friend of those who have none to care for them. The contemplation of a lobster boiled, or eels skinned *alive*, will wring him so, that "all for pity he could die." It will take the savour from his palate, and the rest from his pillow, for days and nights. With the intense feeling of Thomas Clarkson, he wanted only the steadiness of pursuit, and unity of purpose, of that "true yoke-fellow with Time," to have effected as much for the *Animal* as *he* hath done for the *Negro Creation*. But my uncontrollable cousin is but imperfectly formed for purposes which demand co-operation. He cannot wait. His amelioration-

plans must be ripened in a day. For this reason he has cut but an equivocal figure in benevolent societies, and combinations for the alleviation of human sufferings. His zeal constantly makes him to outrun, and put out, his coadjutors. He thinks of relieving,—while they think of debating. He was black-balled out of a society for the Relief of * * * * * * because the fervour of his humanity toiled beyond the formal apprehension and creeping processes of his associates. I shall always consider this distinction as a patent of nobility in the Elia family!

Do I mention these seeming inconsistencies to smile at, or upbraid, my unique cousin? Marry, heaven, and all good manners, and the understanding that should be between kinsfolk, forbid!—With all the strangenesses of this *strangest of the Elias*—I would not have him in one jot or tittle other than he is; neither would I barter or exchange my wild kinsman for the most exact, regular, and every way consistent kinsman breathing.

In my next, reader, I may perhaps give you some account of my cousin Bridget—if you are not already surfeited with cousins—and take you by the hand, if you are willing to go with us, on an excursion which we made a summer or two since, in search of *more cousins—*

Through the green plains of pleasant Hertfordshire.

———

MACKERY END, IN HERTFORDSHIRE.

BRIDGET ELIA has been my housekeeper for many a long year. I have obligations to Bridget, extending beyond the period of memory. We house together, old bachelor and maid, in a sort of double singleness; with such tolerable comfort, upon the whole, that I, for one, find in myself no sort of disposition to go out upon the mountains, with the rash king's offspring, to bewail my celibacy. We agree pretty well in our tastes and habits—yet so, as "with a difference." We are generally in harmony, with occasional bickerings—as it should be among near relations. Our sympathies are rather understood than expressed; and once, upon my dissembling a tone in my voice more kind than ordinary, my cousin burst into tears, and complained that I was altered. We are both great readers in different directions. While I am hanging over (for the thousandth time) some passage in old Burton, or one of his strange contemporaries, she is abstracted in some modern tale or adventure, whereof our common reading-table is daily fed with assiduously fresh supplies. Narrative teases me. I have little concern in the progress of events. She must have a story—well, ill, or indifferently told—so there be life stirring in it, and plenty of good or evil accidents. The fluctuations of fortune in fiction—and almost in real life—have ceased to interest, or operate but dully upon me. Out-of-the-way humours and opinions—heads with some diverting twist in them—the oddities of authorship, please me most. My cousin has a native disrelish of anything that sounds odd or bizarre. Nothing goes down with her that is quaint, irregular, or out of the road of common sympathy. She "holds Nature more clever." I can pardon her blindness to the beautiful obliquities of the Religio Medici; but she must apologize to me for certain disrespectful insinuations, which she has been pleased to throw out latterly, touching the intellectuals of a dear favourite of mine, of the last century but one—the thrice noble, chaste, and virtuous, but again somewhat fantastical and original brained, generous Margaret Newcastle.

It has been the lot of my cousin, oftener perhaps than I could have wished, to have had for her associates and mine, free-thinkers—leaders, and disciples, of novel philosophies and systems; but she neither wrangles with, nor accepts, their opinions. That which was good and venerable to her, when a child, retains its authority over her mind still. She never juggles or plays tricks with her understanding.

We are both of us inclined to be a little too positive; and I have observed the result of our disputes to be almost uniformly this—that in matters of fact, dates, and circumstances, it turns out that I was in the right, and my cousin in the wrong. But where we have differed upon moral points; upon something proper to be done, or let alone; whatever heat of opposition or steadiness of conviction I set out with, I am sure always, in the long-run, to be brought over to her way of thinking.

I must touch upon the foibles of my kinswoman with a gentle hand, for Bridget does not like to be told of her faults. She hath an awkward trick (to say no worse of it) of reading in company: at which times she will answer *yes* or *no* to a question, without fully understanding its purport—which is provoking, and derogatory in the highest degree to the dignity of the putter of the said question. Her presence of mind is equal to the most pressing trials of life, but will sometimes desert her upon trifling occasions. When the purpose requires it, and is a thing of moment, she can speak to it greatly; but in matters which are not stuff of the conscience, she hath been known sometimes to let slip a word less seasonably.

Her education in youth was not much attended to; and she happily missed all that train of female garniture which passeth by the name of accomplishments. She was tumbled early, by accident or design, into a spacious closet of good old English reading, without much selection or prohibition, and browsed at will upon that fair and wholesome pasturage. Had I twenty girls, they should be brought up exactly in this fashion. I know not whether their chance in wedlock might not be diminished by it, but I can answer for it that it makes (if the worst come to the worst) most incomparable old maids.

In a season of distress, she is the truest comforter; but in the teasing accidents and minor perplexities, which do not call out the *will* to meet them, she sometimes maketh matters worse by an excess of participation. If she does not always divide your trouble, upon the pleasanter occasions of life she is sure always to treble your satisfaction. She is excellent to be at a play with, or upon a visit; but best, when she goes a journey with you.

We made an excursion together a few summers since into Hertfordshire, to beat up the quarters of some of our less-known relations in that fine corn country.

The oldest thing I remember is Mackery End, or Mackarel End, as it is spelt, perhaps more properly, in some old maps of Hertfordshire; a farm-house,—delightfully situated within a gentle walk from Wheathampstead. I can just remember having been there, on a visit to a great-aunt, when I was a child, under the care of Bridget; who, as I have said, is older than myself by some ten years. I wish that I could throw into a heap the remainder of our joint existences, that we might share them in equal division. But that is impossible. The house was at that time in the occupation of a substantial yeoman, who had married my grandmother's sister.

6*

His name was Gladman. My grandmother was a Bruton, married to a Field. The Gladmans and the Brutons are still flourishing in that part of the county, but the Fields are almost extinct. More than forty years had elapsed since the visit I speak of; and, for the greater portion of that period, we had lost sight of the other two branches also. Who or what sort of persons inherited Mackery End—kindred or strange folk—we were afraid almost to conjecture, but determined some day to explore.

By somewhat a circuitous route, taking the noble park at Luton in our way from St. Albans, we arrived at the spot of our anxious curiosity about noon. The sight of the old farm-house, though every trace of it was effaced from my recollections, affected me with a pleasure which I had not experienced for many a year. For though *I* had forgotten it, *we* had never forgotten being there together, and we had been talking about Mackery End all our lives, till memory on my part became mocked with a phantom of itself, and I thought I knew the aspect of a place which, when present, O how unlike it was to *that* which I had conjured up so many times instead of it!

Still the air breathed balmily about it; the season was in the "heart of June," and I could say with the poet,

But thou, that didst appear so fair
  To fond imagination,

Dost rival in the light of day
  Her delicate creation!

Bridget's was more a waking bliss than mine, for she easily remembered her old acquaintance again—some altered features, of course, a little grudged at. At first, indeed, she was ready to disbelieve for joy; but the scene soon re-confirmed itself in her affections—and she traversed every outpost of the old mansion, to the wood-house, the orchard, the place where the pigeon-house had stood (house and birds were alike flown) —with a breathless impatience of recognition, which was more pardonable perhaps than decorous at the age of fifty odd. But Bridget in some things is behind her years.

The only thing left was to get into the house—and that was a difficulty which to me singly would have been insurmountable; for I am terribly shy in making myself known to strangers and out-of-date kinsfolk. Love, stronger than scruple, winged my cousin in without me; but she soon returned with a creature that might have sat to a sculptor for the image of Welcome. It was the youngest of the Gladmans; who, by marriage with a Bruton, had become mistress of the old mansion. A comely brood are the Brutons. Six of them, females, were noted as the handsomest young women in the county. But this adopted Bruton, in my mind, was better than they all— more comely. She was born too late to have remembered me. She

just recollected in early life to
have had her cousin Bridget once
pointed out to her, climbing a stile.
But the name of kindred and of
cousinship was enough. Those
slender ties, that prove slight as
gossamer in the reading atmosphere of a metropolis, bind faster,
as we found it, in hearty, homely,
loving Hertfordshire. In five minutes we were as thoroughly acquainted as if we had been born
and bred up together; were familiar, even to the calling each other
by our Christian names. So Christians should call one another. To
have seen Bridget and her—it was
like the meeting of the two scriptural cousins! There was a grace
and dignity, an amplitude of form
and stature, answering to her mind,
in this farmer's wife, which would
have shined in a palace—or so we
thought it. We were made welcome by husband and wife equally
—we, and our friend that was with
us.—I had almost forgotten him—
but B. F. will not so soon forget
that meeting, if peradventure he
shall read this on the far distant
shores where the kangaroo haunts.
The fatted calf was made ready,
or rather was already so, as if in
anticipation of our coming; and,
after an appropriate glass of native wine, never let me forget with
what honest pride this hospitable
cousin made us proceed to Wheathampstead, to introduce us (as
some new-found rarity) to her
mother and sister Gladman, who
did indeed know something more
of us, at a time when she almost
knew nothing.—With what corresponding kindness we were received by them also—how Bridget's
memory, exalted by the occasion,
warmed into a thousand half-
obliterated recollections of things
and persons, to my utter astonishment, and her own—and to the
astoundment of B. F. who sat by,
almost the only thing that was not
a cousin there,—old effaced images
of more than half-forgotten names
and circumstances still crowding
back upon her, as words written
in lemon come out upon exposure
to a friendly warmth,—when I
forget all this, then may my country cousins forget me; and Bridget
no more remember, that in the
days of weakling infancy I was
her tender charge—as I have been
her care in foolish manhood since
—in those pretty pastoral walks,
long ago, about Mackery End, in
Hertfordshire.

MY FIRST PLAY.

At the north end of Cross-court
there yet stands a portal, of some
architectural pretensions, though
reduced to humble use, serving at
present for an entrance to a print-
ing-office. This old door-way, if
you are young, reader, you may
not know was the identical pit
entrance to old Drury—Garrick's
Drury—all of it that is left. I
never pass it without shaking some
forty years from off my shoulders,
recurring to the evening when I
passed through it to see *my first
play*. The afternoon had been wet,
and the condition of our going

(the eider folks and myself) was, that the rain should cease. With what a beating heart did I watch from the window the puddles, from the stillness of which I was taught to prognosticate the desired cessation! I seem to remember the last spurt, and the glee with which I ran to announce it.

We went with orders, which my godfather F. had sent us. He kept the oil shop (now Davies's) at the corner of Featherstone-buildings, in Holborn. F. was a tall grave person, lofty in speech, and had pretensions above his rank. He associated in those days with John Palmer, the comedian, whose gait and bearing he seemed to copy; if John (which is quite as likely) did not rather borrow somewhat of his manner from my godfather. He was also known to and visited by Sheridan. It was to his house in Holborn that young Brinsley brought his first wife on her elopement with him from a boarding-school at Bath—the beautiful Maria Linley. My parents were present (over a quadrille table) when he arrived in the evening with his harmonious charge. From either of these connections it may be inferred that my godfather could command an order for the then Drury-lane theatre at pleasure—and, indeed, a pretty liberal issue of those cheap billets, in Brinsley's easy autograph, I have heard him say was the sole remuneration which he had received for many years nightly illumination of the orchestra and various avenues of that theatre—and he was content it should be so. The honour of Sheridan's familiarity —or supposed familiarity—was better to my godfather than money.

F. was the most gentlemanly of oilmen; grandiloquent, yet courteous. His delivery of the commonest matters of fact was Ciceronian. He had two Latin words almost constantly in his mouth (how odd sounds Latin from an oilman's lips!), which my better knowledge since has enabled me to correct. In strict pronunciation they should have been sounded *vice versâ*—but in those young years they impressed me with more awe than they would now do, read aright from Seneca or Varro—in his own peculiar pronunciation, monosyllabically elaborated, or Anglicised, into something like *verse verse*. By an imposing manner, and the help of these distorted syllables, he climbed (but that was little) to the highest parochial honours which St. Andrew's has to bestow.

He is dead—and thus much I thought due to his memory, both for my first orders (little wondrous talismans!—slight keys, and insignificant to outward sight, but opening to me more than Arabian paradises!) and, moreover, that by his testamentary beneficence I came into possession of the only landed property which I could ever call my own—situate near the road-way village of pleasant Puckeridge, in Hertfordshire. When I journeyed down to take possession, and planted foot on my own ground, the stately habits of the donor descended upon me, and I strode (shall I confess the vanity?) with larger paces over my allotment of three quarters of an acre, with its commodious mansion in the midst, with the feeling of an English freeholder that all betwixt sky and centre was my own. The estate has passed into more prudent hands, and nothing but an agrarian can restore it.

In those days were pit orders. Beshrew the uncomfortable manager who abolished them!—with one of these we went. I remember the waiting at the door—not that which is left—but between that and an inner door in shelter—O when shall I be such an expectant again!—with the cry of nonparcils, an indispensable play-house accompaniment in those days. As near as I can recollect, the fashionable pronunciation of the theatrical fruitcresses then was, "Chase some oranges, chase some numparcls, chase a bill of the play;" —chase *pro* chuse. But when we got in, and I beheld the green curtain that veiled a heaven to my imagination, which was soon to be disclosed—the breathless anticipations I endured! I had seen something like it in the plate prefixed to Troilus and Cressida, in Rowe's Shakspeare—the tent scene with Diomede—and a sight of that plate can always bring back in a measure the feeling of that evening.—The boxes at that time, full of well-dressed women of quality, projected over the pit; and the pilasters reaching down were adorned with a glistening substance (I know not what) under glass (as it seemed), resembling— a homely fancy—but I judged it to be sugarcandy—yet to my raised imagination, divested of its homelier qualities, it appeared a glorified candy!—The orchestra lights at length rose, those "fair Auroras!" Once the bell sounded. It was to ring out yet once again— and, incapable of the anticipation, I reposed my shut eyes in a sort of resignation upon the maternal lap. It rang the second time. The curtain drew up—I was not past six years old, and the play was Artaxerxes!

I had dabbled a little in the Universal History—the ancient part of it—and here was the court of Persia.—It was being admitted to a sight of the past. I took no proper interest in the action going on, for I understood not its import —but I heard the word Darius, and I was in the midst of Daniel. All feeling was absorbed in vision Gorgeous vests, gardens, palaces, princesses, passed before me. I knew not players. I was in Persepolis for the time, and the burning idol of their devotion almost converted me into a worshipper. I was awe-struck, and believed those significations to be something more than elemental fires. It was all enchantment and a dream. No such pleasure has since visited me but in dreams.—Harlequin's invasion followed; where, I remember, the transformation of the magistrates into reverend beldams seemed to me a piece of grave historic justice, and the tailor carrying his own head to be as sober a verity as the legend of St. Denys.

The next play to which I was taken was the Lady of the Manor, of which, with the exception of some scenery, very faint traces are left in my memory. It was followed by a pantomime, called Lun's Ghost—a satiric touch, I apprehend, upon Rich, not long since dead—but to my apprehension (too sincere for satire), Lun was as remote a piece of antiquity as Lud—the father of a line of Harlequins—transmitting his dagger of lath (the wooden sceptre) through countless ages. I saw the primeval Motley come from his silent tomb in a ghastly vest of white patchwork, like the apparition of a dead rainbow. So Harlequins (thought I) look when they are dead.

My third play followed in quick succession. It was the Way of the World. I think I must have sat at it as grave as a judge; for I remember the hysteric affectations of good Lady Wishfort affected me like some solemn tragic passion. Robinson Crusoe followed; in which Crusoe, man Friday, and the parrot, were as good and authentic as in the story.—The clownery and pantaloonery of these pantomimes have clean passed out of my head. I believe, I no more laughed at them, than at the same age I should have been disposed to laugh at the grotesque Gothic heads (seeming to me then replete with devout meaning) that gape, and grin, in stone around the inside of the old Round Church (my church) of the Templars.

I saw these plays in the season 1781-2, when I was from six to seven years old. After the intervention of six or seven other years (for at school all play-going was inhibited) I again entered the doors of a theatre. That old Artaxerxes evening had never done ringing in my fancy. I expected the same feelings to come again with the same occasion. But we differ from ourselves less at sixty and sixteen, than the latter does from six. In that interval what had I not lost! At the first period I knew nothing, understood nothing, discriminated nothing. I felt all, loved all, wondered all—

Was nourished, I could not tell how—

I had left the temple a devotee, and was returned a rationalist. The same things were there materially; but the emblem, the reference, was gone!—The green curtain was no longer a veil, drawn between two worlds, the unfolding of which was to bring back past ages, to present a "royal ghost," —but a certain quantity of green baize, which was to separate the audience for a given time from certain of their fellow-men who were to come forward and pretend those parts. The lights—the orchestra lights—came up a clumsy machinery. The first ring, and the second ring, was now but a trick of the prompter's bell—which had been, like the note of the cuckoo, a phantom of a voice, no hand seen or guessed at which ministered to its warning. The actors were men and women painted. I thought the fault was in them; but it was in myself, and the alteration which those many centuries—of six short twelve-months—had wrought in me.— Perhaps it was fortunate for me that the play of the evening was but an indifferent comedy, as it gave me time to crop some unreasonable expectations, which might have interfered with the genuine emotions with which I was soon after enabled to enter upon the first appearance to me of Mrs. Siddons in Isabella. Comparison and retrospection soon yielded to the present attraction of the scene; and the theatre became to me, upon a new stock, the most delightful of recreations.

MODERN GALLANTRY.

In comparing modern with ancient manners, we are pleased to compliment ourselves upon the point of gallantry; a certain obsequiousness, or deferential respect, which we are supposed to pay to females, as females.

I shall believe that this principle actuates our conduct, when I can forget, that in the nineteenth century of the era from which we date our civility, we are but just beginning to leave off the very frequent practice of whipping females in public, in common with the coarsest male offenders.

I shall believe it to be influential, when I can shut my eyes to the fact, that in England women are still occasionally— hanged.

I shall believe in it, when actresses are no longer subject to be hissed off a stage by gentlemen.

I shall believe in it, when Dorimant hands a fish-wife across the kennel; or assists the apple-woman to pick up her wandering fruit, which some unlucky dray has just dissipated.

I shall believe in it, when the Dorimants in humbler life, who would be thought in their way notable adepts in this refinement, shall act upon it in places where they are not known, or think themselves not observed—when I shall see the traveller for some rich tradesman part with his admired box-coat, to spread it over the defenceless shoulders of the poor woman, who is passing to her parish on the roof of the same stage-coach with him, drenched in the rain—when I shall no longer see a woman standing up in the pit of a London theatre, till she is sick and faint with the exertion, with men about her, seated at their ease, and jeering at her distress; till one, that seems to have more manners or conscience than the rest, significantly declares "she should be welcome to his seat, if she were a little younger and handsomer." Place this dapper warehouseman, or that rider, in a circle of their own female acquaintance, and you shall confess you have not seen a politer-bred man in Lothbury.

Lastly, I shall begin to believe that there is some such principle influencing our conduct, when more than one-half of the drudgery and coarse servitude of the world shall cease to be performed by women.

Until that day comes, I shall never believe this boasted point to be anything more than a conventional fiction; a pageant got up between the sexes, in a certain rank, and at a certain time of life, in which both find their account equally.

I shall be even disposed to rank it among the salutary fictions of life, when in polite circles I shall see the same attentions paid to age as to youth, to homely features as to handsome, to coarse complexions as to clear —to the woman, as she is a woman, not as she is a beauty, a fortune, or a title.

I shall believe it to be something more than a name, when a well-dressed gentleman in a well-dressed company can advert to the topic of *female old age* without exciting, and intending to excite, a sneer:—when the phrases "antiquated virginity," and such a one has "overstood her market," pronounced in good company, shall raise immediate offence in man, or woman, that shall hear them spoken.

Joseph Paice, of Bread-street-hill, merchant, and one of the Directors of the South Sea company—the same to whom Edwards, the Shakspeare commentator, has addressed a fine sonnet—was the only pattern of consistent gallantry I have met with. He took me under his shelter at an early age, and bestowed some pains upon me. I owe to his precepts and example whatever there is of the man of business (and that is not much) in my composition. It was not his fault that I did not profit more. Though bred a Presbyterian, and brought up a merchant, he was the finest gentleman of his time. He had not *one* system of attention to females in the drawing-room, and *another* in the shop, or at the stall. I do not mean that he made no distinction. But he never lost sight of sex, or overlooked it in the casualties of a disadvantageous situation. I have seen him stand bareheaded—smile if you please—to a poor servant-girl, while she has been inquiring of him the way to some street—in such a posture of unforced civility, as neither to embarrass her in the acceptance, nor himself in the offer, of it. He was no dangler, in the common acceptation of the word, after women; but he reverenced and upheld, in every form in which it came before him, *womanhood*. I have seen him—nay, smile not—tenderly escorting a market-woman, whom he had encountered in a shower, exalting his umbrella over her poor basket of fruit, that it might receive no damage, with as much carefulness as if she had been a countess. To the reverend form of Female Eld he would yield the wall (though it were to an ancient beggar-woman) with more ceremony than we can afford to show our grandams. He was the Preux Chevalier of Age; the Sir Calidore, or Sir Tristan, to those who have no Calidores or Tristans to defend them. The roses, that had long faded thence, still bloomed for him in those withered and yellow cheeks.

He was never married, but in his youth he paid his addresses to the beautiful Susan Winstanley—old Winstanley's daughter of Clapton—who dying in the early days of their courtship, confirmed in him the resolution of perpetual bachelorship. It was during their short courtship, he told me, that he had been one day treating his mistress with a profusion of civil speeches—the common gallantries—to which kind of thing she had hitherto manifested no repugnance—but in this instance with no effect. He could not obtain from her a decent acknowledgment in return. She rather seemed to resent his compliments. He could not set it down to caprice, for the lady had always shown herself above that littleness. When he ventured on the following day, finding her a little better humoured, to expostulate with her on her coldness of yesterday, she confessed, with her usual frankness, that she had

no sort of dislike to his attentions; that she could even endure some high-flown compliments; that a young woman placed in her situation had a right to expect all sort of civil things said to her; that she hoped she could digest a dose of adulation, short of insincerity, with as little injury to her humility as most young women; but that—a little before he had commenced his compliments—she had overheard him by accident, in rather rough language, rating a young woman, who had not brought home his cravats quite to the appointed time, and she thought to herself, "As I am Miss Susan Winstanley, and a young lady—a reputed beauty, and known to be a fortune—I can have my choice of the finest speeches from the mouth of this very fine gentleman who is courting me—but if I had been poor Mary Such-a-one (*naming the milliner*),—and had failed of bringing home the cravats to the appointed hour—though perhaps I had sat up half the night to forward them—what sort of compliments should I have received then?—And my woman's pride came to my assistance; and I thought, that if it were only to do *me* honour, a female, like myself, might have received handsomer usage; and I was determined not to accept any fine speeches, to the compromise of that sex, the belonging to which was after all my strongest claim and title to them."

I think the lady discovered

both generosity, and a just way of thinking, in this rebuke which she gave her lover; and I have sometimes imagined, that the uncommon strain of courtesy, which through life regulated the actions and behaviour of my friend towards all of womankind indiscriminately, owed its happy origin to this seasonable lesson from the lips of his lamented mistress.

I wish the whole female world would entertain the same notion of these things that Miss Winstanley showed. Then we should see something of the spirit of consistent gallantry; and no longer witness the anomaly of the same man—a pattern of true politeness to a wife—of cold contempt, or rudeness, to a sister—the idolater of his female mistress—the disparager and despiser of his no less female aunt, or unfortunate—still female—maiden cousin. Just so much respect as a woman derogates from her own sex, in whatever condition placed—her hand-maid, or dependent—she deserves to have diminished from herself on that score; and probably will feel the diminution, when youth, and beauty, and advantages, not inseparable from sex, shall lose of their attraction. What a woman should demand of a man in courtship, or after it, is first—respect for her as she is a woman;—and next to that—to be respected by him above all other women. But let her stand upon her female character as upon a foundation; and let the attentions, incident to individual preference, be so many pretty additaments and ornaments—as many, and as fanciful, as you please—to that main structure. Let her first lesson be with sweet Susan Winstanley—to *reverence her sex*.

THE OLD BENCHERS OF THE INNER TEMPLE.

I was born, and passed the first seven years of my life, in the Temple. Its church, its halls, its gardens, its fountains, its river, I had almost said—for in those young years, what was this king of rivers to me but a stream that watered our pleasant places?—these are of my oldest recollections. I repeat, to this day, no verses to myself more frequently, or with kindlier emotion, than those of Spenser, where he speaks of this spot:

There when they came, whereas those
    bricky towers,
The which on Themmes brode aged back
    doth ride,
Where now the studious lawyers have
    their bowers,
There whylome wont the Templer knights
    to bide,
Till they decayed through pride.

Indeed, it is the most elegant spot in the metropolis. What a transition for a countryman visiting London for the first time—the passing from the crowded Strand or Fleet Street, by unexpected avenues, into its magnificent ample squares, its classic green recesses! What a cheerful, liberal look hath that portion of it, which, from three sides, overlooks the greater garden; that goodly pile

Of building strong, albeit of Paper hight,

confronting with massy contrast, the lighter, older, more fantastically-shrouded one, named of Harcourt, with the cheerful Crown Office-row (place of my kindly engendure), right opposite tho stately stream, which washes the garden-foot with her yet scarcely trade-polluted waters, and seems but just weaned from her Twickenham Naïades! a man would give something to have been born in such places. What a collegiate aspect has that fine Elizabethan hall, where the fountain plays, which I have made to rise and fall, how many times! to the astoundment of the young urchins, my contemporaries, who, not being able to guess at its recondite machinery, were almost tempted to hail the wondrous work as magic! What an antique air had the now almost effaced sun-dials, with their moral inscriptions, seeming coevals with that Time which they measured, and to take their revelations of its flight immediately from heaven, holding correspondence with the fountain of light! How would the dark line steal imperceptibly on, watched by the eye of childhood, eager to detect its movement, never catched, nice as an evanescent cloud, or the first arrests of sleep!

Ah! yet doth beauty like a dial hand
Steal from his figure, and no pace perceived!

What a dead thing is a clock, with its ponderous embowelments of lead and brass, its pert or solemn dulness of communication, compared with the simple altar-like structure and silent heart-language of the old dial! It stood as the garden god of Christian gardens. Why is it almost everywhere vanished? If its business-use be superseded by more elaborate inventions, its moral uses, its beauty, might have pleaded for its continuance. It spoke of moderate labours, of pleasures not protracted after sunset, of temperance, and good hours. It was the primitive clock, the horologe of the first world. Adam could scarce have missed it in Paradise. It was the measure appropriate for sweet plants and flowers to spring by, for the birds to apportion their silver warblings by, for flocks to pasture and be led to fold by. The shepherd "carved it out quaintly in the sun;" and, turning philosopher by the very occupation, provided it with mottoes more touching than tombstones. It was a pretty device of the gardener, recorded by Marvell, who, in the days of artificial gardening, made a dial out of herbs and flowers. I must quote his verses a little higher up, for they are full, as all his serious poetry was, of a witty delicacy. They will not come in awkwardly, I hope, in a talk of fountains and sun-dials. He is speaking of sweet garden scenes:—

What wondrous life is this I lead!
Ripe apples drop about my head.
The luscious clusters of the vine
Upon my mouth do crush their wine.
The nectarine, and curious peach,
Into my hands themselves do reach.
Stumbling on melons, as I pass,
Insnared with flowers, I fall on grass.
Meanwhile the mind from pleasure less
Withdraws into its happiness.
The mind, that ocean, where each kind
Does straight its own resemblance find;
Yet it creates, transcending these,
Far other worlds and other seas;
Annihilating all that's made
To a green thought in a green shade.
Here at the fountain's sliding foot,
Or at some fruit-tree's mossy root,
Casting the body's vest aside,
My soul into the boughs does glide;
There, like a bird, it sits and sings,
Then whets and claps its silver wings,
And, till prepared for longer flight,
Waves in its plumes the various light.
How well the skilful gardener drew
Of flowers and herbs, this dial new!
Where, from above, the milder sun
Does through a fragrant zodiac run:
And, as it works, the industrious bee
Computes its time as well as we.
How could such sweet and wholesome
    hours
Be reckoned, but with herbs and
    flowers?*

The artificial fountains of the metropolis are, in like manner, fast vanishing. Most of them are dried up or bricked over. Yet, where one is left, as in that little green nook behind the South-Sea House, what a freshness it gives to the dreary pile! Four little winged marble boys used to play their virgin fancies, spouting out ever fresh streams from their innocent-wanton lips in the square of Lincoln's Inn, when I was no

bigger than they were figured. They are gone, and the spring choked up. The fashion, they tell me, is gone by, and these things are esteemed childish. Why not, then, gratify children, by letting them stand? Lawyers, I suppose, were children once. They are awakening images to them at least. Why must everything smack of man, and mannish? Is the world all grown up? Is childhood dead? Or is there not in the bosoms of the wisest and the best some of the child's heart left, to respond to its earliest enchantments? The figures were grotesque. Are the stiff-wigged living figures, that still flitter and chatter about that area, less Gothic in appearance? or is the splutter of their hot rhetoric one-half so refreshing and innocent as the little cool playful streams those exploded cherubs uttered?

They have lately gothicised the entrance to the Inner Temple-hall, and the library front; to assimilate them, I suppose, to the body of the hall, which they do not at all resemble. What is become of the winged horse that stood over the former? a stately arms! and who has removed those frescoes of the Virtues, which Italianised the end of the Paper-buildings?—my first hint of allegory! They must account to me for these things, which I miss so greatly.

The terrace is, indeed, left, which we used to call the parade; but the traces are passed away of the footsteps which made its pavement awful! It is become common and profane. The old benchers had it almost sacred to themselves, in the forepart of the day at least. They might not be sided or jostled. Their air and dress asserted the parade. You left wide spaces betwixt you when you passed them. We walk on even terms with their successors. The roguish eye of J——ll, ever ready to be delivered of a jest, almost invites a stranger to vie a repartee with it. But what insolent familiar durst have mated Thomas Coventry?—whose person was a quadrate, his step massy and elephantine, his face square as the lion's, his gait peremptory and path-keeping, indivertible from his way as a moving column, the scarecrow of his inferiors, the browbeater of equals and superiors, who made a solitude of children wherever he came, for they fled his insufferable presence, as they would have shunned an Elisha bear. His growl was as thunder in their ears, whether he spake to them in mirth or in rebuke; his invitatory notes being, indeed, of all, the most repulsive and horrid. Clouds of snuff, aggravating the natural terrors of his speech, broke from each majestic nostril, darkening the air. He took it, not by pinches, but a palmful at once,—diving for it under the mighty flaps of his old-fashioned waistcoat pocket; his waistcoat red and angry, his coat dark rappee, tinctured by dye original, and by adjuncts, with buttons of obsolete gold. And so he paced the terrace.

By his side a milder form was sometimes to be seen; the pensive gentility of Samuel Salt. They were coevals, and had nothing but that and their benchership in common. In politics Salt was a whig, and Coventry a staunch tory. Many a sarcastic growl did the latter cast out—for Coventry had a rough spinous humour—at the political confederates of his associate, which rebounded from the gentle bosom of the latter like cannon-balls from wool. You could not ruffle Samuel Salt.

S. had the reputation of being a very clever man, and of excellent discernment in the chamber practice of the law. I suspect his knowledge did not amount to much. When a case of difficult disposition of money, testamentary or otherwise, came before him, he ordinarily handed it over, with a few instructions, to his man Lovel, who was a quick little fellow, and would despatch it out of hand by the light of natural understanding, of which he had an uncommon share. It was incredible what repute for talents S. enjoyed by the mere trick of gravity. He was a shy man; a child might pose him in a minute—indolent and procrastinating to the last degree. Yet men would give him credit for vast application, in spite of himself. He was not to be trusted with himself with impunity. He never dressed for a dinner party but he forgot his sword—they wore swords then—or some other necessary part of his equipage. Lovel had his eye upon him on all these occasions, and ordinarily gave him his cue. If there was anything which he could speak unseasonably, he was sure to do it.—He was to dine at a relative's of the unfortunate Miss Blandy on the day of her execution;—and L., who had a wary foresight of his probable hallucinations, before he set out schooled him, with great anxiety, not in any possible manner to allude to her story that day. S. promised faithfully to observe the injunction. He had not been seated in the parlour, where the company was expecting the dinner summons, four minutes, when, a pause in the conversation ensuing, he got up, looked out of window, and pulling down his ruffles—an ordinary motion with him—observed, "it was a gloomy day," and added, "Miss Blandy must be hanged by this time, I suppose." Instances of this sort are perpetual. Yet S. was thought by some of the greatest men of his time a fit person to be consulted, not alone in matters pertaining to the law, but in the ordinary niceties and embarrassments of conduct—from force of manner entirely. He never laughed. He had the same good fortune among the female world, —was a known toast with the ladies, and one or two are said to have died for love of him—I suppose, because he never trifled or talked gallantly with them, or paid them, indeed, hardly common attentions. He had a fine face and person, but wanted, methought, the spirit that should have shown them off with advantage to the women. His eye lacked lustre.—Not so, thought Susan P——; who, at the advanced age of sixty, was seen, in the cold evening time, unaccompanied, wetting the pavement of B——d Row, with tears that fell in drops which might be heard, because her friend had died that day—he, whom she had pursued with a hopeless passion for the last forty years—a passion which years could not extinguish or abate; nor the long-resolved, yet gently-enforced, puttings off of unrelenting bachelorhood dissuade from its cherished purpose. Mild Susan P——, thou hast now thy friend in heaven!

Thomas Coventry was a cadet of the noble family of that name. He passed his youth in contracted circumstances, which gave him early those parsimonious habits which in after life never forsook him; so that with one windfall or another, about the time I knew him, he was master of four or five hundred thousand pounds; nor did he look or walk worth a moidore less. He lived in a gloomy house opposite the pump in Serjeant's-inn, Fleet-street. J., the counsel, is doing self-imposed penance in it, for what reason I divine not, at this day. C. had an agreeable seat at North Cray, where he seldom spent above a day or two at a time in the summer; but preferred, during the hot months, standing at his window in this damp, close, well-like mansion, to watch, as he said, "the maids drawing water all day long." I suspect he had his within-door reasons for the preference. *Hic currus et arma fuère.* He might think his treasures more safe. His house had the aspect of a strong box. C. was a close hunks—a hoarder rather than a miser—or, if a miser, none of the mad Elwes breed, who have brought discredit upon a character which cannot exist without certain admirable points of steadiness and unity of purpose. One may hate a true miser, but cannot, I suspect, so easily despise him. By taking care of the pence he is often enabled to part with the pounds, upon a scale that leaves us careless generous fellows halting at an immeasurable distance behind. C. gave away 30,000*l.* at once in his lifetime to a blind charity. His house-keeping was severely looked after, but he kept the table of a gentleman. He would know who came in and who went out of his house, but his kitchen chimney was never suffered to freeze.

Salt was his opposite in this, as in all—never knew what he was worth in the world; and having but a competency for his rank, which his indolent habits were little calculated to improve, might have suffered severely if he had not had honest people about him. Lovel took care of everything. He was at once his clerk, his good servant, his dresser, his friend, his "flapper," his guide, stop-watch, auditor, treasurer. He did nothing without consulting Lovel, or failed in anything without expecting and fearing his admonishing. He put himself almost too much in his hands, had they not been the purest in the world. He resigned his title almost to respect as a master, if L. could ever have forgotten for a moment that he was a servant.

I knew this Lovel. He was a man of incorrigible and losing honesty. A good fellow withal, and "would strike." In the cause of the oppressed he never considered inequalities, or calculated the number of his opponents. He once wrested a sword out of the hand of a man of quality that had drawn upon him, and pommelled him severely with the hilt of it. The swordsman had offered insult to a female—an occasion upon which no odds against him could have prevented the interference of Lovel. He would stand next day bareheaded to the same person modestly to excuse his interference—for L. never forgot rank where something better was not concerned. L. was the liveliest little fellow breathing, had a face as gay as Garrick's, whom he was said greatly to resemble (I have a portrait of him which confirms it), possessed a fine turn for humorous poetry—next to Swift and Prior—moulded heads in clay and plaster of Paris to admiration, by the dint of natural genius merely; turned cribbage boards, and such small cabinet toys, to perfection; took a hand at quadrille or bowls with equal facility; made punch better than any man of his degree in England; had the merriest quips and conceits; and was altogether as brimful of rogueries and inventions as you could desire. He was a brother of the angle, moreover, and just such a free, hearty, honest companion as Mr. Izaak Walton would have chosen to go a-fishing with. I saw him in his old age and the decay of his faculties, palsy-smitten, in the last sad stage of human weakness—"a remnant most forlorn of what he was,"—yet even then his eye would light up upon the mention of his favourite Garrick. He was greatest, he would say, in Bayes—"was upon the stage nearly throughout the whole performance, and as busy as a bee." At intervals, too, he would speak of his former life, and how he came up a little boy from Lincoln, to go to service, and how his mother cried at parting with him, and how he returned, after some few years' absence, in a smart new livery, to see her, and she blest herself at the change, and could hardly be brought to believe that it was "her own bairn." And then, the excitement subsiding, he would weep, till I have wished the sad second-childhood might have a mother still to lay its head upon her lap. But the common mother of us all in no long time after received him gently into hers.

With Coventry and with Salt, in their walks upon the terrace, most commonly Peter Pierson would join to make up a third. They did not walk linked arm-in-arm in those days—"as now our stout triumvirs sweep the streets," —but generally with both hands folded behind them for state, or with one at least behind, the other carrying a cane. P. was a benevolent, but not prepossessing man. He had that in his face which you could not term unhappiness; it rather implied an incapacity of being happy. His cheeks were colourless, even to whiteness. His look was uninviting, resembling (but without his sourness) that of our great philanthropist. I know that he *did* good acts, but I could never make out what he *was*. Contemporary with these, but subordinate, was Daines Barrington—another oddity—he walked burly and square—in imitation, I think, of Coventry—howbeit he attained not to the dignity of his prototype. Nevertheless, he did pretty well, upon the strength of being a tolerable antiquarian, and having a brother a bishop. When the account of his year's treasurership came to be audited, the following singular charge was unanimously disallowed by the bench: "Item, disbursed Mr. Allen, the gardener, twenty shillings for stuff to poison the sparrows, by my orders." Next to him was old Barton—a jolly negation, who took upon him the ordering of the bills of fare for the parliament chamber, where the benchers dine—answering to the combination rooms at College—much to the easement of his less epicurean brethren. I know nothing more of him.—Then Read, and Twopeny—Read, good-humoured and personable — Twopeny, good-humoured, but thin, and felicitous in jests upon his own figure. If T. was thin, Wharry was attenuated and fleeting. Many must remember him (for he was rather of later date) and his singular gait, which was performed by three steps and a jump regularly succeeding. The steps were little efforts, like that of a child beginning to walk; the jump comparatively vigorous, as a foot to an inch. Where he learned this figure, or what occasioned it, I could never discover. It was neither graceful in itself, nor seemed to answer the purpose any better than common walking. The extreme tenuity of his frame, I suspect, set him upon it. It was a trial of poising. Twopeny would often rally him upon his leanness, and hail him as Brother Lusty; but W. had no relish of a joke. His features were spiteful. I have heard that he would pinch his cat's ears extremely when anything had offended him. Jackson—the omniscient Jackson, he was called—was of this period. He had the reputation of possessing more multifarious knowledge than any man of his time. He was the Friar Bacon of the less literate portion of the Temple. I remember a pleasant passage of the cook applying to him, with much formality of apology, for instructions how to write down *edge* bone of beef in the bill of commons. He was supposed to know, if any man in the world did. He decided the orthography to be—as I have given it—fortifying his authority with such anatomical reasons as dismissed the manciple (for the time) learned and happy. Some do spell it yet, perversely, *aitch* bone, from a fanciful resemblance between its shape and that of the aspirate so denominated. I had almost forgotten Mingay with the iron hand · but he was somewhat later. He had lost his right hand by some accident, and supplied it with a grappling-hook, which he wielded with a tolerable adroitness. I detected the substitute before I was old enough to reason whether it were artificial or not. I remember the astonishment it raised in me. He was a blustering, loud-talking person; and I reconciled the phenomenon to my ideas as an emblem of power—somewhat like the horns in the forehead of Michael Angelo's Moses. Baron Maseres, who walks (or did till very lately) in the costume of the reign of George the Second, closes my imperfect recollections of the old benchers of the Inner Temple.

Fantastic forms, whither are ye fled? Or, if the like of you exist, why exist they no more for me? Ye inexplicable, half-understood appearances, why comes in reason to tear away the preternatural mist, bright or gloomy, that enshrouded you? Why make ye so sorry a figure in my relation, who made up me—to my childish eyes—the mythology of the Temple? In those days I saw Gods, as "old men covered with a mantle," walking upon the earth. Let the dream of classic idolatry perish,—extinct be the fairies and fairy trumpery of legendary fabling, in the heart of childhood there will, for ever, spring up a well of innocent or wholesome superstition—the seeds of exaggeration will be busy there, and vital—from every-day forms educing the unknown and the uncommon. In that little Goshen there will be light when the grown world flounders about in the darkness of sense and materiality. While childhood, and while dreams, reducing childhood, shall be left, imagination shall not have spread her holy wings totally to fly the earth.

P.S.—I have done injustice to the soft shade of Samuel Salt. See what it is to trust to imperfect memory, and the erring notices of childhood! Yet I protest I always thought that he had been a bachelor! This gentleman, R. N. informs me, married young, and losing his lady in childbed, within the first year of their union, fell into a deep melancholy, from the effects of which, probably, he never thoroughly recovered. In what a new light does this place his rejection (O call it by a gentler name!) of mild Susan P——, unravelling into beauty certain peculiarities of this very shy and retiring character! Henceforth let no one receive the narratives of Elia for true records! They are, in truth, but shadows of fact—verisimilitudes, not verities—or sitting but upon the remote edges and outskirts of history. He is no such honest chronicler as R. N., and would have done better perhaps to have consulted that gentleman before he sent these incondite reminiscences to press. But the worthy subtreasurer—who respects his old and new masters—would but have been puzzled at the indecorous liberties of Elia. The good man wots not, peradventure, of the licence which *Magazines* have arrived at in this plain-speaking age, or hardly dreams of their existence beyond the *Gentleman's*—his furthest monthly excursions in this nature having been long confined to the holy ground of honest *Urban's* obituary. May it be long before his own name shall help to swell those columns of unenvied flattery!—Meantime, O ye New Benchers of the Inner Temple, cherish him kindly, for he is himself the kindliest of human creatures. Should infirmities overtake him—he is yet in green and vigorous senility—make allowances for them, remembering that "ye yourselves are old." So may the Winged Horse, your ancient badge and cognizance, still flourish! so may future Hookers and Seldens illustrate your church and chambers! so may the sparrows, in default of more melodious quiristers, unpoisoned hop about your walks! so may the fresh-coloured and cleanly nursery-maid, who, by leave, airs her playful charge in your stately gardens, drop her prettiest blushing courtesy as ye pass, reductive of juvenescent emotion! so may the younkers of this generation eye you, pacing your stately terrace, with the same superstitious veneration with which the child Elia gazed of the Old Worthies that solemnized the parade before ye!

——

GRACE BEFORE MEAT.

THE custom of saying grace at meals had, probably, its origin in the early times of the world, and the hunterstate of man, when dinners were precarious things, and a full meal was something more than a common blessing! when a belly-full was a wind-fall, and looked like a special providence. In the shouts and triumphal songs with which, after a season of sharp abstinence, a lucky booty of deer's or goat's flesh would naturally be ushered home, existed, perhaps, the germ of the modern grace. It is not otherwise easy to be understood, why the blessing of food—the act of eating—should have had a particular expression of thanksgiving annexed to it, distinct from that implied and silent gratitude with which we are expected to enter upon the enjoyment of the many other various gifts and good things of existence.

I own that I am disposed to say grace upon twenty other occasions in the course of the day besides my dinner. I want a form for setting out upon a pleasant walk, for a moonlight ramble, for a friendly meeting, or a solved problem. Why have we none for books, those spiritual repasts—a grace before Milton—a grace before Shakspeare—a devotional exercise proper to be said before reading the Fairy Queen?—but the received ritual having prescribed these forms to the solitary ceremony of manducation, I shall confine my observations to the experience which I have had of the grace, properly so called; commending my new scheme for extension to a niche in the grand philosophical, poetical, and perchance in part heretical, liturgy, now compiling by my friend Homo Humanus, for the use of a certain snug congregation of Utopian Rabelæsian Christians, no matter where assembled.

Then form, then, of the benediction before eating has its beauty at a poor man's table, or at the simple and unprovocative repast of children. It is here that the grace becomes exceedingly graceful. The indigent man, who hardly knows whether he shall have a meal the next day or not, sits down to his fare with a present sense of the blessing, which can be but feebly acted by the rich, into whose minds the conception of wanting a dinner could never, but by some extreme theory, have entered. The proper end of food—the animal sustenance—is barely contemplated by them. The poor man's bread is his daily bread, literally his bread for the day. Their courses are perennial.

Again, the plainest diet seems the fittest to be preceded by the grace. That which is least stimulative to appetite, leaves the mind most free for foreign considerations. A man may feel thankful, heartily thankful, over a dish of plain mutton with turnips, and have leisure to reflect upon the ordinance and institution of eating; when he shall confess a perturbation of mind, inconsistent with the purposes of the grace, at the presence of venison or turtle. When I have sate (a *rarus hospes*) at rich men's tables, with the savoury soup and messes steaming up the nostrils, and moistening the lips of the guests with desire and a distracted choice, I have felt the introduction of that ceremony to be unseasonable. With the ravenous orgasm upon you, it seems impertinent to interpose a religious sentiment. It is a confusion of purpose to mutter out praises from a mouth that waters. The heats of epicurism put out the gentle flame of devotion. The incense which rises round is pagan, and the belly-god intercepts it for its own. The very excess of the provision beyond the needs, takes away all sense of proportion between the end and means. The giver is veiled by his gifts. You are startled at the injustice of returning thanks—for what?—for having too much while so many starve. It is to praise the Gods amiss.

I have observed this awkwardness felt, scarce consciously perhaps, by the good man who says the grace. I have seen it in clergymen and others—a sort of shame —a sense of the co-presence of circumstances which unhallow the blessing. After a devotional tone put on for a few seconds, how rapidly the speaker will fall into his common voice! helping himself or his neighbour, as if to get rid of some uneasy sensation of hypocrisy. Not that the good man was a hypocrite, or was not most conscientious in the discharge of the duty; but he felt in his inmost mind the incompatibility of the scene and the viands before him with the exercise of a calm and rational gratitude.

I hear somebody exclaim,— Would you have Christians sit down at table, like hogs to their troughs, without remembering the Giver?—no—I would have them sit down as Christians, remembering the Giver, and less like hogs. Or, if their appetites must run riot, and they must pamper themselves with delicacies for which east and west are ransacked, I would have them postpone their benediction to a fitter season, when appetite is laid; when the still small voice can be heard, and the reason of the grace returns— with temperate diet and restricted dishes. Gluttony and surfeiting are no proper occasions for thanksgiving. When Jeshurun waxed fat, we read that he kicked. Virgil knew the harpy-nature better, when he put into the mouth of Celæno anything but a blessing. We may be gratefully sensible of the deliciousness of some kinds of food beyond others, though that is a meaner and inferior gratitude: but the proper object of the grace is sustenance, not relishes; daily bread, not delicacies; the means of life, and not the means of pampering the carcass. With what frame or composure, I wonder, can a city chaplain pronounce his benediction at some great Hall-feast, when he knows that his last concluding pious word—and that in all probability, the sacred name which he preaches—is but the signal for so many impatient harpies to commence their foul orgies, with as little sense of true thankfulness(which is temperance) as those Virgilian fowl! It is well if the good man himself does not feel his devotions a little clouded, those foggy sensuous steams mingling with and polluting the pure altar sacrifice.

The severest satire upon full tables is the banquet which Satan, in the "Paradise Regained," provides for a temptation in the wilderness:

A table richly spread in regal mode
With dishes piled, and meats of noblest
   sort
And savour; beasts of chase, or fowl of
   game,
In pastry built, or from the spit, or
   boiled,
Gris-amber-steamed; and fish from sea
   or shore,
Freshet or purling brook, for which was
   drained
Pontus, and Lucrine bay, and Afric
   coast.

The Tempter, I warrant you, thought these cates would go down without the recommendatory preface of a benediction. They are like to be short graces where the devil plays the host. I am afraid the poet wants his usual decorum in this place. Was he thinking of the old Roman luxury, or of a gaudy day at Cambridge? This was a temptation fitter for a Heliogabalus. The whole banquet is too civic and culinary, and the accompaniments altogether a profanation of that deep, abstracted, holy scene. The mighty artillery of sauces, which the cook-fiend conjures up, is out of proportion to the simple wants and plain hunger of the guest. He that disturbed him in his dreams, from his dreams might have been taught better. To the temperate fantasies of the famished Son of God, what sort of feasts presented themselves?—He dreamed indeed,

——As appetite is wont to dream,
Of meats and drinks, nature's refreshment sweet.

But what meats?—

Him thought he by the brook of Cherith
   stood,
And saw the ravens with their horny
   beaks
Food to Elijah bringing even and morn;
Though ravenous, taught to abstain from
   what they brought;
He saw the prophet also how he fled
Into the desert, and how there he slept
Under a juniper; then how awaked
He found his supper on the coals prepared,
And by the angel was bid rise and eat,
And ate the second time after repose,
The strength whereof sufficed him forty
   days:
Sometimes, that with Elijah he partook,
Or as a guest with Daniel at his pulse.

Nothing in Milton is finelier fancied than these temperate dreams of the divine Hungerer. To which of these two visionary banquets, think you, would the introduction of what is called the grace have been the most fitting and pertinent?

Theoretically I am no enemy to graces; but practically I own that (before meat especially) they seem to involve something awkward and unseasonable. Our appetites, of one or another kind, are excellent spurs to our reason, which might otherwise but feebly set about the great ends of preserving and continuing the species. They are fit blessings to be contemplated at a distance with a becoming gratitude; but the moment of appetite (the judicious reader will apprehend me) is, perhaps, the least fit season for that exercise. The Quakers, who go about their business of every description with more calmness than we, have more title to the use of these benedictory prefaces. I have always admired their silent grace, and more because I have observed their applications to the meat and drink following to be less passionate and sensual than ours. They are neither gluttons nor wine-bibbers as a people. They eat, as a horse bolts his chopped hay, with indifference, calmness, and cleanly circumstances. They neither grease nor slop themselves. When I see a citizen in his bib and tucker, I cannot imagine it a surplice.

I am no Quaker at my food. I confess I am not indifferent to the kinds of it. Those unctuous morsels of deer's flesh were not made to be received with dispassionate services. I hate a man who swallows it, affecting not to know what he is eating. I suspect his taste in higher matters. I shrink instinctively from one who professes to like minced veal. There is a physiognomical character in the tastes for food. C—— holds that a man cannot have a pure mind who refuses apple-dumplings. I am not certain but he is right. With the decay of my first innocence, I confess a less and less relish daily for those innocuous cates. The whole vegetable tribe have lost their gust with me. Only I stick to asparagus, which still seems to inspire gentle thoughts. I am impatient and querulous under culinary disappointments, as to come home at the dinner hour, for instance, expecting some savoury mess, and to find one quite tasteless and sapidless. Butter ill-melted—that commonest of kitchen failures—puts me beside my tenor.—The author of the Rambler used to make inarticulate animal noises over a favourite food. Was this the music quite proper to be preceded by the grace? or would the pious man have done better to postpone his devotions to a season when the blessing might be contemplated with less perturbation? I quarrel with no man's tastes, nor would set my thin face against those excellent things, in their way, jollity and feasting. But as these exercises, however laudable, have little in them of grace or gracefulness, a man should be sure, before he ventures so to grace them, that while he is pretending his devotions otherwhere, he is not secretly kissing his hand to some great fish—his Dagon—with a special consecration of no ark but the fat tureen before him. Graces are the sweet preluding strains to the banquets of angels and children; to the roots and severer repasts of the Chartreuse; to the slender, but not slenderly acknowledged, refection of the poor and humble man: but at the heaped-up boards of the pampered and the luxurious they become of dissonant mood, less timed and tuned to the occasion, methinks, than the noise of those better befitting organs would be which children hear tales of, at Hog's Norton. We sit too long at our meals, or are too curious in the study of them, or too disordered in our application to them, or engross too great a portion of those good things (which should be common) to our share, to be able with any grace to say grace. To be thankful for what we grasp exceeding our proportion, is to add hypocrisy to injustice. A lurking sense of this truth is what makes the performance of this duty so cold and spiritless a service at most tables. In houses where the grace is as indispensable as the napkin, who has not seen that never-settled question arise, as to *who shall say it?* while the good man of the house and the visitor clergyman, or some other guest belike of next authority, from years or gravity, shall be bandying about the office between them as a matter of compliment, each of them not un-willing to shift the awkward burthen of an equivocal duty from his own shoulders?

I once drank tea in company with two Methodist divines of different persuasions, whom it was my fortune to introduce to each other for the first time that evening. Before the first cup was handed round, one of these reverend gentlemen put it to the other, with all due solemnity, whether he chose to *say anything.* It seems it is the custom with some sectaries to put up a short prayer before this meal also. His reverend brother did not at first quite apprehend him, but upon an explanation, with little less importance he made answer that it was not a custom known in his church: in which courteous evasion the other acquiescing for good manners' sake, or in compliance with a weak brother, the supplementary or tea grace was waived altogether. With what spirit might not Lucian have painted two priests, of *his* religion, playing into each other's hands the compliment of performing or omitting a sacrifice,—the hungry God meantime, doubtful of his incense, with expectant nostrils hovering over the two flamens, and (as between two stools) going away in the end without his supper.

A short form upon these occasions is felt to want reverence; a long one, I am afraid, cannot escape the charge of impertinence. I do not quite approve of the epigrammatic conciseness with which that equivocal wag (but my pleasant school-fellow) C. V. L., when importuned for a grace, used to inquire, first slyly leering down the table, "Is there no clergyman here?"—significantly adding, "Thank G—." Nor do I think our old form at school quite pertinent, where we were used to preface our bald bread-and-cheese-suppers with a preamble, connecting with that humble blessing a recognition of benefits the most awful and overwhelming to the imagination which religion has to offer. *Non tunc illis erat locus.* I remember we were put to it to reconcile the phrase "good creatures," upon which the blessing rested, with the fare set before us, wilfully understanding that expression in a low and animal sense,—till some one recalled a legend, which told how, in the golden days of Christ's, the young Hospitallers were wont to have smoking joints of roast meat upon their nightly boards, till some pious benefactor, commiserating the decencies, rather than the palates, of the children, commuted our flesh for garments, and gave us—*horresco referens*—trousers instead of mutton.

DREAM CHILDREN; A REVERIE.

Children love to listen to stories about their elders, when *they* were children; to stretch their imagination to the conception of a traditionary great-uncle, or grandame, whom they never saw. It was in this spirit that my little ones crept about me the other evening to hear about their great-grandmother Field, who lived in a great house in Norfolk (a hundred times bigger than that in which they and papa lived) which had been the scene—so at least it was generally believed in that part of the country—of the tragic incidents which they had lately become familiar with from the ballad of the Children in the Wood. Certain it is that the whole story of the children and their cruel uncle was to be seen fairly carved out in wood upon the chimney-piece of the great hall, the whole story down to the Robin Redbreasts; till a foolish rich person pulled it down to set up a marble one of modern invention in its stead, with no story upon it. Here Alice put out one of her dear mother's looks, too tender to be called upbraiding. Then I went on to say, how religious and how good their great-grandmother Field was, how beloved and respected by everybody, though she **was** not indeed the mistress of this great house, but had only the charge of it (and yet in some respects she might be said to be the mistress of it too) committed to her by the owner, who preferred living in a newer and more fashionable mansion which he had purchased somewhere in the adjoining county; but still she lived in it in a manner as if it had been her own, and kept up the dignity of the great house in a sort while she lived, which afterwards came to decay, and was nearly pulled down, and all its old ornaments stripped and carried away to the owner's other house, where they were set up, and looked as awkward as if some one were to carry away the old tombs they had seen lately at the Abbey, and stick them up in Lady C.'s tawdry gilt drawing-room. Here John smiled, as much as to say, "that would be foolish indeed." And then I told how, when she came to die, her funeral was attended by a concourse of all the poor, and some of the gentry too, of the neighbourhood for many miles round, to show their respect for her memory, because she had been such a good and religious woman; so good indeed that she knew all the Psaltery by heart, ay, and a great part of the Testament besides. Here little Alice spread her hands. Then I told what a tall, upright, graceful person their great-grandmother Field once was; and how in her youth she was esteemed the best dancer—here Alice's little right foot played an involuntary movement, till, upon my looking grave, it desisted—the best dancer, I was saying, in the county, till a cruel disease, called a cancer, came, and bowed her down with pain; but it could never bend her good spirits, or make them stoop, but they were still upright, because she was so good and religious. Then I told how she was used to sleep by herself in a lone chamber of the great lone house; and how she believed that an apparition of two infants was to be seen at midnight gliding up and down the great staircase near where she slept, but she said "those innocents would do her no harm;" and how frightened I used to be, though in those days I had my maid to sleep with me, because I was never half so good or religious as she—and yet I never saw the infants. Here John expanded all his eyebrows and tried to look courageous. Then I told how good she was to all her grand-children, having us to the great house in the holydays, where I in particular used to spend many hours by myself, in gazing upon the old busts of the twelve Cæsars, that had been Emperors of Rome, till the old marble heads would seem to live again, or I to be turned into marble with them; how I never could be tired with roaming about that huge mansion, with its vast empty rooms, with their worn-out hangings, fluttering tapestry, and carved oaken panels, with the gilding almost rubbed out—sometimes in the spacious old-fashioned gardens, which I had almost to myself, unless when now and then a solitary gardening man would cross me—and how the nectarines and peaches hung upon the walls, without my ever offering to pluck them, because they were forbidden fruit, unless now and then,—and because I had more pleasure in strolling about among the old melancholy-looking yew-trees, or the firs, and picking up the red berries, and the fir-apples, which were good for nothing but to look at—or in lying about upon the fresh grass with all the fine garden smells around me—or basking in the orangery, till I could almost fancy myself ripening too along with the oranges and the limes in that grateful warmth—or in watching the dace that darted to and fro in the fish-pond, and the bottom of the garden, with here and there a great sulky pike hanging midway down the water in silent state, as if it mocked at their impertinent friskings,—I had more pleasure in these busy-idle diversions than in all the sweet flavours of peaches, nectarines, oranges, and such-like common baits of children. Here John slyly deposited back upon the plate a bunch of grapes, which, not unobserved by Alice, he had meditated dividing with her, and both seemed willing to relinquish them for the present as irrelevant. Then, in somewhat a more heightened tone, I told how, though their great-grandmother Field loved all her grandchildren, yet in an especial manner she might be said to love their uncle, John L——, because he was so handsome and spirited a youth, and a king to the rest of us; and, instead of moping about in solitary corners, like some of us, he would mount the most mettlesome horse he could get, when but an imp no bigger than themselves, and make it carry him half over the county in a morning, and join the hunters when there were any

out—and yet he loved the old great house and gardens too, but had too much spirit to be always pent up within their boundaries —and how their uncle grew up to man's estate as brave as he was handsome, to the admiration of everybody, but of their great-grandmother Field most especially; and how he used to carry me upon his back when I was a lame-footed boy—for he was a good bit older than me—many a mile when I could not walk for pain;—and how in after life he became lame-footed to, and I did not always (I fear) make allowances enough for him when he was impatient and in pain, nor remember sufficiently how considerate he had been to me when I was lame-footed; and how when he died, though he had not been dead an hour, it seemed as if he had died a great while ago, such a distance there is betwixt life and death; and how I bore his death as I thought pretty well at first, but afterwards it haunted and haunted me; and though I did not cry or take it to heart as some do, and as I think he would have done if I had died, yet I missed him all day long, and knew not till then how much I had loved him. I missed his kindness, and I missed his crossness, and wished him to be alive again, to be quarrelling with him (for we quarrelled sometimes), rather than not have him again, and was as uneasy without him, as he, their poor uncle, must have been when the doctor took off his limb.—Here the children fell a-crying, and asked if their little mourning which they had on was not for uncle John, and they looked up, and prayed me not to go on about their uncle, but to tell them some stories about their pretty dead mother. Then I told how for seven long years, in hope sometimes, sometimes in despair, yet persisting ever, I courted the fair Alice W——n; and as much as children could understand, I explained to them what coyness, and difficulty, and denial, meant in maidens—when suddenly turning to Alice, the soul of the first Alice looked out at her eyes with such a reality of representment, that I became in doubt which of them stood there before me, or whose that bright hair was; and while I stood gazing, both the children gradually grew fainter to my view, receding, and still receding, till nothing at last but two mournful features were seen in the uttermost distance, which, without speech, strangely impressed upon me the effects of speech: "We are not of Alice, nor of thee, nor are we children at all. The children of Alice call Bartrum father. We are nothing; less than nothing, and dreams. We are only what might have been, and must wait upon the tedious shores of Lethe millions of ages before we have existence, and a name"——and immediately awaking, I found myself quietly seated in my bachelor arm-chair, where I had fallen asleep, with the faithful Bridget unchanged by my side—but John L. (or James Elia) was gone for ever.

DISTANT CORRESPONDENTS.

IN A LETTER TO B. F. ESQ., AT SYDNEY, NEW SOUTH WALES.

My dear F.—When I think how welcome the sight of a letter from the world where you were born must be to you in that strange one to which you have been transplanted, I feel some compunctious visitings at my long silence. But, indeed, it is no easy effort to set about a correspondence at our distance. The weary world of waters between us oppresses the imagination. It is difficult to conceive how a scrawl of mine should ever stretch across it. It is a sort of presumption to expect that one's thought should live so far. It is like writing for posterity; and reminds me of one of Mrs. Rowe's superscriptions, "Alcander to Strephon in the shades." Cowley's Post-Angel is no more than would be expedient in such an intercourse. One drops a packet at Lombard Street, and in twenty-four hours a friend in Cumberland gets it as fresh as if it came in ice. It is only like whispering through a long trumpet. But suppose a tube let down from the moon, with yourself at one end and *the man* at the other; it would be some balk to the spirit of conversation, if you knew that the dialogue exchanged with that interesting theosophist would take two or three revolutions of a higher luminary in its passage. Yet, for aught I know, you may be some parasangs nigher that primitive idea—Plato's man—than we in England here have the honour to reckon ourselves.

Epistolary matter usually compriseth three topics; news, sentiment, and puns. In the latter, I include all non-serious subjects; or subjects serious in themselves, but treated after my fashion, non-seriously.—And first, for news. In them the most desirable circumstance, I suppose, is that they shall be true. But what security can I have that what I now send you for truth shall not, before you get it, unaccountably turn into a lie? For instance, our mutual friend P. is at this present writing —*my Now*—in good health, and enjoys a fair share of worldly reputation. You are glad to hear it. This is natural and friendly. But at this present reading—*your Now* —he may possibly be in the Bench, or going to be hanged, which in reason ought to abate something of your transport (*i. e.*, at hearing he was well, &c.), or at least considerably to modify it. I am going to the play this evening, to have a laugh with Munden. You have no theatre, I think you told me, in your land of d——d realities. You naturally lick your lips, and envy me my felicity. Think but a moment, and you will correct the hateful emotion. Why, it is Sunday morning with you, and

1823. This confusion of tenses, this grand solecism of *two presents*, is in a degree common to all postage. But if I sent you word to Bath or Devizes, that I was expecting the aforesaid treat this evening, though at the moment you received the intelligence my full feast of fun would be over, yet there would be for a day or two after, as you would well know, a smack, a relish left upon my mental palate, which would give rational encouragement for you to foster a portion, at least, of the disagreeable passion, which it was in part my intention to produce. But ten months hence, your envy or your sympathy would be as useless as a passion spent upon the dead. Not only does truth, in these long intervals, unessence herself, but (what is harder) one cannot venture a crude fiction, for the fear that it may ripen into a truth upon the voyage. What a wild improbable banter I put upon you, some three years since,—— of Will Weatherall having married a servant-maid! I remember gravely consulting you how we were to receive her—for Will's wife was in no case to be rejected; and your no less serious replication in the matter; how tenderly you advised an abstemious introduction of literary topics before the lady, with a caution not to be too forward in bringing on the carpet matters more within the sphere of her intelligence; your deliberate judgment, or rather wise suspension of sentence, how far jacks, and spits, and mops, could, with propriety, be introduced as subjects; whether the conscious avoiding of all such matters in discourse would not have a worse look than the taking of them casually in our way; in what manner we should carry ourselves to our maid Becky, Mrs. William Weatherall being by; whether we should show more delicacy, and a truer sense of respect for Will's wife, by treating Becky with our customary chiding before her, or by an unusual deferential civility paid to Becky, as to a person of great worth, but thrown by the caprice of fate into a humble station. There were difficulties, I remember, on both sides, which you did me the favour to state with the precision of a lawyer, united to the tenderness of a friend. I laughed in my sleeve at your solemn pleadings, when lo! while I was valuing myself upon this flam put upon you in New South Wales, the devil in England, jealous possibly of any lie-children not his own, or working after my copy, has actually instigated our friend (not three days since) to the commission of a matrimony, which I had only conjured up for your diversion. William Weatherall had married Mrs. Cotterel's maid. But to take it in its truest sense, you will see, my dear F., that news from me must become history to you; which I neither profess to write, nor indeed care much for reading. No person, under a diviner, can, with any prospect of veracity, conduct a correspondence at such an arm's length. Two prophets, indeed, might thus interchange intelligence with effect; the epoch of the writer (Habakkuk) falling in with the true present time of the receiver (Daniel); but then we are no prophets.

Then as to sentiment. It fares little better with that. This kind of dish, above all, requires to be served up hot, or sent off in water-plates, that your friend may have it almost as warm as yourself. If it have time to cool, it is the most tasteless of all cold meats. I have often smiled at a conceit of the late Lord C. It seems that travelling somewhere about Geneva, he came to some pretty green spot, or nook, where a willow, or something, hung so fantastically and invitingly over a stream—was it?—or a rock?—no matter—but the stillness and the repose, after a weary journey, 'tis likely, in a languid moment of his Lordship's hot, restless life, so took his fancy that he could imagine no place so proper, in the event of his death, to lay his bones in. This was all very natural and excusable as a sentiment, and shows his character in a very pleasing light. But when from a passing sentiment it came to be an act; and when, by a positive testamentary disposal, his remains were actually carried all that way from England; who was there, some desperate sentimentalists excepted, that did not ask the question, Why could not his Lordship have found a spot as solitary, a nook as romantic, a tree as green and pendent, with a stream as emblematic to his purpose, in Surrey, in Dorset, or in Devon? Conceive the sentiment boarded up, freighted, entered at the Custom House (startling the tide-waiters with the novelty), hoisted into a ship. Conceive it pawed about and handled between the rude jests of tarpaulin ruffians—a thing of its delicate texture—the salt bilge wetting it till it became as vapid as a damaged lustring. Suppose it in material danger (mariners have some superstition about sentiments) of being tossed over in a fresh gale to some propitiatory shark (spirit of Saint Gothard, save us from a quietus so foreign to the deviser's purpose!) but it has happily evaded a fishy consummation. Trace it then to its lucky landing—at Lyons shall we say?—I have not the map before me—jostled upon four men's shoulders—baiting at this town—stopping to refresh at t'other village—waiting a passport here, a license there; the sanction of the magistracy in this district, the concurrence of the ecclesiastics in that canton; till at length it arrives at its destination, tired out and jaded, from a brisk sentiment into a feature of silly pride or tawdry senseless affectation. How few sentiments, my dear F., I am afraid we can set down, in the sailor's phrase, as quite seaworthy.

Lastly, as to the agreeable levities, which though contemptible in bulk, are the twinkling corpuscula which should irradiate a right friendly epistle—your puns and small jests are, I apprehend, extremely circumscribed in their sphere of action. They are so far from a capacity of being packed up and sent beyond sea, they will scarce endure to be transported by hand from this room to the next. Their vigour is as the instant of their birth. Their nutriment for their brief existence is the intellectual atmosphere of the by-standers: or this last is the fine slime of Nilus—the *melior lutus*—whose maternal recipiency is as necessary as the *sol pater* to their equivocal generation. A pun hath a hearty kind of present ear-kissing smack with it; you can no more transmit it in its pristine flavour than you can send a kiss. —Have you not tried in some instances to palm off a yesterday's pun upon a gentleman, and has it answered? Not but it was new to his hearing, but it did not seem to come new from you. It did not hitch in. It was like picking up at a village ale-house a two days'-old newspaper. You have not seen it before, but you resent the stale thing as an affront. This sort of merchandize above all requires a quick return. A pun, and its recognitory laugh, must be co-instantaneous. The one is the brisk lightning, the other the fierce thunder. A moment's interval, and the link is snapped. A pun is reflected from a friend's face as from a mirror. Who would consult his sweet visnomy, if the polished surface were two or three minutes (not to speak of twelve months, my dear F.) in giving back its copy?

I cannot image to myself whereabout you are. When I try to fix it, Peter Wilkins's island comes across me. Sometimes you seem to be in the *Hades of Thieves.* I see Diogenes prying among you with his perpetual fruitless lantern. What must you be willing by this time to give for the sight of an honest man! You must almost have forgotten how *we* look. And tell me what your Sydneyites do? are they th**v*ng all day long? Merciful Heaven! what property can stand against such a depredation! The kangaroos—your Aborigines — do they keep their primitive simplicity un Europe-tainted, with those little short fore puds, looking like a lesson framed by nature to the pick-pocket! Marry, for diving into fobs they are rather lamely provided *à priori;* but if the hue and cry were once up, they would show as fair a pair of hind-shifters as the expertest loco-motor in the colony. We bear the most improbable tales at this distance. Pray is it true that the young Spartans among you are born with six fingers, which spoils their scanning?—It must look very odd; but use reconciles. For their scansion, it is less to regretted; for if they take it into their heads to be poets, it is odds but they turn out, the greater part of them, vile plagiarists. Is there much difference to see, too, between the son of a th**f and the grandson? or where does the taint stop? Do you bleach in three or in four generations? I have many questions to put, but ten Delphic voyages can be made in a shorter time than it will take to satisfy my scruples. Do you grow your own hemp?—What is your staple trade,—exclusive of the national profession, I mean? Your locksmiths, I take it, are some of your great capitalists.

I am insensibly chatting to you as familiarly as when we used to exchange good-morrows out of our old contiguous windows, in pump-famed Hare Court in the Temple. Why did you ever leave that quiet corner?—Why did I?—with its complement of four poor elms, from whose smoke-dyed barks, the theme of jesting ruralists, I picked my first lady-birds! My heart is as dry as that spring sometimes proves in a thirsty August, when I revert to the space that is between us; a length of passage enough to render obsolete the phrases of our English letters before they can reach you. But while I talk I think you hear me, —thoughts dallying with vain surmise—

Aye me! while thee the seas and sounding shores
Hold far away.

Come back, before I am grown into a very old man, so as you shall hardly know me. Come, before Bridget walks on crutches. Girls whom you left children have become sage matrons while you are tarrying there. The blooming Miss W—r (you remember Sally W—r) called upon us yesterday, an aged crone. Folks whom you knew die off every year. Formerly, I thought that death was wearing out,—I stood ramparted about with so many healthy friends. The departure of J. W., two springs back, corrected my delusion. Since then the old divorcer has been busy. If you do not make haste to return, there will be little left to greet you, of me, or mine.

[Something of home matters I could add; but *that*, with certain remembrances never to be omitted, I reserve for the grave postscript to this light epistle; which postscript, for weighty reasons, justificatory in any court of feeling, I think better omitted in this first edition.]

THE PRAISE OF CHIMNEY-SWEEPERS.

I LIKE to meet a sweep—understand me—not a grown sweeper— old chimney-sweepers are by no means attractive—but one of those tender novices, blooming through their first nigritude, the maternal washings not quite effaced from the cheek—such as come forth with the dawn, or somewhat earlier, with their little professional notes sounding like the *peep-peep* of a young sparrow; or liker to the matin lark should I pronounce them, in their aërial ascents not seldom anticipating the sun-rise?

I have a kindly yearning towards these dim specks—poor blots—innocent blacknesses—

I reverence these young Africans of our own growth—these almost clergy imps, who sport their cloth without assumption; and from their little pulpits (the tops of chimneys), in the nipping air of a December morning, preach a lesson of patience to mankind.

When a child, what a mysterious pleasure it was to witness their operation! to see a chit no bigger than one's self, enter, one knew not by what process, into what seemed the *fauces Averni*— to pursue him in imagination, as he went sounding on through so many dark stifling caverns, horrid shades! to shudder with the idea that "now, surely, he must be lost for ever!"—to revive at hearing his feeble shout of discovered daylight—and then (O fulness of delight!) running out of doors, to come just in time to see the sable phenomenon emerge in safety, the brandished weapon of his art victorious like some flag waved over a conquered citadel! I seem to remember having been told, that a bad sweep was once left in a stack with his brush, to indicate which way the wind blew. It was an awful spectacle, certainly; not much unlike the old stage direction in Macbeth, where the "Apparition of a child crowned, with a tree in his hand, rises."

Reader, if thou meetest one of these small gentry in thy early rambles, it is good to give him a penny,—it is better to give him two-pence. If it be starving weather, and to the proper troubles of his hard occupation, a pair of kibed heels (no unusual accompaniment) be superadded, the demand on thy humanity will surely rise to a tester.

There is a composition, the ground-work of which I have understood to be the sweet wood 'yclept sassafras. This wood boiled down to a kind of tea, and tempered with an infusion of milk and sugar, hath to some tastes a delicacy beyond the China luxury. I know not how thy palate may relish it; for myself, with every deference to the judicious Mr. Read, who hath time out of mind kept open a shop (the only one he avers in London) for the vending of this "wholesome and pleasant beverage," on the south side of Fleet Street, as thou approachest Bridge Street—*the only Salopian house*—I have never yet adventured to dip my own particular lip in a basin of his commended ingredients—a cautious premonition to the olfactories constantly whispering to me, that my stomach must infallibly, with all due courtesy, decline it. Yet I have seen palates, otherwise not uninstructed in dietetical elegancies, sup it up with avidity.

I know not by what particular conformations of the organ it happens, but I have always found that this composition is surprisingly gratifying to the palate of a young chimney-sweeper—whether the oily particles (sassafras is slightly oleaginous) do attenuate and soften the fuliginous concretions, which are sometimes found (in dissections) to adhere to the roof of the mouth in these unfledged practitioners; or whether Nature, sensible that she had mingled too much of bitter wood in the lot of these raw victims, caused to grow out of the earth her sassafras for a sweet lenitive—but so it is, that no possible taste or odour to the senses of a young chimney-sweeper can convey a delicate excitement comparable to this mixture. Being penniless, they will yet hang their black heads over the ascending steam, to gratify one sense if possible, seemingly no less pleased than those domestic animals—cats —when they purr over a new-found sprig of valerian. There is something more in these sympathies than philosophy can inculcate.

Now albeit Mr. Read boasteth, not without reason, that his is the *only Salopian house;* yet be it known to thee, reader—if thou art one who keepest what are called good hours, thou art haply ignorant of the fact—he hath a race of industrious imitators, who from stalls, and under open sky, dispense the same savoury mess to humbler customers, at that dead time of the dawn, when (as extremes meet) the rake, reeling home from his midnight cups, and the hard-handed artisan leaving his bed to resume the premature labours of the day, jostle, not unfrequently to the manifest disconcerting of the former, for the honours of the pavement. It is the time when, in summer, between the expired and the not yet relumined kitchen-fires, the kennels of our fair metropolis give forth their least satisfactory odours. The rake, who wisheth to dissipate his o'ernight vapours in more grateful coffee, curses the ungenial fume, as he passeth; but the artisan stops to taste, and blesses the fragrant breakfast.

This is *saloop*—the precocious herb-woman's darling—the delight of the early gardener, who transports his smoking cabbages by break of day from Hammersmith to Covent Garden's famed piazzas—the delight, and oh! I fear, too often the envy, of the unpennied sweep. Him shouldst thou haply encounter, with his dim visage pendent over the grateful steam, regale him with a sumptuous basin (it will cost but three-halfpennies) and a slice of delicate bread and butter (an added halfpenny—so may thy culinary fires, eased of the o'ercharged secretions from thy worse-placed hospitalities, curl up a lighter volume to the welkin—so may the descending soot never taint thy costly well-ingredienced soups—nor the odious cry, quick-reaching from street to street, of the *fired chimney*, invite the rattling engines from ten adjacent parishes, to disturb for a casual scintillation thy peace and pocket!

I am by nature extremely susceptible of street affronts; the jeers and taunts of the populace; the low-bred triumph they display over the casual trip, or splashed stocking, of a gentleman. Yet can I endure the jocularity of a young sweep with something more than forgiveness.—In the last winter but one, pacing along Cheapside with my accustomed precipitation when I walk westward, a treacherous slide brought me upon my back in an instant. I scrambled up with pain and shame enough—yet outwardly trying to face it down, as if nothing had happened—when the roguish grin of one of these young wits encountered me. There he stood, pointing me out with his dusky finger to the mob, and to a poor woman (I suppose his mother) in particular, till the tears for the exquisiteness of the fun (so he thought it) worked themselves out at the corners of his poor red eyes, red from many a previous weeping, and soot-inflamed, yet twinkling through all with such a joy, snatched out of desolation, that Hogarth—— but Hogarth has got him already (how could he miss him?) in the March to Finchley, grinning at the pieman—there he stood, as he stands in the picture, irremovable, as if the jest was to last for ever—with such a maximum of glee, and minimum of mischief, in his mirth—for the grin of a genuine sweep hath absolutely no malice in it—that I could have been content, if the honour of a gentleman might endure it, to have remained his butt and his mockery till midnight.

I am by theory obdurate to the seductiveness of what are called a fine set of teeth. Every pair of rosy lips (the ladies must pardon me) is a casket presumably holding such jewels; but, methinks they should take leave to "air" them as frugally as possible. The fine lady, or fine gentleman, who show me their teeth, show me bones. Yet must I confess, that from the mouth of a true sweep a display (even to ostentation) of those white and shiny ossifications, strikes me as an agreeable anomaly in manners, and an allowable piece of foppery. It is, as when

> A sable cloud
> **Turns forth her silver lining on the night.**

It is like some remnant of gentry not quite extinct; a badge of better days; a hint of nobility:—and, doubtless, under the obscuring darkness and double night of their forlorn disguisement, oftentimes lurketh good blood, and gentle conditions, derived from lost ancestry, and a lapsed pedigree. The premature apprenticements of these tender victims give but too much encouragement, I fear, to clandestine and almost infantile abductions; the seeds of civility and true courtesy, so often discernible in these young grafts (not otherwise to be accounted for) plainly hint at some forced adoptions; many noble Rachels mourning for their children, even in our days, countenance the fact; the tales of fairy spiriting may shadow a lamentable verity, and the recovery of the young Montagu be but a solitary instance of good fortune out of many irreparable and hopeless *defiliations*.

In one of the state-beds at Arundel Castle, a few years since —under a ducal canopy—(that seat of the Howards is an object of curiosity to visitors, chiefly for its beds, in which the late duke was especially a connoisseur)—encircled with curtains of delicatest crimson, with starry coronets inwoven—folded between a pair of sheets whiter and softer than the lap where Venus lulled Ascanius —was discovered by chance, after all methods of search had failed, at noon-day, fast asleep, a lost chimney-sweeper. The little creature, having somehow confounded his passage among the intricacies of those lordly chimneys, by some unknown aperture had alighted upon this magnificent chamber; and, tired with his tedious explorations, was unable to resist the delicious invitement to repose, which he there saw exhibited; so creeping between the sheets very quietly, laid his black head upon the pillow, and slept like a young Howard.

Such is the account given to the visitors at the Castle.—But I cannot help seeming to perceive a confirmation of what I had just hinted at in this story. A high instinct was at work in the case, or I am mistaken. Is it probable that a poor child of that description, with whatever weariness he might be visited, would have ventured, under such a penalty as be would be taught to expect, to uncover the sheets of a Duke's bed, and deliberately to lay himself down between them, when the rug, or the carpet, presented an obvious couch, still far above his pretensions—is this probable, I would ask, if the great power of nature, which I contend for, had not been manifested within him, prompting to the adventure? Doubtless this young nobleman (for such my mind misgives me that he must be) was allured by some memory, not amounting to full consciousness, of his condition in infancy, when he was used to be lapped by his mother, or his nurse, in just such sheets as he there found, into which he was now but creeping back as into his proper *incunabula*, and resting-place.—By no other theory than by this sentiment of a pre-existent state (as I may call it), can I explain a deed so venturous, and, indeed, upon any other system, so indecorous, in this tender, but unseasonable, sleeper.

My pleasant friend Jem White was so impressed with a belief of metamorphoses like this frequently taking place, that in some sort to reverse the wrongs of fortune in these poor changelings, he instituted an annual feast of chimney-sweepers, at which it was his pleasure to officiate as host and waiter. It was a solemn supper held in Smithfield, upon the yearly return of the fair of St. Bartholomew. Cards were issued a week before to the master-sweeps in and about the metropolis, confining the invitation to their younger fry. Now and then an elderly stripling would get in among us, and be good-naturedly winked at; but our main body were infantry. One unfortunate wight, indeed, who, relying upon his dusky suit, had intruded himself into our party, but by tokens was providentially discovered in time to be no chimney-sweeper, (all is not soot which looks so,) was quoited out of the presence with universal indignation, as not having on the wedding garment; but in general the greatest harmony prevailed. The place chosen was a convenient spot among the pens, at the north side of the fair, not so far distant as to be impervious to the agreeable hubbub of that vanity, but remote enough not to be obvious to the interruption of every gaping spectator in it. The guests assembled about seven. In those little temporary parlours three tables were spread with napery, not so fine as substantial, and at every board a comely hostess presided with her pan of hissing sausages. The nostrils of the young rogues dilated at the savour. James White, as head waiter, had charge of the first table; and myself, with our trusty companion Bigod, ordinarily ministered to the other two. There was clambering and jostling, you may be sure, who should get at the first table, for Rochester in his maddest days could not have done the humours of the scene with more spirit than my friend. After some general expression of thanks for the honour the company had done him, his inaugural ceremony was to clasp the greasy waist of old dame Ursula (the fattest of the three), that stood frying and fretting, half-blessing, half-cursing "the gentleman," and imprint upon her chaste lips a tender salute, whereat the universal host would set up a shout that tore the concave, while hundreds of grinning teeth startled the night with their brightness. O it was a pleasure to see the sable younkers lick in the unctuous meat, with *his* more unctuous sayings—how he would fit the tit-bits to the puny mouths, reserving the lengthier links for the seniors—how he would intercept a morsel even in the jaws of some young desperado, declaring it "must to the pan again to be browned, for it was not fit for a gentleman's eating"—how he would recommend this slice of white bread, or that piece of kissing-crust, to a tender juvenile, advising them all to have a care of cracking their teeth, which were their best patrimony,—how genteely he would deal about the small ale, as if it were wine, naming the brewer, and protesting, if it were not good, he should lose their custom; with a special recommendation to wipe the lip before drinking. Then we had our toasts—"the King,"—"the Cloth,"—which, whether they understood or not, was equally diverting and flattering; and for a crowning sentiment, which never failed, "May the Brush supersede the Laurel!" All these, and fifty other fancies, which were rather felt than comprehended by his guests, would be utter, standing upon tables, and prefacing every sentiment with a "Gentlemen, give me leave to propose so and so," which was a prodigious comfort to those young orphans; every now and then stuffing into his mouth (for it did not do to be squeamish on these occasions) indiscriminate pieces of those reeking sausages, which pleased them mightily, and was the savouriest part, you may believe, of the entertainment.

Golden lads and lasses must,
As chimney-sweepers, come to dust—

James White is extinct, and with him these suppers have long ceased. He carried away with him half the fun of the world when he died—of my world at least. His old clients look for him among the pens; and, missing him, reproach the altered feast of St. Bartholomew, and the glory of Smithfield departed for ever.

———

A COMPLAINT OF THE DECAY OF BEGGARS.

IN THE METROPOLIS.

THE all-sweeping besom of societarian reformation—your only modern Alcides' club to rid the time of its abuses—is uplift with many-handed sway to extirpate the last fluttering tatters of the bugbear MENDICITY from the metropolis. Scrips, wallets, bags—staves, dogs, and crutches—the whole mendicant fraternity, with all their baggage, are fast posting out of the purlieus of this eleventh persecution From the crowded crossing, from the corners of streets and turnings of alleys, the parting Genius of Beggary is "with sighing sent."

I do not approve of this wholesale going to work, this impertinent crusado, or *bellum ad exterminationem*, proclaimed against a species. Much good might be sucked from these Beggars.

They were the oldest and the honourablest form of pauperism. Their appeals were to our common nature; less revolting to an ingenuous mind than to be a suppliant to the particular humours or caprice of any fellow-creature, or set of fellow-creatures, parochial or societarian. Theirs were the only rates uninvidious in the levy, ungrudged in the assessment.

There was a dignity springing from the very depth of their desolation; as to be naked is to be so much nearer to the being a man, than to go in livery.

The greatest spirits have felt this in their reverses; and when Dionysius from king turned schoolmaster, do we feel anything towards him but contempt? Could Vandyke have made a picture of him, swaying a ferula for a sceptre, which would have affected our minds with the same heroic pity, the same compassionate admiration, with which we regard his Belisarius begging for an *obolum!* Would the moral have been more graceful, more pathetic?

The Blind Beggar in the legend —the father of pretty Bessy— whose story doggrel rhymes and ale-house signs cannot so degrade or attenuate but that some sparks of a lustrous spirit will shine through the disguisements—this noble Earl of Cornwall (as indeed he was) and memorable sport of fortune, fleeing from the unjust sentence of his liege lord, stript of all, and seated on the flowering green of Bethnal, with his more fresh and springing daughter by his side, illumining his rags and his beggary—would the child and parent have cut a better figure doing the honours of a counter, or expiating their fallen condition upon the three-foot eminence of some sempstering shop-board?

In tale or history your Beggar is ever the just antipode to your King. The poets and romancical writers (as dear Margaret Newcastle would call them,) when they would most sharply and feelingly paint a reverse of fortune, never stop till they have brought down their hero in good earnest to rags and the wallet. The depth of the descent illustrates the height he falls from. There is no medium which can be presented to the imagination without offence. There is no breaking the fall. Lear, thrown from his palace, must divest him of his garments, till he answer "mere nature;" and Cresseid, fallen from a prince's love, must extend her pale arms, pale with other whiteness than of beauty, supplicating lazar arms with bell and clap-dish.

The Lucian wits knew this very well; and, with a converse policy, when they would express scorn of greatness without the pity, they show us an Alexander in the shades cobbling shoes, or a Semiramis getting up foul linen.

How would it sound in song, that a great monarch had declined his affections upon the daughter of a baker! yet do we feel the imagination at all violated when we read the "true ballad," where King Cophetua woos the beggar maid?

Pauperism, pauper, poor man, are expressions of pity, but pity alloyed with contempt. No one properly contemns a Beggar. Poverty is a comparative thing, and each degree of it is mocked by its "neighbour grice." Its poor rents and comings-in are soon summed up and told. Its pretences to property are almost ludicrous. Its pitiful attempts to save excite a smile. Every scornful companion can weigh his trifle-bigger purse against it. Poor man reproaches poor man in the street with impolitic mention of his condition, his own being a shade better, while the rich pass by and jeer at both. No rascally comparative insults a Beggar, or thinks of weighing purses with him. He is not in the scale of comparison. He is not under the measure of property. He confessedly hath none, any more than a dog or a sheep. No one twitteth him with ostentation above his means. No one accuses him of pride, or upbraideth him with mock humility. None jostle with him for the wall, or pick quarrels for precedency. No wealthy neighbour seeketh to eject him from his tenement. No man sues him. No man goes to law with him. If I were not the independent gentleman that I am, rather than I would be a retainer to the great, a led captain, or a poor relation, I would choose, out of the delicacy and true greatness of my mind, to be a Beggar.

Rags, which are the reproach of poverty, are the Beggar's robes, and graceful *insignia* of his profession, his tenure, his full dress, the suit in which he is expected to show himself in public. He is never out of the fashion, or limpeth awkwardly behind it. He is not required to put on court mourning. He weareth all colours, fearing none. His costume hath undergone less change than the Quaker's. He is the only man in the universe who is not obliged to study appearances. The ups and downs of the world concern him no longer. He alone continueth in one stay. The price of stock or land affecteth him not. The fluctuations of agricultural or commercial prosperity touch him not, or at worst but change his customers. He is not expected to become bail or surety for any one. No man troubleth him with questioning his religion or politics. He is the only free man in the universe.

The Mendicants of this great city were so many of her sights, her lions. I can no more spare them than I could the Cries of London. No corner of a street is complete without them. They are as indispensable as the Ballad

Singer; and in their picturesque attire as ornamental as the signs of old London. They were the standing morals, emblems, mementos, dial-mottos, the spital sermons, the books for children, the salutary checks and pauses to the high and rushing tide of greasy citizenry—

——————— Look
Upon that poor and broken bankrupt
        there.

Above all, those old blind Tobits that used to line the wall of Lincoln's-inn Garden, before modern fastidiousness had expelled them, casting up their ruined orbs to catch a ray of pity, and (if possible) of light, with their faithful Dog Guide at their feet,—whither are they fled? or into what corners, blind as themselves, have they been driven, out of the wholesome air and sun-warmth? immersed between four walls, in what withering poor-house do they endure the penalty of double darkness, where the chink of the dropt halfpenny no more consoles their forlorn bereavement, far from the sound of the cheerful and hope-stirring tread of the passenger? Where hang their useless staves? and who will farm their dogs?—Have the overseers of St. L— caused them to be shot? or were they tied up in sacks and dropt into the Thames, at the suggestion of B—, the mild rector of——?

Well fare the soul of unfastidious Vincent Bourne,—most classical, and, at the same time, most English of the Latinists!—who has treated of this human and quadrupedal alliance, this dog and man friendship, in the sweetest of his poems, the *Epitaphium in Canem*, or, *Dog's Epitaph*. Reader, peruse it; and say, if customary sights, which could call up such gentle poetry as this, were of a nature to do more harm or good to the moral sense of the passengers through the daily thoroughfares of a vast and busy metropolis.

Pauperis hic Iri requiesco Lyciscus,
        herilis,
Dum vixi, tutela vigil columenque se-
        nectæ,
Dux cæco fidus: nec, me ducente, solebat,
Prætenso huc atque huc baculo, per
        iniqua locorum
Incertam explorare viam; sed fila secutus,
Quæ dubios regerent passûs, vestigia tuta
Fixit inoffenso gressu; gelidumque sedile
In nudo nactus saxo, quâ prætereuntium
Unda frequens confluxit, ibi miseriæque
        tenebras
Lamentis, noctemque oculis ploravit
        obortam.
Ploravit nec frustra; obolum dedit alter
        et alter,
Queis corda et mentem indiderat natura
        benignam.
Ad latus interea jacui sopitus herile,
Vel mediis vigil in somnis; ad herilia
        jussa
Aureisque atque animum arrectus, seu
        frustula amicâ
Porrexit sociasque dapes, seu longa diei
Tædia perpessus, reditum sub nocte
        parabat.
   Hi mores, hæc vita fuit, dum fata sine-
        bant,
Dum neque languebam morbis, nec inerte
        senectâ
Quæ tandem obrepsit, veterique satellite
        cæcum
Orbavit dominum; prisci sed gratia facti
Ne tota intereat, longos deleta per annos,
Exiguum hunc Irus tumulum de cespite
        fecit,
Etsi inopis, non ingratæ, munuscula
        dextræ;

Carmine signavitque brevi, dominumque
   canemque,
Quod memoret, idumque Canem dominumque Benignum.

Poor Irus' faithful wolf-dog here I lie,
That wont to tend my old blind master's
   steps,
His guide and guard; nor, while my ser-
   vice lasted,
Had he occasion for that staff, with
   which
He now goes picking out his path in fear
Over the highways and crossings; but
   would plant,
Safe in the conduct of my friendly string,
A firm foot forward still, till he had
   reach'd
His poor seat on some stone, nigh where
   the tide
Of passers-by in thickest confluence
   flow'd:
To whom with loud and passionate la-
   ments
From morn to eve his dark estate he
   wail'd.
Nor wail'd to all in vain: some here and
   there,
The well-disposed and good, their pen-
   nies gave.
I meantime at his feet obsequious slept;
Not all-asleep in sleep, but heart and ear
Prick'd up at his least motion; to receive
At his kind hand my customary crumbs,
And common portion in his feast of
   scraps;
Or when night warn'd us homeward,
   tired and spent
With our long day and tedious beggary.
  These were my manners, this my way
   of life
Till age and slow disease me overtook,
And sever'd from my sightless master's
   side.
But lest the grace of so good deeds
   should die,
Through tract of years in mute oblivion
   lost,
This slender tomb of turf hath Irus
   rear'd,
Cheap monument of no ungrudging hand,
And with short verse inscribed it, to
   attest,
In long and lasting union to attest,
The virtues of the Beggar and his Dog.

These dim eyes have in vain explored for some months past a well-known figure, or part of the figure, of a man, who used to glide his comely upper half over the pavements of London, wheeling along with most ingenious celerity upon a machine of wood; a spectacle to natives, to foreigners, and to children. He was of a robust make, with a florid sailor-like complexion, and his head was bare to the storm and sunshine. He was a natural curiosity, a speculation to the scientific, a prodigy to the simple. The infant would stare at the mighty man brought down to his own level. The common cripple would despise his own pusillanimity, viewing the hale stoutness, and hearty heart, of this half-limbed giant. Few but must have noticed him; for the accident which brought him low took place during the riots of 1780, and he has been a groundling so long. He seemed earth-born, an Antæus, and to suck in fresh vigour from the soil which he neighboured. He was a grand fragment; as good as an Elgin marble. The nature, which should have recruited his reft legs and thighs, was not lost, but only retired into his upper parts, and he was half a Hercules. I heard a tremendous voice thundering and growling, as before an earthquake, and casting down my eyes, it was this mandrake reviling a steed that had started at his portentous appearance. He seemed to want but his just stature to have rent the offending quadruped in shivers. He was as the man-part of a centaur, from which the horse-half had been cloven in some dire Lapithan controversy. He moved on, as if he could have made shift with yet half of the body-portion which was left him. The *os sublime* was not wanting; and he threw out yet a jolly countenance upon the heavens. Forty-and-two years had he driven this out-of-door trade, and now that his hair is grizzled in the service, but his good spirits no way impaired, because he is not content to exchange his free air and exercise for the restraints of a poor-house, he is expiating his contumacy in one of those houses (ironically christened) of Correction.

Was a daily spectacle like this to be deemed a nuisance, which called for legal interference to remove? or not rather a salutary and a touching object to the passers-by in a great city? Among her shows, her museums, and supplies for ever-gaping curiosity (and what else but an accumulation of sights—endless sights—*is* a great city; or for what else is it desirable?) was there not room for one *Lusus* (not *Naturæ*, indeed, but) *Accidentium?* What if in forty-and-two-years' going about, the man had scraped together enough to give a portion to his child (as the rumour ran) of a few hundreds—whom had he injured? —whom had he imposed upon? The contributors had enjoyed their *sight* for their pennies. What if after being exposed all day to the heats, the rains, and the frosts of heaven—shuffling his ungainly trunk along in an elaborate and painful motion—he was enabled to retire at night to enjoy himself at a club of his fellow cripples over a dish of hot meat and vegetables, as the charge was gravely brought against him by a clergyman deposing before a House of Commons' Committee— was *this*, or was his truly paternal consideration, which (if a fact) deserved a statue rather than a whipping-post, and is inconsistent, at least, with the exaggeration of nocturnal orgies which he has been slandered with—a reason that he should be deprived of his chosen, harmless, nay, edifying way of life, and be committed in hoary age for a sturdy vagabond?—

There was a Yorick once, whom it would not have shamed to have sate down at the cripples' feast, and to have thrown in his benediction, ay, and his mite too, for a companionable symbol. "Age, thou hast lost thy breed."—

Half of these stories about the prodigious fortunes made by begging are (I verily believe) misers' calumnies. One was much talked of in the public papers some time since, and the usual charitable inferences deduced. A clerk in the Bank was surprised with the announcement of a five hundred-pound legacy left him by a person whose name he was a stranger to. It seems that in his daily morning walks from Peckham (or some village thereabouts) where he lived, to his office, it had been his practice for the last twenty years to drop his halfpenny duly into the hat of some blind Bartimeus, that sate begging alms by the way-side in the Borough. The good old beggar recognised his daily benefactor by the voice only; and, when he died, left all the amassings of his alms (that had been half a century perhaps in the accumulating) to his old Bank friend. Was this a story to purse up people's hearts, and pennies, against giving an alms to the blind?—or not rather a beautiful moral of well-directed charity on the one part, and noble gratitude upon the other?

I sometimes wish I had been that Bank clerk.

I seem to remember a poor old grateful kind of creature, blinking, and looking up with his no eyes in the sun—

Is it possible I could have steeled my purse against him?

Perhaps I had no small change.

Reader, do not be frightened at the hard words imposition, imposture—*give, and ask no questions.* Cast thy bread upon the waters. Some have unawares (like this Bank clerk) entertained angels.

Shut not thy purse-strings always against painted distress. Act a charity sometimes. When a poor creature (outwardly and visibly such) comes before thee, do not stay to inquire whether the "seven small children," in whose name he implores thy assistance, have a veritable existence. Rake not into the bowels of unwelcome truth to save a halfpenny. It is good to believe him. If he be not all that he pretendeth, *give,* and under a personate father of a family, think (if thou pleasest) that thou hast relieved an indigent bachelor. When they come with their counterfeit looks, and mumping tones, think them players. You pay your money to see a comedian feign these things, which, concerning these poor people, thou canst not certainly tell whether they are feigned or not.

["Pray God, your honour, relieve me," said a poor beadswoman to my friend L—— one day: "I have seen better days." "So have I, my good woman," retorted he, looking up at the welkin, which was just then threatening a storm—and the jest (he will have it) was as good to the beggar as a tester. It was, at all events, kinder than consigning her to the stocks, or the parish beadle.—

But L. has a way of viewing things in rather a paradoxical light on some occasions.]

A DISSERTATION UPON ROAST PIG.

MANKIND, says a Chinese manuscript, which my friend M. was obliging enough to read and explain to me, for the first seventy thousand ages ate their meat raw, clawing or biting it from the living animal, just as they do in Abyssinia to this day. This period is not obscurely hinted at by their great Confucius in the second chapter of his Mundane Mutations, where he designates a kind of golden age by the term Cho-fang, literally the Cooks' Holiday. The manuscript goes on to say, that the art of roasting, or rather broiling (which I take to be the elder brother) was accidentally discovered in the manner following. The swine-herd, Ho-ti, having gone out into the woods one morning, as his manner was, to collect mast for his hogs, left his cottage in the care of his eldest son Bo-bo, a great lubberly boy, who being fond of playing with fire, as younkers of his age commonly are, let some sparks escape into a bundle of straw, which kindling quickly, spread the conflagration over every part of their poor mansion, till it was reduced to ashes. Together with the cottage (a sorry antediluvian make-shift of a building, you may think it), what was of much more importance, a fine litter of new-farrowed pigs, no less than nine in number, perished. China pigs have been esteemed a luxury all over the East, from the remotest periods that we read of. Bo-bo was in the utmost consternation, as you may think, not so much for the sake of the tenement, which his father and he could easily build up again with a few dry branches, and the labour of an hour or two, at any time, as for the loss of the pigs. While he was thinking what he should say to his father, and wringing his hands over the smoking remnants of one of those untimely sufferers, an odour assailed his nostrils, unlike any scent which he had before experienced. What could it proceed from?—not from the burnt cottage—he had smelt that smell before—indeed, this was by no means the first accident of the kind which had occurred through the negligence of this unlucky young firebrand. Much less did it resemble that of any known herb, weed, or flower. A premonitory moistening at the same time overflowed his nether lip. He knew not what to think. He next stooped down to feel the pig, if there were any signs of life in it. He burnt his fingers, and to cool them he applied them in his booby fashion to his mouth. Some of the crumbs of the scorched skin had come away with his fingers, and for the first time in his life (in the world's life indeed, for before him no man had known it) he tasted—*crackling!* Again he felt and fumbled at the pig. It did not burn him so much now, still he licked his fingers from a sort of habit. The truth at length broke into his slow understanding, that it was the pig that smelt so, and the pig that tasted so delicious; and surrendering himself up to the new-born pleasure, he fell to tearing up whole handfuls of the scorched skin with the flesh next it, and was cramming it down his throat in his beastly fashion, when his sire entered amid the smoking rafters, armed with retributory cudgel, and finding how affairs stood, began to rain blows upon the young rogue's shoulders, as thick as hail-stones, which Bo-bo heeded not any more than if they had been flies. The tickling pleasure, which he experienced in his lower regions, had rendered him quite callous to any inconveniences he might feel in those remote quarters. His father might lay on, but he could not beat him from his pig, till he had fairly made an end of it, when, becoming a little more sensible of his situation, something like the following dialogue ensued.

"You graceless whelp, what have you got there devouring? Is it not enough that you have burnt me down three houses with your dog's tricks, and be hanged to you! but you must be eating fire, and I know not what—what have you got there, I say?"

"O father, the pig, the pig! do come and taste how nice the burnt pig eats."

The ears of Ho-ti tingled with horror. He cursed his son, and he cursed himself that ever he should beget a son that should eat burnt pig.

Bo-bo, whose scent was wonderfully sharpened since morning, soon raked out another pig, and fairly rending it asunder, thrust the lesser half by main force into the fists of Ho-ti, still shouting out, "Eat, eat, eat the burnt pig, father, only taste—O Lord!"—with such-like barbarous ejaculations, cramming all the while as if he would choke.

Ho-ti trembled every joint while he grasped the abominable thing, wavering whether he should not put his son to death for an unnatural young monster, when the crackling scorching his fingers, as it had done his son's, and applying the same remedy to them, he in his turn tasted some of its flavour, which, make what sour mouths he would for a pretence, proved not altogether displeasing to him. In conclusion (for the manuscript here is a little tedious), both father and son fairly set down to the mess, and never left off till they had despatched all that remained of the litter.

Bo-bo was strictly enjoined not to let the secret escape, for the neighbours would certainly have stoned them for a couple of abominable wretches, who could think of improving upon the good meat which God had sent them. Nevertheless, strange stories got about. It was observed that Ho-ti's cottage was burnt down now more frequently than ever. Nothing but fires from this time forward. Some would break out in broad day, others in the night-time. As often as the sow farrowed, so sure was the house of Ho-ti to be in a blaze; and Ho-ti himself, which was the more remarkable, instead of chastising his son, seemed to grow more indulgent to him than ever. At length they were watched, the terrible mystery discovered, and father and son summoned to take their trial at Pekin, then an inconsiderable assize town. Evidence was given, the obnoxious food itself produced in court, and verdict about to be pronounced, when the foreman of the jury begged that some of the burnt pig, of which the culprits stood accused, might be handed into the box. He handled it, and they all handled it; and burning their fingers, as Bo-bo and his father had done before them, and nature prompting to each of them the same remedy, against the face of all the facts, and the clearest charge which judge had ever given,—to the surprise of the whole court, townsfolk, strangers, reporters, and all present—without leaving the box, or any manner of consultation whatever, they brought in a simultaneous verdict of Not Guilty.

The judge, who was a shrewd fellow, winked at the manifest iniquity of the decision: and when the court was dismissed, went privily and bought up all the pigs that could be had for love or money. In a few days his lordship's town-house was observed to be on fire. The thing took wing, and now there was nothing to be seen but fires in every direction. Fuel and pigs grew enormously dear all over the district. The insurance-offices one and all shut up shop. People built slighter and slighter every day, until it was feared that the very science of architecture would in no long time be lost to the world. Thus this custom of firing houses continued, till in process of time, says my manuscript, a sage arose, like our Locke, who made a discovery that the flesh of swine, or indeed of any other animal, might be cooked (*burnt*, as they called it) without the necessity of consuming a whole house to dress it. Then first began the rude form of a gridiron. Roasting by the string or spit came in a century or two later, I forget in whose dynasty. By such slow degrees, concludes the manuscript, do the most useful, and seemingly the most obvious, arts make their way among mankind——

Without placing too implicit faith in the account above given, it must be agreed that if a worthy pretext for so dangerous an experiment as setting houses on fire (especially in these days) could be assigned in favour of any culinary object, that pretext and excuse might be found in ROAST PIG.

Of all the delicacies in the whole *mundus edibilis*, I will maintain it to be the most delicate—*princeps obsoniorum*.

I speak not of your grown porkers—things between pig and pork—those hobbledehoys—but a young and tender suckling—under a moon old—guiltless as yet of the sty—with no original speck of the *amor immunditiæ*, the hereditary failing of the first parent, yet manifest—his voice as yet not broken, but something between a childish treble and a grumble—the mild forerunner or *præludium* of a grunt.

He must be roasted. I am not ignorant that our ancestors ate them seethed, or boiled—but what a sacrifice of the exterior tegument!

There is no flavour comparable, I will contend, to that of the crisp, tawny, well-watched, not over-roasted *crackling*, as it is well called—the very teeth are invited to their share of the pleasure at this banquet in overcoming the coy, brittle resistance—with the adhesive oleaginous—O call it not fat! but an indefinable sweetness growing up to it - the tender blossoming of fat—fat cropped in the bud - taken in the shoot—in the first innocence—the cream and quintessence of the child-pig's yet pure food—the lean, no lean, but a kind of animal manna—or, rather, fat and lean (if it must be so) so blended and running into each other, that both together make but one ambrosian result or common substance.

Behold him while he is "doing" —it seemeth rather a refreshing warmth, than a scorching heat, that he is so passive to. How equably he twirleth round the string! Now he is just done. To see the extreme sensibility of that tender age! he hath wept out his pretty eyes—radiant jellies— shooting stars.—

See him in the dish, his second cradle, how meek he lieth!— wouldst thou have had this· innocent grow up to the grossness and indocility which too often accompany maturer swinehood? Ten to one he would have proved a glutton, a sloven, an obstinate, disagreeable animal—wallowing in all manner of filthy conversation—from these sins he is happily snatched away—

Ere sin could blight or sorrow fade,
Death came with timely care—
Elia and Eliana.

his memory is odoriferous—no clown curseth, while his stomach half rejecteth, the rank bacon— no coalheaver bolteth him in reeking sausages—he hath a fair sepulchre in the grateful stomach of the judicious epicure—and for such a tomb might be content to die.

He is the best of sapors. Pineapple is great. She is indeed almost too transcendent a delight, if not sinful, yet so like to sinning, that really a tender-conscienced person would do well to pause—too ravishing for mortal taste, she woundeth and excoriateth the lips that approach her—like lovers' kisses, she biteth —she is a pleasure bordering on pain from the fierceness and insanity of her relish - but she stoppeth at the palate - she meddleth not with the appetite—and the coarsest hunger might barter her consistently for a muttonchop.

Pig—let me speak his praise— is no less provocative of the appetite than he is satisfactory to the criticalness of the censorious palate. The strong man may batten on him, and the weakling refuseth not his mild juices.

Unlike to mankind's mixed characters, a bundle of virtues and vices, inexplicably intertwisted, and not to be unravelled without hazard, he is - good throughout. No part of him is better or worse than another. He helpeth, as far as his little means extend, all around. He is the least envious of banquets. He is all neighbours' fare.

I am one of those who freely and ungrudgingly impart a share of the good things of this life which fall to their lot (few as mine are in this kind) to a friend. I protest I take as great an interest in my friend's pleasures, his relishes, and proper satisfactions, as in mine own. "Presents," I often say, "endear Absents." Hares, pheasants, partridges, snipes, barn-door chickens (those "tame villatic fowl"), capons, plovers, brawn, barrels of oysters, I dispense as freely as I receive them. I love to taste them, as it were, upon the tongue of my friend. But a stop must be put somewhere. One would not, like Lear, "give everything." I make my stand upon pig. Methinks it is an ingratitude to the Giver of all good flavours to extra-domiciliate, or send out of the house slightingly (under pretext of friendship, or I know not what) a blessing so particularly adapted, predestined, I may say, to my individual palate.—It argues an insensibility.

I remember a touch of conscience in this kind at school. My good old aunt, who never parted from me at the end of a holiday without stuffing a sweetmeat, or some nice thing, into my pocket, had dismissed me one evening with a smoking plum-cake, fresh from the oven. In my way to school (it was over London Bridge) a grey-headed old beggar saluted me (I have no doubt, at this time

of day, that he was a counterfeit). I had no pence to console him with, and in the vanity of self-denial, and the very coxcombry of charity, school-boy like, I made him a present of—the whole cake! I walked on a little, buoyed up, as one is on such occasions, with a sweet soothing of self-satisfaction; but, before I had got to the end of the bridge, my better feelings returned, and I burst into tears, thinking how ungrateful I had been to my good aunt, to go and give her good gift away to a stranger that I had never seen before, and who might be a bad man for aught I knew; and then I thought of the pleasure my aunt would be taking in thinking that I—I myself, and not another—would eat her nice cake—and what should I say to her the next time I saw her—how naughty I was to part with her pretty present!—and the odour of that spicy cake came back upon my recollection, and the pleasure and the curiosity I had taken in seeing her make it, and her joy when she sent it to the oven, and how disappointed she would feel that I had never had a bit of it in my mouth at last—and I blamed my impertinent spirit of alms-giving, and out-of-place hypocrisy of goodness; and above all I wished never to see the face again of that insidious, good-for-nothing, old grey impostor.

Our ancestors were nice in their method of sacrificing these tender victims. We read of pigs whipt to death with something of a shock, as we hear of any other obsolete custom. The age of discipline is gone by, or it would be curious to inquire (in a philosophical light merely) what effect this process might have towards intenerating and dulcifying a substance, naturally so mild and dulcet as the flesh of young pigs. It looks like refining a violet. Yet we should be cautious, while we condemn the inhumanity, how we censure the wisdom of the practice. It might impart a gusto.—

I remember an hypothesis, argued upon by the young students, when I was at St. Omer's, and maintained with much learning and pleasantry on both sides, "Whether, supposing that the flavour of a pig who obtained his death by whipping (*per flagellationem extremam*) superadded a pleasure upon the palate of a man more intense than any possible suffering we can conceive in the animal, is man justified in using that method of putting the animal to death?" I forget the decision.

His sauce should be considered. Decidedly, a few bread crumbs, done up with his liver and brains, and a dash of mild sage. But banish, dear Mrs. Cook, I beseech you, the whole onion tribe. Barbecue your whole hogs to your palate, steep them in shalots, stuff them out with plantations of the rank and guilty garlic; you cannot poison them, or make them stronger than they are—but consider, he is a weakling—a flower.

———

A BACHELOR'S COMPLAINT OF THE BEHAVIOUR OF MARRIED PEOPLE.

As a single man, I have spent a good deal of my time in noting down the infirmities of Married People, to console myself for those superior pleasures, which they tell me I have lost by remaining as I am.

I cannot say that the quarrels of men and their wives ever made any great impression upon me, or had much tendency to strengthen me in those anti-social resolutions which I took up long ago upon more substantial considerations. What oftenest offends me at the houses of married persons where I visit, is an error of quite a different description;—it is that they are too loving.

Not too loving neither: that does not explain my meaning. Besides, why should that offend me? The very act of separating themselves from the rest of the world, to have the fuller enjoyment of each other's society, implies that they prefer one another to all the world.

But what I complain of is, that they carry this preference so undisguisedly, they perk it up in the faces of us single people so shamelessly, you cannot be in their company a moment without being made to feel, by some indirect hint or open avowal, that *you* are not the object of this preference. Now there are some things which give no offence, while implied or taken for granted merely; but expressed, there is much offence in them. If a man were to accost the first homely-featured or plain-dressed young woman of his acquaintance, and tell her bluntly, that she was not handsome or rich enough for him, and he could not marry her, he would deserve to be kicked for his ill-manners; yet no less is implied in the fact, that having access and opportunity of putting the question to her, he has never yet thought fit to do it. The young woman understands this as clearly as if it were put into words; but no reasonable young woman would think of making this the ground of a quarrel. Just as little right have a married couple to tell me by speeches, and looks that are scarce less plain than speeches, that I am not the happy man,—the lady's choice. It is enough that I know I am not: I do not want this perpetual reminding.

The display of superior knowledge or riches may be made sufficiently mortifying, but these admit of a palliative. The knowledge which is brought out to insult me, may accidentally improve me; and in the rich man's houses and pictures,—his parks and gardens, I have a temporary usufruct at least. But the display of married happiness has none of these palliatives: it is throughout pure, unrecompensed, unqualified insult.

Marriage by its best title is a monopoly, and not of the least invidious sort. It is the cunning of most possessors of any exclusive privilege to keep their advantage as much out of sight as possible, that their less favoured neighbours, seeing little of the benefit, may the less be disposed to question the right. But these married monopolists thrust the most obnoxious part of their patent into our faces.

Nothing is to me more distasteful than that entire complacency and satisfaction which beam in the countenances of a new-married couple,—in that of the lady particularly: it tells you, that her lot is disposed of in this world: that you can have no hopes of her. It is true, I have none: nor wishes either, perhaps: but this is one of those truths which ought, as I said before, to be taken for granted, not expressed.

The excessive airs which those people give themselves, founded on the ignorance of us unmarried people, would be more offensive if they were less irrational. We will allow them to understand the mysteries belonging to their own craft better than we, who have not had the happiness to be made free of the company: but their arrogance is not content within these limits. If a single person presume to offer his opinion in their presence, though upon the most indifferent subject, he is immediately silenced as an incompetent person. Nay, a young married lady of my acquaintance, who, the best of the jest was, had not changed her condition above a fortnight before, in a question on which I had the misfortune to differ from her, respecting the properest mode of breeding oysters for the London market, had the assurance to ask with a sneer, how such an old Bachelor as I could pretend to know anything about such matters!

But what I have spoken of hitherto is nothing to the airs which these creatures give themselves when they come, as they generally do, to have children. When I consider how little of a rarity children are,—that every street and blind alley swarms with them,—that the poorest people commonly have them in most abundance,—that there are few marriages that are not blest with at least one of these bargains,—how often they turn out ill, and defeat the fond hopes of their parents, taking to vicious courses, which end in poverty, disgrace, the gallows, &c.—I cannot for my life tell what cause for pride there can possibly be in having them. If they were young phœnixes, indeed, that were born but one in a year, there might be a pretext. But when they are so common—

I do not advert to the insolent merit which they assume with their husbands on these occasions. Let *them* look to that. But why *we*, who are not their natural-born subjects, should be expected to bring our spices, myrrh, and incense,—our tribute and homage of admiration,—I do not see.

"Like as the arrows in the hand of the giant, even so are the young children;" so says the ex-cellent office in our Prayer-book appointed for the churching of women. "Happy is the man that hath his quiver full of them." So say I; but then don't let him discharge his quiver upon us that are weaponless;—let them be arrows, but not to gall and stick us. I have generally observed that these arrows are double-headed: they have two forks, to be sure to hit with one or the other. As for instance, when you come into a house which is full of children, if you happen to take no notice of them (you are thinking of something else, perhaps, and turn a deaf ear to their innocent caresses), you are set down as untractable, morose, a hater of children. On the other hand, if you find them more than usually engaging,—if you are taken with their pretty manners, and set about in earnest to romp and play with them,—some pretext or other is sure to be found for sending them out of the room; they are too noisy or boisterous, or Mr.— does not like children. With one or other of these forks the arrow is sure to hit you.

I could forgive their jealousy, and dispense with toying with their brats, if it gives them any pain; but I think it unreasonable to be called upon to *love* them, where I see no occasion,—to love a whole family, perhaps eight, nine, or ten, indiscriminately,— to love all the pretty dears, because children are so engaging!

I know there is a proverb, "Love me, love my dog:" that is

not always so very practicable, particularly if the dog be set upon you to tease you or snap at you in sport. But a dog, or a lesser thing—any inanimate substance, as a keepsake, a watch or a ring, a tree, or the place where we last parted when my friend went away upon a long absence, I can make shift to love, because I love him, and anything that reminds me of him; provided it be in its nature indifferent, and apt to receive whatever hue fancy can give it. But children have a real character, and an essential being of themselves: they are amiable or unamiable *per se;* I must love or hate them as I see cause for either in their qualities. A child's nature is too serious a thing to admit of its being regarded as a mere appendage to another being, and to be loved or hated accordingly; they stand with me upon their own stock, as much as men and women do. Oh! but you will say, sure it is an attractive age,—there is something in the tender years of infancy that of itself charms us? That is the very reason why I am more nice about them. I know that a sweet child is the sweetest thing in nature, not even excepting the delicate creatures which bear them; but the prettier the kind of thing is, the more desirable it is that it should be pretty of its kind. One daisy differs not much from another in glory; but a violet should look and smell the daintiest.—I was always rather squeamish in my women and children.

But this is not the worst: one must be admitted into their familiarity at least, before they can complain of inattention. It implies visits, and some kind of intercourse. But if the husband be a man with whom you have lived on a friendly footing before marriage—if you did not come in on the wife's side—if you did not sneak into the house in her train, but were an old friend in fast habits of intimacy before their courtship was so much as thought on,—look about you—your tenure is precarious—before a twelvemonth shall roll over your head, you shall find your old friend gradually grow cool and altered towards you, and at last seek opportunities of breaking with you. I have scarce a married friend of my acquaintance, upon whose firm faith I can rely, whose friendship did not commence *after the period of his marriage.* With some limitations, they can endure that; but that the good man should have dared to enter into a solemn league of friendship in which they were not consulted, though it happened before they knew him,—before they that are now man and wife ever met,—this is intolerable to them. Every long friendship, every old authentic intimacy, must be brought into their office to be new stamped with their currency, as a sovereign prince calls in the good old money that was coined in some reign before he was born or thought of, to be new marked and minted with the stamp of his authority, before he will let it pass current in the world. You may guess what luck generally befalls such a rusty piece of metal as I am in these *new mintings*.

Innumerable are the ways which they take to insult and worm you out of their husband's confidence. Laughing at all you say with a kind of wonder, as if you were a queer kind of fellow that said good things, *but an oddity*, is one of the ways;—they have a particular kind of stare for the purpose;—till at last the husband, who used to defer to your judgment, and would pass over some excrescences of understanding and manner for the sake of a general vein of observation (not quite vulgar) which he perceived in you, begins to suspect whether you are not altogether a humorist, —a fellow well enough to have consorted with in his bachelor days, but not quite so proper to be introduced to ladies. This may be called the staring way; and is that which has oftenest been put in practice against me.

Then there is the exaggerating way, or the way of irony; that is, where they find you an object of especial regard with their husband, who is not so easily to be shaken from the lasting attachment founded on esteem which he has conceived towards you, by never qualified exaggerations to cry up all that you say or do, till the good man, who understands well enough that it is all done in compliment to him, grows weary of the debt of gratitude which is due to so much candour, and by relaxing a little on his part, and taking down a peg or two in his enthusiasm, sinks at length to the kindly level of moderate esteem —that "decent affection and complacent kindness" towards you, where she herself can join in sympathy with him without much stretch and violence to her sincerity.

Another way (for the ways they have to accomplish so desirable a purpose are infinite) is, with a kind of innocent simplicity, continually to mistake what it was which first made their husband fond of you. If an esteem for something excellent in your moral character was that which riveted the chain which she is to break, upon any imaginary discovery of a want of poignancy in your conversation, she will cry, "I thought, my dear, you described your friend, Mr.——, as a great wit?" If, on the other hand, it was for some supposed charm in your conversation that he first grew to like you, and was content for this to overlook some trifling irregularities in your moral deportment, upon the first notice of any of these she as readily exclaims, "This, my dear, is your good Mr.——!" One good lady whom I took the liberty of expostulating with for not showing me quite so much respect as I thought due to her husband's old friend, had the candour to confess to me that she had often heard Mr.—— speak of me before marriage, and that she had conceived a great desire to be acquainted with me, but that the sight of me had very much disappointed her expectations; for, from her husband's representations of me, she had formed a notion that she was to see a fine, tall. officer-like looking man (I use her very words), the very reverse of which proved to be the truth. This was candid; and I had the civility not to ask her in return, how she came to pitch upon a standard of personal accomplishments for her husband's friends which differed so much from his own; for my friend's dimensions as near as possible approximate to mine; he standing five feet five in his shoes, in which I have the advantage of him by about half an inch; and he no more than myself exhibiting any indications of a martial character in his air or countenance.

These are some of the mortifications which I have encountered in the absurd attempt to visit at their houses. To enumerate them all would be a vain endeavour; I shall therefore just glance at the very common impropriety of which married ladies are guilty,—of treating us as if we were their husbands, and *vice versâ*. I mean, when they use us with familiarity, and their husbands with ceremony. *Testacea*, for instance, kept me the other night two or three hours beyond my usual time of supping, while she was fretting because Mr.—— did not come home, till the oysters were all spoiled, rather than she would be guilty of the impoliteness of touching one in his absence. This was reversing the point of good manners: for ceremony is an invention to take off the uneasy feeling which we derive from knowing ourselves to be less the object of love and esteem with a fellow-creature than some other person is. It endeavours to make up, by superior attentions in little points, for that invidious preference which it is forced to deny in the greater. Had *Testacea* kept the oysters back for me, and withstood her husband's importunities to go to supper, she would have acted according to the strict rules of propriety. I know no ceremony that ladies are bound to observe to their husbands, beyond the point of a modest behaviour and decorum: therefore I must protest against the vicarious gluttony of *Cerasia*, who at her own table sent away a dish of Morellas, which I was applying to with great good-will, to her husband at the other end of the table, and recommended a plate of less extraordinary gooseberries to my unwedded palate in their stead. Neither can I excuse the wanton affront of——

But I am weary of stringing up all my married acquaintance by Roman denominations. Let them amend and change their manners, or I promise to record the full-length English of their names, to the terror of all such desperate offenders in future.

——

ON SOME OF THE OLD ACTORS.

The casual sight of an old Play Bill, which I picked up the other day—I know not by what chance it was preserved so long—tempts me to call to mind a few of the Players, who make the principal figure in it. It presents the cast of parts in the Twelfth-Night, at the old Drury-lane Theatre two-and-thirty years ago. There is something very touching in these old remembrances. They make us think how we *once* used to read a Play Bill—not, as now peradventure, singling out a favourite performer, and casting a negligent eye over the rest; but spelling out every name, down to the very mutes and servants of the scene; when it was a matter of no small moment to us whether Whitfield, or Packer, took the part of Fabian; when Benson, and Burton, and Phillimore—names of small account—had an importance, beyond what we can be content to attribute now to the time's best actors.—"Orsino, by Mr. Barrymore."—What a full Shaksperian sound it carries! how fresh to memory arise the image and the manner of the gentle actor! Those who have only seen Mrs. Jordan within the last ten or fifteen years, can have no adequate notion of her performance of such parts as Ophelia; Helena, in All's Well that Ends Well; and Viola, in this play. Her voice had latterly acquired a coarseness, which suited well enough with her Nells and Hoydens, but in those days it sank, with her steady, melting eye, into the heart. Her joyous parts—in which her memory now chiefly lives—in her youth were outdone by her plaintive ones. There is no giving an account how she delivered the disguised story of her love for Orsino. It was no set speech, that she had foreseen, so as to weave it into an harmonious period, line necessarily following line, to make up the music—yet I have heard it so spoken, or rather *read*, not without its grace and beauty—but, when she had declared her sister's history to be a "blank," and that she "never told her love," there was a pause, as if the story had ended—and then the image of the "worm in the bud" came up as a new suggestion—and the heightened image of "Patience" still followed after that, as by some growing (and not mechanical) process, thought springing up after thought, I would almost say, as they were watered by her tears. So in those fine lines—

Right loyal cantons of contemned love—
Halloo your name to the reverberate
hills—

there was no preparation made in the foregoing image for that which was to follow. She used no rhetoric in her passion; or it was nature's own rhetoric, most legitimate then, when it seemed altogether without rule or law.

Mrs. Powel (now Mrs. Renard), then in the pride of her beauty, made an admirable Olivia. She was particularly excellent in her unbending scenes in conversation with the Clown. I have seen some Olivias—and those very sensible actresses too—who in these inter-locutions have seemed to set their wits at the jester, and to vie conceits with him in downright emulation. But she used him for her sport, like what he was, to trifle a leisure sentence or two with, and then to be dismissed, and she to be the Great Lady still. She touched the imperious fantastic humour of the character with nicety. Her fine spacious person filled the scene.

The part of Malvolio has, in my judgment, been so often misunderstood, and the *general merits* of the actor, who then played it, so unduly appreciated, that I shall hope for pardon, if I am a little prolix upon these points.

Of all the actors who flourished in my time—a melancholy phrase if taken aright, reader Bensley had most of the swell of soul, was greatest in the delivery of heroic conceptions, the emotions consequent upon the presentment of a great idea to the fancy. He had the true poetical enthusiasm—the rarest faculty among players. None that I remember possessed even a portion of that fine madness which he threw out in Hotspur's famous rant about glory, or the transports of the Venetian incendiary at the vision of the fired city. His voice had the dissonance, and at times the inspiriting effect, of the trumpet. His gait was uncouth and stiff, but no way embarrassed by affectation;

and the thorough-bred gentleman was uppermost in every movement. He seized the moment of passion with greatest truth; like a faithful clock, never striking before the time; never anticipating or leading you to anticipate. He was totally destitute of trick and artifice. He seemed come upon the stage to do the poet's message simply, and he did it with as genuine fidelity as the nuncios in Homer deliver the errands of the gods. He let the passion or the sentiment do its own work without prop or bolstering. He would have scorned to mountebank it; and betrayed none of that *cleverness* which is the bane of serious acting. For this reason, his Iago was the only endurable one which I remember to have seen. No spectator, from his action, could divine more of his artifice than Othello was supposed to do. His confessions in soliloquy alone put you in possession of the mystery. There were no by-intimations to make the audience fancy their own discernment so much greater than that of the Moor — who commonly stands like a great helpless mark, set up for mine Ancient, and a quantity of barren spectators, to shoot their bolts at. The Iago of Bensley did not go to work so grossly. There was a triumphant tone about the character, natural to a general consciousness of power; but none of that petty vanity which chuckles and cannot contain itself upon any little successful stroke of its knavery—as is common with your small villains, and green probationers in mischief. It did not clap or crow before its time. It was not a man setting his wits at a child, and winking all the while at other children, who are mightily pleased at being let into the secret; but a consummate villain entrapping a noble nature into toils against which no discernment was available, where the manner was as fathomless as the purpose seemed dark, and without motive. The part of Malvolio, in the Twelfth Night, was performed by Bensley with a richness and a dignity, of which (to judge from some recent castings of that character) the very tradition must be worn out from the stage. No manager in those days would have dreamed of giving it to Mr. Baddely, or Mr. Parsons; when Bensley was occasionally absent from the theatre, John Kemble thought it no derogation to succeed to the part. Malvolio is not essentially ludicrous. He becomes comic but by accident. He is cold, austere, repelling; but dignified, consistent, and, for what appears, rather of an over-stretched morality. Maria describes him as a sort of Puritan; and he might have worn his gold chain with honour in one of our old roundhead families, in the service of a Lambert, or a Lady Fairfax. But his morality and his manners are misplaced in Illyria. He is opposed to the proper *levities* of the piece, and falls in the unequal contest. Still his pride, or his gravity (call it which you will), is inherent, and native to the man, not mock or affected, which latter only are the fit objects to excite laughter. His quality is at the best unlovely, but neither buffoon nor contemptible. His bearing is lofty, a little above his station, but probably not much above his deserts. We see no reason why he should not have been brave, honourable, accomplished. His careless committal of the ring to the ground (which he was commissioned to restore to Cesario), bespeaks a generosity of birth and feeling. His dialect on all occasions is that of a gentleman and a man of education. We must not confound him with the eternal old, low steward of comedy. He is master of the household to a great princess; a dignity probably conferred upon him for other respects than age or length of service. Olivia, at the first indication of his supposed madness, declares that she "would not have him miscarry for half of her dowry." Does this look as if the character was meant to appear little or insignificant? Once, indeed, she accuses him to his face —of what?—of being "sick of self-love,"—but with a gentleness and considerateness, which could not have been, if she had not thought that this particular infirmity shaded some virtues. His rebuke to the knight and his sottish revellers, is sensible and spirited; and when we take into consideration the unprotected condition of his mistress, and the strict regard with which her state of real or dissembled mourning would draw the eyes of the world upon her house-affairs, Malvolio might feel the honour of the family in some sort in his keeping; as it appears not that Olivia had any more brothers, or kinsmen, to look to it—for Sir Toby had dropped all such nice respects at the buttery-hatch. That Malvolio was meant to be represented as possessing estimable qualities, the expression of the Duke, in his anxiety to have him reconciled, almost infers: "Pursue him, and entreat him to a peace." Even in his abused state of chains and darkness, a sort of greatness seems never to desert him. He argues highly and well with the supposed Sir Topas, and philosophizes gallantly upon his straw.* There must have been some shadow of worth about the man; he must have been something more than a mere vapour—a thing of straw, or Jack in office—before Fabian and Maria could have ventured sending him upon a courting-errand to Olivia. There was some consonancy (as he would say) in the undertaking, or the jest would have been too bold even for that house of misrule.

Bensley, accordingly, threw over the part an air of Spanish loftiness. He looked, spake, and moved like an old Castilian. He was starch, spruce, opinionated, but his superstructure of pride seemed bottomed upon a sense of worth There was something in it beyond the coxcomb. It was big and swelling, but you could not be sure that it was hollow. You might wish to see it taken down, but you felt that it was upon an elevation. He was magnificent from the outset; but when the decent sobrieties of the character began to give way, and the poison of self-love, in his conceit of the Countess's affection, gradually to work, you would have thought that the hero of La Mancha in person stood before you. How he went smiling to himself! with what ineffable carelessness would he twirl his gold chain! what a dream it was! you were infected with the illusion, and did not wish that it should be removed! you had no room for laughter! if an unseasonable reflection of morality obtruded itself, it was a deep sense of the pitiable infirmity of man's nature, that can lay him open to such frenzies—but, in truth, you rather admired than pitied the lunacy while it lasted—you felt that an hour of such mistake was worth an age with the eyes open. Who would not wish to live but for a day in the conceit of such a lady's love as Olivia? Why, the Duke would have given his principality but for a quarter of a minute, sleeping or waking, to have been so deluded. The man seemed to tread

* *Clown.* What is the opinion of Pythagoras concerning wild fowl?
  Mal. That the soul of our grandam might haply inhabit a bird.
  Clown. What thinkest thou of his opinion?
  Mal. I think nobly of the soul, and no way approve of his opinion.

upon air, to taste manna, to walk with his head in the clouds, to mate Hyperion. O! shake not the castles of his pride—endure yet for a season, bright moments of confidence—"stand still, ye watches of the element," that Malvolio may be still in fancy fair Olivia's lord!—but fate and retribution say no—I hear the mischievous titter of Maria—the witty taunts of Sir Toby—the still more insupportable triumph of the foolish knight—the counterfeit Sir Topas is unmasked—and "thus the whirligig of time," as the true clown hath it, "brings in his revenges." I confess that I never saw the catastrophe of this character, while Bensley played it, without a kind of tragic interest. There was good foolery too. Few now remember Dodd. What an Aguecheek the stage lost in him! Lovegrove, who came nearest to the old actors, revived the character some few seasons ago, and made it sufficiently grotesque; but Dodd was *it*, as it came out of nature's hands. It might be said to remain *in puris naturalibus*. In expressing slowness of apprehension, this actor surpassed all others. You could see the first dawn of an idea stealing slowly over his countenance, climbing up by little and little, with a painful process, till it cleared up at last to the fulness of a twilight conception—its highest meridian. He seemed to keep back his intellect, as some have had the power to retard their pulsation. The balloon takes less time in filling than it took to cover the expansion of his broad moony face over all its quarters with expression. A glimmer of understanding would appear in a corner of his eye, and for lack of fuel go out again. A part of his forehead would catch a little intelligence, and be a long time in communicating it to the remainder.

I am ill at dates, but I think it is now better than five-and-twenty years ago, that walking in the gardens of Gray's Inn—they were then far finer than they are now—the accursed Verulam Buildings had not encroached upon all the east side of them, cutting out delicate green crankles, and shouldering away one or two of the stately alcoves of the terrace—the survivor stands gaping and relationless as if it remembered its brother —they are still the best gardens of any of the Inns of Court, my beloved Temple not forgotten— have the gravest character; their aspect being altogether reverend and law-breathing—Bacon has left the impress of his foot upon their gravel walks—taking my afternoon solace on a summer day upon the aforesaid terrace, a comely sad personage came towards me, whom, from his grave air and deportment, I judged to be one of the old Benchers of the Inn. He had a serious, thoughtful forehead, and seemed to be in meditations of mortality. As I have an instinctive awe of old Benchers, I was passing him with that sort of sub-indicative token of respect which one is apt to demonstrate towards a venerable stranger, and which rather denotes an inclination to greet him, than any positive motion of the body to that effect—a species of humility and will-worship which I observe, nine times out of ten, rather puzzles than pleases the person it is offered to—when the face turning full upon me strangely identified itself with that of Dodd. Upon close inspection I was not mistaken. But could this sad thoughtful countenance be the same vacant face of folly which I had hailed so often under circumstances of gaiety; which I had never seen without a smile, or recognized but as the usher of mirth; that looked out so formally flat in Foppington, so frothily pert in Tattle, so impotently busy in Backbite; so blankly divested of all meaning, or resolutely expressive of none, in Acres, in Fribble, and a thousand agreeable impertinences? Was this the face —full of thought and carefulness —that had so often divested itself at will of every trace of either to give me diversion, to clear my cloudy face for two or three hours at least of its furrows! Was this the face—manly, sober, intelligent —which I had so often despised, made mocks at, made merry with! The remembrance of the freedoms which I had taken with it came upon me with a reproach of insult. I could have asked it pardon. I thought it looked upon me with a sense of injury. There is something strange as well as sad in seeing actors—your pleasant fellows particularly—subjected to and suffering the common lot;— their fortunes, their casualties, their deaths, seem to belong to the scene, their actions to be amenable to poetic justice only. We can hardly connect them with more awful responsibilities. The death of this fine actor took place shortly after this meeting. He had quitted the stage some months; and, as I learned afterwards, had been in the habit of resorting daily to these gardens, almost to the day of his decease. In these serious walks, probably, he was divesting himself of many scenic and some real vanities—weaning himself from the frivolities of the lesser and the greater theatre— —doing gentle penance for a life of no very reprehensible fooleries —taking off by degrees the buffoon mask which he might feel he had worn too long—and rehearsing for a more solemn cast of part. Dying, he "put on the weeds of Dominic." *

If few can remember Dodd, many yet living will not easily

* Dodd was a m.n of reading, and left at his death a choice collection of old English literature. I should judge him to have been a man of wit. I know one instance of an impromptu which no length of study could have bettered. My merry friend, Jem White, had seen him one evening in Aguecheek, and recognising Dodd the next day in Fleet Street, was irresistibly impelled to take off his hat and salute him as the identical Knight of the preceding evening with a "Save you, *Sir Andrew*." Dodd, not at all disconcerted at this unusual address from a stranger, with a courteous half-rebuking wave of the hand, put him off with an "Away, *Fool*."

forget the pleasant creature, who in those days enacted the part of the Clown to Dodd's Sir Andrew. —Richard, or rather Dicky Suett —for so in his life-time he delighted to be called, and time hath ratified the appellation— lieth buried on the north side of the cemetery of Holy Paul, to whose service his nonage and tender years were dedicated. There are who do yet remember him at that period—his pipe clear and harmonious. He would often speak of his chorister days, when he was "cherub Dicky."

What clipped his wings, or made it expedient that he should exchange the holy for the profane state; whether he had lost his good voice (his best recommendation to that office), like Sir John, "with hallooing and singing of anthems;" or whether he was adjudged to lack something, even in those early years, of the gravity indispensable to an occupation which professeth to "commerce with the skies,"—I could never rightly learn; but we find him, after the probation of a twelve-month or so, reverting to a secular condition and become one of us.

I think he was not altogether of that timber out of which cathedral seats and sounding-boards are hewed. But if a glad heart —kind, and therefore glad—be any part of sanctity, then might the robe of Motley, with which he invested himself with so much humility after his deprivation, and which he wore so long with so much blameless satisfaction to himself and to the public, be accepted for a surplice—his white stole, and *albe*.

The first fruits of his secularization was an engagement upon the boards of Old Drury, at which theatre he commenced, as I have been told, with adopting the manner of Parsons in old men's characters. At the period in which most of us knew him, he was no more an imitator than he was in any true sense himself imitable.

He was the Robin Goodfellow of the stage. He came in to trouble all things with a welcome perplexity, himself no whit troubled for the matter. He was known, like Puck, by his note— *Ha! Ha! Ha!*—sometimes deepening to *Ho! Ho! Ho!* with an irresistible accession, derived, perhaps, remotely from his ecclesiastical education, foreign to his prototype of—*O La!* Thousands of hearts yet respond to the chuckling *O La!* of Dicky Suett, brought back to their remembrance by the faithful transcript of his friend Mathews's mimicry. The "force of nature could no further go." He drolled upon the stock of these two syllables richer than the cuckoo.

Care, that troubles all the world, was forgotten in his composition. Had he had but two grains (nay, half a grain) of it, he could never have supported himself upon those two spider's strings, which served him (in the latter part of his unmixed existence) as legs. A doubt or a scruple must have made him totter, a sigh have puffed him down; the weight of a frown had staggered him, a wrinkle made him lose his balance. But on he went, scrambling upon those airy stilts of his, with Robin Good-fellow, "thorough brake, thorough briar," reckless of a scratched face or a torn doublet.

Shakspeare foresaw him, when he framed his fools and jesters. They have all the true Suett stamp, a loose and shambling gait, a slippery tongue, this last the ready midwife to a without-pain-delivered jest; in words, light as air, venting truths deep as the centre; with idlest rhymes tagging conceit when busiest, singing with Lear in the tempest, or Sir Toby at the buttery-hatch.

Jack Bannister and he had the fortune to be more of personal favourites with the town than any actors before or after. The difference, I take it, was this:—Jack was more *beloved* for his sweet, good-natured, moral pretensions. Dicky was more *liked* for his sweet, good-natured, no pretensions at all. Your whole conscience stirred with Bannister's performance of Walter in the Children in the Wood—but Dicky seemed like a thing, as Shakspeare says of Love, too young to know what conscience is. He put us into Vesta's days. Evil fled before him—not as from Jack, as from an antagonist,—but because it could not touch him, any more than a cannon-ball a fly. He was delivered from the burthen of that death; and, when Death came himself, not in metaphor, to fetch Dicky, it is recorded of him by Robert Palmer, who kindly watched his exit, that he received the last stroke, neither varying his accustomed tranquillity, nor tune, with the simple exclamation, worthy to have been recorded in his epitaph—*O La! O La! Bobby!*

The elder Palmer (of stage-treading celebrity) commonly played Sir Toby in those days; but there is a solidity of wit in the jests of that half-Falstaff which he did not quite fill out. He was as much too showy as Moody (who sometimes took the part) was dry and sottish. In sock or buskin there was an air of swaggering gentility about Jack Palmer. He was a *gentleman* with a slight infusion of *the footman*. His brother Bob (of recenter memory), who was his shadow in everything while he lived, and dwindled into less than a shadow afterwards—was a *gentleman* with a little stronger infusion of the *latter ingredient;* that was all. It is amazing how a little of the more or less makes a difference in these things. When you saw Bobby in the Duke's Servant,* you said, "What a pity such a pretty fellow was only a servant!" When you saw Jack figuring in Captain Absolute, you thought you could trace his promotion to some lady of quality who fancied the handsome fellow in his top-knot, and had bought him a commission. Therefore Jack in Dick Amlet was insuperable.

* High Life Below Stairs.

Jack had two voices, both plausible, hypocritical, and insinuating; but his secondary or supplemental voice still more decisively histrionic than his common one. It was reserved for the spectator; and the *dramatis personæ* were supposed to know nothing at all about it. The *lies* of Young Wilding, and the *sentiments* in Joseph Surface, were thus marked out in a sort of italics to the audience. This secret correspondence with the company before the curtain (which is the bane and death of tragedy) has an extremely happy effect in some kinds of comedy, in the more highly artificial comedy of Congreve or of Sheridan especially, where the absolute sense of reality (so indispensable to scenes of interest) is not required, or would rather interfere to diminish your pleasure. The fact is, you do not believe in such characters as Surface—the villain of artificial comedy—even while you read or see them. If you did, they would shock and not divert you. When Ben, in Love for Love, returns from sea, the following exquisite dialogue occurs at his first meeting with his father:—

Sir Sampson. Thou hast been many a weary league, Ben, since I saw thee.

Ben. Ey, ey, been. Been far enough, an that be all.—Well, father, and how do all at home? how does brother Dick and brother Val?

Sir Sampson. Dick! body o' me, Dick has been dead these two years. I writ you word when you were at Leghorn.

Ben. Mess, that's true; Marry, I had forgot. Dick's dead, as you say—well, and how?—I have a many questions to ask you—

Mia and Mima.

Here is an instance of insensibility which in real life would be revolting, or rather in real life could not have coexisted with the warm-hearted temperament of the character. But when you read it in the spirit with which such playful selections and specious combinations rather than strict *metaphrases* of nature should be taken, or when you saw Bannister play it, it neither did, nor does, wound the moral sense at all. For what is Ben—the pleasant sailor which Bannister gives us—but a piece of satire—a creation of Congreve's fancy—a dreamy combination of all the accidents of a sailor's character—his contempt of money—his credulity to women —with that necessary estrangement from home which it is just within the verge of credibility to suppose *might* produce such an hallucination as is here described. We never think the worse of Ben for it, or feel it as a stain upon his character. But when an actor comes, and instead of the delightful phantom—the creature dear to half-belief—which Bannister exhibited—displays before our eyes a downright concretion of a Wapping sailor—a jolly warmhearted Jack Tar—and nothing else—when instead of investing it with a delicious confusedness of the head, and a veering undirected goodness of purpose—he gives to it a downright daylight understanding, and a full consciousness of its actions; thrusting forward the sensibilities of the character with a pretence as if it stood upon

10

nothing else, and was to be judged by them alone—we feel the discord of the thing; the scene is disturbed; a real man has got in among the *dramatis personæ*, and puts them out. We want the sailor turned out. We feel that his true place is not behind the curtain, but in the first or second gallery.

ON THE ARTIFICIAL COMEDY OF THE LAST CENTURY.

THE artificial Comedy, or Comedy of manners, is quite extinct on our stage. Congreve and Farquhar show their heads once in seven years only, to be exploded and put down instantly. The times cannot bear them. Is it for a few wild speeches, an occasional license of dialogue? I think not altogether. The business of their dramatic characters will not stand the moral test. We screw everything up to that. Idle gallantry in a fiction, a dream, the passing pageant of an evening, startles us in the same way as the alarming indications of profligacy in a son or ward in real life should startle a parent or guardian. We have no such middle emotions as dramatic interests left. We see a stage libertine playing his loose pranks of two hours' duration, and of no after consequence, with the severe eyes which inspect real vices with their bearings upon two worlds. We are spectators to a plot or intrigue (not reducible in life to the point of strict morality),

and take it all for truth. We substitute a real for a dramatic person, and judge him accordingly. We try him in our courts, from which there is no appeal to the *dramatis personæ*, his peers. We have been spoiled with—not sentimental comedy—but a tyrant far more pernicious to our pleasures which has succeeded to it, the exclusive and all-devouring drama of common life; where the moral point is everything; where, instead of the fictitious half-believed personages of the stage (the phantoms of old comedy), we recognise ourselves, our brothers, aunts, kinsfolk, allies, patrons, enemies,—the same as in life,—with an interest in what is going on so hearty and substantial, that we cannot afford our moral judgment, in its deepest and most vital results, to compromise or slumber for a moment. What is *there* transacting, by no modification is made to affect us in any other manner than the same events or characters would do in our relationships of life. We carry our fire-side concerns to the theatre with us. We do not go thither like our ancestors, to escape from the pressure of reality, so much as to confirm our experience of it; to make assurance double, and take a bond of fate. We must live our toilsome lives twice over, as it was the mournful privilege of Ulysses to descend twice to the shades. All that neutral ground of character, which stood between vice and virtue; or which in fact was indifferent to neither, where neither properly was called in question; that happy breathing-place from the burthen of a perpetual moral questioning—the sanctuary and quiet Alsatia of hunted casuistry—is broken up and disfranchised, as injurious to the interests of society. The privileges of the place are taken away by law. We dare not dally with images, or names, of wrong. We bark like foolish dogs at shadows. We dread infection from the scenic representation of disorder, and fear a painted pustule. In our anxiety that our morality should not take cold, we wrap it up in a great blanket surtout of precaution against the breeze and sunshine.

I confess for myself that (with no great delinquencies to answer for) I am glad for a season to take an airing beyond the diocese of the strict conscience,—not to live always in the precincts of the law-courts,—but now and then, for a dream-while or so, to imagine a world with no meddling restrictions—to get into recesses, whither the hunter cannot follow me -

        - —————— Secret shades
Of woody Ida's inmost grove,
While yet there was no fear of Jove.

I come back to my cage and my restraint the fresher and more healthy for it. I wear my shackles more contentedly for having respired the breath of an imaginary freedom. I do not know how it is with others, but I feel the better always for the perusal of one of Congreve's—nay, why should I not add even of Wycher-ley's—comedies. I am the gayer at least for it; and I could never connect those sports of a witty fancy in any shape with any result to be drawn from them to imitation in real life. They are a world of themselves almost as much as fairy land. Take one of their characters, male or female (with few exceptions they are alike), and place it in a modern play, and my virtuous indignation shall rise against the profligate wretch as warmly as the Catos of the pit could desire; because in a modern play I am to judge of the right and the wrong. The standard of *police* is the measure of *political justice*. The atmosphere will blight it; it cannot live here. It has got into a moral world, where it has no business, from which it must needs fall headlong; as dizzy, and incapable of making a stand, as a Swedenborgian bad spirit that has wandered unawares into the sphere of one of his Good Men, or Angels. But in its own world do we feel the creature is so very bad?—The Fainalls and the Mirabels, the Dorimants and the Lady Touchwoods, in their own sphere, do not offend my moral sense; in fact, they do not appeal to it at all. They seem engaged in their proper element. They break through no laws or conscientious restraints. They know of none. They have got out of Christendom into the land—what shall I call it?—of cuckoldry—the Utopia of gallantry, where pleasure is duty, and the manners perfect freedom. It is altogether a speculative scene of things, which has no reference whatever to the world that is. No good person can be justly offended as a spectator, because no good person suffers on the stage. Judged morally, every character in these plays—the few exceptions only are *mistakes*—is alike essentially vain and worthless. The great art of Congreve is especially shown in this, that he has entirely excluded from his scenes—some little generosities in the part of Angelica perhaps excepted—not only anything like a faultless character, but any pretensions to goodness or good feelings whatsoever. Whether he did this designedly, or instinctively, the effect is as happy as the design (if design) was bold. I used to wonder at the strange power which his Way of the World in particular possesses of interesting you all along in the pursuits of characters, for whom you absolutely care nothing —for you neither hate nor love his personages—and I think it is owing to this very indifference for any, that you endure the whole. He has spread a privation of moral light, I will call it, rather than by the ugly name of palpable darkness, over his creations; and his shadows flit before you without distinction or preference. Had he introduced a good character, a single gush of moral feeling, a revulsion of the judgment to actual life and actual duties, the imperti-nent Goshen would have only lighted to the discovery of deformities, which now are none, because we think them none.

Translated into real life, the characters of his, and his friend Wycherley's dramas, are profligates and strumpets,—the business of their brief existence, the undivided pursuit of lawless gallantry. No other spring of action, or possible motive of conduct, is recognised; principles which, universally acted upon, must reduce this frame of things to a chaos. But we do them wrong in so translating them. No such effects are produced, in *their* world. When we are among them, we are amongst a chaotic people. We are not to judge them by our usages. No reverend institutions are insulted by their proceedings —for they have none amongst them. No peace of families is violated— for no family ties exist among them. No purity of the marriage bed is stained—for none is supposed to have a being. No deep affections are disquieted, no holy wedlock bands are snapped asunder—for affection's depth and wedded faith are not of the growth of that soil. There is neither right nor wrong,—gratitude or its opposite,—claim or duty,—paternity or sonship. Of what consequence is it to Virtue, or how is she at all concerned about it, whether Sir Simon or Dapperwit steal away Miss Martha; or who is the father of Lord Froth's or Sir Paul Pliant's children?

The whole is a passing pageant, where we should sit as unconcerned at the issues, for life or death, as at the battle of the frogs and mice. But, like Don Quixote, we take part against the puppets, and quite as impertinently. We dare not contemplate an Atlantis, a scheme, out of which our coxcombical moral sense is for a little transitory ease excluded. We have not the courage to imagine a state of things for which there is neither reward nor punishment. We cling to the painful necessities of shame and blame. We would indict our very dreams.

Amidst the mortifying circumstances attendant upon growing old, it is something to have seen the School for Scandal in its glory. This comedy grew out of Congreve and Wycherley, but gathered some allays of the sentimental comedy which followed theirs. It is impossible that it should be now *acted*, though it continues, at long intervals, to be announced in the bills. Its hero, when Palmer played it at least, was Joseph Surface. When I remember the gay boldness, the graceful solemn plausibility, the measured step, the insinuating voice—to express it in a word—the downright *acted* villany of the part, so different from the pressure of conscious actual wickedness,—the hypocritical assumption of hypocrisy,—which made Jack so deservedly a favourite in that character, I must needs conclude the present generation of playgoers more virtuous than myself, or more dense. I freely confess that he divided the palm with me with his better

brother; that, in fact, I liked him quite as well. Not but there are passages,—like that, for instance, where Joseph is made to refuse a pittance to a poor relation,—incongruities which Sheridan was forced upon by the attempt to join the artificial with the sentimental comedy, either of which must destroy the other—but over these obstructions Jack's manner floated him so lightly, that a refusal from him no more shocked you, than the easy compliance of Charles gave you in reality any pleasure; you got over the paltry question as quickly as you could, to get back into the regions of pure comedy, where no cold moral reigns. The highly artificial manner of Palmer in this character counteracted every disagreeable impression which you might have received from the contrast, supposing them real, between the two brothers. You did not believe in Joseph with the same faith with which you believed in Charles. The latter was a pleasant reality, the former a no less pleasant poetical foil to it. The comedy, I have said, is incongruous; a mixture of Congreve with sentimental incompatibilities; the gaiety upon the whole is buoyant; but it required the consummate art of Palmer to reconcile the discordant elements.

A player with Jack's talents, if we had one now, would not dare to do the part in the same manner. He would instinctively avoid every turn which might tend to unrealise, and so to make the character fascinating. He must take his cue from his spectators, who would expect a bad man and a good man as rigidly opposed to each other as the deathbeds of those geniuses are contrasted in the prints, which I am sorry to say have disappeared from the windows of my old friend Carrington Bowles, of St. Paul's Church-yard memory—(an exhibition as venerable as the adjacent cathedral, and almost coeval) of the bad and good man at the hour of death; where the ghastly apprehensions of the former,—and truly the grim phantom with his reality of a toasting-fork is not to be despised,—so finely contrast with the meek complacent kissing of the rod,—taking it in like honey and butter,—with which the latter submits to the scythe of the gentle bleeder, Time, who wields his lancet with the apprehensive finger of a popular young ladies' surgeon. What flesh, like loving grass, would not covet to meet half-way the stroke of such a delicate mower?—John Palmer was twice an actor in this exquisite part. He was playing to you all the while that he was playing upon Sir Peter and his lady. You had the first intimation of a sentiment before it was on his lips. His altered voice was meant to you, and you were to suppose that his fictitious co-flutterers on the stage perceived nothing at all of it. What was it to you if that half reality, the husband, was overreached by the puppetry—or the thin thing (Lady Teazle's re-putation) was persuaded it was dying of a plethory? The fortunes of Othello and Desdemona were not concerned in it. Poor Jack has passed from the stage in good time, that he did not live to this our age of seriousness. The pleasant old Teazle *King*, too, is gone in good time. His manner would scarce have passed current in our day. We must love or hate—acquit or condemn—censure or pity—exert our detestable coxcombry of moral judgment upon everything. Joseph Surface, to go down now, must be a downright revolting villain—no compromise—his first appearance must shock and give horror—his specious plausibilities, which the pleasurable faculties of our fathers welcomed with such hearty greetings, knowing that no harm (dramatic harm even) could come, or was meant to come, of them, must inspire a cold and killing aversion. Charles (the real canting person of the scene—for the hypocrisy of Joseph has its ulterior legitimate ends, but his brother's professions of a good heart centre in down-right self-satisfaction) must be *loved*, and Joseph *hated*. To balance one disagreeable reality with another, Sir Peter Teazle must be no longer the comic idea of a fretful old bachelor bridegroom, whose teasings (while King acted it) were evidently as much played off at you, as they were meant to concern anybody on the stage,—he must be a real person, capable in law of sustaining an injury—a person towards whom duties are to be acknowledged—the genuine crim. con. antagonist of the villanous seducer Joseph. To realise him more, his sufferings under his unfortunate match must have the downright pungency of life—must (or should) make you not mirthful but uncomfortable, just as the same predicament would move you in a neighbour or old friend.

The delicious scenes which give the play its name and zest, must affect you in the same serious manner as if you heard the reputation of a dear female friend attacked in your real presence. Crabtree and Sir Benjamin—those poor snakes that live but in the sunshine of your mirth—must be ripened by this hot-bed process of realization into asps or amphisbænas; and Mrs. Candour—O! frightful!—become a hooded serpent. Oh! who that remembers Parsons and Dodd—the wasp and butterfly of the School for Scandal—in those two characters; and charming natural Miss Pope, the perfect gentlewoman as distinguished from the fine lady of comedy, in the latter part—would forego the true scenic delight—the escape from life—the oblivion of consequences—the holiday barring out of the pedant Reflection—those Saturnalia of two or three brief hours, well won from the world—to sit instead at one of our modern plays—to have his coward conscience (that forsooth must not be left for a moment) stimulated with perpetual appeals - dulled rather, and blunted, as a faculty without repose must be—and his moral vanity pampered with images of notional justice, notional beneficence, lives saved without the spectator's risk, and fortunes given away that cost the author nothing?

No piece was, perhaps, ever so completely cast in all its parts as this *manager's comedy*. Miss Farren had succeeded to Mrs. Abington in Lady Teazle; and Smith, the original Charles, had retired when I first saw it. The rest of the characters, with very slight exceptions, remained. I remember it was then the fashion to cry down John Kemble, who took the part of Charles after Smith; but, I thought, very unjustly. Smith, I fancy, was more airy, and took the eye with a certain gaiety of person. He brought with him no sombre recollections of tragedy. He had not to expiate the fault of having pleased beforehand in lofty declamation. He had no sins of Hamlet or of Richard to atone for. His failure in these parts was a passport to success in one of so opposite a tendency. But, as far as I could judge, the weighty sense of Kemble made up for more personal incapacity than he had to answer for. His harshest tones in this part came steeped and dulcified in good-humour. He made his defects a grace. His exact declamatory manner, as he managed it, only served to convey the points of his dialogue with more precision. It seemed to head the shafts to carry them deeper. Not one of his sparkling sentences was lost. I remember minutely how he delivered each in succession, and cannot by any effort imagine how any of them could be altered for the better. No man could deliver brilliant dialogue—the dialogue of Congreve or of Wycherley—because none understood it—half so well as John Kemble. His Valentine, in Love for Love, was, to my recollection, faultless. He flagged sometimes in the intervals of tragic passion. He would slumber over the level parts of an heroic character. His Macbeth has been known to nod. But he always seemed to me to be particularly alive to pointed and witty dialogue. The relaxing levities of tragedy have not been touched by any since him—the playful court-bred spirit in which he condescended to the players in Hamlet —the sportive relief which he threw into the darker shades of Richard—disappeared with him. [Tragedy is become a uniform dead weight. They have fastened lead to her buskins. She never pulls them off for the ease of a moment. To invert a commonplace from Niobe, she never forgets herself to liquefaction.] He had his sluggish moods, his torpors —but they were the halting-stones and resting-place of his tragedy —politic savings, and fetches of the breath - husbandry of the lungs, where nature pointed him to be an economist—rather, I think, than errors of the judgment. They were, at worst, less painful than the eternal tormenting unappeas-able vigilance, — the "lidless dragon eyes," of present fashionable tragedy.

[The story of his swallowing opium pills to keep him lively on the first night of a certain tragedy, we may presume to be a piece of retaliatory pleasantry on the part of the suffering author; but, indeed, John had the art of diffusing a complacent equable dulness (which you knew not where to quarrel with), over a piece which he did not like, beyond any of his contemporaries. John Kemble had made up his mind early, that all the good tragedies which could be written, had been written; and he resented any new attempt. His shelves were full. The old standards were scope enough for his ambition. He ranged in them absolute—and fair "in Otway, full in Shakspeare shone." He succeeded to the old lawful thrones, and did not care to adventure bottomry with a Sir Edward Mortimer or any casual speculator that offered. I remember, too acutely for my peace, the deadly extinguisher which he put upon my friend G.'s "Antonio." G., satiate with visions of political justice (possibly not to be realized in our time), or willing to let the sceptical worldlings see that his anticipations of the future did not preclude a warm sympathy for men as they are and have been— wrote a tragedy. He chose a story, affecting, romantic, Spanish —the plot simple, without being naked—the incidents uncommon, without being overstrained. Antonio, who gives the name to the piece, is a sensitive young Castilian, who, in a fit of his country honour, immolates his sister—

But I must not anticipate the catastrophe—the play, reader, is extant in choice English—and you will employ a spare half-crown not injudiciously in the quest of it.

The conception was bold, and the *dénouement*—the time and place in which the hero of it existed, considered—not much out of keeping; yet it must be confessed, that it required a delicacy of handling both from the author and the performer, so as not much to shock the prejudices of a modern English audience. G., in my opinion, had done his part.

John, who was in familiar habits with the philosopher, had undertaken to play Antonio. Great expectations were formed. A philosopher's first play was a new era. The night arrived. I was favoured with a seat in an advantageous box, between the author and his friend M——. G. sat cheerful and confident. In his friend M.'s looks, who had perused the manuscript, I read some terror. Antonio, in the person of John Philip Kemble, at length appeared, starched out in a ruff which no one could dispute, and in most irreproachable moustachios. John always dressed most provokingly correct, on these occasions. The first act swept by, solemn and silent. It went off, as G. assured M., exactly as the opening act of a piece – the protasis—should do. The cue of the spectators was, to be mute. The characters were but in their introduction. The passions and the incidents would be developed hereafter. Applause hitherto would be impertinent. Silent attention was the effect all-desirable. Poor M. acquiesced—but in his honest, friendly face I could discern a working which told how much more acceptable the plaudit of a single hand (however misplaced) would have been than all this reasoning. The second act (as in duty bound) rose a little in interest, but still John kept his forces under—in policy, as G. would have it—and the audience were most complacently attentive. The protasis, in fact, was scarcely unfolded. The interest would warm in the next act, against which a special incident was provided. M. wiped his cheek, flushed with a friendly perspiration—'tis M.'s way of showing his zeal— "from every pore of him a perfume falls"—I honour it above Alexander's. He had once or twice during this act joined his palms, in a feeble endeavour to elicit a sound—they emitted a solitary noise, without an echo— there was no deep to answer to his deep. G. repeatedly begged him to be quiet. The third act at length brought on the scene which was to warm the piece, progressively, to the final flaming forth of the catastrophe. A philosophic calm settled upon the clear brow of G., as it approached. The lips of M. quivered. A challenge was held forth upon the stage, and there was a promise of a fight. The pit roused themselves on this extraordinary occasion, and, as their manner is, seemed disposed to make a ring,—when suddenly, Antonio, who was the challenged, turning the tables upon the hot challenger, Don Gusman (who, by the way, should have had his sister) baulks his humour, and the pit's reasonable expectation at the same time, with some speeches out of the 'New Philosophy against Duelling.' The audience were here fairly caught—their courage was up, and on the alert —a few blows, *ding-dong*, as R—s, the dramatist, afterwards expressed it to me, might have done the business, when their most exquisite moral sense was suddenly called in to assist in the mortifying negation of their own pleasure. They could not applaud for disappointment; they would not condemn for morality's sake. The interest stood stone still; and John's manner was not at all calculated to unpetrify it. It was Christmas time, and the atmosphere furnished some pretext for asthmatic affections. One began to cough—his neighbour sympathized with him—till a cough became epidemical. But when, from being half artificial in the pit, the cough got frightfully naturalised among the fictitious persons of the drama, and Antonio himself (albeit it was not set down in the stage directions) seemed more intent upon relieving his own lungs than the distresses of the author

and his friends,—then G. "first knew fear;" and, mildly turning to M., intimated that he had not been aware that Mr. K. laboured under a cold; and that the performance might possibly have been postponed with advantage for some nights further — still keeping the same serene countenance, while M. sweat like a bull. It would be invidious to pursue the fates of this ill-starred evening. In vain did the plot thicken in the scenes that followed; in vain the dialogue waxed more passionate and stirring, and the progress of the sentiment point more and more clearly to the arduous development which impended. In vain the action was accelerated, while the acting stood still. From the beginning John had taken his stand; had wound himself up to an even tenor of stately declamation, from which no exigence of dialogue or person could make him swerve for an instant. To dream of his rising with the scene (the common trick of tragedians) was preposterous; for, from the onset, he had planted himself, as upon a terrace, on an eminence vastly above the audience, and he kept that sublime level to the end. He looked from his throne of elevated sentiment upon the under-world of spectators with a most sovereign and becoming contempt. There was excellent pathos delivered out to them: an they would receive it, so; an they would not receive it, so; there was no offence against decorum in all this; nothing to condemn, to damn. Not an irreverent symptom of a sound was to be heard. The procession of verbiage stalked on through four and five acts, no one venturing to predict what would come of it, when, towards the winding up of the latter, Antonio, with an irrelevancy that seemed to stagger Elvira herself—for she had been coolly arguing the point of honour with him—suddelny whips out a poniard, and stabs his sister to the heart. The effect was as if a murder had been committed in cold blood. The whole house rose up in clamorous indignation, demanding justice. The feeling rose far above hisses. I believe at that instant, if they could have got him, they would have torn the unfortunate author to pieces. Not that the act itself was so exorbitant, or of a complexion different from what they themselves would have applauded upon another occasion, in a Brutus or an Appius, but for want of attending to Antonio's *words*, which palpably led to the expectation of no less dire an event, instead of being seduced by his *manner*, which seemed to promise a sleep of a less alarming nature than it was his cue to inflict upon Elvira: they found themselves betrayed into an accompliceship of murder, a perfect misprision of parricide, while they dreamed of nothing less. M. I believe, was the only person who suffered acutely from the failure; for G. thenceforward, with a serenity unattainable but by the true philosophy, abandoning a precarious popularity, retired into his fasthold of speculation,—the drama in which the world was to be his tiring-room, and remote posterity his applauding spectators, at once, and actors.]

——

ON THE ACTING OF MUNDEN.

Not many nights ago I had come home from seeing this extraordinary performer in Cockletop; and when I retired to my pillow, his whimsical image still stuck by me, in a manner as to threaten sleep. In vain I tried to divest myself of it, by conjuring up the most opposite associations. I resolved to be serious. I raised up the gravest topics of life; private misery, public calamity. All would not do:

> There the antic sate
> Mocking our state   -

his queer visnomy—his bewildering costume—all the strange things which he had raked together—his serpentine rod swagging about in his pocket—Cleopatra's tear, and the rest of his relics—O'Keefe's wild farce, and *his* wilder commentary—till the passion of laughter, like grief in excess, relieved itself by its own weight, inviting the sleep which in the first instance it had driven away.

But I was not to escape so easily. No sooner did I fall into slumbers, than the same image, only more perplexing, assailed me in the shape of dreams. Not one Munden, but five hundred, were dancing before me, like the faces which, whether you will or no, come when you have been taking opium—all the strange combinations, which this strangest of all strange mortals ever shot his proper countenance into, from the day he came commissioned to dry up the tears of the town for the loss of the now almost forgotten Edwin. O for the power of the pencil to have fixed them when I awoke! A season or two since, there was exhibited a Hogarth gallery. I do not see why there should not be a Munden gallery. In richness and variety, the latter would not fall short of the former.

There is one face of Farley, one face of Knight, one (but what a one it is!) of Liston; but Munden has none that you can properly pin down, and call *his*. When you think he has exhausted his battery of looks, in unaccountable warfare with your gravity, suddenly he sprouts out an entirely new set of features, like Hydra. He is not one, but legion; not so much a comedian, as a company. If his name could be multiplied like his countenance, it might fill a play-bill. He, and he alone, literally *makes faces:* applied to any other person, the phrase is a mere figure, denoting certain modifications of the human countenance. Out of some invisible wardrobe he dips for faces, as his friend Suett used for wigs, and fetches them out as easily. I should not be surprised to see him some day put out the head of a river-horse: or come forth a pewitt, or lapwing, some feathered metamorphosis.

I have seen this gifted actor in Sir Christopher Curry—in old Dornton—diffuse a glow of sentiment which has made the pulse of a crowded theatre beat like that of one man; when he has come in aid of the pulpit, doing good to the moral heart of a people. I have seen some faint approaches to this sort of excellence in other players. But in the grand grotesque of farce, Munden stands out as single and unaccompanied as Hogarth. Hogarth, strange to tell, had no followers. The school of Munden began, and must end, with himself.

Can any man *wonder*, like him? can any man *see ghosts*, like him? or *fight with his own shadow*—"SESSA" —as he does in that strangely-neglected thing, the Cobbler of Preston—where his alternations from the Cobbler to the Magnifico, and from the Magnifico to the Cobbler, keep the brain of the spectator in as wild a ferment, as if some Arabian Night were being acted before him. Who like him can throw, or ever attempted to throw, a preternatural interest over the commonest daily-life objects? A table or a joint-stool, in his conception, rises into a dignity equivalent to Cassiopeia's chair. It is invested with constellatory importance. You could not speak of it with more deference, if it were mounted into the firmament.

A beggar in the hands of Michael Angelo, says Fuseli, rose the Patriarch of Poverty. So the gusto of Munden antiquates and ennobles what it touches. His pots and his ladles are as grand and primal as the seething-pots and hooks seen in old prophetic vision. A tub of butter, contemplated by him, amounts to a Platonic idea. He understands a leg of mutton in its quiddity. He stands wondering, amid the commonplace materials of life, like primæval man with the sun and stars about him.

———

BLAKESMOOR IN H—SHIRE.

I do not know a pleasure more affecting than to range at will over the deserted apartments of some fine old family mansion. The traces of extinct grandeur admit of a better passion than envy: and contemplations on the great and good, whom we fancy in succession to have been its inhabitants, weave for us illusions, incompatible with the bustle of modern occupancy, and vanities of foolish present aristocracy. The same difference of feeling, I think, attends us between entering an empty and a crowded church. In the latter it is chance but some present human frailty—an act of inattention on the part of some of the auditory—or a trait of affectation, or worse, vainglory, on that of the preacher, puts us by our best thoughts, disharmonising the place and the occasion. But wouldst thou know the beauty of holiness?—go alone on some week-day, borrowing the keys of good Master Sexton, traverse the cool aisles of some country church: think of the piety that has kneeled there—the congregations, old and young, that have found consolation there—the meek pastor—the docile parishioner. With no disturbing emotions, no cross conflicting comparisons, drink in the tranquillity of the place, till thou thyself become as fixed and motionless as the marble effigies that kneel and weep around thee.

Journeying northward lately, I could not resist going some few miles out of my road to look upon the remains of an old great house with which I had been impressed in this way in infancy. I was apprised that the owner of it had lately pulled it down; still I had a vague notion that it could not all have perished,—that so much solidity with magnificence could not have been crushed all at once into the mere dust and rubbish which I found it.

The work of ruin had proceeded with a swift hand indeed, and the demolition of a few weeks had reduced it to—an antiquity.

I was astonished at the indistinction of everything. Where had stood the great gates? What bounded the court-yard? Whereabout did the out-houses commence? A few bricks only lay as representatives of that which was so stately and so spacious.

Death does not shrink up his human victim at this rate. The burnt ashes of a man weigh more in their proportion.

Had I seen these brick-and-mortar knaves at their process of destruction, at the plucking of every panel I should have felt the varlets at my heart. I should have cried out to them to spare a plank at least out of the cheerful store-room, in whose hot window-seat I used to sit and read Cowley, with the grass-plot before, and the hum and flappings of that one solitary wasp that ever haunted it about me—it is in mine ears now, as oft as summer returns; or a panel of the yellow-room.

Why, every plank and panel of that house for me had magic in it. The tapestried bedrooms—tapestry so much better than paint-ing—not adorning merely, but peopling the wainscots—at which childhood ever and anon would steal a look, shifting its coverlid (replaced as quickly) to exercise its tender courage in a momentary eye-encounter with those stern bright visages, staring recipro-cally—all Ovid on the walls, in colours vivider than his descrip-tion. Actæon in mid sprout, with the unappeasable prudery of Diana; and the still more provok-ing and almost culinary coolness of Dan Phœbus, eel-fashion, de-liberately divesting of Marsyas.

Then, that haunted room—in which old Mrs. Battle died—whereinto I have crept, but al-' ways in the daytime, with a pas-sion of fear; and a sneaking curi-osity, terror-tainted, to hold com-munication with the past.—*How shall they build it up again?*

It was an old deserted place, yet not so long deserted that the traces of the splendour of past in-mates were everywhere apparent Its furniture was still standing—even to the tarnished gilt leather battledores, and crumbling feathers of shuttlecocks in the nursery, which told that children had once played there. But I was a lonely child, and had the range at will of every apartment, knew every nook and corner, wondered and worshipped every-where.

The solitude of childhood is not so much the mother of thought as it is the feeder of love, of silence, and admiration. So strange a passion for the place possessed me in those years, that, though there lay—I shame to say how few roods distant from the man-sion—half hid by trees, what I judged some romantic lake, such was the spell which bound to the house, and such my carefulness not to pass its strict and proper precincts, that the idle waters lay unexplored for me; and not till late in life, curiosity prevailing over elder devotion, I found, to my astonishment, a pretty brawl-ing brook had been the Lacus Incognitus of my infancy. Varie-gated views, extensive prospects - and those at no great distance from the house—I was told of such —what were they to me, being out of the boundaries of my Eden? So far from a wish to roam, I would have drawn, me-thought, still closer the fences of my chosen prison, and have been hemmed in by a yet securer cincture of those excluding garden walls. I could have exclaimed with the garden-loving poet—

Bind me, ye woodbines, in your twines;
Curl me about, ye gadding vines;
And oh so close your circles lace,
That I may never leave this place;
But, lest your fetters prove too weak,
Ere I your silken bondage break,
Do you, O brambles, chain me too,
And, courteous briars, nail me through.*

I was here as in a lonely temple. Snug fire-sides—the low-built roof—parlours ten feet by ten—frugal boards, and all the homeliness of home—these were the condition of my birth—the wholesome soil which I was planted in. Yet, without impeachment to their tenderest lessons, I am not sorry to have had glances of something beyond, and to have taken, if but a peep, in childhood, at the contrasting accidents of a great fortune.

To have the feeling of gentility, it is not necessary to have been born gentle. The pride of ancestry may be had on cheaper terms than to be obliged to an unfortunate race of ancestors; and the coatless antiquary in his unemblazoned cell, revolving the long line of a Mowbray's or De Clifford's pedigree, at those sounding names may warm himself into as gay a vanity as those who do

inherit them. The claims of birth are ideal merely, and what herald shall go about to strip me of an idea? Is it trenchant to their swords? can it be hacked off as a spur can? or torn away like a tarnished garter?

What, else, were the families of the great to us? what pleasure should we take in their tedious genealogies, or their capitulatory brass monuments? What to us the uninterrupted current of their bloods, if our own did not answer within us to a cognate and corresponding elevation?

Or wherefore, else, O tattered and diminished 'Scutcheon that hung upon the time-worn walls of thy princely stairs, BLAKESMOOR! have I in childhood so oft stood poring upon thy mystic characters—thy emblematic supporters, with their prophetic "Resurgam"—till, every dreg of peasantry purging off, I received into myself Very Gentility? Thou wert first in my morning eyes; and of nights hast detained my steps from bedward, till it was but a step from gazing at thee to dreaming on thee.

This is the only true gentry by adoption: the veritable change of blood, and not as empirics have fabled, by transfusion.

Who it was by dying that had earned the splendid trophy, I know not, I inquired not; but its fading rags, and colours cobweb-stained, told that its subject was of two centuries back.

And what if my ancestor at that date was some Dæmœtas,—feed-

* [Marvell, on Appleton House, to the Lord Fairfax.]

ing flocks, not his own, upon the hills of Lincoln—did I in less earnest vindicate to myself the family trappings of this once proud Ægon? repaying by a backward triumph the insults he might possibly have heaped in his life-time upon my poor pastoral progenitor.

If it were presumption so to speculate, the present owners of the mansion had least reason to complain. They had long forsaken the old house of their fathers for a newer trifle; and I was left to appropriate to myself what images I could pick up, to raise my fancy, or to soothe my vanity.

I was the true descendant of those old W——s, and not the present family of that name, who had fled the old waste places.

Mine was that gallery of good old family portraits, which as I have gone over, giving them in fancy my own family name, one —and then another—would seem to smile, reaching forward from the canvas, to recognise the new relationship; while the rest looked grave, as it seemed, at the vacancy in their dwelling, and thoughts of fled posterity.

The Beauty with the cool blue pastoral drapery, and a lamb— that hung next the great bay window—with the bright yellow H——shire hair, and eye of watchet hue—so like my Alice!— I am persuaded she was a true Elia—Mildred Elia, I take it.

[From her, and from my passion for her—for I first learned love from a picture—Bridget took the hint of those pretty whimsical lines, which thou mayst see, if haply thou hast never seen them, Reader, in the margin.* But my Mildred grew not old, like the imaginary Helen.]

Mine, too, BLAKESMOOR, was thy noble Marble Hall, with its mosaic pavements, and its Twelve Cæsars —stately busts in marble—ranged round; of whose countenances, young reader of faces as I was, the frowning beauty of Nero, I remember, had most of my wonder; but the mild Galba had my love. There they stood in the coldness of death, yet freshness of immortality.

Mine, too, thy lofty Justice Hall, with its one chair of authority, high-backed and wickered, once the terror of luckless poacher, or self-forgetful maiden—so common since, that bats have roosted in it.

Mine, too,—whose else?—thy costly fruit-garden, with its sunbaked southern wall; the ampler pleasure-garden, rising backwards from the house in triple terraces, with flower-pots now of palest lead, save that a speck here and there, saved from the elements, bespake their pristine state to have been gilt and glittering; the verdant quarters backwarder still; and, stretching still beyond, in old formality, thy firry wilderness, the haunt of the squirrel, and the day-long murmuring wood-pigeon, with that antique image

* Here was inserted the little poem by Mary Lamb, called "Helen."—Ed.

in the centre, God or Goddess I wist not; but child of Athens or old Rome paid never a sincerer worship to Pan or to Sylvanus in their native groves, than I to that fragmental mystery.

Was it for this that I kissed my childish hands too fervently in your idol-worship, walks and windings of BLAKESMOOR! for this, or what sin of mine, has the plough passed over your pleasant places? I sometimes think that as men, when they die, do not die all, so of their extinguished habitations there may be a hope—a germ to be revivified.

POOR RELATIONS.

A POOR RELATION—is the most irrelevant thing in nature,—a piece of impertinent correspondency,—an odious approximation, —a haunting conscience,—a preposterous shadow, lengthening in the noon-tide of our prosperity,— an unwelcome remembrancer,—a perpetually recurring mortification,—a drain on your purse,—a more intolerable dun upon your pride,—a drawback upon success, —a rebuke to your rising,—a stain in your blood,—a blot on your 'scutcheon,—a rent in your garment,—a death's head at your banquet,—Agathocles' pot,—a Mordecai in your gate,—a Lazarus at your door,—a lion in your path, —a frog in your chamber,—a fly in your ointment,—a mote in your eye,—a triumph to your enemy, —an apology to your friends,—

the one thing not needful,—the hail in harvest,—the ounce of sour in a pound of sweet.

He is known by his knock. Your heart telleth you "That is Mr. ——." A rap, between familiarity and respect; that demands, and at the same time seems to despair of, entertainment. He entereth smiling and—embarrassed. He holdeth out his hand to you to shake, and—draweth it back again. He casually looketh in about dinner-time—when the table is full. He offereth to go away, seeing you have company—but is induced to stay. He filleth a chair, and your visitor's two children are accommodated at a side-table. He never cometh upon open days, when your wife says, with some complacency, "My dear, perhaps Mr. —— will drop in to-day." He remembereth birth-days—and professeth he is fortunate to have stumbled upon one. He declareth against fish, the turbot being small —yet suffereth himself to be importuned into a slice, against his first resolution. He sticketh by the port—yet will be prevailed upon to empty the remainder glass of claret, if a stranger press it upon him. He is a puzzle to the servants, who are fearful of being too obsequious, or not civil enough, to him. The guests think "they have seen him before." Every one speculateth upon his condition; and the most part take him to be a—tide-waiter. He calleth you by your Christian name, to imply that his other is the same with your own. He is too familiar by half, yet you wish he had less diffidence. With half the familiarity, he might pass for a casual dependent; with more boldness, he would be in no danger of being taken for what he is. He is too humble for a friend; yet taketh on him more state than befits a client. He is a worse guest than a country tenant, inasmuch as he bringeth up no rent—yet 'tis odds, from his garb and demeanour, that your guests take him for one. He is asked to make one at the whist table; refuseth on the score of poverty, and—resents being left out. When the company break up, he proffereth to go for a coach—and lets the servant go. He recollects your grandfather; and will thrust in some mean and quite unimportant anecdote—of the family. He knew it when it was not quite so flourishing as "he is blest in seeing it now." He reviveth past situations, to institute what he calleth—favourable comparisons. With a reflecting sort of congratulation, he will inquire the price of your furniture: and insults you with a special commendation of your window-curtains. He is of opinion that the urn is the more elegant shape; but, after all, there was something more comfortable about the old tea-kettle—which you must remember. He dare say you must find a great convenience in having a carriage of your own, and appealeth to your lady if it is not so. Inquireth if you have had your arms done on vellum yet; and did not know, till lately,

that such-and-such had been the crest of the family. His memory is unseasonable; his compliments perverse; his talk a trouble; his stay pertinacious; and when he goeth away, you dismiss his chair into a corner as precipitately as possible, and feel fairly rid of two nuisances.

There is a worse evil under the sun, and that is—a female Poor Relation. You may do something with the other; you may pass him off tolerably well; but your indigent she-relative is hopeless. "He is an old humorist," you may say, "and affects to go threadbare. His circumstances are better than folks would take them to be. You are fond of having a Character at your table, and truly he is one." But in the indications of female poverty there can be no disguise. No woman dresses below herself from caprice. The truth must out without shuffling. "She is plainly related to the L——'s; or what does she at their house?" She is, in all probability, your wife's cousin. Nine times out of ten, at least, this is the case.—Her garb is something between a gentlewoman and a beggar, yet the former evidently predominates. She is most provokingly humble, and ostentatiously sensible to her inferiority. He may require to be repressed sometimes—*aliquando sufflaminandus erat*—but there is no raising her. You send her soup at dinner, and she begs to be helped—after the gentlemen. Mr. —— requests the honour of taking wine with her; she hesitates between Port and Madeira, and chooses the former—because he does. She calls the servant *Sir;* and insists on not troubling him to hold her plate. The house-keeper patronises her. The children's governess takes upon her to correct her, when she has mistaken the piano for a harpsichord.

Richard Amlet, Esq., in the play, is a notable instance of the disadvantages to which this chimerical notion of *affinity constituting a claim to acquaintance,* may subject the spirit of a gentleman. A little foolish blood is all that is betwixt him and a lady with a great estate. His stars are perpetually crossed by the malignant maternity of an old woman, who persists in calling him "her son Dick." But she has wherewithal in the end to recompense his indignities, and float him again upon the brilliant surface, under which it had been her seeming business and pleasure all along to sink him. All men, besides, are not of Dick's temperament. I knew an Amlet in real life, who, wanting Dick's buoyancy, sank indeed. Poor W—— was of my own standing at Christ's, a fine classic, and a youth of promise. If he had a blemish, it was too much pride; but its quality was inoffensive; it was not of that sort which hardens the heart, and serves to keep inferiors at a distance; it only sought to ward off derogation from itself. It was the principle of self-respect carried as far as it could go, without infringing upon that respect, which he would have every one else equally maintain for himself. He would have you to think alike with him on this topic. Many a quarrel have I had with him, when we were rather older boys, and our tallness made us more obnoxious to observation in the blue clothes, because I would not thread the alleys and blind ways of the town with him to elude notice, when we have been out together on a holiday in the streets of this sneering and prying metropolis. W—— went, sore with these notions, to Oxford, where the dignity and sweetness of a scholar's life, meeting with the alloy of a humble introduction, wrought in him a passionate devotion to the place, with a profound aversion from the society. The servitor's gown (worse than his school array) clung to him with Nessian venom. He thought himself ridiculous in a garb, under which Latimer must have walked erect, and in which Hooker, in his young days, possibly flaunted in a vein of no discommendable vanity. In the depth of college shades, or in his lonely chamber, the poor student shrunk from observation. He found shelter among books, which insult not; and studies, that ask no questions of a youth's finances. He was lord of his library, and seldom cared for looking out beyond his domains. The healing influence of studious pursuits was upon him to soothe and to abstract. He was almost a healthy man, when the waywardness of his fate broke out against him with a second and worse malignity. The father of W—— had hitherto exercised the humble profession of house-painter, at N——, near Oxford. A supposed interest with some of the heads of colleges had now induced him to take up his abode in that city, with the hope of being employed upon some public works which were talked of. From that moment I read in the countenance of the young man the determination which at length tore him from academical pursuits for ever. To a person unacquainted with our universities, the distance between the gownsmen and the townsmen, as they are called—the trading part of the latter especially—is carried to an excess that would appear harsh and incredible. The temperament of W——'s father was diametrically the reverse of his own. Old W—— was a little, busy, cringing tradesman, who, with his son upon his arm, would stand bowing and scraping, cap in hand, to anything that wore the semblance of a gown – insensible to the winks and opener remonstrances of the young man, to whose chamber-fellow, or equal in standing, perhaps, he was thus obsequiously and gratuitously_ducking. Such a state of things could not last. W—— must change the air of Oxford, or be suffocated. He chose the former; and let the sturdy moralist, who strains the point of the filial duties as high as they can bear, censure the dereliction; he cannot estimate the struggle. I stood with W——, the last afternoon I ever saw him, under the eaves of his paternal dwelling. It was in the fine lane leading from the High Street to the back of * * * * college, where W—— kept his rooms. He seemed thoughtful and more reconciled. I ventured to rally him—finding him in a better mood—upon a representation of the Artist Evangelist, which the old man, whose affairs were beginning to flourish, had caused to be set up in a splendid sort of frame over his really handsome shop, either as a token of prosperity or badge of gratitude to his saint. W—— looked up at the Luke, and, like Satan, "knew his mounted sign—and fled." A letter on his father's table, the next morning, announced that he had accepted a commission in a regiment about to embark for Portugal. He was among the first who perished before the walls of St. Sebastian.

I do not know how, upon a subject which I began with treating half seriously, I should have fallen upon a recital so eminently painful; but this theme of poor relationship is replete with so much matter for tragic as well as comic associations, that it is difficult to keep the account distinct without blending. The earliest impressions which I received on this matter are certainly not attended with anything painful, or very humiliating, in the recalling. At my father's table (no very splendid one) was to be found, every Saturday, the mysterious figure of an aged gentleman, clothed in neat black, of a sad yet comely appearance. His deportment was of the essence of gravity; his words few or none; and I was not to make a noise in his presence. I had little inclination to have done so—for my cue was to admire in silence. A particular elbow-chair was appropriated to him, which was in no case to be violated. A peculiar sort of sweet pudding, which appeared on no other occasion, distinguished the days of his coming. I used to think him a prodigiously rich man. All I could make out of him was, that he and my father had been schoolfellows, a world ago, at Lincoln, and that he came from the Mint. The Mint I knew to be a place where all the money was coined—and I thought he was the owner of all that money. Awful ideas of the Tower twined themselves about his presence. He seemed above human infirmities and passions. A sort of melancholy grandeur invested him. From some inexplicable doom I fancied him obliged to go about in an eternal suit of mourning; a captive—a stately being let out of the Tower on Saturdays. Often have I wondered at the temerity of my father, who, in spite of an habitual general respect which we all in common manifested towards him, would venture now and then to stand up against him in some argument touching their youthful days. The houses of the ancient city of Lincoln are divided (as most of my readers know) between the dwellers on the hill and in the valley. This marked distinction formed an obvious division between the boys who lived above (however brought together in a common school) and the boys whose paternal residence was on the plain; a sufficient cause of hostility in the code of these young Grotiuses. My father had been a leading Mountaineer; and would still maintain the general superiority in skill and hardihood of the *Above Boys* (his own faction) over the *Below Boys* (so were they called), of which party his contemporary had been a chieftain. Many and hot were the skirmishes on this topic—the only one upon which the old gentleman was ever brought out—and bad blood bred; even sometimes almost to the recommencement (so I expected) of actual hostilities. But my father, who scorned to insist upon advantages, generally contrived to turn the conversation upon some adroit by-commendation of the old Minster; in the general preference of which, before all other cathedrals in the island, the dweller on the hill, and the plain-born, could meet on a conciliating level, and lay down their less important differences. Once only I saw the old gentleman really ruffled, and I remember with anguish the thought that came over me: "Perhaps he will never come here again." He had been pressed to take another plate of the viand, which I have already mentioned as the indispensable concomitant of his visits. He had refused with a resistance amounting to rigour, when my aunt, an old Lincolnian, but who had something of this, in common with my cousin Bridget, that she would sometimes press civility out of season · uttered the following memorable application—"Do take another slice, Mr. Billet, for you do not get pudding every day." The old gentleman said nothing at the time but he took occasion in the course of the evening, when some argument had intervened between them, to utter with an emphasis which chilled the company, and which chills me now as I write it—"Woman, you are superannuated!" John Billet did not survive long, after the digesting of this affront; but he survived long enough to assure me that peace was actually restored! and if I remember aright, another pudding was discreetly substituted in the place of that which had occasioned the offence. He died at the Mint (anno 1781) where he had long held, what he accounted, a comfortable independence; and with five pounds, fourteen shillings, and a penny, which were found in his escritoir after his decease, left the world, blessing God that he had enough to bury him, and that he had never been obliged to any man for a sixpence. This was—a Poor Relation.

———

DETACHED THOUGHTS ON BOOKS AND READING.

To mind the inside of a book is to entertain one's self with the forced product of another man's brain. Now I think a man of quality and breeding may be much amused with the natural sprouts of his own.—*Lord Foppington, in "The Relapse."*

An ingenious acquaintance of my own was so much struck with this bright sally of his Lordship, that he has left off reading altogether, to the great improvement of his originality. At the hazard of losing some credit on this head, I must confess that I dedicate no inconsiderable portion of my time to other people's thoughts. I dream away my life in others' speculations. I love to lose myself in other men's minds. When I am not walking, I am reading; I cannot sit and think. Books think for me.

I have no repugnances. Shaftesbury is not too genteel for me, nor Jonathan Wild too low. I can read anything which I call *a book.* There are things in that shape which I cannot allow for such.

In this catalogue of *books which are no books—biblia a-biblia—*I reckon Court Calendars, Directories, Pocket Books [the Literary excepted], Draught Boards, bound and lettered on the back, Scientific Treatises, Almanacs, Statutes at Large: the works of Hume, Gibbon, Robertson, Beattie, Soame Jenyns, and generally, all those volumes which "no gentleman's library should be without:" the Histories of Flavius Josephus (that learned Jew), and Paley's Moral Philosophy. With these exceptions, I can read almost anything. I bless my stars for a taste so catholic, so unexcluding.

I confess that it moves my spleen to see these *things in books' clothing* perched upon shelves, like false saints, usurpers of true shrines, intruders into the sanctuary, thrusting out the legitimate occupants. To reach down a well-bound semblance of a volume, and hope it some kind-hearted play-book, then, opening what "seem its leaves," to come bolt upon a withering Population Essay. To expect a Steele or a Farquhar, and find—Adam Smith. To view a well-arranged assortment of blockheaded Encyclopædias (Anglicanas or Metropolitanas) set out in an array of russia, or morocco, when a tithe of that good leather would comfortably re-clothe my shivering folios, would renovate Paracelsus himself, and enable old Raymund Lully to look like himself again in the world. I never see these impostors, but I long to strip them, to warm my ragged veterans in their spoils.

To be strong-backed and neat-bound is the desideratum of a volume. Magnificence comes after. This, when it can be afforded, is not to be lavished upon all kinds of books indiscriminately. I would not dress a set of magazines, for instance, in full suit. The dishabille, or half-binding (with russia backs ever) is *our* costume. A Shakspeare or a Milton (unless the first editions), it were mere foppery to trick out in gay apparel. The possession of them confers no distinction. The exterior of them (the things themselves being so common), strange to say, raises no sweet emotions, no tickling sense of property in the owner. Thomson's Seasons, again, looks best (I maintain it) a little torn and dog's-eared. How beautiful to a genuine lover of reading are the sullied leaves, and worn-out appearance, nay, the very odour (beyond russia) if we would not forget kind feelings in fastidiousness, of an old "Circulating Library" Tom Jones, or Vicar of Wakefield! How they speak of the thousand thumbs that have turned over their pages with delight!—of the lone sempstress, whom they may have cheered (milliner, or harder-working mantua-maker) after her long day's needle-toil, running far into midnight, when she has snatched an hour, ill spared from sleep, to steep her cares, as in some Lethean cup, in spelling out their enchanting contents! Who would have them a whit less soiled? What better condition could we desire to see them in?

In some respects the better a book is, the less it demands from binding. Fielding, Smollett, Sterne, and all that class of perpetually self-reproductive volumes —Great Nature's Stereotypes— we see them individually perish with less regret, because we know the copies of them to be "eterne." But where a book is at once both good and rare—where the individual is almost the species, and when *that* perishes,

We know not where is that Promethean
      torch
That can its light relumine,—

such a book, for instance, as the Life of the Duke of Newcastle, by his Duchess—no casket is rich enough, no casing sufficiently durable, to honour and keep safe such a jewel.

Not only rare volumes of this description, which seem hopeless ever to be reprinted, but old editions of writers, such as Sir Philip Sydney, Bishop Taylor, Milton in his prose works, Fuller—of whom we *have* reprints, yet the books themselves, though they go about, and are talked of here and there, we know have not endenizened themselves (nor possibly ever will) in the national heart, so as to become stock books—it is good to possess these in durable and costly covers. I do not care for a First Folio of Shakspeare. ⌈[You cannot make a *pet* book of ⌊an author whom everybody reads.] I rather prefer the common editions of Rowe and Tonson, without notes, and with *plates*, which, being so execrably bad, serve as maps or modest remembrancers, to the text; and, without pretending to any supposable emulation with it, are so much better than the Shakspeare gallery *engravings*, which *did*. I have a community of feeling with my countrymen about his Plays, and I like those editions of him best which have

been oftenest tumbled about and handled. On the contrary, I cannot read Beaumont and Fletcher but in Folio. The Octavo editions are painful to look at. I have no sympathy with them. If they were as much read as the current editions of the other poet, I should prefer them in that shape to the older one. I do not know a more heartless sight than the reprint of the Anatomy of Melancholy. What need was there of unearthing the bones of that fantastic old great man, to expose them in a winding-sheet of the newest fashion to modern censure? what hapless stationer could dream of Burton ever becoming popular?—The wretched Malone could not do worse, when he bribed the sexton of Stratford church to let him whitewash the painted effigy of old Shakspeare, which stood there, in rude but lively fashion depicted, to the very colour of the cheek, the eye, the eyebrow, hair, the very dress he used to wear—the only authentic testimony we had, however imperfect, of these curious parts and parcels of him. They covered him over with a coat of white paint. By——, if I had been a justice of peace for Warwickshire, I would have clapt both commentator and sexton fast in the stocks, for a pair of meddling sacrilegious varlets.

I think I see them at their work—these sapient trouble-tombs.

Shall I be thought fantastical if I confess that the names of some of our poets sound sweeter, and have a finer relish to the ear —to mine, at least—than that of Milton or of Shakspeare? It may be that the latter are more staled and rung upon in common discourse. The sweetest names, and which carry a perfume in the mention, are, Kit Marlowe, Drayton, Drummond of Hawthornden, and Cowley.

Much depends upon *when* and *where* you read a book. In the five or six impatient minutes, before the dinner is quite ready, who would think of taking up the Fairy Queen for a stop-gap, or a volume of Bishop Andrewes' sermons?

Milton almost requires a solemn service of music to be played before you enter upon him. But he brings his music, to which, who listens, had need bring docile thoughts, and purged ears.

Winter evenings—the world shut out—with less of ceremony the gentle Shakspeare enters. At such a season the Tempest, or his own Winter's Tale—

These two poets you cannot avoid reading aloud—to yourself, or (as it chances) to some single person listening. More than one —and it degenerates into an audience.

Books of quick interest, that hurry on for incidents, are for the eye to glide over only. It will not do to read them out. I could never listen to even the better kind of modern novels without extreme irksomeness.

A newspaper, read out, is intolerable. In some of the Bank offices it is the custom (to save so much individual time) for one of the clerks—who is the best scholar —to commence upon the *Times* or the *Chronicle* and recite its entire contents aloud, *pro bono publico*. With every advantage of lungs and elocution, the effect is singularly vapid. In barbers' shops and public-houses a fellow will get up and spell out a paragraph, which he communicates as some discovery. Another follows with *his* selection. So the entire journal transpires at length by piecemeal. Seldom-readers are slow readers, and, without this expedient, no one in the company would probably ever travel through the contents of a whole paper.

Newspapers always excite curiosity. No one ever lays one down without a feeling of disappointment.

What an eternal time that gentleman in black, at Nando's, keeps the paper! I am sick of hearing the waiter bawling out incessantly, "The *Chronicle* is in hand, Sir."

[As in these little diurnals I generally skip the Foreign News, the Debates and the Politics, I find the *Morning Herald* by far the most entertaining of them. It is an agreeable miscellany rather than a newspaper.]

Coming into an inn at night— having ordered your supper— what can be more delightful than to find lying in the window-seat, left there time out of mind by the carelessness of some former guest

—two or three numbers of the old Town and Country Magazine, with its amusing *tête-à-tête* pictures—"The Royal Lover and Lady G——;" "The Melting Platonic and the old Beau,"—and such-like antiquated scandal? Would you exchange it—at that time, and in that place—for a better book?

Poor Tobin, who latterly fell blind, did not regret it so much for the weightier kinds of reading—the Paradise Lost, or Comus, he could have *read* to him—but he missed the pleasure of skimming over with his own eye a magazine, or a light pamphlet.

I should not care to be caught in the serious avenues of some cathedral alone, and reading *Candide*.

I do not remember a more whimsical surprise than having been once detected—by a familiar damsel—reclined at my ease upon the grass, on Primrose Hill (her Cythera) reading—*Pamela*. There was nothing in the book to make a man seriously ashamed at the exposure; but as she seated herself down by me, and seemed determined to read in company, I could have wished it had been—any other book. We read on very sociably for a few pages; and, not finding the author much to her taste, she got up, and—went away. Gentle casuist, I leave it to thee to conjecture, whether the blush (for there was one between us) was the property of the nymph or the swain in this dilemma. From me you shall never get the secret.

I am not much a friend to out-of-doors reading. I cannot settle my spirits to it. I knew a Unitarian minister, who was generally to be seen upon Snow Hill (as yet Skinner's Street *was not*), between the hours of ten and eleven in the morning, studying a volume of Lardner. I own this to have been a strain of abstraction beyond my reach. I used to admire how he sidled along, keeping clear of secular contacts. An illiterate encounter with a porter's knot, or a bread basket, would have quickly put to flight all the theology I am master of, and have left me worse than indifferent to the five points.

[I was once amused—there is a pleasure in *affecting* affectation—at the indignation of a crowd that was jostling in with me at the pit-door of Covent Garden Theatre, to have a sight of Master Betty—then at once in his dawn and his meridian—in *Hamlet*. I had been invited, quite unexpectedly, to join a party, whom I met near the door of the playhouse, and I happened to have in my hand a large octavo of Johnson and Steevens's *Shakspeare*, which, the time not admitting of my carrying it home, of course went with me to the theatre. Just in the very heat and pressure of the doors opening—the *rush*, as they term it—I deliberately held the volume over my head, open at the scene in which the young Roscius had been most cried up, and quietly read by the lamp-light. The clamour became universal. "The affectation of the fellow," cried one. "Look at that gentleman *reading, papa,*" squeaked a young lady, who, in her admiration of the novelty, almost forgot her fears. I read on. "He ought to have his book knocked out of his hand," exclaimed a pursy cit, whose arms were too fast pinioned to his side to suffer him to execute his kind intention. Still I read on—and, till the time came to pay my money, kept as unmoved as Saint Anthony at his holy offices, with the satyrs, apes, and hobgoblins, mopping, and making mouths at him, in the picture, while the good man sits as undisturbed at the sight as if he were the sole tenant of the desert.—The individual rabble (I recognised more than one of their ugly faces) had damned a slight piece of mine a few nights before, and I was determined the culprits should not a second time put me out of countenance.]

There is a class of street readers, whom I can never contemplate without affection—the poor gentry, who, not having wherewithal to buy or hire a book, filch a little learning at the open stalls—the owner, with his hard eye, casting envious looks at them all the while, and thinking when they will have done. Venturing tenderly, page after page, expecting every moment when he shall interpose his interdict, and yet unable to deny themselves the gratification, they "snatch a fearful joy." Martin B——, in this way, by daily fragments, got through two volumes of Clarissa, when the stall-keeper damped his laudable ambition, by asking him (it was in his younger days) whether he meant to purchase the work. M. declares, that under no circumstance in his life did he ever peruse a book with half the satisfaction which he took in those uneasy snatches. A quaint poetess of our day has moralised upon this subject in two very touching but homely stanzas:

I saw a boy with eager eye
Open a book upon a stall,
And read, as he'd devour it all;
Which, when the stall-man did espy,
Soon to the boy I heard him call,
"You Sir, you never buy a book,
Therefore in one you shall not look."
The boy pass'd slowly on, and with a
    sigh
He wish'd he never had been taught to
    read,
Then of the old churl's books he should
    have had no need.

Of sufferings the poor have many,
Which never can the rich annoy:
I soon perceived another boy,
Who look'd as if he had not any
Food, for that day at least—enjoy
The sight of cold meat in a tavern larder.
This boy's case, then thought I, is surely
    harder,
Thus hungry, longing, thus without a
    penny,
Beholding choice of dainty-dress'd meat;
No wonder if he wish he ne'er had learn'd
    to eat.

STAGE ILLUSION.

A PLAY is said to be well or ill acted, in proportion to the scenical illusion produced. Whether such illusion can in any case be perfect, is not the question. The nearest approach to it, we are told, is when the actor appears wholly unconscious of the presence of spectators. In tragedy —in all which is to affect the feelings—this undivided attention to his stage business seems indispensable. Yet it is, in fact, dispensed with every day by our cleverest tragedians; and while these references to an audience, in the shape of rant or sentiment, are not too frequent or palpable, a sufficient quantity of illusion for the purposes of dramatic interest may be said to be produced in spite of them. But, tragedy apart, it may be inquired whether, in certain characters in comedy, especially those which are a little extravagant, or which involve some notion repugnant to the moral sense, it is not a proof of the highest skill in the comedian when, without absolutely appealing to an audience, he keeps up a tacit understanding with them; and makes them, unconsciously to themselves, a party in the scene. The utmost nicety is required in the mode of doing this; but we speak only of the great artists in the profession.

The most mortifying infirmity in human nature, to feel in ourselves, or to contemplate in another, is, perhaps, cowardice. To see a coward *done to the life* upon a stage would produce anything but mirth. Yet we most of us remember Jack Bannister's cowards. Could anything be more agreeable, more pleasant? We loved the rogues. How was this effected but by the exquisite art of the actor in a perpetual sub-insinuation to us, the spectators, even in the extremity of the shaking fit, that he was not half such a coward as we took him for? We saw all the common symptoms of the malady upon him; the quivering lip, the cowering knees, the teeth chattering; and could have sworn "that man was frightened." But we forgot all the while—or kept it almost a secret to ourselves— that he never once lost his self-possession; that he let out, by a thousand droll looks and gestures —meant at *us*, and not at all supposed to be visible to his fellows in the scene, that his confidence in his own resources had never once deserted him. Was this a genuine picture of a coward; or not rather a likeness, which the clever artist contrived to palm upon us instead of an original; while we secretly connived at the delusion for the purpose of greater pleasure, than a more genuine counterfeiting of the imbecility, helplessness, and utter self-desertion, which we know to be concomitants of cowardice in real life, could have given us?

Why are misers so hateful in the world, and so endurable on the stage, but because the skilful actor, by a sort of subreference, rather than direct appeal to us, disarms the character of a great deal of its odiousness, by seeming to engage *our* compassion for the insecure tenure by which he holds his money-bags and parchments? By this subtle vent half of the hatefulness of the character—the self-closeness with which in real life it coils itself up from the sympathies of men—evaporates. The miser becomes sympathetic; *i.e.*, is no genuine miser. Here again a diverting likeness is substituted for a very disagreeable reality.

Spleen, irritability—the pitiable infirmities of old men, which produce only pain to behold in the realities, counterfeited upon a stage, divert not altogether for the comic appendages to them, but in part from an inner conviction that they are *being acted* before us; that a likeness only is going on, and not the thing itself. They please by being done under the life, or beside it; not *to the life.* When Gattic acts an old man, is he angry indeed? or only a pleasant counterfeit, just enough of a likeness to recognise, without pressing upon us the uneasy sense of a reality?

Comedians, paradoxical as it may seem, may be too natural. It was the case with a late actor. Nothing could be more earnest or true than the manner of Mr. Emery; this told excellently in his Tyke, and characters of a tragic cast. But when he carried the same rigid exclusiveness of attention to the stage business, and wilful blindness and oblivion of everything before the curtain into his comedy, it produced a harsh and dissonant effect. He was out of keeping with the rest of the *dramatis personæ.* There was as little link between him and them, as betwixt himself and the audience. He was a third estate—dry, repulsive, and unsocial to all. Individually considered, his execution was masterly. But comedy is not this unbending thing; for this reason, that the same degree of credibility is not required of it as to serious scenes. The degrees of credibility demanded to the two things may be illustrated by the different sort of truth which we expect when a man tells us a mournful or a merry story. If we suspect the former of falsehood in any one tittle, we reject it altogether. Our tears refuse to flow at a suspected imposition. But the teller of a mirthful tale has latitude allowed him. We are content with less than absolute truth. 'Tis the same with dramatic illusion. We confess we love in comedy to see an audience naturalised behind the scenes—taken into the interest of the drama, welcomed as bystanders, however. There is something ungracious in a comic actor holding himself aloof from all participation or concern with those who are come to be diverted by him. Macbeth must see the dagger, and no ear but his own be told of it; but an old fool in farce may think he *sees something*, and by conscious words and looks express it, as plainly as he can speak, to pit, box, and gallery. When an impertinent in tragedy, an Osric, for instance, breaks in upon the serious passions of the scene, we approve of the contempt with which he is treated. But when the pleasant impertinent of comedy, in a piece purely meant to give delight, and raise mirth out of whimsical perplexities, worries the studious man with taking up his leisure, or making his house his home, the same sort of contempt expressed (however *natural*) would destroy the balance of delight in the spectators. To make the intrusion comic, the actor who plays the annoyed man must a little desert nature; he must, in short, be thinking of the audience, and express only so much dissatisfaction and peevishness as is consistent with the pleasure of comedy. In other words, his perplexity must seem half put on. If he repel the intruder with the sober set face of a man in earnest, and more especially if he deliver his expostulations in a tone which in the world must necessarily provoke a duel, his real-life manner will destroy the whimsical and purely dramatic existence of the other character (which to render it comic demands an antagonist comicality on the part of the character opposed to it), and convert what was meant for mirth, rather than belief, into a downright piece of impertinence indeed, which would raise no diversion in us, but rather stir pain, to see in-flicted in earnest upon any worthy person. A very judicious actor (in most of his parts) seems to have fallen into an error of this sort in his playing with Mr. Wrench in the farce of Free and Easy.

Many instances would be tedious; these may suffice to show that comic acting at least does not always demand from the performer that strict abstraction from all reference to an audience which is exacted of it; but that in some cases a sort of compromise may take place, and all the purposes of dramatic delight be attained by a judicious understanding, not too openly announced, between the ladies and gentlemen—on both sides of the curtain.

TO THE SHADE OF ELLISTON.

Joyousest of once embodied spirits, whither at length hast thou flown? to what genial region are we permitted to conjecture that thou hast flitted?

Art thou sowing the WILD OATS yet (the harvest-time was still to come with thee) upon casual sands of Avernus? or art thou enacting ROVER (as we would gladlier think) by wandering Elysian streams?

This mortal frame, while thou didst play thy brief antics amongst us, was in truth anything but a prison to thee, as the vain Platonist dreams of this *body* to be no better than a county gaol, forsooth, or some house of durance vile, whereof the five senses are the fetters. Thou knewest better than to be in a hurry to cast off these gyves; and had notice to quit, I fear, before thou wert quite ready to abandon this fleshy tenement. It was thy Pleasure-House, thy Palace of Dainty Devices: thy Louvre, or thy White-Hall.

What new mysterious lodgings dost thou tenant now? or when may we expect thy aërial house-warming?

Tartarus we know, and we have read of the Blessed Shades; now cannot I intelligibly fancy thee in either.

Is it too much to hazard a conjecture, that (as the schoolmen admitted a receptacle apart for Patriarchs and unchrisom babes) there may exist—not far perchance from that store-house of all vanities, which Milton saw in visions,—a Limbo somewhere for PLAYERS? and that

Up thither like aërial vapours fly
Both all Stage things, and all that in
    Stage things
Built their fond hopes of glory, or lasting
    fame?
All the unaccomplished works of Authors'
    hands,
Abortive, monstrous, or unkindly mixed,
Damn'd upon earth, fleet thither—
Play, Opera, Farce; with all their
    trumpery.—

There, by the neighbouring moon (by some not improperly supposed thy Regent Planet upon earth), mayst thou not still be acting thy managerial pranks, great disembodied Lessee? but Lessee still, and still a manager.

In Green Rooms, impervious to mortal eye, the muse beholds thee wielding posthumous empire.

Thin ghosts of Figurantes (never plump on earth) circle thee in endlessly, and still their song is *Fie on sinful Phantasy!*

Magnificent were thy capriccios on this globe of earth, ROBERT WILLIAM ELLISTON! for as yet we know not thy new name in heaven.

It irks me to think, that, stript of thy regalities, thou shouldst ferry over, a poor forked shade, in crazy Stygian wherry. Methinks I hear the old boatman, paddling by the weedy wharf, with raucid voice, bawling "SCULLS, SCULLS!" to which, with waving hand, and majestic action, thou deignest no reply, other than in two curt monosyllables, "No: Oars."

But the laws of Pluto's kingdom know small difference between king and cobbler; manager and call-boy; and, if haply your dates of life were conterminant, you are quietly taking your passage, cheek by cheek (O ignoble levelling of Death) with the shade of some recently departed candle-snuffer.

But mercy! what strippings, what tearing off of histrionic robes, and private vanities! what denudations to the bone, before the surly Ferryman will admit you to set a foot within his battered lighter.

Crowns, sceptres; shield, sword, and truncheon; thy own coronation robes (for thou hast brought the whole property-man's wardrobe with thee, enough to sink a navy); the judge's ermine; the coxcomb's wig; the snuff-box à *la Foppington*—all must overboard, he positively swears—and that Ancient Mariner brooks no denial; for, since the tiresome monodrame of the old Thracian Harper, Charon, it is to be believed, hath shown small taste for theatricals.

Ay, now 'tis done. You are just boat-weight; *pura et puta anima*.

But, bless me, how *little* you look!

So shall we all look—kings and keysars—stripped for the last voyage.

But the murky rogue pushes off. Adieu pleasant, and thrice pleasant shade! with my parting thanks for many a heavy hour of life lightened by thy harmless extravaganzas, public or domestic.

Rhadamanthus, who tries the lighter causes below, leaving to his two brethren the heavy calendars—honest Rhadamanth, always partial to players, weighing their parti-coloured existence here upon earth,—making account of the few foibles, that may have shaded thy *real life*, as we call it, (though, substantially, scarcely less a vapour than thy idlest vagaries upon the boards of the Drury,) as but of so many echoes, natural re-percussions, and results to be expected from the assumed extravagancies of thy *secondary* or *mock life*, nightly upon a stage —after a lenient castigation with rods lighter than of those Medusean ringlets, but just enough to "whip the offending Adam out of thee," shall courteously dismiss thee at the right hand gate—the o. p. side of Hades—that conducts to masques and merry-makings in the Theatre Royal of Proserpine.

PLAUDITO, ET VALETO.

ELLISTONIANA.

My acquaintance with the pleasant creature, whose loss we all deplore, was but slight.

My first introduction to E., which afterwards ripened into an acquaintance a little on this side of intimacy, was over a counter in the Leamington Spa Library, then newly entered upon by a branch of his family. E., whom nothing misbecame—to auspicate, I suppose, the filial concern, and set it a-going with a lustre—was serving in person two damsels fair, who had come into the shop ostensibly to inquire for some new publication, but in reality to have a sight of the illustrious shopman, hoping some conference. With what an air did he reach down the volume, dispassionately giving his opinion of the worth of the work in question, and launching out into a dissertation on its comparative merits with those of certain publications of a similar stamp, its rivals! his enchanted customers fairly hanging on his lips, subdued to their authoritative sentence. So have I seen a gentleman in comedy *acting* the shopman. So Lovelace sold his gloves in King Street. I admired the histrionic art, by which he contrived to carry clean away every notion of disgrace, from the occupation he had so generously submitted to; and from that hour I judged him, with no after repentance, to be a person with whom it would be a felicity to be more acquainted.

To descant upon his merits as a Comedian would be superfluous. With his blended private and professional habits alone I have to do: that harmonious fusion of the manners of the player into those of every-day life, which brought the stage boards into streets and dining-parlours, and kept up the play when the play was ended.— "I like Wrench," a friend was saying to him one day, "because he is the same natural, easy creature, *on* the stage, that he is *off*." "My case exactly," retorted Elliston—with a charming forgetfulness, that the converse of a proposition does not always lead to the same conclusion—"I am the same person *off* the stage that I am *on*." The inference, at first sight, seems identical; but examine it a little, and it confesses only, that the one performer was never, and the other always, *acting*.

And in truth this was the charm of Elliston's private deportment. You had spirited performance always going on before your eyes, with nothing to pay As where a monarch takes up his casual abode for the night, the poorest hovel which he honours by his sleeping in it, becomes *ipso facto* for that time a palace; so wherever Elliston walked, sate, or stood still, there was the theatre. He carried about with him his pit, boxes, and galleries, and set up his portable play-house at corners of streets, and in the market-places. Upon flintiest pavements he trod the boards still; and if his theme chanced to be passionate, the green baize carpet of tragedy spontaneously rose beneath his feet. Now this was hearty, and showed a love for his art. So Apelles *always* painted— in thought. So G. D. *always* poetises. I hate a lukewarm artist. I have known actors—and some of them of Elliston's own stamp—who shall have agreeably been amusing you in the part of a rake or a coxcomb, through the two or three hours of their dramatic existence; but no sooner does the curtain fall with its leaden clatter, but a spirit of lead seems to seize on all their faculties. They emerge sour, morose persons, intolerable to their families, servants, &c. Another shall have been expanding your heart with generous deeds and sentiments, till it even beats with yearnings of universal sympathy; you absolutely long to go home and do some good action. The play seems tedious, till you can get fairly out of the house, and realise your laudable intentions. At length the final bell rings, and this cordial representative of all that is amiable in human breasts steps forth—a miser. Elliston was more of a piece. Did he *play* Ranger? and did Ranger fill the general bosom of the town with satisfaction? why should *he* not be Ranger, and diffuse the same cordial satisfaction among his private circles? with *his* temperament, *his* animal spirits, *his* good nature, *his* follies perchance, could he do better than identify himself with his impersonation? Are we to like a pleasant rake, or coxcomb, on the stage, and give ourselves airs of aversion for the identical character, presented to us in actual life? or what would the performer have gained by divesting himself of the impersonation? Could the man Elliston have been essentially different from his part, even if he had avoided to reflect to us studiously, in private circles, the airy briskness, the forwardness, the 'scape-goat trickeries of the prototype?

"But there is something not natural in this everlasting *acting;* we want the real man."

Are you quite sure that it is not the man himself, whom you cannot, or will not see, under some adventitious trappings which, nevertheless, sit not at all inconsistently upon him? What if it is the nature of some men to be highly artificial? The fault is least reprehensible in *players.* Cibber was his own Foppington, with almost as much wit as Vanbrugh could add to it.

"My conceit of his' person,"—it is Ben Jonson speaking of Lord Bacon,—"was never increased towards him by his *place* or *honours.* But I have, and do reverence him for the *greatness*, that was only proper to himself; in that he seemed to me ever one of the *greatest* men, that had been in many ages. In his adversity I ever prayed that Heaven would give him strength; for *greatness* he could not want."

The quality here commended was scarcely less conspicuous in the subject of these idle reminiscences than in my Lord Verulam. Those who have imagined that an unexpected elevation to the direction of a great London Theatre affected the consequence of Elliston, or at all changed his nature, knew not the essential *greatness* of the man whom they disparage. It was my fortune to encounter him near St. Dunstan's Church (which, with its punctual giants, is now no more than dust and a shadow), on the morning of his election to that high office. Grasping my hand with a look of significance, he only uttered,—"Have you heard the news?"—then, with another look following up the blow, he subjoined, "I am the future manager of Drury Lane Theatre."—Breathless as he saw me, he stayed not for congratulation or reply, but mutely stalked away, leaving me to chew upon his new-blown dignities at leisure. In fact, nothing could be said to it. Expressive silence alone could muse his praise. ' This was in his *great* style.

But was he less *great* (be witness, O ye powers of Equanimity, that supported in the ruins of Carthage the consular exile, and more recently transmuted, for a more illustrious exile, the barren constableship of Elba into an image of Imperial France), when, in melancholy after-years, again, much nearer the same spot, I met him, when that sceptre had been wrested from his hand, and his dominion was curtailed to the petty managership, and part proprietorship, of the small Olympic, *his Elba?* He still played nightly upon the boards of Drury, but in parts, alas! allotted to him, not magnificently distributed by him. Waiving his great loss as nothing, and magnificently sinking the sense of fallen *material* grandeur in the more liberal resentment of depreciations done to his more lofty *intellectual* pretensions, "Have you heard" (his customary exordium)—"have you heard," said he, "how they treat me? they put me in *comedy*." Thought I—but his finger on his lips forbade any verbal interruption— "where could they have put you better?" Then, after a pause— "Where I formerly played Romeo, I now play Mercutio,"—and so again he stalked away, neither staying, nor caring for, responses.

O, it was a rich scene,—but Sir A—— C——, the best of story-tellers and surgeons, who mends a lame narrative almost as well as he sets a fracture, alone could do justice to it,—that I was a witness to, in the tarnished room (that had once been green) of that same little Olympic. There, after his deposition from Imperial Drury, he substituted a throne. That Olympic Hill was his "highest heaven;" himself "Jove in his chair." There he sat in state, while before him, on complaint of prompter, was brought for judgment—how shall I describe her? —one of those little tawdry things that flirt at the tails of choruses —a probationer for the town, in either of its senses—the pertest little drab—a dirty fringe and appendage of the lamp's smoke— who, it seems, on some disapprobation expressed by a "highly respectable" audience—had precipitately quitted her station on the boards, and withdrawn her small talents in disgust.

"And how dare you," said her manager,—assuming a censorial severity, which would have crushed the confidence of a Vestris, and disarmed that beautiful Rebel herself of her professional caprices—I verily believe, he thought *her* standing before him—"how dare you, Madam, withdraw yourself, without a notice, from your theatrical duties?" "I was hissed, Sir." "And you have the presumption to decide upon the taste of the town?" "I don't know that, Sir, but I will never stand to be hissed," was the subjoinder of young Confidence— when gathering up his features into one significant mass of wonder, pity, and expostulatory indignation—in a lesson never to have been lost upon a creature less forward than she who stood before him—his words were these: "They have hissed *me*."

'Twas the identical argument *à fortiori*, which the son of Peleus uses to Lycaon trembling under his lance, to persuade him to take his destiny with a good grace. "I too am mortal." And it is to be believed that in both cases the rhetoric missed of its application, for want of a proper understanding with the faculties of the respective recipients.

"Quite an Opera pit," he said to me, as he was courteously conducting me over the benches of his Surrey Theatre, the last retreat, and recess, of his every-day waning grandeur.

Those who knew Elliston, will know the *manner* in which he pronounced the latter sentence of the few words I am about to record. One proud day to me he took his roast mutton with us in the Temple, to which I had superadded a preliminary haddock. After a rather plentiful partaking of the meagre banquet, not unrefreshed with the humbler sort of liquors, I made a sort of apology for the humility of the fare, observing that for my own part I never ate but of one dish at dinner. "I too never eat but one thing at dinner,"—was his reply—then after a pause—"reckoning fish as nothing." The manner was all. It was as if by one peremptory sentence he had decreed the annihilation of all the savoury esculents, which the plea-sant and nutritious-food-giving Ocean pours forth upon poor humans from her watery bosom. This was *greatness*, tempered with considerate *tenderness* to the feelings of his scanty but welcoming entertainer.

Great wert thou in thy life, Robert William Elliston! and *not lessened* in thy death, if report speak truly, which says that thou didst direct that thy mortal remains should repose under no inscription but one of pure *Latinity*. Classical was thy bringing up! and beautiful was the feeling on thy last bed, which, connecting the man with the boy, took thee back to thy latest exercise of imagination, to the days when, undreaming of Theatres and Managerships, thou wert a scholar, and an early ripe one, under the roofs builded by the munificent and pious Colet. For thee the Pauline Muses weep. In elegies, that shall silence this crude prose, they shall celebrate thy praise.

THE OLD MARGATE HOY.

I am fond of passing my vacations (I believe I have said so before) at one or other of the Universities. Next to these my choice would fix me at some woody spot, such as the neighbourhood of Henley affords in abundance, on the banks of my beloved Thames. But somehow or other my cousin contrives to wheedle me, once in three or four seasons, to a water-ing-place. Old attachments cling to her in spite of experience. We have been dull at Worthing one summer, duller at Brighton another, dullest at Eastbourn a third, and are at this moment doing dreary penance at—Hastings!—and all because we were happy many years ago for a brief week at Margate. That was our first sea-side experiment, and many circumstances combined to make it the most agreeable holiday of my life. We had neither of us seen the sea, and we had never been from home so long together in company.

Can I forget thee, thou old Margate Hoy, with thy weather-beaten, sorn-burnt captain, and his rough accommodations—ill exchanged for the foppery and fresh-water niceness of the modern steam-packet? To the winds and waves thou committedst thy goodly freightage, and didst ask no aid of magic fumes, and spells, and boiling cauldrons. With the gales of heaven thou wentest swimmingly; or, when it was their pleasure, stoodest still with sailor-like patience. Thy course was natural, not forced, as in a hot-bed; nor didst thou go poisoning the breath of ocean with sulphureous smoke—a great sea chimera, chimneying and furnacing the deep; or liker to that fire-god parching up Scamander.

Can I forget thy honest, yet slender crew, with their coy reluctant responses (yet to the suppression of anything like contempt) to the raw questions, which we of the great city would be ever and anon putting to them, as to the uses of this or that strange naval implement? 'Specially can I forget thee, thou happy medium, thou shade of refuge between us and them, conciliating interpreter of their skill to our simplicity, comfortable ambassador between sea and land!—whose sailor-trousers did not more convincingly assure thee to be an adopted denizen of the former, than thy white cap, and whiter apron over them, with thy neat-fingered practice in thy culinary vocation, bespoke thee to have been of inland nurture heretofore—a master cook of Eastcheap? How busily didst thou ply thy multifarious occupation, cook, mariner, attendant, chamberlain; here, there, like another Ariel, flaming at once about all parts of the deck, yet with kindlier ministrations—not to assist the tempest, but, as if touched with a kindred sense of our infirmities, to soothe the qualms which that untried motion might haply raise in our crude land-fancies. And when the o'erwashing billows drove us below deck (for it was far gone in October, and we had stiff and blowing weather), how did thy officious ministerings, still catering for our comfort, with cards, and cordials, and thy more cordial conversation, alleviate the closeness and the confinement of thy else (truth to say) not very savoury, nor very inviting, little cabin!

With these additaments to boot, we had on board a fellow-passenger, whose discourse in verity might have beguiled a longer voyage than we meditated, and have made mirth and wonder abound as far as the Azores. He was a dark, Spanish-complexioned young man, remarkably handsome, with an officer-like assurance, and an insuppressible volubility of assertion. He was, in fact, the greatest liar I had met with then, or since. He was none of your hesitating, half story-tellers (a most painful description of mortals) who go on sounding your belief, and only giving you as much as they see you can swallow at a time—the nibbling pickpockets of your patience—but one who committed downright, daylight depredations upon his neighbour's faith. He did not stand shivering upon the brink, but was a hearty, thorough-paced liar, and plunged at once into the depths of your credulity. I partly believe, he made pretty sure of his company. Not many rich, not many wise, or learned, composed at that time the common stowage of a Margate packet. We were, I am afraid, a set of as unseasoned Londoners (let our enemies give it a worse name) as Aldermanbury, or Watling Street, at that time of day could have supplied. There might be an exception or two among us, but I scorn to make any invidious distinctions among such a jolly, companionable ship's company as those were whom I sailed with. Something too must be conceded to the *Genius Loci.* Had the confident fellow told us half the legends on land which he favoured us with on the other element, I flatter myself the good sense of most of us would have revolted. But we were in a new world, with everything unfamiliar about us, and the time and place disposed us to the reception of any prodigious marvel whatsoever. Time has obliterated from my memory much of his wild fablings; and the rest would appear but dull, as written, and to be read on shore. He had been Aide-de-camp (among other rare accidents and fortunes) to a Persian Prince, and at one blow had stricken off the head of the King of Carimania on horseback. He, of course, married the Prince's daughter. I forget what unlucky turn in the politics of that court, combining with the loss of his consort, was the reason of his quitting Persia; but, with the rapidity of a magician, he transported himself, along with his hearers, back to England, where we still found him in the confidence of great ladies. There was some story of a princess—Elizabeth, if I remember—having intrusted to his care an extraordinary casket of jewels, upon some extraordinary occasion—but, as I am not certain of the name or circumstance at this distance of time, I must leave it to the Royal daughters of England to settle the honour among themselves in private. I cannot call to mind half his pleasant wonders; but I perfectly remember that, in the course of his travels, he had seen a phœnix; and he obligingly undeceived us of the vulgar error, that there is but one of that species at a time, assuring us that they were not uncommon in some parts of Upper Egypt. Hitherto he had found the most implicit listeners. His dreaming fancies had transported us beyond the "ignorant present." But when (still hardying more and more in his triumphs over our simplicity) he went on to affirm that he had actually sailed through the legs of the Colossus at Rhodes, it really became necessary to make a stand. And here I must do justice to the good sense and intrepidity of one of our party, a youth, that had hitherto been one of his most deferential auditors, who, from his recent reading, made bold to assure the gentleman, that there must be some mistake, as "the Colossus in question had been destroyed long since;" to whose opinion, delivered with all modesty, our hero was obliging enough to concede thus much, that "the figure was indeed a little damaged." This was the only opposition he met with, and it did not at all seem to stagger him, for he proceeded with his fables, which the same youth appeared to swallow with still more complacency than ever,—confirmed, as it were, by the extreme candour of that concession. With these prodigies he wheedled us on till we came in sight of the Reculvers, which one of our own company (having been the voyage before) immediately recognizing, and pointing out to us, was con-

sidered by us as no ordinary seaman.

All this time sat upon the edge of the deck quite a different character. It was a lad, apparently very poor, very infirm, and very patient. His eye was ever on the sea, with a smile; and, if he caught now and then some snatches of these wild legends, it was by accident, and they seemed not to concern him. The waves to him whispered more pleasant stories. He was as one being with us, but not of us. He heard the bell of dinner ring without stirring; and when some of us pulled out our private stores—our cold meat and our salads—he produced none, and seemed to want none. Only a solitary biscuit he had laid in; provision for the one or two days and nights, to which these vessels then were oftentimes obliged to prolong their voyage. Upon a nearer acquaintance with him, which he seemed neither to court nor decline, we learned that he was going to Margate, with the hope of being admitted into the Infirmary there for sea-bathing. His disease was a scrofula, which appeared to have eaten all over him. He expressed great hopes of a cure; and when we asked him whether he had any friends where he was going, he replied, "he *had* no friends."

These pleasant, and some mournful passages, with the first sight of the sea, co-operating with youth, and a sense of holidays, and out-of-door adventure, to me that had been pent up in populous cities for many months before,—have left upon my mind the fragrance as of summer days gone by, bequeathing nothing but their remembrance for cold and wintry hours to chew upon.

Will it be thought a digression (it may spare some unwelcome comparisons) if I endeavour to account for the *dissatisfaction* which I have heard so many persons confess to have felt (as I did myself feel in part on this occasion), *at the sight of the sea for the first time?* I think the reason usually given—referring to the incapacity of actual objects for satisfying our preconceptions of them—scarcely goes deep enough into the question. Let the same person see a lion, an elephant, a mountain for the first time in his life, and he shall perhaps feel himself a little mortified. The things do not fill up that space which the idea of them seemed to take up in his mind. But they have still a correspondency to his first notion, and in time grow up to it, so as to produce a very similar impression: enlarging themselves (if I may say so) upon familiarity. But the sea remains a disappointment.—Is it not, that in *the latter* we had expected to behold (absurdly, I grant, but, I am afraid, by the law of imagination, unavoidably) not a definite object, as those wild beasts, or that mountain compassable by the eye, but *all the sea at once*, THE COMMENSURATE ANTAGONIST OF THE EARTH? I do not say we tell ourselves so much, but the craving of the mind is to be satisfied with nothing less. I will suppose the case of a young person of fifteen (as I then was) knowing nothing of the sea, but from description. He comes to it for the first time—all that he has been reading of it all his life, and *that* the most enthusiastic part of life, —all he has gathered from narratives of wandering seamen,—what he has gained from true voyages, and what he cherishes as credulously from romance and poetry, —crowding their images, and exacting strange tributes from expectation.—He thinks of the great deep, and of those who go down unto it; of its thousand isles, and of the vast continents it washes; of its receiving the mighty Plata, or Orellana, into its bosom, without disturbance, or sense of augmentation; of Biscay swells, and the mariner

For many a day, and many a dreadful
      night,
Incessant labouring round the stormy
      Cape;

of fatal rocks, and the "still-vexed Bermoothes;" of great whirlpools, and the water-spout; of sunken ships, and sumless treasures swallowed up in the unrestoring depths; of fishes and quaint monsters, to which all that is terrible on earth—

Be but as buggs to frighten babes withal,
Compared with the creatures in the sea's
      entral;

of naked savages, and Juan Fernandez; of pearls, and shells; of coral beds, and of enchanted isles; of mermaids' grots—

I do not assert that in sober earnest he expects to be shown all these wonders at once, but he is under the tyranny of a mighty faculty, which haunts him with confused hints and shadows of all these; and when the actual object opens first upon him, seen (in tame weather, too, most likely) from our unromantic coasts—a speck, a slip of sea-water, as it shows to him—what can it prove but a very unsatisfying and even diminutive entertainment? Or if he has come to it from the mouth of a river, was it much more than the river widening? and, even out of sight of land, what had he but a flat watery horizon about him, nothing comparable to the vast o'ercurtaining sky, his familiar object, seen daily without dread or amazement?—Who, in similar circumstances, has not been tempted to exclaim with Charoba, in the poem of Gebir,

Is this the mighty ocean? is this all?

I love town or country; but this detestable Cinque Port is neither. I hate these scrubbed shoots, thrusting out their starved foliage from between the horrid fissures of dusty innutritious rocks; which the amateur calls "verdure to the edge of the sea." I require woods, and they show me stunted coppices. I cry out for the water-brooks, and pant for fresh streams, and inland murmurs. I cannot stand all day on the naked beach, watching the capricious hues of the sea, shifting like the colours of a dying mullet. I am tired of looking out at the windows of this island-prison. I would fain retire into the interior of my cage. While I gaze upon the sea, I want to be on it, over it, across it. It binds me in with chains, as of iron. My thoughts are abroad. I should not so feel in Staffordshire. There is no home for me here. There is no sense of home at Hastings. It is a place of fugitive resort, an heterogeneous assemblage of sea-mews and stock-brokers, Amphitrites of the town, and misses that coquet with the Ocean. If it were what it was in its primitive shape, and what it ought to have remained, a fair, honest fishing-town, and no more, it were something—with a few straggling fishermen's huts scattered about, artless as its cliffs, and with their materials filched from them, it were something. I could abide to dwell with Meshech; to assort with fisher-swains, and smugglers. There are, or I dream there are, many of this latter occupation here. Their faces become the place. I like a smuggler. He is the only honest thief. He robs nothing but the revenue—an abstraction I never greatly cared about. I could go out with them in their mackerel boats, or about their less ostensible business, with some satisfaction. I can even tolerate those poor victims to monotony, who from day to day pace along the beach, in endless progress and recurrence, to watch their illicit countrymen—townsfolk or brethren, perchance—whistling to the sheathing and unsheathing of their cutlasses (their only solace), who, under the mild name of preventive service, keep up a legitimated civil warfare in the deplorable absence of a foreign one, to show their detestation of run hollands, and zeal for Old England. But it is the visitants from town, that come here to *say* that they have been here, with no more relish of the sea than a pond-perch or a dace might be supposed to have, that are my aversion. I feel like a foolish dace in these regions, and have as little toleration for myself here as for them. What can they want here? If they had a true relish of the ocean, why have they brought all this land luggage with them? or why pitch their civilized tents in the desert? What mean these scanty book-rooms—marine libraries as they entitle them—if the sea were, as they would have us believe, a book "to read strange matter in?" what are their foolish concert-rooms, if they come, as they would fain be thought to do, to listen to the music of the waves? All is false and hollow pretension. They come because it is the fashion, and to spoil the nature of the place. They are, mostly, as I have said, stock-brokers; but I have watched the better sort of them—now and then, an honest citizen (of the old stamp), in the simplicity of his heart, shall bring down his wife and daughters to taste the sea breezes. I always know the date of their arrival. It is easy to see it in their countenance. A day or two they go wandering on the shingles, picking up cockle-shells, and thinking them great things; but, in a poor week, imagination slackens: they begin to discover that cockles produce no pearls, and then—O then!—if I could interpret for the pretty creatures (I know they have not the courage to confess it themselves), how gladly would they exchange their sea-side rambles for a Sunday walk on the green sward of their accustomed Twickenham meadows!

I would ask one of these sea-charmed emigrants, who think they truly love the sea, with its wild usages, what would their feelings be if some of the unsophisticated aborigines of this place, encouraged by their courteous questionings here, should venture, on the faith of such assured sympathy between them, to return the visit, and come up to see—London. I must imagine them with their fishing-tackle on their back, as we carry our town necessaries. What a sensation would it cause in Lothbury! What vehement laughter would it not excite among

The daughters of Cheapside, and wives of Lombard-street!

I am sure that no town-bred or inland-born subjects can feel their true and natural nourishment at these sea-places. Nature, where she does not mean us for mariners and vagabonds, bids us stay at home. The salt foam seems to nourish a spleen. I am not half so good-natured as by the milder waters of my natural river. I would exchange these sea-gulls for swans, and scud a swallow for ever about the banks of Thamesis.

THE CONVALESCENT.

A PRETTY severe fit of indisposition which, under the name of a nervous fever, has made a prisoner of me for some weeks past, and is but slowly leaving me, has reduced me to an incapacity of reflecting upon any topic foreign to itself. Expect no healthy conclusions from me this month, reader; I can offer you only sick men's dreams.

And truly the whole state of sickness is such; for what else is it but a magnificent dream for a man to lie a-bed, and draw daylight curtains about him; and, shutting out the sun, to induce a total oblivion of all the works which are going on under it? To become insensible to all the operations of life, except the beatings of one feeble pulse?

If there be a regal solitude, it is a sick bed. How the patient lords it there; what caprices he acts without control! how kinglike he sways his pillow—tumbling, and tossing, and shifting, and lowering, and thumping, and flatting, and moulding it, to the ever-varying requisitions of his throbbing temples.

He changes *sides* oftener than a politician. Now he lies full length, then half length, obliquely, transversely, head and feet quite across the bed; and none accuses him of tergiversation. Within the four curtains he is absolute. They are his Mare Clausum.

How sickness enlarges the dimensions of a man's self to himself! he is his own exclusive object. Supreme selfishness is inculcated upon him as his only duty. 'Tis the Two Tables of the Law to him. He has nothing to think of but how to get well. What passes out of doors, or within them, so he hear not the jarring of them, affects him not.

A little while ago he was greatly concerned in the event of a lawsuit, which was to be the making or the marring of his dearest friend. He was to be seen trudging about upon this man's errand to fifty quarters of the town at once, jogging this witness, refreshing that solicitor. The cause was to come on yesterday. He is absolutely as indifferent to the decision as if it were a question to be tried at Pekin. Peradventure from some whispering, going on about the house, not intended for his hearing, he picks up enough to make him understand that things went cross-grained in the court yesterday, and his friend is ruined. But the word "friend," and the word "ruin," disturb him no more than so much jargon. He is not to think of anything but how to get better.

What a world of foreign cares are merged in that absorbing consideration!

He has put on the strong armour of sickness, he is wrapped in the callous hide of suffering; he keeps his sympathy, like some curious vintage, under trusty lock and key, for his own use only.

He lies pitying himself, honing and moaning to himself; he yearneth over himself; his bowels are even melted within him, to think what he suffers; he is not ashamed to weep over himself.

He is for ever plotting how to do some good to himself; studying little stratagems and artificial alleviations.

He makes the most of himself; dividing himself, by an allowable fiction, into as many distinct individuals as he hath sore and sorrowing members. Sometimes he meditates—as of a thing apart from him—upon his poor aching head, and that dull pain which, dozing or waking, lay in it all the past night like a log, or palpable substance of pain, not to be removed without opening the very skull, as it seemed, to take it thence. Or he pities his long, clammy, attenuated fingers. He compassionates himself all over; and his bed is a very discipline of humanity, and tender heart.

He is his own sympathizer; and instinctively feels that none can so well perform that office for him. He cares for few spectators to his tragedy. Only that punctual face of the old nurse pleases him, that announces his broths and his cordials. He likes it because it is so unmoved, and because he can pour forth his feverish ejaculations before it as unreservedly as to his bed-post.

To the world's business he is dead. He understands not what the callings and occupations of mortals are; only he has a glimmering conceit of some such thing, when the doctor makes his daily call; and even in the lines on that busy face he reads no multiplicity of patients, but solely conceives of himself as *the sick man*. To what other uneasy couch the good man is hastening, when he slips out of his chamber, folding up his thin douceur so carefully, for fear of rustling—is no speculation which he can at present entertain. He thinks only of the regular return of the same phenomenon at the same hour to-morrow.

Household rumours touch him not. Some faint murmur, indicative of life going on within the house, soothes him, while he knows not distinctly what it is. He is not to know anything, not to think of anything. Servants gliding up or down the distant staircase, treading as upon velvet, gently keep his ear awake, so long as he troubles not himself further than with some feeble guess at their errands. Exacter knowledge would be a burthen to him: he can just endure the pressure of conjecture. He opens his eye faintly at the dull stroke of the muffled knocker, and closes it again without asking "Who was it?" He is flattered by a general notion that inquiries are making after him, but he cares not to know the name of the inquirer. In the general stillness, and awful hush of the house, he lies in state, and feels his sovereignty.

To be sick is to enjoy monarchal prerogatives. Compare the silent tread and quiet ministry, almost by the eye only, with which he is served—with the careless demeanour, the unceremonious goings in and out (slapping of doors, or leaving them open) of the very same attendants, when he is getting a little better—and you will confess, that from the bed of sickness(throne let me rather call it) to the elbow-chair of convalescence, is a fall from dignity, amounting to a deposition.

How convalescence shrinks a man back to his pristine stature! Where is now the space, which he occupied so lately, in his own, in the family's eye?

The scene of his regalities, his sick room, which was his presence-chamber, where he lay and acted his despotic fancies—how is it reduced to a common bedroom! The trimness of the very bed has something petty and unmeaning about it. It is *made* every day. How unlike to that wavy, many-furrowed, oceanic surface, which it presented so short a time since, when to *make* it was a service not to be thought of at oftener than three or four day revolutions, when the patient was with pain and grief to be lifted for a little while out of it, to submit to the encroachments of unwelcome neatness, and decencies which his shaken frame deprecated; then to be lifted into it again, for another three or four days' respite, to flounder it out of shape again, while every fresh furrow was an historical record of some shifting posture, some uneasy turning, some seeking for a little ease; and the shrunken skin scarce told a truer story than the crumpled coverlid.

Hushed are those mysterious sighs—those groans—so much more awful, while we knew not from what caverns of vast hidden suffering they proceeded. The Lernean pangs are quenched. The riddle of sickness is solved; and Philoctetes is become an ordinary personage.

Perhaps some relic of the sick man's dream of greatness survives in the still lingering visitations of the medical attendant. But how is he, too, changed with everything else! Can this be he —this man of news—of chat—of anecdote—of everything but physic—can this be he, who so lately came between the patient and his cruel enemy, as on some solemn embassy from Nature, erecting herself into a high mediating party?—Pshaw! 'tis some old woman.

Farewell with him all that made sickness pompous—the spell that hushed the household—the desert-like stillness, felt throughout its inmost chambers—the mute attendance—the inquiry by looks—the still softer delicacies of self-attention—the sole and single eye of distemper alonely fixed upon itself—world-thoughts excluded—the man a world unto himself—his own theatre—

What a speck is he dwindled into!

In this flat swamp of convalescence, left by the ebb of sickness, yet far enough from the terra-firma of established health, your note, dear Editor, reached me, requesting—an article. In Articulo Mortis, thought I; but it is something hard—and the quibble, wretched as it was, relieved me. The summons, unseasonable as it appeared, seemed to link me on again to the petty businesses of life, which I had lost sight of; a gentle call to activity, however trivial; a wholesome weaning from that preposterous dream of self-absorption—the puffy state of sickness—in which I confess to have lain so long, insensible to the magazines and monarchies of the world alike; to its laws, and to its literature. The hypochondriac flatus is subsiding; the acres, which in imagination I had spread over—for the sick man swells in the sole contemplation of his single sufferings, till he becomes a Tityus to himself—are wasting to a span; and for the giant of self-importance, which I was so lately, you have me once again in my natural pretensions—the lean and meagre figure of your insignificant Essayist.

———

SANITY OF TRUE GENIUS.

So far from the position holding true, that great wit (or genius, in our modern way of speaking) has a necessary alliance with insanity, the greatest wits, on the contrary, will ever be found to be the sanest writers. It is impossible for the mind to conceive of a mad Shakspeare. The greatness of wit, by which the poetic talent is here chiefly to be understood, manifests itself in the admirable balance of all the faculties. Madness is the disproportionate straining or excess of any one of them. "So strong a wit," says Cowley, speaking of a poetical friend,

"———— did Nature to him frame,
As all things but his judgment overcame;
His judgment like the heavenly moon did show,
Tempering that mighty sea below."

The ground of the mistake is, that men, finding in the raptures of the higher poetry a condition of exaltation, to which they have no parallel in their own experience, besides the spurious resemblance of it in dreams and fevers, impute a state of dreaminess and fever to the poet. But the true poet dreams being awake. He is not possessed by his subject, but has dominion over it. In the groves of Eden he walks familiar as in his native paths. He ascends the empyrean heaven, and is not intoxicated. He treads the burning marl without dismay; he wins his flight without self-loss through realms of chaos "and old night." Or if, abandoning himself to that severer chaos of a "human mind untuned," he is content awhile to be mad with Lear, or to hate mankind (a sort of madness) with Timon, neither is that madness, nor this misanthropy, so un-checked, but that,—never letting the reins of reason wholly go, while most he seems to do so,—he has his better genius still whispering at his ear, with the good servant Kent suggesting saner counsels, or with the honest steward Flavius recommending kindlier resolutions. Where he seems most to recede from human-ity, he will be found the truest to it. From beyond the scope of Nature if he summon possible existences, he subjugates them to the law of her consistency. He is beautifully loyal to that sover-eign directress, even when he ap-pears most to betray and desert her. His ideal tribes submit to policy; his very monsters are tamed to his hand, even as that wild sea-brood, shepherded by Proteus. He tames, and he clothes them with attributes of flesh and blood, till they wonder at them-selves, like Indian Islanders forced to submit to European vesture. Caliban, the Witches, are as true to the laws of their own nature (ours with a difference), as Othello, Hamlet, and Macbeth. Herein the great and the little wits are differenced; that if the latter wander ever so little from nature or actual existence, they lose themselves and their readers. Their phantoms are lawless; their visions nightmares. They do not create, which implies shaping and consistency. Their imaginations are not active—for to be active is to call something into act and form—but passive, as men in sick dreams. For the super-natural, or something super-added to what we know of nature, they give you the plainly non-natural. And if this were all, and that these men-tal hallucinations were discover-able only in the treatment of sub-jects out of nature, or transcend-ing it, the judgment might with some plea be pardoned if it ran riot, and a little wantonized: but even in the describing of real and every-day life, that which is be-fore their eyes, one of these lesser wits shall more deviate from na-ture—show more of that incon-sequence, which has a natural alliance with frenzy,—than a great genius in his "maddest fits," as Wither somewhere calls them. We appeal to any one that is ac-quainted with the common run of Lane's novels,—as they existed some twenty or thirty years back, —those scanty intellectual viands of the whole female reading public, till a happier genius arose, and expelled for ever the innutritious phantoms,—whether he has not found his brain more "betossed," his memory more puzzled, his sense of when and where more confounded, among the improb-able events, the incoherent inci-dents, the inconsistent characters, or no characters, of some third-rate love-intrigue—where the per-sons shall be a Lord Glendamour and a Miss Rivers, and the scene only alternate between Bath and Bond Street—a more bewildering dreaminess induced upon him than he has felt wandering over all the fairy-grounds of Spenser.

In the productions we refer to, nothing but names and places is familiar; the persons are neither of this world nor of any other conceivable one; an endless stream of activities without purpose, of purposes destitute of motive:—we meet phantoms in our known walks; *fantasques* only christened. In the poet we have names which announce fiction; and we have absolutely no place at all, for the things and persons of the Fairy Queen prate not of their "where-about." But in their inner nature, and the law of their speech and actions, we are at home, and upon acquainted ground. The one turns life into a dream; the other to the wildest dreams gives the sobrieties of every-day occurrences. By what subtle art of tracing the mental processes it is effected, we are not philosophers enough to explain, but in that wonderful episode of the cave of Mammon, in which the Money God appears first in the lowest form of a miser, is then a worker of metals, and becomes the god of all the treasures of the world; and has a daughter, Ambition, before whom all the world kneels for favours—with the Hesperian fruit, the waters of Tantalus, with Pilate washing his hands vainly, but not impertinently, in the same stream—that we should be at one moment in the cave of an old hoarder of treasures, at the next at the forge of the Cyclops, in a palace and yet in hell, all at once, with the shifting mutations of the most rambling dream, and our judgment yet all the time awake, and neither able nor willing to detect the fallacy,—is a proof of that hidden sanity which still guides the poet in the wildest seeming-aberrations.

It is not enough to say that the whole episode is a copy of the mind's conceptions in sleep; it is, in some sort—but what a copy! Let the most romantic of us, that has been entertained all night with the spectacle of some wild and magnificent vision, recombine it in the morning, and try it by his waking judgment. That which appeared so shifting, and yet so coherent, while that faculty was passive, when it comes under cool examination shall appear so reasonless and so unlinked, that we are ashamed to have been so deluded; and to have taken, though but in sleep, a monster for a god. But the transitions in this episode are every whit as violent as in the most extravagant dream, and yet the waking judgment ratifies them.

CAPTAIN JACKSON.

AMONG the deaths in our obituary for this month, I observe with concern "At his cottage on the Bath Road, Captain Jackson." The name and attribution are common enough; but a feeling like reproach persuades me that this could have been no other in fact than my dear old friend, who some five-and-twenty years ago rented a tenement, which he was pleased to dignify with the appellation here used, about a mile from Westbourn Green. Alack, how good men, and the good turns they do us, slide out of memory, and are recalled but by the surprise of some such sad memento as that which now lies before us!

He whom I mean was a retired half-pay officer, with a wife and two grown-up daughters, whom he maintained with the port and notions of gentlewomen upon that slender professional allowance. Comely girls they were too.

And was I in danger of forgetting this man?—his cheerful suppers—the noble tone of hospitality, when first you set your foot in *the cottage*—the anxious ministerings about you, where little or nothing (God knows) was to be ministered.—Althea's horn in a poor platter—the power of self enchantment, by which, in his magnificent wishes to entertain you, he multiplied his means to bounties.

You saw with your bodily eyes indeed what seemed a bare scrag —cold savings from the foregone meal—remnant hardly sufficient to send a mendicant from the door contented. But in the copious will—the revelling imagination of your host—the "mind, the mind, Master Shallow," whole beeves were spread before you—hecatombs—no end appeared to the profusion.

It was the widow's cruse—the loaves and fishes; carving could not lessen, nor helping diminish it—the stamina were left—the elemental bone still flourished, divested of its accidents.

"Let us live while we can," methinks I hear the open-handed creature exclaim; "while we have, let us not want," "here is plenty left;" "want for nothing"—with many more such hospitable sayings, the spurs of appetite, and old concomitants of smoking boards and feast-oppressed chargers. Then sliding a slender ratio of Single Gloucester upon his wife's plate, or the daughters', he would convey the remanent rind into his own, with a merry quirk of "the nearer the bone," &c., and declaring that he universally preferred the outside. For we had our table distinctions, you are to know, and some of us in a manner sate above the salt. None but his guest or guests dreamed of tasting flesh luxuries at night, the fragments were *verè hospitibus sacra.* But of one thing or another there was always enough, and leavings: only he would sometimes finish the remainder crust, to show that he wished no savings.

Wine we had none; nor, except on very rare occasions, spirits; but the sensation of wine was there. Some thin kind of ale I remember—"British beverage," he would say! "Push about, my boys;" "Drink to your sweethearts, girls." At every meagre draught a toast must ensue, or a song. All the forms of good liquor were there, with none of the effects wanting. Shut your eyes, and you would swear a capacious bowl of punch was foaming in the centre, with beams of generous Port or Madeira radiating to it from each of the table corners. You got flustered, without knowing whence; tipsy upon words; and reeled under the potency of his unperforming Bacchanalian encouragements.

We had our songs—"Why, Soldiers, why,"—and the "British Grenadiers"—in which last we were all obliged to bear chorus. Both the daughters sang. Their proficiency was a nightly theme—the masters he had given them—the "no-expense" which he spared to accomplish them in a science "so necessary to young women." But then—they could not sing "without the instrument."

Sacred, and, by me, never-to-be-violated, secrets of Poverty! Should I disclose your honest aims at grandeur, your makeshift efforts of magnificence? Sleep, sleep, with all thy broken keys, if one of the bunch be extant; thrummed by a thousand ancestral thumbs; dear, cracked spinnet of dearer Louisa! Without mention of mine, be dumb, thou thin accompanier of her thinner warble! A veil be spread over the dear delighted face of the well-deluded father, who now haply listening to cherubic notes, scarce feels sincerer pleasure than when she awakened thy time-shaken chords responsive to the twitterings of that slender image of a voice.

We were not without our literary talk either. It did not extend far, but as far as it went it was good. It was bottomed well; had good grounds to go upon. In *the cottage* was a room, which tradition authenticated to have been the same in which Glover, in his occasional retirements, had penned the greater part of his Leonidas. This circumstance was nightly quoted, though none of the present inmates, that I could discover, appeared ever to have met with the poem in question. But that was no matter. Glover had written there, and the anecdote was pressed into the account of the family importance. It diffused a learned air through the apartment, the little side casement of which (the poet's study window), opening upon a superb view as far as the pretty spire of Harrow, over domains and patrimonial acres, not a rood nor square yard whereof our host could call his own, yet gave occasion to an immoderate expansion of—vanity shall I call it?—in his bosom, as he showed them in a glowing summer evening. It was all his, he took it all in, and communicated rich portions of it to his guests. It was a part of his largess, his hospitality; it was going over his grounds; he was lord for the time of showing them, and you the implicit lookers-up to his magnificence.

He was a juggler, who threw mists before your eyes—you had no time to detect his fallacies. He would say, "Hand me the *silver* sugar-tongs;" and before you could discover it was a single spoon, and that *plated*, he would disturb and captivate your imagination by a misnomer of "the urn" for a tea-kettle; or by calling a homely bench a sofa. Rich men direct you to their furniture, poor ones divert you from it; he neither did one nor the other, but by simply assuming that everything was handsome about him, you were positively at a demur what you did, or did not see, at *the cottage*. With nothing to live on, he seemed to live on everything. He had a stock of wealth in his mind; not that which is properly termed *Content*, for in truth he was not to be *contained* at all, but overflowed all bounds by the force of a magnificent self-delusion.

Enthusiasm is catching; and even his wife, a sober native of North Britain, who generally saw things more as they were, was not proof against the continual collision of his credulity. Her daughters were rational and discreet young women; in the main, perhaps, not insensible to their true circumstances. I have seen them assume a thoughtful air at times. But such was the preponderating opulence of his fancy, that I am persuaded not for any half hour together did they ever look their own prospects fairly in the face. There was no resisting the vortex of his temperament. His riotous imagination conjured up handsome settlements before their eyes, which kept them up in the eye of the world too, and seem at last to have realized themselves; for they both have married since, I am told, more than respectably.

It is long since, and my memory waxes dim on some subjects, or I should wish to convey some notion of the manner in which the pleasant creature described the circumstances of his own wedding-day. I faintly remember something of a chaise-and-four, in which he made his entry into Glasgow on that morning to fetch the bride home, or carry her thither, I forget which. It so completely made out the stanza of the old ballad—

When we came down through Glasgow
   town,
  We were a comely sight to see;
My love was clad in black velvet,
  And I myself in cramasie.

I suppose it was the only occasion upon which his own actual splendour at all corresponded with the world's notions on that subject. In homely cart, or travelling caravan, by whatever humble vehicle they chanced to be transported in less prosperous days, the ride through Glasgow came back upon his fancy, not as a humiliating contrast, but as a fair occasion for reverting to that one day's state. It seemed an "equipage etern" from which no power of fate or fortune, once mounted, had power thereafter to dislodge him.

There is some merit in putting a handsome face upon indigent circumstances. To bully and swagger away the sense of them before strangers, may not be always discommendable. Tibbs, and Bobadil, even when detected, have more of our admiration than contempt. But for a man to put the cheat upon himself; to play the Bobadil at home; and, steeped in poverty up to the lips, to fancy himself all the while chin-deep in riches, is a strain of constitutional philosophy, and a mastery over fortune, which was reserved for my old friend Captain Jackson.

THE SUPERANNUATED MAN.

Sera tamen respexit
Libertas.   VIRGIL.
A Clerk I was in London gay.—O'KEEFE.

IF peradventure, Reader, it has been thy lot to waste the golden years of thy life—thy shining youth—in the irksome confinement of an office; to have thy prison days prolonged through middle age down to decrepitude and silver hairs, without hope of release or respite; to have lived to forget that there are such things as holidays, or to remember them but as the prerogatives of childhood; then, and then only, will you be able to appreciate my deliverance.

It is now six-and-thirty years since I took my seat at the desk in Mincing Lane. Melancholy was the transition at fourteen from the abundant playtime, and the frequently-intervening vacations of school days, to the eight, nine, and sometimes ten hours' a-day attendance at the counting-house. But time partially recon-ciles us to anything. I gradually became content—doggedly contented, as wild animals in cages.

It is true I had my Sundays to myself; but Sundays, admirable as the institution of them is for purposes of worship, are for that very reason the very worst adapted for days of unbending and recreation.* In particular, there is a gloom for me attendant upon a city Sunday, a weight in the air. I miss the cheerful cries of London, the music, and the ballad-singers—the buzz and stirring murmur of the streets. Those eternal bells depress me. The closed shops repel me. Prints, pictures, all the glittering and endless succession of knacks and gewgaws, and ostentatiously displayed wares of tradesmen, which make a week-day saunter through the less busy parts of the metropolis so delightful—are shut out. No book-stalls deliciously to idle over—no busy faces to recreate the idle man who contemplates them ever passing by—the very face of business a charm by contrast to his temporary relaxation

* [Our ancestors, the noble old Puritans of Cromwell's day, could distinguish between a day of religious rest and a day of recreation; and while they exacted a rigorous abstinence from all amusements (even to the walking out of nurserymaids with their little charges in the fields) upon the Sabbath; in the lieu of the superstitious observance of the saints' days, which they abrogated, they humanely gave to the apprentices and poorer sort of people every alternate Thursday for a day of entire sport and recreation. A strain of piety and policy to be commended above the profane mockery of the Stuarts and their book of sports.]

from it. Nothing to be seen but unhappy countenances—or half-happy at best—of emancipated 'prentices and little trades-folks, with here and there a servant-maid that has got leave to go out, who, slaving all the week, with the habit has lost almost the capacity of enjoying a free hour; and livelily expressing the hollowness of a day's pleasuring. The very strollers in the fields on that day look anything but comfortable.

But besides Sundays, I had a day at Easter, and a day at Christmas, with a full week in the summer to go and air myself in my native fields of Hertfordshire. This last was a great indulgence; and the prospect of its recurrence, I believe, alone kept me up through the year, and made my durance tolerable. But when the week came round, did the glittering phantom of the distance keep touch with me? or rather was it not a series of seven uneasy days, spent in restless pursuit of pleasure, and a wearisome anxiety to find out how to make the most of them? Where was the quiet, where the promised rest? Before I had a taste of it, it was vanished. I was at the desk again, counting upon the fifty one tedious weeks that must intervene before such another snatch would come. Still the prospect of its coming threw something of an illumination upon the darker side of my captivity. Without it, as I have said, I could scarcely have sustained my thraldom.

Independently of the rigours of attendance, I have ever been haunted with a sense (perhaps a mere caprice) of incapacity for business. This, during my latter years, had increased to such a degree, that it was visible in all the lines of my countenance. My health and my good spirits flagged. I had perpetually a dread of some crisis, to which I should be found unequal. Besides my daylight servitude, I served over again all night in my sleep, and would awake with terrors of imaginary false entries, errors in my accounts, and the like. I was fifty years of age, and no prospect of emancipation presented itself. I had grown to my desk, as it were; and the wood had entered into my soul.

My fellows in the office would sometimes rally me upon the trouble legible in my countenance; but I did not know that it had raised the suspicions of any of my employers, when, on the fifth of last month, a day ever to be remembered by me, L——, the junior partner in the firm, calling me on one side, directly taxed me with my bad looks, and frankly inquired the cause of them. So taxed, I honestly made confession of my infirmity, and added that I was afraid I should eventually be obliged to resign his service. He spoke some words of course to hearten me, and there the matter rested. A whole week I remained labouring under the impression that I had acted imprudently in my disclosure; that I had foolishly given a handle against myself, and had been anticipating my own dismissal. A week passed in this manner—the most anxious one, I verily believe, in my whole life—when on the evening of the 12th of April, just as I was about quitting my desk to go home (it might be about eight o'clock), I received an awful summons to attend the presence of the whole assembled firm in the formidable back parlour. I thought now my time is surely come, I have done for myself, I am going to be told that they have no longer occasion for me. L——, I could see, smiled at the terror I was in, which was a little relief to me,—when to my utter astonishment B——, the eldest partner, began a formal harangue to me on the length of my services, my very meritorious conduct during the whole of the time (the deuce, thought I, how did he find out that? I protest I never had the confidence to think as much). He went on to descant on the expediency of retiring at a certain time of life (how my heart panted!), and asking me a few questions as to the amount of my own property, of which I have a little, ended with a proposal, to which his three partners nodded a grave assent, that I should accept from the house, which I had served so well, a pension for life to the amount of two-thirds of my accustomed salary—a magnificent offer! I do not know what I answered between surprise and gratitude, but it was understood that I accepted their proposal, and I was told that I was free from that hour to leave their service. I stammered out a bow, and at just ten minutes after eight I went home—for ever. This noble benefit—gratitude forbids me to conceal their names—I owe to the kindness of the most munificent firm in the world—the house of Boldero, Merryweather, Bosanquet, and Lacy.

Esto perpetua!

For the first day or two I felt stunned—overwhelmed. I could only apprehend my felicity; I was too confused to taste it sincerely. I wandered about, thinking I was happy, and knowing that I was not. I was in the condition of a prisoner in the old Bastile, suddenly let loose after a forty years' confinement. I could scarce trust myself with myself. It was like passing out of Time into Eternity —for it is a sort of Eternity for a man to have all his Time to himself. It seemed to me that I had more time on my hands than I could ever manage. From a poor man, poor in Time, I was suddenly lifted up into a vast revenue; I could see no end of my possessions; I wanted some steward, or judicious bailiff, to manage my estates in Time for me. And here let me caution persons grown old in active business, not lightly, nor without weighing their own resources, to forego their customary employment all at once, for there may be danger in it. I feel it by myself, but I know that my resources are sufficient; and now that those first giddy raptures have subsided, I have a quiet home-feeling of the blessedness of my condition. I am in no hurry. Having all holidays, I am as though I had none. If Time hung heavy upon me, I could walk it away; but I do *not* walk all day long, as I used to do in those old transient holidays, thirty miles a day, to make the most of them. If Time were troublesome, I could read it away; but I do *not* read in that violent measure, with which, having no Time my own but candle-light Time, I used to weary out my head and eyesight in bygone winters. I walk, read, or scribble (as now) just when the fit seizes me. I no longer hunt after pleasure; I let it come to me. I am like the man

———— that's born, and has his years
    come to him,
In some green desert.

"Years!" you will say; "what is this superannuated simpleton calculating upon? He has already told us he is past fifty."

I have indeed lived nominally fifty years, but deduct out of them the hours which I have lived to other people, and not to myself, and you will find me still a young fellow. For *that* is the only true Time, which a man can properly call his own—that which he has all to himself; the rest, though in some sense he may be said to live it, is other people's Time, not his. The remnant of my poor days, long or short, is at least multiplied for me threefold. My ten next years, if I stretch so far, will be as long as any preceding thirty. 'Tis a fair rule-of-three sum.

Among the strange fantasies which beset me at the commencement of my freedom, and of which all traces are not yet gone, one was, that a vast tract of time had intervened since I quitted the Counting House. I could not conceive of it as an affair of yesterday. The partners, and the clerks with whom I had for so many years, and for so many hours in each day of the year, been closely associated—being suddenly removed from them—they seemed as dead to me. There is a fine passage, which may serve to illustrate this fancy, in a Tragedy by Sir Robert Howard, speaking of a friend's death:—

———— 'Twas but just now he went
    away;
I have not since had time to shed a tear;
And yet the distance does the same
    appear
As if he had been a thousand years
    from me.
Time takes no measure in Eternity.

To dissipate this awkward feeling, I have been fain to go among them once or twice since; to visit my old desk-fellows—my co-brethren of the quill—that I had left below in the state militant. Not all the kindness with which they received me could quite restore to me that pleasant familiarity, which I had heretofore enjoyed among them. We cracked some of our old jokes, but methought they went off but faintly. My old desk; the peg where I hung my hat, were appropriated to another. I knew it must be, but I could not take it kindly. D——l take me, if I did not feel some remorse—beast, if I had not—at quitting my old compeers, the faithful partners of my toils for six-and-thirty years, that smoothed for me with their jokes and conundrums the ruggedness of my professional road. Had it been so rugged then, after all? or was I a coward simply? Well, it is too late to repent; and I also know that these suggestions are a common fallacy of the mind on such occasions. But my heart smote me. I had violently broken the bands betwixt us. It was at least not courteous. I shall be some time before I get quite reconciled to the separation. Farewell, old cronies, yet not for long, for again and again I will come among ye, if I shall have your leave. Farewell, Ch——, dry, sarcastic, and friendly! Do——, mild, slow to move, and gentlemanly! Pl——, officious to do, and to volunteer, good services!—and thou, thou dreary pile, fit mansion for a Gresham or a Whittington of old, stately house of Merchants; with thy labyrinthine passages, and light-excluding, pent-up offices, where candles for one-half the year supplied the place of the sun's light; unhealthy contributor to my weal, stern fosterer of my living, farewell! In thee remain, and not in the obscure collection of some wandering bookseller, my "works!" There let them rest, as I do from my labours, piled on thy massy shelves, more MSS. in folio than ever Aquinas left, and full as usefull! My mantle I bequeath among ye.

A fortnight has passed since the date of my first communication. At that period I was approaching to tranquillity, but had not reached it. I boasted of a calm indeed, but it was comparative only. Something of the first flutter was left; an unsettling sense of novelty; the dazzle to weak eyes of unaccustomed light. I missed my old chains, forsooth, as if they had been some necessary part of my apparel. I was a poor Carthusian, from strict cellular discipline suddenly by some revolution returned upon the world. I am now as if I had never been other than my own master. It is natural for me to go where I please, to do what I please. I find myself at 11 o'clock in the day in Bond Street, and it seems to me that I have been sauntering there at that very hour for years past. I digress into Soho, to explore a bookstall. Methinks I have been thirty years a collector. There is nothing strange nor new in it. I find myself before a fine picture in the morning. Was it ever otherwise? What is become of Fish Street Hill? Where is Fenchurch Street? Stones of old Mincing Lane, which I have worn with my daily pilgrimage for six-and-thirty years, to the footsteps of what toil-worn clerk are your everlasting flints now vocal? I indent the gayer flags of Pall Mall. It is 'Change time, and I am strangely among the Elgin marbles. It was no hyperbole when I ventured to compare the change in my condition to passing into another world. Time stands still in a manner to me. I have lost all distinction of season. I do not know the day of the week or of the month. Each day used to be individually felt by me in its reference to the foreign post days; in its distance from, or propinquity to, the next Sunday. I had my Wednesday feelings, my Saturday nights' sensations. The genius of each day was upon me distinctly during the whole of it, affecting my appetite, spirits, &c. The phantom of the next day, with the dreary five to follow, sate as a load upon my poor Sabbath recreations. What charm has washed that Ethiop white? What is gone of Black Monday? All days are the same. Sunday itself—that unfortunate failure of a holiday, as it too often proved, what with my sense of its fugitiveness, and over-care to get the greatest quantity of pleasure out of it—is melted down into a week-day. I can spare to go to church now, without grudging the huge cantle which it used to seem to cut out of the holiday. I have time for everything. I can visit a sick friend. I can interrupt the man of much occupation when he is busiest. I can insult over him with an invitation to take a day's pleasure with me to Windsor this fine May-morning. It is Lucretian pleasure to behold the poor drudges, whom I have left behind in the world, carking and caring; like horses in a mill, drudging on in the same eternal round—and what is it all for? A man can never have too much Time to himself, nor too little to do. Had I a little son, I would christen him NOTHING-TO-DO; he should do nothing. Man, I verily believe, is out of his element as long as he is operative. I am altogether for the life contemplative. Will no kindly earthquake come and swallow up those accursed cotton-mills? Take me that lumber of a desk there, and bowl it down

As low as to the fiends.

I am no longer ******, clerk to the Firm of, &c. I am Retired Leisure. I am to be met with in trim gardens. I am already come to be known by my vacant face and careless gesture, perambulating at no fixed pace, nor with any settled purpose. I walk about; not to and from. They tell me, a certain *cum dignitate* air, that has been buried so long with my other good parts, has begun to shoot forth in my person. I grow into gentility perceptibly. When I take up a newspaper, it is to read the state of the opera. *Opus operatum est.* I have done all that I came into this world to do. I have worked task-work, and have the rest of the day to myself.

———

THE GENTEEL STYLE IN WRITING.

It is an ordinary criticism, that my Lord Shaftesbury and Sir William Temple are models of the genteel style in writing. We should prefer saying—of the lordly, and the gentlemanly. Nothing can be more unlike, than the inflated finical rhapsodies of Shaftesbury and the plain natural chit-chat of Temple. The man of rank is discernible in both writers; but in the one it is only insinuated gracefully, in the other it stands out offensively. The peer seems to have written with his coronet on, and his Earl's mantle before him; the commoner in his elbow-chair and undress.—What can be more pleasant than the way in which the retired statesman peeps out in his essays, penned by the latter in his delightful retreat at Shene? They scent of Nimeguen and the Hague. Scarce an authority is quoted under an ambassador. Don Francisco de Melo, a "Portugal Envoy in England," tells him it was frequent in his country for men, spent with age and other decays, so as they could not hope for above a year or two of life, to ship themselves away in a Brazil fleet, and after their arrival there to go on a great length, sometimes of twenty or thirty years, or more, by the force of that vigour they recovered with that remove. "Whether such an effect (Temple beautifully adds) might grow from the air, or the fruits of that climate, or by ap-proaching nearer the sun, which is the fountain of light and heat, when their natural heat was so far decayed; or whether the piecing out of an old man's life were worth the pains; 1 cannot tell: perhaps the play is not worth the candle." Monsieur Pompone, "French Ambassador in his (Sir William's) time at the Hague," certifies him, that in his life he had never heard of any man in France that arrived at a hundred years of age; a limitation of life which the old gentleman imputes to the excellence of their climate, giving them such a liveliness of temper and humour, as disposes them to more pleasures of all kinds than in other countries; and moralizes upon the matter very sensibly. The "late Robert Earl of Leicester" furnishes him with a story of a Countess of Desmond, married out of England in Edward the Fourth's time, and who lived far in King James's reign. The "same noble person" gives him an account, how such a year, in the same reign, there went about the country a set of morrice-dancers, composed of ten men who danced, a Maid Marian, and a tabor and pipe; and how these twelve, one with another, made up twelve hundred years. "It was not so much (says Temple) that so many in one small county (Hertfordshire) should live to that age, as that they should be in vigour and in humour to travel and to dance." Monsieur Zulichem, one of his "colleagues at the Hague," informs him of a cure for the gout; which is confirmed by another "Envoy," Monsieur Serinchamps, in that town, who had tried it.—Old Prince Maurice of Nassau recommends to him the use of hammocks in that complaint; having been allured to sleep, while suffering under it himself, by the "constant motion or swinging of those airy beds." Count Egmont, and the Rhinegrave who "was killed last summer before Macstricht," impart to him their experiences.

But the rank of the writer is never more innocently disclosed, than where he takes for granted the compliments paid by foreigners to his fruit-trees. For the taste and perfection of what we esteem the best, he can truly say, that the French, who have eaten his peaches and grapes at Shene in no very ill year, have generally concluded that the last are as good as any they have eaten in France on this side Fontainebleau; and the first as good as any they have eat in Gascony. Italians have agreed his white figs to be as good as any of that sort in Italy, which is the earlier kind of white fig there; for in the latter kind and the blue, we cannot come near the warm climates, no more than in the Frontignac or Muscat grape. His orange-trees, too, are as large as any he saw when he was young in France, except those of Fontainebleau; or what he had seen since in the Low Countries, except some very old ones of the Prince of Orange's. Of grapes he had the honour of bringing over four sorts into England, which he enumerates, and supposes that they are all by this time pretty common among some gardeners in his neighbourhood, as well as several persons of quality; for he ever thought all things of this kind "the commoner they are made the better." The garden pedantry with which he asserts that 'tis to little purpose to plant any of the best fruits, as peaches or grapes, hardly, he doubts, beyond Northamptonshire at the farthest northwards; and praises the "Bishop of Munster at Cosevelt," for attempting nothing beyond cherries in that cold climate; is equally pleasant and in character. "I may perhaps" (he thus ends his sweet Garden Essay with a passage worthy of Cowley) "be allowed to know something of this trade, since I have so long allowed myself to be good for nothing else, which few men will do, or enjoy their gardens, without often looking abroad to see how other matters play, what motions in the state, and what invitations they may hope for into other scenes. For my own part, as the country life, and this part of it more particularly, were the inclination of my youth itself, so they are the pleasures of my age; and I can truly say that, among many great employments that have fallen to my share, I have never asked or sought for any of them, but have often endeavoured to escape from them, into the ease and freedom of a private scene, where a man may go his own way and his own pace in the common paths and circles of life. The measure of choosing well is whether a man likes what he has chosen, which, I thank God, has befallen me; and though among the follies of my life, building and planting have not been the least, and have cost me more than I have the confidence to own; yet they have been fully recompensed by the sweetness and satisfaction of this retreat, where, since my resolution taken of never entering again into any public employments, I have passed five years without ever once going to town, though I am almost in sight of it, and have a house there always ready to receive me. Nor has this been any sort of affectation, as some have thought it, but a mere want of desire or humour to make so small a remove; for when I am in this corner I can truly say with Horace, *Me quoties refi-cit*, &c.

'Me, when the cold Digentian stream
   revives,
What does my friend believe I think or
   ask?
Let me yet less possess, so I may live,
Whate'er of life remains, unto myself.
May I have books enough; and one
   year's store,
Not to depend upon each doubtful hour:
This is enough of mighty Jove to pray,
Who, as he pleases, gives and takes
   away.'"

The writings of Temple are, in general, after this easy copy. On one occasion, indeed, his wit, which was mostly subordinate to nature and tenderness, has seduced him into a string of felicitous antitheses; which, it is ob-vious to remark, have been a model to Addison and succeeding essayists. "Who would not be covetous, and with reason," he says, "if health could be purchased with gold? who not ambitious, if it were at the command of power, or restored by honour? but, alas! a white staff will not help gouty feet to walk better than a common cane; nor a blue riband bind up a wound so well as a fillet. The glitter of gold, or of diamonds, will but hurt sore eyes instead of curing them; and an aching head will be no more eased by wearing a crown than a common nightcap." In a far better style, and more accordant with his own humour of plainness, are the concluding sentences of his "Discourse upon Poetry." Temple took a part in the controversy about the ancient and the modern learning; and, with that partiality so natural and so graceful in an old man, whose state engagements had left him little leisure to look into modern productions, while his retirement gave him occasion to look back upon the classic studies of his youth decided in favour of the latter. "Certain it is," he says, "that, whether the fierceness of the Gothic humours, or noise of their perpetual wars, frighted it away, or that the unequal mixture of the modern languages would not bear it—the great heights and excellency both of poetry and music fell with the Roman learning and empire, and have never since recovered the admiration and applauses that before attended them. Yet, such as they are amongst us, they must be confessed to be the softest and the sweetest, the most general and most innocent amusements of common time and life. They still find room in the courts of princes, and the cottages of shepherds. They serve to revive and animate the dead calm of poor and idle lives, and to allay or divert the violent passions and perturbations of the greatest and the busiest men. And both these effects are of equal use to human life; for the mind of man is like the sea, which is neither agreeable to the beholder nor the voyager, in a calm or in a storm, but is so to both when a little agitated by gentle gales; and so the mind, when moved by soft and easy passions or affections. I know very well that many who pretend to be wise by the forms of being grave, are apt to despise both poetry and music, as toys and trifles too light for the use or entertainment of serious men. But whoever find themselves wholly insensible to their charms, would, I think, do well to keep their own counsel, for fear of reproaching their own temper, and bringing the goodness of their natures, if not of their understandings, into question. While this world lasts, I doubt not but the pleasure and request of these two entertainments will do so too; and happy those that content themselves with these, or any other so easy and so innocent, and do not trouble the world or other men, because they cannot be quiet themselves, though nobody hurts them." "When all is done (he concludes), human life is at the greatest and the best but like a froward child, that must be played with, and humoured a little, to keep it quiet, till it falls asleep, and then the care is over."

———

BARBARA S——.

On the noon of the 14th of November, 1743 or 4, I forget which it was, just as the clock had struck one, Barbara S——, with her accustomed punctuality, ascended the long rambling staircase, with awkward interposed landing-places, which led to the office, or rather a sort of box with a desk in it, whereat sat the then treasurer of (what few of our readers may remember) the old Bath Theatre. All over the island it was the custom, and remains so I believe to this day, for the players to receive their weekly stipend on the Saturday. It was not much that Barbara had to claim.

The little maid had just entered her eleventh year; but her important station at the theatre, as it seemed to her, with the benefits which she felt to accrue from her pious application of her small earnings, had given an air of womanhood to her steps and to her behaviour. You would have taken her to have been at least five years older.

Till latterly she had merely

been employed in choruses, or where children were wanted to fill up the scene. But the manager, observing a diligence and adroitness in her above her age, had for some few months past intrusted to her the performance of whole parts. You may guess the self-consequence of the promoted Barbara. She had already drawn tears in young Arthur; had rallied Richard with infantine petulance in the Duke of York; and in her turn had rebuked that petulance when she was Prince of Wales. She would have done the elder child in Morton's pathetic afterpiece to the life; but as yet the "Children in the Wood" was not.

Long after this little girl was grown an aged woman, I have seen some of these small parts, each making two or three pages at most, copied out in the rudest hand of the then prompter, who doubtless transcribed a little more carefully and fairly for the grown-up tragedy ladies of the establishment. But such as they were, blotted and scrawled, as for a child's use, she kept them all; and in the zenith of her after reputation it was a delightful sight to behold them bound up in costliest morocco, each single—each small part making a *book*—with fine clasps, gilt-splashed, &c. She had conscientiously kept them as they had been delivered to her; not a blot had been effaced or tampered with. They were precious to her for their affecting remembrancings. They were her principia, her rudiments; the elementary atoms; the little steps by which she pressed forward to perfection. "What," she would say, "could India-rubber, or a pumice-stone, have done for these darlings?"

I am in no hurry to begin my story—indeed, I have little or none to tell—so I will just mention an observation of hers connected with that interesting time.

Not long before she died I had been discoursing with her on the quantity of real present emotion which a great tragic performer experiences during acting. I ventured to think, that though in the first instance such players must have possessed the feelings which they so powerfully called up in others, yet by frequent repetition those feelings must become deadened in great measure, and the performer trust to the memory of past emotion, rather than express a present one. She indignantly repelled the notion, that with a truly great tragedian the operation, by which such effects were produced upon an audience, could ever degrade itself into what was purely mechanical. With much delicacy, avoiding to instance in her *self*-experience, she told me, that so long ago as when she used to play the part of the Little Son to Mrs. Porter's Isabella (I think it was), when that impressive actress has been bending over her in some heart-rending colloquy, she has felt real hot tears come trickling from her, which (to use her powerful expression) have perfectly scalded her back.

I am not quite so sure that it was Mrs. Porter; but it was some great actress of that day. The name is indifferent; but the fact of the scalding tears I most distinctly remember.

I was always fond of the society of players, and am not sure that an impediment in my speech (which certainly kept me out of the pulpit), even more than certain personal disqualifications, which are often got over in that profession, did not prevent me at one time of life from adopting it. I have had the honour (I must ever call it) once to have been admitted to the tea-table of Miss Kelly. I have played at serious whist with Mr. Liston. I have chattered with ever good-humoured Mrs. Charles Kemble. I have conversed as friend to friend with her accomplished husband. I have been indulged with a classical conference with Macready; and with a sight of the Player-picture gallery, at Mr. Mathews's, when the kind owner, to remunerate me for my love of the old actors (whom he loves so much), went over it with me, supplying to his capital collection, what alone the artist could not give them—voice; and their living motion. Old tones, half-faded, of Dodd, and Parsons, and Baddeley, have lived again for me at his bidding. Only Edwin he could not restore to me. I have supped with——; but I am growing a coxcomb.

As I was about to say—at the desk of the then treasurer of the old Bath Theatre—not Diamond's —presented herself the little Barbara S——.

The parents of Barbara had been in reputable circumstances. The father had practised, I believe, as an apothecary in the town. But his practice, from causes which I feel my own infirmity too sensibly that way to arraign—or perhaps from that pure infelicity which accompanies some people in their walk through life, and which it is impossible to lay at the door of imprudence—was now reduced to nothing. They were, in fact, in the very teeth of starvation, when the manager, who knew and respected them in better days, took the little Barbara into his company.

At the period I commenced with, her slender earnings were the sole support of the family, including two younger sisters. I must throw a veil over some mortifying circumstances. Enough to say, that her Saturday's pittance was the only chance of a Sunday's (generally their only) meal of meat.

One thing I will only mention, that in some child's part, where in her theatrical character she was to sup off a roast fowl (O joy to Barbara!) some comic actor, who was for the night caterer for this dainty—in the misguided humour of his part, threw over the dish such a quantity of salt (O grief and pain of heart to Barbara!) that when she crammed a portion of it into her mouth, she was obliged sputteringly to reject it; and what with shame of her ill-acted part, and pain of real appetite at missing such a dainty, her little heart sobbed almost to breaking, till a flood of tears, which the well-fed spectators were totally unable to comprehend, mercifully relieved her.

This was the little starved, meritorious maid, who stood before old Ravenscroft, the treasurer, for her Saturday's payment.

Ravenscroft was a man, I have heard many old theatrical people besides herself say, of all men least calculated for a treasurer. He had no head for accounts, paid away at random, kept scarce any books, and summing up at the week's end, if he found himself a pound or so deficient, blest himself that it was no worse.

Now Barbara's weekly stipend was a bare half-guinea.—By mistake he popped into her hand—a whole one.

Barbara tripped away.

She was entirely unconscious at first of the mistake: God knows, Ravenscroft would never have discovered it.

But when she had got down to the first of those uncouth landing-places, she became sensible of an unusual weight of metal pressing in her little hand.

Now mark the dilemma.

She was by nature a good child. From her parents and those about her, she had imbibed no contrary influence. But then they had taught her nothing. Poor men's smoky cabins are not always porticoes of moral philosophy. This little maid had no instinct to evil, but then she might be said to have no fixed principle. She had heard honesty commended, but never dreamed of its application to herself. She thought of it as something which concerned grown-up people, men and women. She had never known temptation, or thought of preparing resistance against it.

Her first impulse was to go back to the old treasurer, and explain to him his blunder. He was already so confused with age, besides a natural want of punctuality, that she would have had some difficulty in making him understand it. She saw *that* in an instant. And then it was such a bit of money! and then the image of a larger allowance of butcher's meat on their table the next day came across her, till her little eyes glistened, and her mouth moistened. But then Mr. Ravenscroft had always been so good-natured, had stood her friend behind the scenes, and even recommended her promotion to some of her little parts. But again the old man was reputed to be worth a world of money. He was supposed to have fifty pounds a-year clear of the theatre. And then came staring upon her the figures of her little stockingless and shoeless sisters. And when she looked at her own neat white cotton stockings, which her situation at the theatre had made it indispensable for her mother to provide for her, with hard straining and pinching from the family stock, and thought how glad she should be to cover their poor feet with the same—and how then they could accompany her to rehearsals, which they had hitherto been precluded from doing, by reason of their unfashionable attire,—in these thoughts she reached the second landing-place—the second, I mean, from the top—for there was still another left to traverse.

Now virtue support Barbara!

And that never-failing friend *did* step in—for at that moment a strength not her own, I have heard her say, was revealed to her—a reason above reasoning—and without her own agency, as it seemed (for she never felt her feet to move), she found herself transported back to the individual desk she had just quitted, and her hand in the old hand of Ravenscroft, who in silence took back the refunded treasure, and who had been sitting (good man) insensible to the lapse of minutes, which to her were anxious ages, and from that moment a deep peace fell upon her heart, and she knew the quality of honesty.

A year or two's unrepining application to her profession brightened up the feet and the prospects of her little sisters, set the whole family upon their legs again, and released her from the difficulty of discussing moral dogmas upon a landing-place.

I have heard her say that it was a surprise, not much short of mortification to her, to see the coolness with which the old man pocketed the difference, which had caused her such mortal throes.

This anecdote of herself I had in the year 1800, from the mouth of the late Mrs. Crawford,[*] then sixty-seven years of age (she died soon after); and to her struggles upon this childish occasion I have sometimes ventured to think her indebted for that power of rending the heart in the representation of conflicting emotions, for which in after years she was considered as little inferior (if at all so in the part of Lady Randolph) even to Mrs. Siddons.

THE TOMBS IN THE ABBEY.

IN A LETTER TO R— S—, ESQ.

THOUGH in some points of doctrine, and perhaps of discipline, I am diffident of lending a perfect assent to that church which you have so worthily *historified*, yet may the ill time never come to me, when with a chilled heart or a portion of irreverent sentiment, I shall enter her beautiful and time-hallowed Edifices. Judge, then, of my mortification when, after attending the choral anthems of last Wednesday at Westminster, and being desirous of renewing my acquaintance, after

---

[*] The maiden name of this lady was Street, which she changed, by successive marriages, for those of Dancer, Barry, and Crawford. She was Mrs. Crawford, a third time a widow, when I knew her.

lapsed years, with the tombs and antiquities there, I found myself excluded; turned out, like a dog, or some profane person, into the common street, with feelings not very congenial to the place, or to the solemn service which I had been listening to. It was a jar after that music.

You had your education at Westminster; and doubtless among those dim aisles and cloisters, you must have gathered much of that devotional feeling in those young years, on which your purest mind feeds still—and may it feed! The antiquarian spirit, strong in you, and gracefully blending ever with the religious, may have been sown in you among those wrecks of splendid mortality. You owe it to the place of your education; you owe it to your learned fondness for the architecture of your ancestors; you owe it to the venerableness of your ecclesiastical establishment, which is daily lessened and called in question through these practices—to speak aloud your sense of them; never to desist raising your voice against them, till they be totally done away with and abolished; till the doors of Westminster Abbey be no longer closed against the decent, though low-in-purse, enthusiast, or blameless devotee, who must commit an injury against his family economy, if he would be indulged with a bare admission within its walls. You owe it to the decencies which you wish to see maintained in its impressive services, that our Cathedral be no longer an object of inspection to the poor at those times only, in which they must rob from their attendance on the worship every minute which they can bestow upon the fabric. In vain the public prints have taken up this subject,—in vain such poor, nameless writers as myself express their indignation. A word from you, sir,—a hint in your Journal —would be sufficient to fling open the doors of the Beautiful Temple again, as we can remember them when we were boys. At that time of life, what would the imaginative faculty (such as it is) in both of us, have suffered, if the entrance to so much reflection had been obstructed by the demand of so much silver!—If we had scraped it up to gain an occasional admission (as we certainly should have done), would the sight of those old tombs have been as impressive to us (while we have been weighing anxiously prudence against sentiment) as when the gates stood open as those of the adjacent Park; when we could walk in at any time, as the mood brought us, for a shorter or longer time, as that lasted? Is the being shown over a place the same as silently for ourselves detecting the genius of it? In no part of our beloved Abbey now can a person find entrance (out-of-service-time) under the sum of *two shillings*. The rich and the great will smile at the anti-climax, presumed to lie in these two short words. But you can tell them, sir, how much quiet worth, how much capacity for enlarged feeling, how much taste and genius, may co-exist, especially in youth, with a purse incompetent to this demand. A respected friend of ours, during his late visit to the metropolis, presented himself for admission to St. Paul's. At the same time a decently-clothed man, with as decent a wife and child, were bargaining for the same indulgence. The price was only two-pence each person. The poor but decent man hesitated, desirous to go in; but there were three of them, and he turned away reluctantly. Perhaps he wished to have seen the tomb of Nelson. Perhaps the Interior of the Cathedral was his object. But in the state of his finances, even sixpence might reasonably seem too much. Tell the Aristocracy of the country (no man can do it more impressively); instruct them of what value these insignificant pieces of money, these minims to their sight, may be to their humbler brethren. Shame these Sellers out of the Temple. Stifle not the suggestions of your better nature with the pretext, that an indiscriminate admission would expose the Tombs to violation. Remember your boy-days. Did you ever see, or hear, of a mob in the Abbey, while it was free to all? Do the rabble come there, or trouble their heads about such speculations? It is all that you can do to drive them into your churches; they do not voluntarily offer themselves. They have, alas! no passion for antiquities; for tomb of king or prelate, sage or poet. If they had, they would be no longer the rabble.

For forty years that I have known the Fabric, the only well-attested charge of violation adduced, has been—a ridiculous dismemberment committed upon the effigy of that amiable spy, Major André. And is it for this—the wanton mischief of some schoolboy, fired perhaps with raw notions of Transatlantic Freedom—or the remote possibility of such a mischief occurring again, so easily to be prevented by stationing a constable within the walls, if the vergers are incompetent to the duty—is it upon such wretched pretences that the people of England are made to pay a new Peter's Pence, so long abrogated; or must content themselves with contemplating the ragged Exterior of their Cathedral? The mischief was done about the time that you were a scholar there. Do you know anything about the unfortunate relic?—

AMICUS REDIVIVUS.

Where were ye, Nymphs, when the remorseless deep
   Closed o'er the head of your loved Lycidas?

I do not know when I have experienced a stranger sensation than on seeing my old friend, G. D., who had been paying me a morning visit, a few Sundays back, at my cottage at Islington, upon taking leave, instead of turning down the right-hand path by which he had entered—with staff in hand, and at noonday, deliberately march right forwards into the midst of the stream that runs by us, and totally disappear.

A spectacle like this at dusk would have been appalling enough; but in the broad, open daylight, to witness such an unreserved motion towards self-destruction in a valued friend, took from me all power of speculation.

How I found my feet I know not. Consciousness was quite gone. Some spirit, not my own, whirled me to the spot. I remember nothing but the silvery apparition of a good white head emerging; nigh which a staff (the hand unseen that wielded it) pointed upwards, as feeling for the skies. In a moment (if time was in that time) he was on my shoulders, and I—freighted with a load more precious than his who bore Anchises.

And here I cannot but do justice to the officious zeal of sundry passers-by, who, albeit arriving a little too late to participate in the honours of the rescue, in philanthropic shoals came thronging to communicate their advice as to the recovery; prescribing variously the application, or non-application, of salt, &c., to the person of the patient. Life, meantime, was ebbing fast away, amidst the stifle of conflicting judgments, when one, more sagacious than the rest, by a bright thought, proposed sending for the Doctor. Trite as the counsel was, and impossible, as one should think, to be missed on, shall I confess?—in this emergency it was to me as if an Angel had spoken. Great previous exertions—and mine had not been inconsiderable—are commonly followed by a debility of purpose. This was a moment of irresolution.

Monoculus—for so, in default of catching his true name, I choose to designate the medical gentleman who now appeared—is a grave, middle-aged person, who, without having studied at the college, or truckled to the pedantry of a diploma, hath employed a great portion of his valuable time in experimental processes upon the bodies of unfortunate fellow-creatures, in whom the vital spark, to mere vulgar thinking, would seem extinct and lost for ever. He omitteth no occasion of obtruding his services, from a case of common surfeit suffocation to the ignobler obstructions, sometimes induced by a too wilful application of the plant *cannabis* outwardly. But though he declineth not altogether these drier extinctions, his occupation tendeth, for the most part, to water-practice; for the convenience of which, he hath judiciously fixed his quarters near the grand repository of the stream mentioned, where day and night, from his little watch-tower, at the Middleton's Head, he listeneth to detect the wrecks of drowned mortality —partly, as he saith, to be upon the spot—and partly, because the liquids which he useth to pre-scribe to himself and his patients, on these distressing occasions, are ordinarily more conveniently to be found at these common hostel-ries than in the shops and phials of the apothecaries. His ear hath arrived to such finesse by practice, that it is reported he can dis-tinguish a plunge, at half a fur-long distance; and can tell if it be casual or deliberate. He weareth a medal, suspended over a suit, originally of a sad brown, but which, by time and frequency of nightly divings, has been dinged into a true professional sable. He passeth by the name of Doctor, and is remarkable for wanting his left eye. His remedy after a sufficient application of warm blankets, friction, &c., is a simple tumbler, or more, of the purest Cognac, with water, made as hot as the convalescent can bear it. Where he findeth, as in the case of my friend, a squeamish subject, he condescendeth to be the taster; and showeth, by his own example, the innocuous na-ture of the prescription. Nothing can be more kind or encouraging than this procedure. It addeth confidence to the patient, to see his medical adviser go hand in hand with himself in the remedy. When the doctor swalloweth his own draught, what peevish invalid can refuse to pledge him in the potion? In fine, MONOCULUS is a human, sensible man, who, for a slender pittance, scarce enough to sustain life, is content to wear it out in the endeavour to save the lives of others—his pretensions so moderate, that with difficulty I could press a crown upon him, for the price of restoring the ex-istence of such an invaluable crea-ture to society as G. D.

It was pleasant to observe the effect of the subsiding alarm upon the nerves of the dear absentee. It seemed to have given a shake to memory, calling up notice after notice, of all the providential de-liverances he had experienced in the course of his long and innocent life. Sitting up on my couch—my couch which, naked and void of furniture hitherto, for the salu-tary repose which it administered, shall be honoured with costly val-ance, at some price, and hence-forth be a state-bed at Colebrook, —he discoursed of marvellous es-capes—by carelessness of nurses —by pails of gelid, and kettles of the boiling element, in infancy—by orchard pranks, and snapping twigs, in schoolboy frolics—by descent of tiles at Trumpington, and of heavier tomes at Pembroke —by studious watchings, inducing frightful vigilance—by want, and the fear of want, and all the sore throbbings of the learned head.—Anon, he would burst out into little fragments of chanting—of songs long ago—ends of deliver-ance hymns, not remembered be-fore since childhood, but coming up now, when his heart was made tender as a child's—for the *tremor cordis*, in the retrospect of a re-cent deliverance, as in a case of impending danger, acting upon an innocent heart, will produce a self-tenderness, which we should do ill to christen cowardice; and Shakspeare, in the latter crisis, had made his good Sir Hugh to remember the sitting by Babylon, and to mutter of shallow rivers.

Waters of Sir Hugh Middleton—what a spark you were like to have extinguished for ever! Your insalubrious streams to this City, for now near two centuries, would hardly have atoned for what you were in a moment washing away. Mockery of a river—liquid artifice—wretched conduit! henceforth rank with canals and sluggish aqueducts. Was it for this that, smit in boyhood with the explorations of that Abyssinian traveller, I paced the vales of Amwell to explore your tributary springs, to trace your salutary waters sparkling through green Hertfordshire, and cultured Enfield parks?—Ye have no swans—no Naïads—no river God—or did the benevolent hoary aspect of my friend tempt ye to suck him in, that ye also might have the tutelary genius of your waters?

Had he been drowned in Cam, there would have been some consonancy in it; but what willows had ye to wave and rustle over his moist sepulture?—or, having no *name*, besides that unmeaning assumption of *eternal novity*, did ye think to get one by the noble prize, and henceforth to be termed the STREAM DYERIAN?

And could such spacious virtue find a
 grave
Beneath the imposthumed bubble of a
 wave?

I protest, George, you shall not venture out again—no, not by daylight—without a sufficient pair of spectacles—in your musing moods especially. Your absence of mind we have borne, till your presence of body came to be called in question by it. You shall not go wandering into Euripus with Aristotle, if we can help it. Fie, man, to turn dipper at your years, after your many tracts in favour of sprinkling only!

I have nothing but water in my head o'nights since this frightful accident. Sometimes I am with Clarence in his dream. At others, I behold Christian beginning to sink, and crying out to his good brother Hopeful (that is, to me), "I sink in deep waters; the billows go over my head, all the waves go over me. Selah." Then I have before me Palinurus, just letting go the steerage. I cry out too late to save. Next follow—a mournful procession—*suicidal faces*, saved against their will from drowning; dolefully trailing a length of reluctant gratefulness, with ropy weeds pendent from locks of watchet hue—constrained Lazari—Pluto's half-subjects—stolen fees from the grave—bilking Charon of his fare. At their head Arion—or is it G. D.?—in his singing garments marcheth singly, with harp in hand, and votive garland, which Machaon (or Dr. Hawes) snatcheth straight, intending to suspend it to the stern God of Sea. Then follow dismal streams of Lethe, in which the half-drenched on earth are constrained to drown downright, by wharfs where Ophelia twice acts her muddy death.

And, doubtless, there is some notice in that invisible world when one of us approacheth (as my friend did so lately) to their inexorable precincts. When a soul knocks once, twice, at Death's door, the sensation aroused within the palace must be considerable; and the grim Feature, by modern science so often dispossessed of his prey, must have learned by this time to pity 'Tantalus.

A pulse assuredly was felt along the line of the Elysian shades, when the near arrival of G. D. was announced by no equivocal indications. From their seats of Asphodel arose the gentler and the graver ghosts—poet, or historian—of Grecian or of Roman lore —to crown with unfading chaplets the half-finished love-labours of their unwearied scholiast. Him Markland expected—him Tyrwhitt hoped to encounter—him the sweet lyrist of Peter House, whom he had barely seen upon earth,* with newest airs prepared to greet——; and patron of the gentle Christ's boy,—who should have been his patron through life —the mild Askew, with longing aspirations leaned foremost from his venerable Æsculapian chair, to welcome into that happy company the matured virtues of the man, whose tender scions in the boy he himself upon earth had so prophetically fed and watered.

* Graium tantum vidit.

Sydney's Sonnets—I speak of the best of them—are among the very best of their sort. They fall below the plain moral dignity, the sanctity, and high yet modest spirit of self-approval, of Milton, in his compositions of a similar structure. They are in truth what Milton, censuring the Arcadia, says of that work (to which they are a sort of after-tune or application), "vain and amatorious" enough, yet the things in their kind (as he confesses to be true of the romance) may be "full of worth and wit." They savour of the Courtier, it must be allowed, and not of the Commonwealthsman. But Milton was a Courtier when he wrote the Masque at Ludlow Castle, and still more a Courtier when he composed the Arcades. When the national struggle was to begin, he becomingly cast these vanities behind him; and if the order of time had thrown Sir Philip upon the crisis which preceded the revolution, there is no reason why he should not have acted the same part in that emergency, which has glorified the name of a later Sydney. He did not want for plainness or boldness of spirit. His letter on the French match may testify he could speak his mind freely to Princes. The times did not call him to the scaffold.

The Sonnets which we oftenest call to mind of Milton were the compositions of his maturest years. Those of Sydney, which I am about to produce, were written in the very heyday of his blood. They are stuck full of amorous fancies—far-fetched conceits, befitting his occupation; for True Love thinks no labour too send out Thoughts upon the vast and more than Indian voyages, to bring home rich pearls, outlandish wealth, gums, jewels, spicery, to sacrifice in self-depreciating similitudes, as shadows of true amiabilities in the Beloved. We must be Lovers—or at least the cooling touch of time, the *circum præcordia frigus*, must not have so damped our faculties, as to take away our recollection that we were once so—before we can duly appreciate the glorious vanities and graceful hyperboles of the passion. The images which lie before our feet (though by som accounted the only natural) are least natural for the high Sydnean love to express its fancies by. They may serve for the loves of Tibullus, or the dear Author of the Schoolmistress; for passions that creep and whine in Elegies and Pastoral Ballads. I am sure Milton never loved at this rate. I am afraid some of his addresses (*ad Leonoram* I mean) have rather erred on the farther side; and that the poet came not much short of a religious indecorum, when he could thus apostrophize a singing-girl:—

Angelus unicuique suus (sic credite gentes)
 Obtigit ætherei ales ab ordinibus.
Quid mirum, Leonora, tibi si gloria major,
 Nam tua præsentem vox sonat ipsa Deum?

Aut Deus, aut vacui certe mens tertia cœli
 Per tua secreta guttura serpit agens:
Serpit agens, facilisque docet mortalia
  corda
Sensim immortali assuescere posse sono.
QUOD SI CUNCTA QUIDEM DEUS EST, PER
  CUNCTAQUE FUSUS,
IN TE UNA LOQUITUR, CÆTERA MUTUS
 HABET.

This is loving in a strange fashion; and it requires some candour of construction (besides the slight darkening of a dead language) to cast a veil over the ugly appearance of something very like blasphemy in the last two verses. I think the Lover would have been staggered if he had gone about to express the same thought in English. I am sure Sydney has no flights like this. His extravaganzas do not strike at the sky, though he takes leave to adopt the pale Dian into a fellowship with his mortal passions:

i.

With how sad steps, O Moon, thou climb'st
  the skies;
How silently; and with how wan a face!
What! may it be, that even in heavenly
  place,
That busy Archer his sharp arrow tries?
Sure, if that long-with-love-acquainted
  eyes
Can judge of love, then feel'st a lover's
  case;
I read it in thy looks; thy languisht grace
To me, that feel the like, thy state descries.
Then, even of fellowship, O Moon, tell me,
Is constant love deem'd there but want
  of wit?
Are beauties there as proud as here they
  be?
Do they above love to be loved, and yet
Those lovers scorn, whom that love doth
  possess?
Do they call virtue there—ungratefulness!

The last line of this poem is a

little obscured by transposition.
He means, Do they call ungratefulness there a virtue?

II.

Come, Sleep, O Sleep, the certain knot of
  peace,
The baiting-place of wit, the balm of woe,
The poor man's wealth, the prisoner's re-
  lease,
The indifferent judge between the high
  and low;
With shield of proof shield me from out
  the prease*
Of those fierce darts despair at me doth
  throw;
O make in me those civil wars to cease:
I will g od tribute pay if thou do so.
Take thou of me sweet pillows, sweetest
  bed;
A chamber deaf to noise, and blind to
  light;
A rosy garland, and a weary head.
And if these things, as being thine by
  right,
Move not thy heavy grace, thou shalt in
  me,
Livelier than elsewhere, Stella's image
  see.

III.

The curious wits, seeing dull pensiveness
Bewray itself in my long-settled eyes,
Whence those same fumes of melancholy
  rise,
With idle pains, and missing aim, do
  guess.
Some, that know how my spring I did
  address,
Deem that my Muse some fruit of know-
  ledge plies;
Others, because the Prince my service
  tries,
Think, that I think state errors to re-
  dress;
But harder judges judge, ambition's rage,
Scourge of itself, still climbing slippery
  place,
Holds my young brain captiv'd in golden
  cage.
O fools, or over-wise! alas, the race
Of all my thoughts hath neither stop nor
  start,
But only Stella's eyes, and Stella's
  heart.

* Press.

IV.

Because I oft in dark abstracted guise
Seem most alone in greatest company,
With dearth of words, or answers quite
  awry,
To them that would make speech of
  speech arise;
They deem, and of their doom the rumour
  flies,
That poison foul of bubbling *Pride* doth
  lie
So in my swelling breast, that only I
Fawn on myself, and others do despise;
Yet *Pride*, I think, doth not my soul pos-
  sess,
Which looks too oft in his unflattering
  glass:
But one worse fault—*Ambition*—I confess,
That makes me oft my best friends over-
  pass,
Unseen, unheard—while Thought to high-
  est place
Bends all his powers, even unto Stella's
  grace.

V.

Having this day, my horse, my hand, my
  lance,
Guided so well that I obtained the prize,
Both by the judgment of the English eyes,
And of some sent from that sweet enemy,
  —France;
Horseman my skill in horsemanship ad-
  vance;
Townsfolk my strength; a daintier judge
  applies
His praise to sleight, which from good
  use doth rise;
Some lucky wits impute it but to chance:
Others, because of both sides I do take
My blood from them, who did excel in
  this,
Think Nature me a man of arms did make.
How far they shot awry! the true cause is,
Stella look'd on, and from her heavenly
  face
Sent forth the beams which made so fair
  my race.

VI.

In martial sports I had my cunning tried,
And yet to break more staves did me address,
While with the people's shouts (I must
  confess)
Youth, luck, and praise, even fill'd my
  veins with pride--

When Cupid having me (his slave) de-
    serted
In Mars's livery, prancing in the press,
"What now, Sir Fool!" said he; "I
    would no less:
Look here, I say." I look'd, and STELLA
    spied,
Who hard by made a window send forth
    light.
My heart then quaked, then dazzled were
    mine eyes;
One hand forgot to rule, th'other to fight;
Nor trumpet's sound I heard, nor friendly
    cries.
My foe came on, and beat the air for me—
Till that her blush made me my shame
    to see.

VII.

No more, my dear, no more these coun-
    sels try;
O give my passions leave to run their race;
Let Fortune lay on me her worst disgrace;
Let folk o'ercharged with brain against
    me cry;
Let clouds bedim my face, break in mine
    eye;
Let me no steps, but of lost labour, trace;
Let all the earth with scorn recount my
    case—
But do not will me from my love to fly.
I do not envy Aristotle's wit,
Nor do aspire to Cæsar's bleeding fame;
Nor aught do care, though some above
    me sit;
Nor hope, nor wish, another course to
    frame.
But that which once may win thy cruel
    heart:
Thou art my wit, and thou my virtue art.

VIII.

Love still a boy, and oft a wanton, is,
School'd only by his mother's tender eye;
What wonder, then, if he his lesson miss,
When for so soft a rod dear play he try?
And yet my STAR, because a sugar'd kiss
In sport I suck'd, while she asleep did lie,
Doth lour, nay chide, nay threat, for only
    this.
Sweet, it was saucy LOVE, not humble I.
But no 'scuse serves; she makes her wrath
    appear
In Beauty's throne—see now who dares
    come near
Those scarlet judges, threat'ning bloody
    pain?
O heav'nly Fool, thy most kiss-worthy face

Anger invests with such a lovely grace,
That anger's self I needs must kiss again.

IX.

I never drank of Aganippe well,
Nor ever did in shade of Tempe sit,
And Muses scorn with vulgar brains to
    dwell;
Poor lay-man I, for sacred rights unfit,
Some do I hear of Poet's fury tell,
But (God wot) wot not what they mean
    by it;
And this I swear by blackest brook of hell,
I am no pick-purse of another's wit.
How falls it then, that with so smooth an
    ease
My thoughts I speak, and what I speak
    doth flow
In verse, and that my verse best wits doth
    please?
Guess me the cause—what is it thus?—
    fye, no!
Or so?—much less. How then? sure thus
    it is,
My lips are sweet, inspir'd with STELLA's
    kiss.

X.

Of all the kings that ever here did reign,
Edward, named Fourth, as first in praise
    I name.
Not for his fair outside, nor well-lined
    brain—
Although less gifts imp feathers oft on
    Fame.
Nor that he could, young-wise, wise-
    valiant, frame
His sire's revenge, join'd with a king-
    dom's gain;
And, gain'd by Mars could yet mad Mars
    so tame,
That Balance weigh'd what Sword did
    late obtain
Nor that he made the Floure-de-lnce so
    'fraid,
Though strongly hedged, of bloody Lions'
    paws,
That witty Lewis to him a tribute paid.
Nor this, nor that, nor any such small
    cause—
But only, for this worthy knight durst prove
To lose his crown rather than fail his love.

XI.

O happy Thames, that didst my STELLA
    bear,
I saw thyself, with many a smiling line
Upon thy cheerful face, Joy's livery wear,

While those fair planets on thy streams
   did shine;
The boat for joy could not to dance
   forbear,
While wanton winds, with beauty so
   divine
Ravish'd, stay'd not, till in her golden hair
They did themselves (O sweetest prison)
   twine.
And fain those Æol's youth there would
   their stay
Have made; but, forced by nature still
   to fly,
First did with puffing kiss those locks
   display.
She, so dishevell'd, blush'd; from window I
With sight thereof cried out, O fair disgrace,
Let Honour's self 'to thee grant highest
   place!

XII.

Highway, since you my chief Parnassus be;
And that my Muse, to some ears not un-
   sweet,
Tempers her words to trampling horses'
   feet,
More soft than to a chamber melody;
Now blessed You bear onward blessed Me
To Her, where I my heart safe left shall
   meet,
My Muse and I must you of duty greet
With thanks and wishes, wishing thank-
   fully.
Be you still fair, honour'd by public heed,
By no encroachment wrong'd, nor time
   forgot;
Nor blamed for blood, nor ashamed for
   sinful deed.
And that you know, I envy you no lot
Of highest wish, I wish you so much bliss,
Hundreds of years you STELLA'S feet
   may kiss.

Of the foregoing, the first, the second, and the last sonnet, are my favourites. But the general beauty of them all is, that they are so perfectly characteristical. The spirit of "learning and of chivalry,"—of which union, Spenser has entitled Sydney to have been the "president,"—shines through them. I confess I can see nothing of the "jejune" or "frigid" in them; much less of the "stiff" and "cumbrous"— which I have sometimes heard objected to the Arcadia. The verse runs off swiftly and gallantly. It might have been tuned to the trumpet; or tempered (as himself expresses it) to "trampling horses' feet." They abound in felicitous phrases—

O heav'nly Fool, thy most kiss-worthy
   face—
8th Sonnet.

... ———— Sweet pillows, sweetest bed;
A chamber deaf to noise, and blind to
   light;
A rosy garland, and a weary head.
2nd Sonnet.

.. ————————— That sweet enemy,—France—
5th Sonnet.

But they are not rich in words only, in vague and unlocalised feelings—the failing too much of some poetry of the present day— they are full, material, and circumstantiated. Time and place appropriates every one of them. It is not a fever of passion wasting itself upon a thin diet of dainty words, but a transcendent passion pervading and illuminating action, pursuits, studies, feats of arms, the opinions of contemporaries, and his judgment of them. An historical thread runs through them, which almost affixes a date to them; marks the *when* and *where* they were written.

I have dwelt the longer upon what I conceive the merit of these poems, because I have been hurt by the wantonness (I wish I could treat it by a gentler name) with which W. H. takes every occasion of insulting the memory of Sir Philip Sydney. But the decisions of the Author of Table Talk, &c. (most profound and subtle where they are, as for the most part, just) are more safely to be relied upon, on subjects and authors he has a partiality for, than on such as he has conceived an accidental prejudice against. Milton wrote sonnets, and was a king-hater; and it was congenial perhaps to sacrifice a courtier to a patriot. But I was unwilling to lose a *fine idea* from my mind. The noble images, passions, sentiments, and poetical delicacies of character, scattered all over the Arcadia (spite of some stiffness and encumberment), justify to me the character which his contemporaries have left us of the writer. I cannot think with the *Critic*, that Sir Philip Sydney was that *opprobrious thing* which a foolish nobleman in his insolent hostility chose to term him. I call to mind the epitaph made on him, to guide me to juster thoughts of him; and I repose upon the beautiful lines in the "Friend's Passion for his Astrophel," printed with the Elegies of Spenser and others:

You knew—who knew not Astrophel?
(That I should live to say I knew,
And have not in possession still I)—
Things known permit me to renew—
  Of him you know his merit such,
  I cannot say—you hear—too much.

Within these woods of Arcady
He chief delight and pleasure took;
And on the mountain Partheny,
Upon the crystal liquid brook,
  The Muses met him every day,
  That taught him sing, to write, and say.

When he descended down the mount,
His personage seemed most divine:
A thousand graces one might count
Upon his lovely cheerful eyne.
  To hear him speak, and sweetly smile,
  You were in Paradise the while.

A sweet attractive kind of grace;
A full assurance given by looks;
Continual comfort in a face,
The lineaments of Gospel books—
  I trow that count'nance cannot lye,
  Whose thoughts are legible in the eye.

*   *   *   *   *   *   *   *

Above all others this is he,
Which erst approved in his song,
That love and honour might agree,
And that pure love will do no wrong.
  Sweet saints, it is no sin or blame
  To love a man of virtuous name.

Did never love so sweetly breathe
In any mortal breast before,
Did never Muse inspire beneath
A Poet's brain with finer store!
  He wrote of Love with high conceit,
  And Beauty rear'd above her height.

Or let any one read the deeper sorrows (grief running into rage) in the Poem,—the last in the collection accompanying the above,—which from internal testimony I believe to be Lord Brooke's—beginning with "Silence augmenteth grief," and then seriously ask himself, whether the subject of such absorbing and confounding regrets could have been *that thing* which Lord Oxford termed him.

—————

NEWSPAPERS THIRTY-FIVE YEARS AGO.

Dan Stuart once told us, that he did not remember that he ever deliberately walked into the Exhibition at Somerset House in his life. He might occasionally have escorted a party of ladies across the way that were going in, but he never went in of his own head. Yet the office of the *Morning Post* newspaper stood then just where it does now—we are carrying you back, Reader, some thirty years or more—with its gilt-globe-topt front facing that emporium of our artists' grand Annual Exposure. We sometimes wish that we had observed the same abstinence with Daniel.

A word or two of D. S. He ever appeared to us one of the finest-tempered of Editors. Perry, of the *Morning Chronicle*, was equally pleasant, with a dash, no slight one either, of the courtier. S. was frank, plain, and English all over. We have worked for both these gentlemen.

It is soothing to contemplate the head of the Ganges; to trace the first little bubblings of a mighty river,

With holy reverence to approach the rocks,
Whence glide the streams renowned in ancient song.

Fired with a perusal of the Abyssinian Pilgrim's exploratory ramblings after the cradle of the infant Nilus, we well remember on one fine summer holyday (a "whole day's leave" we called it at Christ's hospital) sallying forth at rise of sun, not very well provisioned either for such an undertaking, to trace the current of the New River—Middletonian stream!—to its scaturient source, as we had read, in meadows by fair Amwell. Gallantly did we commence our solitary quest—for it was essential to the dignity of a Discovery, that no eye of schoolboy, save our own, should beam on the detection. By flowery spots, and verdant lanes skirting Hornsey, Hope trained us on in many a baffling turn; endless, hopeless meanders, as it seemed; or as if the jealous waters had *dodged* us, reluctant to have the humble spot of their nativity revealed; till spent, and nigh famished, before set of the same sun, we sate down somewhere by Bowes Farm near Tottenham, with a tithe of our proposed labours only yet accomplished; sorely convinced in spirit, that that Brucian enterprise was as yet too arduous for our young shoulders.

Not more refreshing to the thirsty curiosity of the traveller is the tracing of some mighty waters up to their shallow fontlet, than it is to a pleased and candid reader to go back to the inexperienced essays, the first callow flights in authorship, of some established name in literature; from the Gnat which preluded to the Æneid, to the Duck which Samuel Johnson trod on.

In those days, every Morning Paper, as an essential retainer to its establishment, kept an author, who was bound to furnish daily a quantum of witty paragraphs. Sixpence a joke—and it was thought pretty high too—was Dan Stuart's settled remuneration in these cases. The chat of the day—scandal, but, above all, *dress*

—furnished the material. The length of no paragraph was to exceed seven lines. Shorter they might be, but they must be poignant.

A fashion of *flesh*, or rather *pink*-coloured hose for the ladies luckily coming up at the juncture when we were on our probation for the place of Chief Jester to S.'s Paper, established our reputation in that line. We were pronounced a "capital hand." O the conceits which we varied upon *red* in all its prismatic differences! from the trite and obvious flower of Cytherea, to the flaming costume of the lady that has her sitting upon "many waters." Then there was the collateral topic of ankles. What an occasion to a truely chaste writer, like ourself, of touching that nice brink, and yet never tumbling over it, of a seemingly ever approximating something "not quite. proper;" while, like a skilful posturemaster, balancing betwixt decorums and their opposites, he keeps the line, from which a hair's-breadth deviation is destruction; hovering in the confines of light and darkness, or where "both seem either;" a lazy uncertain delicacy; Autolycus-like in the Play, still putting off his expectant auditory with "'Whoop,' do me no harm, good man!" But above all, that conceit arrided us most at that time, and still tickles our midriff to remember, where, allusively to the flight of Astræa—*ultima Cœlestûm terras reliquit*—we pronounced—in reference to the stockings still—that MODESTY, TAKING HER FINAL LEAVE OF MORTALS, HER LAST BLUSH WAS VISIBLE IN HER ASCENT TO THE HEAVENS BY THE TRACT OF THE GLOWING INSTEP. This might be called the crowning conceit: and was esteemed tolerable writing in those days.

But the fashion of jokes, with all other things, passes away; as did the transient mode which had so favoured us. The ankles of our fair friends in a few weeks began to reassume their whiteness, and left us scarce a leg to stand upon. Other female whims followed, but none, methought, so pregnant, so invitatory of shrewd conceits, and more than single meanings.

Somebody has said, that to swallow six cross-buns daily consecutively for a fortnight, would surfeit the stoutest digestion But to have to furnish as many jokes daily, and that not for a fortnight, but for a long twelvemonth, as we were constrained to do, was a little harder exaction. "Man goeth forth to his work until the evening"—from a reasonable hour in the morning, we presume it was meant. Now, as our main occupation took us up from eight till five every day in the City; and as our evening hours, at that time of life, had generally to do with anything rather than business, it follows, that the only time we could spare for this manufactory of jokes—our supplementary livelihood, that supplied us in every want beyond mere bread and cheese—was exactly that part of the day which (as we have heard of No Man's Land) may be fitly denominated No Man's Time; that is, no time in which a man ought to be up, and awake, in. To speak more plainly, it is that time of an hour, or an hour and a half's duration, in which a man, whose occasions call him up so preposterously, has to wait for his breakfast.

O those head-aches at dawn of day, when at five, or half-past five in summer, and not much later in the dark seasons, we were compelled to rise, having been perhaps not above four hours in bed—(for we were no go-to-beds with the lamb, though we anticipated the lark ofttimes in her rising—we like a parting cup at midnight, as all young men did before these effeminate times, and to have our friends about us— we were not constellated under Aquarius that watery sign, and therefore incapable of Bacchus, cold, washy, bloodless—we were none of your Basilian water-sponges, nor had taken our degrees at Mount Ague—we were right toping Capulets, jolly companions, we and they)—but to have to get up, as we said before, curtailed of half our fair sleep, fasting, with only a dim vista of refreshing bohea in the distance —to be necessitated to rouse ourselves at the detestable rap of an old bag of a domestic, who seemed to take a diabolical pleasure in her announcement, that it was "time to rise;" and whose chappy knuckles we have often yearned to amputate, and string them up at our chamber door, to be a terror to all such unseasonable rest-breakers in future——

"Facil" and sweet, as Virgil sings, had been the "descending" of the over-night, balmy the first sinking of the heavy head upon the pillow; but to get up, as he goes on to say,

—revocare gradus, superasque evadere ad auras—

and to get up, moreover, to make jokes with malice prepended— there was the "labour," there the "work."

No Egyptian taskmaster ever devised a slavery like to that, our slavery. No fractious operants ever turned out for half the tyranny which this necessity exercised upon us. Half a dozen jests in a day, (bating Sundays too,) why, it seems nothing! We make twice the number every day in our lives as a matter of course, and claim no Sabbatical exemptions. But then they come into our head. But when the head has to go out to them—when the mountain must go to Mahomet—

Reader, try it for once, only for a short twelvemonth.

It was not every week that a fashion of pink stockings came up; but mostly, instead of it, some rugged untractable subject; some topic impossible to be contorted into the risible; some feature, upon which no smile could play; some flint, from which no process of ingenuity could procure a scintillation. There they lay; there your appointed tale of brick-making was set before you, which you must finish, with or without straw, as it happened. The craving Dragon—*the Public*—like him in Bel's Temple—must be fed; it expected its daily rations; and Daniel, and ourselves, to do us justice, did the best we could on this side bursting him.

While we were wringing out coy sprightlinesses for the *Post*, and writhing under the toil of what is called "easy writing," Bob Allen, our *quondam* school-fellow, was tapping his impracticable brains in a like service for the *Oracle*. Not that Robert troubled himself much about wit. If his paragraphs had a sprightly air about them, it was sufficient. He carried this nonchalance so far at last, that a matter of intelligence, and that no very important one, was not seldom palmed upon his employers for a good jest; for example sake—"*Walking yesterday morning casually down Snow Hill, who should we meet but Mr. Deputy Humphreys! we rejoice to add, that the worthy Deputy appeared to enjoy a good state of health. We do not remember ever to have seen him look better.*" This gentleman so surprisingly met upon Snow Hill, from some peculiarities in gait or gesture, was a constant butt for mirth to the small paragraph-mongers of the day; and our friend thought that he might have his fling at him with the rest. We met A. in Holborn shortly after this extraordinary rencounter, which he told with tears of satisfaction in his eyes, and chuckling at the anticipated effects of its anouncement next day in the paper.

We did not quite comprehend where the wit of it lay at the time; nor was it easy to be detected, when the thing came out advantaged by type and letter-press. He had better have met anything that morning than a Common Council Man. His services were shortly after dispensed with, on the plea that his paragraphs of late had been deficient in point. The one in question, it must be owned, had an air, in the opening especially, proper to awaken curiosity; and the sentiment, or moral, wears the aspect of humanity and good neighbourly feeling. But somehow the conclusion was not judged altogether to answer to the magnificent promise of the premises. We traced our friend's pen afterwards in the *True Briton*, the *Star*, the *Traveller*,—from all which he was successively dismissed, the Proprietors having "no further occasion for his services." Nothing was easier than to detect him. When wit failed, or topics ran low, there constantly appeared the following—"*It is not generally known that the three Blue Balls at the Pawnbrokers' shops are the ancient arms of Lombardy. The Lombards were the first money-brokers in Europe.*" Bob has done more to set the public right on this important point of blazonry, than the whole College of Heralds.

The appointment of a regular wit has long ceased to be a part of the economy of a Morning Paper. Editors find their own jokes, or do as well without them. Parson Este, and Topham, brought up the set custom of "witty paragraphs" first in the *World*. Boaden was a reigning paragraphist in his day, and succeeded poor Allen in the *Oracle*. But, as we said, the fashion of jokes passes away; and it would be difficult to discover in the biographer of Mrs. Siddons, any traces of that vivacity and fancy which charmed the whole town at the commencement of the present century. Even the prelusive delicacies of the present writer—the curt "Astræan allusion"—would be thought pedantic and out of date, in these days.

From the office of the *Morning Post* (for we may as well exhaust our Newspaper Reminiscences at once) by change of property in the paper, we were transferred, mortifying exchange! to the office of the *Albion* Newspaper, late Rackstrow's Museum, in Fleet Street. What a transition—from a handsome apartment, from rosewood desks and silver inkstands, to an office—no office, but a *den* rather, but just redeemed from the occupation of dead monsters, of which it seemed redolent—from the centre of loyalty and fashion, to a focus of vulgarity and sedition! Here in murky closet, inadequate from its square contents to the receipt of the two bodies of Editor and humble paragraph-maker, together at one time, sat in the discharge of his new editorial functions (the "Bigod" of Elia) the redoubted John Fenwick.

F., without a guinea in his pocket, and having left not many in the pockets of his friends whom he might command, had purchased (on tick, doubtless) the whole and sole Editorship, Proprietorship, with all the rights and titles (such as they were worth) of the *Albion* from one Lovell; of whom we know nothing, save that he had stood in the pillory for a libel on the Prince of Wales. With this hopeless concern—for it had been sinking ever since its commencement, and could now reckon upon not more than a hundred subscribers—F. resolutely determined upon pulling down the Government in the first instance, and making both our fortunes by way of corollary. For seven weeks and more did this infatuated democrat go about borrowing seven-shilling pieces, and lesser coin, to meet the daily demands of the Stamp Office, which allowed no credit to publications of that side in politics. An outcast from politer bread, we attached our small talents to the forlorn fortunes of our friend. Our occupation now was to write treason.

Recollections of feelings—which were all that now remained from our first boyish heats kindled by the French Revolution, when, if we were misled, we erred in the company of some who are accounted very good men now—rather than any tendency at this time to Republican doctrines—assisted us in assuming a style of writing, while the paper lasted, consonant in no very undertone to the right earnest fanaticism of F. Our cue was now to insinuate, rather than recommend, possible abdications. Blocks, axes, Whitehall tribunals, were covered with flowers of so cunning a periphrasis—as Mr. Bayes says, never naming the *thing* directly—that the keen eye of an Attorney-General was insufficient to detect the lurking snake among them. There were times, indeed, when we sighed for our more gentleman-like occupation under Stuart. But with change of masters it is ever change of service. Already one paragraph, and another, as we learned afterwards from a gentleman at the Treasury, had begun to be marked at that office, with a view of its being submitted at least to the attention of the proper Law Officers—when an unlucky, or rather lucky epigram from our pen, aimed at Sir J——s M——h, who was on the eve of departing for India to reap the fruits of his apostacy, as F. pronounced it, (it is hardly worth particularizing,) happening to offend the nice sense of Lord (or, as he then delighted to be called Citizen) Stanhope, deprived F. at once of the last hopes of a guinea from the last patron that had stuck by us; and breaking up our establishment, left us to the safe, but somewhat mortifying, neglect of the Crown Lawyers. It was about this time, or a little earlier, that Dan Stuart made that curious confession to us, that he had "never deliberately walked into an Exhibition at Somerset House in his life."

BARRENNESS OF THE IMAGINATIVE FACULTY IN THE PRODUCTIONS OF MODERN ART.

HOGARTH excepted, can we produce any one painter within the last fifty years, or since the humour of exhibiting began, that has treated a story *imaginatively?* By this we mean, upon whom his subject has so acted, that it has seemed to direct *him*—not to be arranged by him? Any upon whom its leading or collateral points have impressed themselves so tyrannically, that he dared not treat it otherwise, lest he should falsify a revelation? Any that has imparted to his compositions, not merely so much truth as is enough to convey a story with clearness, but that individualizing property, which should keep the subject so treated distinct in feature from every other subject, however similar, and to common apprehensions almost identical; so that we might say, this and this part could have found an appropriate place in no other picture in the world but this? Is there anything in modern art—we will not demand that it should be equal—but in any way analogous to what Titian has effected,

15*

in that wonderful bringing to-gether of two times in the "Ariadne," in the National Gallery? Precipitous, with his reeling satyr rout about him, re-peopling and re-illuming suddenly the waste places, drunk with a new fury beyond the grape, Bacchus, born in fire, fire-like flings himself at the Cretan. This is the time present. With this telling of the story, an artist, and no ordinary one, might remain richly proud. Guido, in his harmonious version of it, saw no farther. But from the depths of the imaginative spirit Titian has recalled past time, and laid it contributory with the present to one simultaneous effect. With the desert all ringing with the mad cymbals of his followers, made lucid with the presence and new offers of a god,—as if unconscious of Bacchus, or but idly casting her eyes as upon some unconcerning pageant—her soul undistracted from Theseus—Ariadne is still pacing the solitary shore in as much heart-silence, and in almost the same local solitude, with which she awoke at day-break to catch the forlorn last glances of the sail that bore away the Athenian.

Here are two points miraculously co-uniting; fierce society, with the feeling of solitude still absolute; noon-day revelations, with the accidents of the dull grey dawn unquenched and lingering; the *present* Bacchus, with the *past* Ariadne: two stories, with double Time; separate, and harmonizing.

Had the artist made the woman one shade less indifferent to the God; still more, had she expressed a rapture at his advent, where would have been the story of the mighty desolation of the heart previous? merged in the insipid accident of a flattering offer met with a welcome acceptance. The broken heart for Theseus was not likely to be pieced up by a God.

We have before us a fine rough print, from a picture by Raphael in the Vatican. It is the Presentation of the new-born Eve to Adam by the Almighty. A fairer mother of mankind we might imagine, and a goodlier sire perhaps of men since born. But these are matters subordinate to the conception of the *situation*, displayed in this extraordinary production. A tolerable modern artist would have been satisfied with tempering certain raptures of connubial anticipation, with a suitable acknowledgment to the Giver of the blessing, in the countenance of the first bridegroom: something like the divided attention of the child (Adam was here a child-man) between the given toy, and the mother who had just blest it with the bauble. This is the obvious, the first-sight view, the superficial. An artist of a higher grade, considering the awful presence they were in, would have taken care to subtract something from the expression of the more human passion, and to heighten the more spiritual one. This would be as much as an exhibition-goer, from the opening of Somerset House to last year's show, has been encouraged to look for. It is obvious to hint at a lower expression yet, in a picture that, for respects of drawing and colouring, might be deemed not wholly inadmissible within these art-fostering walls, in which the raptures should be as ninety-nine, the gratitude as one, or perhaps zero! By neither the one passion nor the other has Raphael expounded the situation of Adam. Singly upon his brow sits the absorbing sense of wonder at the created miracle. The *moment* is seized by the intuitive artist, perhaps not self-conscious of his art, in which neither of the conflicting emotions—a moment how abstracted!—have had time to spring up, or to battle for indecorous mastery.—We have seen a landscape of a justly-admired neoteric, in which he aimed at delineating a fiction, one of the most severely beautiful in antiquity—the gardens of the Hesperides. To do Mr. —— justice, he had painted a laudable orchard, with fitting seclusion, and a veritable dragon (of which a Polypheme, by Poussin, is somehow a fac-simile for the situation), looking over into the world shut out backwards, so that none but a "still-climbing Hercules" could hope to catch a peep at the admired Ternary of Recluses. No conventual porter could keep his keys better than this custos with the "lidless eyes." He not only sees that none *do* intrude into that privacy, but, as clear as daylight, that none but *Hercules aut Diabolus* by any

manner of means *can*. So far all is well. We have absolute solitude here or nowhere. *Ab extra*, the damsels are snug enough. But here the artist's courage seems to have failed him. He began to pity his pretty charge, and, to comfort the irksomeness, has peopled their solitude with a bevy of fair attendants, maids of honour, or ladies of the bed-chamber, according to the approved etiquette at a court of the nineteenth century; giving to the whole scene the air of a *fête-champêtre*, if we will but excuse the absence of the gentlemen. This is well, and Watteauish. But what is become of the solitary mystery—the

Daughters three,
That sing around the golden tree?

This is not the way in which Poussin would have treated this subject.

The paintings, or rather the stupendous architectural designs, of a modern artist, have been urged as objections to the theory of our motto. They are of a character, we confess, to stagger it. His towered structures are of the highest order of the material sublime. Whether they were dreams, or transcripts of some elder workmanship—Assyrian ruins old—restored by this mighty artist, they satisfy our most stretched and craving conceptions of the glories of the antique world. It is a pity that they were ever peopled. On that side, the imagination of the artist halts, and appears defective. Let us examine the point of the story in the "Belshazzar's Feast." We will introduce it by an apposite anecdote.

The court historians of the day record, that at the first dinner given by the late King (then Prince Regent) at the Pavilion, the following characteristic frolic was played off. The guests were select and admiring; the banquet profuse and admirable; the lights lustrous and oriental; the eye was perfectly dazzled with the display of plate, among which the great gold salt-cellar, brought from the regalia in the Tower for this especial purpose, itself a tower! stood conspicuous for its magnitude. And now the Rev. * * *, the then admired court Chaplain, was proceeding with the grace, when, at a signal given, the lights were suddenly overcast, and a huge transparency was discovered, in which glittered in gold letters—

"BRIGHTON—EARTHQUAKE— SWALLOW-UP-ALIVE!"

Imagine the confusion of the guests; the Georges and garters, jewels, bracelets, moulted upon the occasion! The fans dropped, and picked up the next morning by the sly court-pages! Mrs. Fitz-what's-her-name fainting, and the Countess of *** holding the smelling-bottle, till the good-humoured Prince caused harmony to be restored, by calling in fresh candles, and declaring that the whole was nothing but a pantomime *hoax*, got up by the ingenious Mr. Farley, of Covent Garden, from hints which his Royal Highness himself had furnished! Then imagine the infinite applause that followed, the mutual rallyings, the declarations that "they were not much frightened," of the assembled galaxy.

The point of time in the picture exactly answers to the appearance of the transparency in the anecdote. The huddle, the flutter, the bustle, the escape, the alarm, and the mock alarm; the prettinesses heightened by consternation; the courtier's fear which was flattery; and the lady's which was affectation; all that we may conceive to have taken place in a mob of Brighton courtiers, sympathizing with the well-acted surprise of their sovereign; all this, and no more, is exhibited by the well-dressed lords and ladies in the Hall of Belus. Just this sort of consternation we have seen among a flock of disquieted wild geese at the report only of a gun having gone off!

But is this vulgar fright, this mere animal anxiety for the preservation of their persons—such as we have witnessed at a theatre, when a slight alarm of fire has been given—an adequate exponent of a supernatural terror? the way in which the finger of God, writing judgments, would have been met by the withered conscience? There is a human fear, and a divine fear. The one is disturbed, restless, and bent upon escape; the other is bowed down, effortless, passive. When the spirit appeared before Eliphaz in the visions of the night, and the hair of his flesh stood up, was it in the thoughts of the Temanite to ring the bell of his chamber, or to call up the servants? But let us see in the text what there is to justify all this huddle of vulgar consternation.

From the words of Daniel it appears that Belshazzar had made a great feast to a thousand of his lords, and drank wine before the thousand. The golden and silver vessels are gorgeously enumerated, with the princes, the king's concubines, and his wives. Then follows—

"In the same hour came forth fingers of a man's hand, and wrote over against the candlestick upon the plaster of the wall of the king's palace; and the *king* saw the part of the hand that wrote. Then the *king's* countenance was changed, and his thoughts troubled him, so that the joints of his loins were loosened, and his knees smote one against another."

This is the plain text. By no hint can it be otherwise inferred, but that the appearance was solely confined to the fancy of Belshazzar, that his single brain was troubled. Not a word is spoken of its being seen by any else there present, not even by the queen herself, who merely undertakes for the interpretation of the phenomenon, as related to her, doubtless, by her husband. The lords are simply said to be astonished; *i. e.* at the trouble and the change of countenance in their sovereign. Even the prophet does not appear to have seen the scroll, which the king saw. He recalls it only, as Joseph did the Dream to the King of Egypt. "Then was the part of the hand sent from him [the Lord], and this writing was written." He speaks of the phantasm as past.

Then what becomes of this needless multiplication of the miracle? this message to a royal conscience, singly expressed—for it was said, "Thy kingdom is divided,"—simultaneously impressed upon the fancies of a thousand courtiers, who were implied in it neither directly nor grammatically?

But, admitting the artist's own version of the story, and that the sight was seen also by the thousand courtiers—let it have been visible to all Babylon—as the knees of Belshazzar were shaken, and his countenance troubled, even so would the knees of every man in Babylon, and their countenances, as of an individual man, have been troubled; bowed, bent down, so would they have remained, stupor-fixed, with no thought of struggling with that inevitable judgment.

Not all that is optically possible to be seen, is to be shown in every picture. The eye delightedly dwells upon the brilliant individualities in a "Marriage at Cana," by Veronese, or Titian, to the very texture and colour of the wedding garments, the ring glittering upon the bride's finger, the metal and fashion of the wine-pots; for at such seasons there is leisure and luxury to be curious. But in a "day of judgment," or in a "day of lesser horrors, yet divine," as at the impious feast of Belshazzar, the eye should see, as the actual eye of an agent or patient in the immediate scene would see, only in masses and indistinction. Not only the female attire and jewelry exposed to the critical eye of the fashion, as minutely as the dresses in a Lady's Magazine, in the criticised picture —but perhaps the curiosities of anatomical science, and studied diversities of posture, in the falling angels and sinners of Michael Angelo,—have no business in their great subjects. There was no leisure for them.

By a wise falsification, the great masters of painting got at their true conclusions; by not showing the actual appearances, that is, all that was to be seen at any given moment by an indifferent eye, but only what the eye might be supposed to see in the doing or suffering of some portentous action. Suppose the moment of the swallowing up of Pompeii. There they were to be seen— houses, columns, architectural proportions, differences of public and private buildings, men and women at their standing occupations, the diversified thousand postures, attitudes, dresses, in some confusion truly, but physically they were visible. But what eye saw them at that eclipsing moment, which reduces confusion to a kind of unity, and when the senses are upturned from their proprieties, when sight and hearing are a feeling only? A thousand years have passed, and we are at leisure to contemplate the weaver fixed standing at his shuttle, the baker at his oven, and to turn over with antiquarian coolness the pots and pans of Pompeii.

"Sun, stand thou still upon Gibeon, and thou, Moon, in the valley of Ajalon." Who, in reading this magnificent Hebraism, in his conception, sees aught but the heroic son of Nun, with the outstretched arm, and the greater and lesser light obsequious? Doubtless there were to be seen hill and dale, and chariots and horsemen, on open plain, or winding by secret defiles, and all the circumstances and stratagems of war. But whose eyes would have been conscious of this array at the interposition of the synchronic miracle? Yet in the picture of this subject by the artist of the "Belshazzar's Feast"—no ignoble work, either—the marshalling and landscape of the war is everything, the miracle sinks into an anecdote of the day; and the eye may "dart through rank and file traverse" for some minutes, before it shall discover, among his armed followers, *which is Joshua!* Not modern art alone, but ancient, where only it is to be found if anywhere, can be detected erring, from defect of this imaginative faculty. The world has nothing to show of the preternatural in painting, transcending the figure of Lazarus bursting his graveclothes, in the great picture at Angerstein's. It seems a thing between two beings. A ghastly horror at itself struggles with newly-apprehending gratitude at second life bestowed. It cannot forget that it was a ghost. It has hardly felt that it is a body. It has to tell of the world of spirits. —Was it from a feeling, that the crowd of half-impassioned by-standers, and the still more irrelevant herd of passers-by at a distance, who have not heard, or but faintly have been told of the passing miracle, admirable as they are in design and hue—for it is a glorified work—do not respond adequately to the action—that the single figure of the Lazarus has been attributed to Michael Angelo, and the mighty Sebastian unfairly robbed of the fame of the greater half of the interest? Now that there were not indifferent passers-by within actual scope of the eyes of those present at the miracle, to whom the sound of it had but faintly, or not at all, reached, it would be hardihood to deny; but would they see them? or can the mind in the conception of it admit of such unconcerning objects; can it think of them at all? or what associating league to the imagination can there be between the seers and the seers not, of a presential miracle?

Were an artist to paint upon demand a picture of a Dryad, we will ask whether, in the present low state of expectation, the patron would not, or ought not be fully satisfied with a beautiful naked figure recumbent under wide-stretched oaks? Dis-seat those woods, and place the same figure among fountains, and falls of pellucid water, and you have a—Naïad! Not so in a rough print we have seen after Julio Romano, we think—for it is long since—there, by no process, with mere change of scene, could the figure have reciprocated characters. Long, grotesque, fantastic, yet with a grace of her own, beautiful in convolution and distortion, linked to her connatural tree, co-twisting with its limbs her own, till both seemed either —these, animated branches; those, disanimated members—yet the animal and vegetable lives sufficiently kept distinct—his Dryad lay—an approximation of two natures, which to conceive, it must be seen; analogous to, not the same with, the delicacies of Ovidian transformations.

To the lowest subjects, and, to a superficial comprehension, the most barren, the Great Masters gave loftiness and fruitfulness. The large eye of genius saw in the meanness of present objects their capabilities of treatment from their relations to some grand Past or Future. How has Raphael —we must still linger about the Vatican—treated the humble craft of the ship-builder, in his "Building of the Ark?" It is in that scriptural series, to which we have referred, and which, judging from some fine rough old graphic sketches of them which we possess, seem to be of a higher and more poetic grade than even the Cartoons. The dim of sight are the timid and the shrinking.

There is a cowardice in modern art. As the Frenchman, of whom Coleridge's friend made the prophetic guess at Rome, from the beard and horns of the Moses of Michael Angelo collected no inferences beyond that of a He Goat and a Cornuto; so from this subject, of mere mechanic promise, it would instinctively turn away, as from one incapable of investiture with any grandeur. The dock-yards at Woolwich would object derogatory associations. The depôt at Chatham would be the mote and the beam in its intellectual eye. But not to the nautical preparations in the ship-yards of Civita Vecchia did Raphael look for instructions, when he imagined the building of the Vessel that was to be conservatory of the wrecks of the species of drowned mankind. In the intensity of the action he keeps ever out of sight the meanness of the operation. There is the Patriarch, in calm forethought, and with holy prescience, giving directions. And there are his agents—the solitary but sufficient Three—hewing, sawing, every one with the might and earnestness of a Demiurgus; under some instinctive rather than technical guidance! giant-muscled; every one a Hercules; or liker to those Vulcanian Three, that in sounding caverns under Mongibello wrought in fire— Brontes, and black Steropes, and Pyracmon. So work the workmen that should repair a world!

Artists again err in the confounding of *poetic* with *pictorial subjects*. In the latter, the exterior accidents are nearly everything, the unseen qualities as nothing. Othello's colour—the infirmities and corpulence of a Sir John Falstaff—do they haunt us perpetually in the reading? or are they obtruded upon our conceptions one time for ninety-nine that we are lost in admiration at the respective moral or intellectual attributes of the character? But in a picture Othello is *always* a Blackamoor; and the other only Plump Jack. Deeply corporealized, and enchained hopelessly in the grovelling fetters of externality, must be the mind, to which, in its better moments, the image of the high-souled, high-intelligenced Quixote —the errant Star of Knighthood, made more tender by eclipse— has never presented itself divested from the unhallowed accompaniment of a Sancho, or a rabblement at the heels of Rosinante. That man has read his book by halves; he has laughed, mistaking his author's purport, which was —tears. The artist that pictures Quixote (and it is in this degrading point that he is every season held up at our Exhibitions) in the shallow hope of exciting mirth, would have joined the rabble at the heels of his starved steed. We wish not to see *that* counterfeited, which we would not have wished to see in the reality. Conscious of the heroic inside of the noble Quixote, who, on hearing that his withered person was passing, would have stepped over his threshold to gaze upon his forlorn habiliments, and the "strange bed-fellows which misery brings a man acquainted with?" Shade of Cervantes! who in thy Second Part could put into the mouth of thy Quixote those high aspirations of a super-chivalrous gallantry, where he replies to one of the shepherdesses, apprehensive that he would spoil their pretty net-works, and inviting him to be a guest with them, in accents like these: "Truly, fairest Lady, Actæon was not more astonished when he saw Diana bathing herself at the fountain, than I have been in beholding your beauty: I commend the manner of your pastime, and thank you for your kind offers; and, if I may serve you, so I may be sure you will be obeyed, you may command me: for my profession is this, To show myself thankful, and a doer of good to all sorts of people, especially of the rank that your person shows you to be; and if those nets, as they take up but a little piece of ground, should take up the whole world, I would seek out new worlds to pass through, rather than break them: and (he adds) that you may give credit to this my exaggeration, behold at least he that promiseth you this, is Don Quixote de la Mancha, if haply this name hath come to your hearing." Illustrious Romancer! were the "fine frenzies," which possessed the brain of thy own Quixote, a fit subject, as in this Second Part, to be exposed to the jeers of Duennas and Serving-men? to be monstered, and shown up at the heartless banquets of *great men?* Was that pitiable infirmity, which in thy First Part misleads him, *always from within*, into half-ludicrous, but more than half-compassionable and admirable errors, not infliction enough from heaven, that men by studied artifices must devise and practise upon the humour, to inflame where they should soothe it? Why, Goneril would have blushed to practise upon the abdicated king at this rate, and the she-wolf Regan not have endured to play the pranks upon his fled wits, which thou hast made thy Quixote suffer in Duchesses' halls, and at the hands of that unworthy nobleman.*

In the First Adventures, even, it needed all the art of the most consummate artist in the Book way that the world hath yet seen, to keep up in the mind of the reader the heroic attributes of the character without relaxing; so as absolutely that they shall suffer no alloy from the debasing fellowship of the clown. If it ever obtrudes itself as a disharmony, are we inclined to laugh; or not, rather, to indulge a contrary emotion?—Cervantes, stung, perchance, by the relish with which *his* Reading Public had received the fooleries of the man, more to their palates than the generosities

* Yet from this Second Part, our cried-up pictures are mostly selected; the waiting-women with beards, &c.

of the master, in the sequel let his pen run riot, lost the harmony and the balance, and sacrificed a great idea to the taste of his contemporaries. We know that in the present day the Knight has fewer admirers than the Squire. Anticipating, what did actually happen to him—as afterwards it did to his scarce inferior follower, the Author of "Guzman de Alfarache"—that some less knowing hand would prevent him by a spurious Second Part; and judging that it would be easier for his competitor to outbid him in the *comicalities*, than in the *romance*, of his work, he abandoned his Knight, and has fairly set up the Squire for his Hero. For what else has he unsealed the eyes of Sancho? and instead of that twilight state of semi-insanity—the madness at second-hand—the contagion, caught from a stronger mind infected—that war between native cunning, and hereditary deference, with which he has hitherto accompanied his master—two for a pair almost—does he substitute a downright Knave, with open eyes, for his own ends only following a confessed Madman; and offering at one time to lay, if not actually laying, hands upon him! From the moment that Sancho loses his reverence, Don Quixote is become—a treatable lunatic. Our artists handle him accordingly.

———

THE WEDDING.

I do not know when I have been better pleased than at being invited last week to be present at the wedding of a friend's daughter. I like to make one at these ceremonies, which to us old people give back our youth in a manner, and restore our gayest season, in the remembrance of our own success, or the regrets, scarcely less tender, of our own youthful disappointments, in this point of a settlement. On these occasions I am sure to be in good-humour for a week or two after, and enjoy a reflected honeymoon. Being without a family, I am flattered with these temporary adoptions into a friend's family; I feel a sort of cousinhood, or uncleship, for the season; I am inducted into degrees of affinity; and, in the participated socialities of the little community, I lay down for a brief while my solitary bachelorship. I carry this humour so far, that I take it unkindly to be left out, even when a funeral is going on in the house of a dear friend. But to my subject.——

The union itself had been long settled, but its celebration had been hitherto deferred, to an almost unreasonable state of suspense in the lovers, by some invincible prejudices which the bride's father had unhappily contracted upon the subject of the too early marriages of females. He has been lecturing any time these five years—for to that length the courtship had been protracted—upon the propriety of putting off the solemnity, till the lady should have completed her five-and-twentieth year. We all began to be afraid that a suit, which as yet had abated of none of its ardours,. might at last be lingered on, till passion had time to cool, and love go out in the experiment. But a little wheedling on the part of his wife, who was by no means a party to these overstrained notions, joined to some serious expostulations on that of his friends, who, from the growing infirmities of the old gentleman, could not promise ourselves many years' enjoyment of his company, and were anxious to bring matters to a conclusion during his lifetime, at length prevailed; and on Monday last the daughter of my old friend, Admiral——, having attained the *womanly* age of nineteen, was conducted to the church by her pleasant cousin J——, who told some few years older.

Before the youthful part of my female readers express their indignation at the abominable loss of time occasioned to the lovers by the preposterous notions of my old friend, they will do well to consider the reluctance which a fond parent naturally feels at parting with his child. To this unwillingness, I believe, in most cases may be traced the difference of opinion on this point between child and parent, whatever pretences of interest or prudence may be held out to cover it. The hard-heartedness of fathers is a fine theme for romance writers, a sure and moving topic; but is there not something untender, to say no more of it, in the hurry which a beloved child is sometimes in to tear herself from the paternal stock, and commit herself to strange graftings? The case is heightened where the lady, as in the present instance, happens to be an only child. I do not understand these matters experimentally, but I can make a shrewd guess at the wounded pride of a parent upon these occasions. It is no new observation, I believe, that a lover in most cases has no rival so much to be feared as the father. Certainly there is a jealousy in *unparallel subjects*, which is little less heartrending than the passion which we more strictly christen by that name. Mothers' scruples are more easily got over; for this reason, I suppose, that the protection transferred to a husband is less a derogation and a loss to their authority than to the paternal. Mothers, besides, have a trembling foresight, which paints the inconveniences (impossible to be conceived in the same degree by the other parent) of a life of forlorn celibacy, which the refusal of a tolerable match may entail upon their child. Mothers' instinct is a surer guide here than the cold reasonings of a father on such a topic. To this instinct may be imputed, and by it alone may be excused, the unbeseeming artifices, by which some wives push on the matrimonial projects of their daughters, which the husband, however approving, shall entertain with comparative indifference. A little shamelessness on this head is pardonable. With this explanation, forwardness becomes a grace, and maternal importunity receives the name of a virtue.—But the parson stays, while I preposterously assume his office; I am preaching, while the bride is on the threshold.

Nor let any of my female readers suppose that the sage reflections which have just escaped me have the obliquest tendency of application to the young lady, who, it will be seen, is about to venture upon a change in her condition, at a *mature and competent age*, and not without the fullest approbation of all parties. I only deprecate *very hasty marriages*.

It had been fixed that the ceremony should be gone through at an early hour, to give time for a little *déjeûné* afterwards, to which a select party of friends had been invited. We were in church a little before the clock struck eight.

Nothing could be more judicious or graceful than the dress of the bride-maids—the three charming Miss Foresters—on this morning. To give the bride an opportunity of shining singly, they had come habited all in green. I am ill at describing female apparel; but while *she* stood at the altar in vestments white and candid as her thoughts, a sacrificial whiteness, *they* assisted in robes such as might become Diana's nymphs—Foresters indeed—as such who had not yet come to the resolution of putting off cold virginity. These young maids, not being so blest as to have a mother living, I am told, keep single for their father's sake, and live altogether so happy with their remaining parent, that the hearts of their lovers are ever broken with the prospect (so inauspicious to their hopes) of such uninterrupted and provoking home-comfort. Gallant girls! each a victim worthy of Iphigenia!

I do not know what business I have to be present in solemn places. I cannot divest me of an unseasonable disposition to levity upon the most awful occasions. I was never cut out for a public functionary. Ceremony and I have long shaken hands; but I could not resist the importunities of the young lady's father, whose gout unhappily confined him at home, to act as parent on this occasion, and *give away the bride.* Something ludicrous occurred to me at this most serious of all moments—a sense of my unfitness to have the disposal, even in imagination, of the sweet young creature beside me. I fear I was betrayed to some lightness, for the awful eye of the parson—and the rector's eye of Saint Mildred's in the Poultry is no trifle of a rebuke—was upon me in an instant, souring my incipient jest to the tristful severities of a funeral.

This was the only misbehaviour which I can plead to upon this solemn occasion, unless what was objected to me after the ceremony,

by one of the handsome Miss
T——s, be accounted a solecism.
She was pleased to say that she
had never seen a gentleman before me give away a bride, in
black. Now black has been my
ordinary apparel so long—indeed,
I take it to be the proper costume
of an author—the stage sanctions
it—that to have appeared in some
lighter colour would have raised
more mirth at my expense than
the anomaly had created censure.
But I could perceive that the
bride's mother, and some elderly
ladies present (God bless them!)
would have been well content, if
I had come in any other colour
than that. But I got over the
omen by a lucky apologue, which
I remembered out of Pilpay, or
some Indian author, of all the
birds being invited to the linnet's
wedding, at which, when all the
rest came in their gayest feathers,
the raven alone apologised for his
cloak because "he had no other."
This tolerably reconciled the
elders. But with the young people
all was merriment, and shaking
of hands, and congratulations,
and kissing away the bride's
tears, and kissing from her in return, till a young lady, who assumed some experience in these
matters, having worn the nuptial
bands some four or five weeks
longer than her friend, rescued
her, archly observing, with half
an eye upon the bridegroom, that
at this rate she would have "none
left."

My friend the Admiral was in
fine wig and buckle on this occasion—a striking contrast to his
usual neglect of personal appearance. He did not once shove up
his borrowed locks (his custom
ever at his morning studies) to
betray the few grey stragglers of
his own beneath them. He wore
an aspect of thoughtful satisfaction. I trembled for the hour,
which at length approached, when
after a protracted *breakfast* of
three hours—if stores of cold
fowls, tongues, hams, botargoes,
dried fruits, wines, cordials, &c.,
can deserve so meagre an appellation—the coach was announced,
which was come to carry off the
bride and bridegroom a for season,
as custom has sensibly ordained,
into the country; upon which design, wishing them a felicitous
journey, let us return to the assembled guests.

As when a well-graced actor leaves the
    stage,
The eyes of men
Are idly bent on him that enters next,

so idly did we bend our eyes upon
one another, when the chief per-
formers in the morning's pageant
had vanished. None told his tale.
None sipped her glass. The poor
Admiral made an effort—it was
not much. I had anticipated so
far. Even the infinity of full satisfaction, that had betrayed itself
through the prim looks and quiet
deportment of his lady, began to
wane into something of misgiving.
No one knew whether to take their
leave or stay. We seemed assembled upon a silly occasion. In
this crisis, betwixt tarrying and
departure, I must do justice to a

foolish talent of mine, which had otherwise like to have brought me into disgrace in the fore-part of the day; I mean a power, in any emergency, of thinking and giving vent to all manner of strange nonsense. In this awkward dilemma I found it sovereign. I rattled off some of my most excellent absurdities. All were willing to be relieved, at any expense of reason, from the pressure of the intolerable vacuum which had succeeded to the morning bustle. By this means I was fortunate in keeping together the better part of the company to a late hour; and a rubber of whist (the Admiral's favourite game) with some rare strokes of chance as well as skill, which came opportunely on his side—lengthened out till midnight—dismissed the old gentleman at last to his bed with comparatively easy spirits.

I have been at my old friend's various times since. I do not know a visiting place where every guest is so perfectly at his ease; nowhere, where harmony is so strangely the result of confusion. Everybody is at cross purposes, yet the effect is so much better than uniformity. Contradictory orders; servants pulling one way; master and mistress driving some other, yet both diverse; visitors huddled up in corners; chairs unsymmetrized; candles disposed by chance; meals at odd hours, tea and supper at once, or the latter preceding the former; the host and the guest conferring, yet each upon a different topic, each understanding himself, neither trying to understand or hear the other; draughts and politics, chess and political economy, cards and conversation on nautical matters, going on at once, without the hope, or indeed the wish, of distinguishing them, make it altogether the most perfect *concordia discors* you shall meet with. Yet somehow the old house is not quite what it should be. The Admiral still enjoys his pipe, but he has no Miss Emily to fill it for him. The instrument stands where it stood, but she is gone, whose delicate touch could sometimes for a short minute appease the warring elements. He has learnt, as Marvel expresses it, to "make his destiny his choice." He bears bravely up, but he does not come out with his flashes of wild wit so thick as formerly. His sea-songs seldomer escape him. His wife, too, looks as if she wanted some younger body to scold and set to rights. Well all miss a junior presence. It is wonderful how one young maiden freshens up, and keeps green, the paternal roof. Old and young seem to have an interest in her, so long as she is not absolutely disposed of. The youthfulness of the house is flown. Emily is married.

———

REJOICINGS UPON THE NEW YEAR'S COMING OF AGE.

THE *Old Year* being dead, and the *New Year* coming of age, which he does, by Calendar Law, as soon as the breath is out of the old gentleman's body, nothing would serve the young spark but he must give a dinner upon the occasion, to which all the *Days* in the year were invited. The *Festivals*, whom he deputed as his stewards, were mightily taken with the notion. They had been engaged time out of mind, they said, in providing mirth and good cheer for mortals below; and it was time they should have a taste of their own bounty. It was stiffly debated among them whether the *Fasts* should be admitted. Some said the appearance of such lean, starved guests, with their mortified faces, would pervert the ends of the meeting. But the objection was overruled by *Christmas Day*, who had a design upon *Ash Wednesday* (as you shall hear), and a mighty desire to see how the old Domine would behave himself in his cups. Only the *Vigils* were requested to come with their lanterns, to light the gentlefolks home at night.

All the *Days* came to their day. Covers were provided for three hundred and sixty-five guests at the principal table; with an occasional knife and fork at the sideboard for the *Twenty-Ninth of February*.

I should have told you that cards of invitation had been issued. The carriers were the *Hours*; twelve little, merry, whirligig foot-pages, as you should desire to see, that went all round, and found out the persons invited well enough, with the exception of *Easter Day*, *Shrove Tuesday*, and a few such *Moveables*, who had lately shifted their quarters.

Well, they all met at last—foul *Days*, fine *Days*, all sorts of *Days*, and a rare din they made of it. There was nothing but, Hail! fellow *Day*, well met—brother *Day* —sister *Day*—only *Lady Day* kept a little on the aloof, and seemed somewhat scornful. Yet some said *Twelfth Day* cut her out and out, for she came in a tiffany suit, white and gold, like a queen on a frost-cake, all royal, glittering, and *Epiphanous*. The rest came, some in green, some in white— but old *Lent and his family* were not yet out of mourning. Rainy *Days* came in, dripping; and sunshiny *Days* helped them to change their stockings. *Wedding Day* was there in his marriage finery, a little the worse for wear. *Pay Day* came late, as he always does; and *Doomsday* sent word—he might be expected.

April Fool (as my young lord's jester) took upon himself to marshal the guests, and wild work he made with it. It would have posed old Erra Pater to have found out any given *Day* in the year to erect a scheme upon— good *Days*, bad *Days*, were so shuffled together, to the confounding of all sober horoscopy.

He had stuck the *Twenty-First of June* next to the *Twenty-Second of December*, and the former looked like a Maypole siding a marrow-bone. *Ash Wednesday* got wedged in (as was concerted) betwixt *Christmas* and *Lord Mayor's Days*. Lord! how he laid about him! Nothing but barons of beef and turkeys would go down with him —to the great greasing and detriment of his new sackcloth bib and tucker. And still *Christmas Day* was at his elbow, plying him with the wassail-bowl, till he roared, and hiccupp'd, and protested there was no faith in dried ling, but commended it to the devil for a sour, windy, acrimonious, censorious, hy-po-crit-crit-critical mess, and no dish for a gentleman. Then he dipt his fist into the middle of the great custard that stood before his *left-hand neighbour*, and daubed his hungry beard all over with it, till you would have taken him for the *Last Day in December*, it so hung in icicles.

At another part of the table, *Shrove Tuesday* was helping the *Second of September* to some cock broth,—which courtesy the latter returned with the delicate thigh of a hen pheasant—so that there was no love lost for that matter. The *Last of Lent* was spunging upon *Shrovetide's* pancakes; which *April Fool* perceiving, told him that he did well, for pancakes were proper to a *good fry-day*.

In another part, a hubbub arose about the *Thirtieth of January*, who, it seems, being a sour, puritonic character, that thought no-body's meat good or sanctified enough for him, had smuggled into the room a calf's head, which he had had cooked at home for that purpose, thinking to feast thereon incontinently; but as it lay in the dish, *March Many-weathers*, who is a very fine lady, and subject to the meagrims, screamed out there was a "human head in the platter," and raved about Herodias' daughter to that degree, that the obnoxious viand was obliged to be removed; nor did she recover her stomach till she had gulped down a *Restora-tive*, confected of *Oak Apple*, which the merry *Twenty-Ninth of May* always carries about with him for that purpose.

The King's health [*] being called for after this, a notable dispute arose between the *Twelfth of August* (a zealous old Whig gentlewoman) and the *Twenty-Third of April* (a new-fangled lady of the Tory stamp), as to which of them should have the honour to propose it. *August* grew hot upon the matter, affirming time out of mind the prescriptive right to have lain with her, till her rival had basely supplanted her; whom she represented as little better than a *kept* mistress, who went about in *fine clothes*, while she (the legitimate BIRTHDAY) had scarcely a rag, &c.

April Fool, being made mediator, confirmed the right, in the strongest form of words, to the appellant, but decided for peace'

[*] King George IV.

sake, that the exercise of it should remain with the present possessor. At the same time, he slyly rounded the first lady in the ear, that an action might lie against the Crown for *bi-geny*.

It beginning to grow a little duskish, *Candlemas* lustily bawled out for lights, which was opposed by all the *Days*, who protested against burning daylight. Then fair water was handed round in silver ewers, and the *same lady* was observed to take an unusual time in *Washing* herself.

May Day, with that sweetness which is peculiar to her, in a neat speech proposing the health of the founder, crowned her goblet (and by her example the rest of the company) with garlands. This being done, the lordly *New Year*, from the upper end of the table, in a cordial but somewhat lofty tone, returned thanks. He felt proud on an occasion of meeting so many of his worthy father's late tenants, promised to improve their farms, and at the same time to abate (if anything was found unreasonable) in their rents.

At the mention of this, the four *Quarter Days* involuntarily looked at each other, and smiled; *April Fool* whistled to an old tune of "New Brooms;" and a surly old rebel at the farther end of the table (who was discovered to be no other than the *Fifth of November*) muttered out, distinctly enough to be heard by the whole company, words to this effect—that "when the old one is gone, he is a fool that looks for a better."

Which rudeness of his, the guests resenting, unanimously voted his expulsion; and the malcontent was thrust out neck and heels into the cellar, as the properest place for such a *boutefeu* and firebrand as he had shown himself to be.

Order being restored—the young lord (who, to say truth, had been a little ruffled, and put beside his oratory) in as few and yet as obliging words as possible, assured them of entire welcome; and, with a graceful turn, singling out poor *Twenty-Ninth of February*, that had sate all this while mumchance at the side-board, begged to couple his health with that of the good company before him—which he drank accordingly; observing that he had not seen his honest face any time these four years—with a number of endearing expressions besides. At the same time removing the solitary *Day* from the forlorn seat which had been assigned him, he stationed him at his own board, somewhere between the *Greek Calends* and *Latter Lammas*.

Ash Wednesday, being now called upon for a song, with his eyes fast stuck in his head, and as well as the Canary he had swallowed would give him leave, struck up a Carol, which *Christmas Day* had taught him for the nonce; and was followed by the latter, who gave "Miserere" in fine style, hitting off the mumping notes and lengthened drawl of *Old Mortification* with infinite humour. *April Fool* swore they had exchanged conditions; but *Good Friday* was observed to look extremely grave; and *Sunday* held her fan before her face that she might not be seen to smile.

Shrove-tide, *Lord Mayor's Day*, and *April Fool*, next joined in a glee—

Which is the properest day to drink?

in which all the *Days* chiming in, made a merry burden.

They next fell to quibbles and conundrums. The question being proposed, who had the greatest number of followers—the *Quarter Days* said, there could be no question as to that; for they had all the creditors in the world dogging their heels. But *April Fool* gave it in favour of the *Forty Days before Easter;* because the debtors in all cases outnumbered the creditors, and they kept *Lent* all the year.

All this while *Valentine's Day* kept courting pretty *May*, who sate next him, slipping amorous *billets-doux* under the table, till the *Dog Days* (who are naturally of a warm constitution) began to be jealous, and to bark and rage exceedingly. *April Fool*, who likes a bit of sport above measure, and had some pretensions to the lady besides, as being but a cousin once removed,—clapped and halloo'd them on; and as fast as their indignation cooled, those mad wags, the *Ember Days*, were at it with their bellows, to blow it into a flame; and all was in a ferment, till old Madam *Septuagesima* (who boasts herself the *Mother of the Days*) wisely diverted the conversation with a tedious tale of the lovers which she could reckon when she was young, and of one Master *Rogation Day* in particular, who was for ever putting the *question* to her; but she kept him at a distance, as the chronicle would tell—by which I apprehend she meant the Almanack. Then she rambled on to the *Days that were gone*, the *good old Days*, and so to the *Days before the Flood*—which plainly showed her old head to be little better than crazed and doited.

Day being ended, the *Days* called for their cloaks and greatcoats, and took their leave. *Lord Mayor's Day* went off in a Mist, as usual; *Shortest Day* in a deep black Fog, that wrapt the little gentleman all round like a hedgehog. Two *Vigils*—so watchmen are called in heaven—saw *Christmas Day* safe home—they had been used to the business before. Another *Vigil*—a stout, sturdy patrole, called the *Eve of St. Christopher*—seeing *Ash Wednesday* in a condition little better than he should be—e'en whipt him over his shoulders, pick-a-back fashion, and *Old Mortification* went floating home singing—

On the bat's back I do fly,

and a number of old snatches besides, between drunk and sober; but very few Aves or Penitentiaries (you may believe me) were among them. *Longest Day* set off westward in beautiful crimson and gold—the rest, some in one fashion, some in another; but

Valentine and pretty *May* took their departure together in one of the prettiest silvery twilights a Lover's Day could wish to set in.

OLD CHINA.

I HAVE an almost feminine partiality for old china. When I go to see any great house, I inquire for the china-closet, and next for the picture-gallery. I cannot defend the order of preference, but by·saying that we have all some taste or other, of too ancient a date to admit of our remembering distinctly that it was an acquired one. I can call to mind the first play, and the first exhibition, that I was taken to; but I am not conscious of a time when china jars and saucers were introduced into my imagination.

I had no repugnance then—why should I now have?—to those little, lawless, azure-tinctured grotesques, that, under the notion of men and women, float about, uncircumscribed by any element, in that world before perspective—a china tea-cup.

I like to see my old friends—whom distance cannot diminish—figuring up in the air (so they appear to our optics), yet on *terra firma* still—for so we must in courtesy interpret that speck of deeper blue, which the decorous artist, to prevent absurdity, had made to spring up beneath their sandals.

I love the men with women's faces, and the women, if possible, with still more womanish expressions.

Here is a young and courtly Mandarin, handing tea to a lady from a salver—two miles off. See how distance seems to set off respect! And here the same lady, or another—for likeness is identity on tea-cups—is stepping into a little fairy boat, moored on the hither side of this calm garden river, with a dainty mincing foot, which in a right angle of incidence (as angles go in our world) must infallibly land her in the midst of a flowery mead—a furlong off on the other side of the same strange stream!

Farther on—if far or near can be predicated of their world—see horses, trees, pagodas, dancing the hays.

Here—a cow and rabbit couchant, and co-extensive—so objects show, seen through the lucid atmosphere of fine Cathay.

I was pointing out to my cousin last evening, over our Hyson (which we are old-fashioned enough to drink unmixed still of an afternoon), some of these *speciosa miracula* upon a set of extraordinary old blue china (a recent purchase) which we were now for the first time using; and could not help remarking, how favourable circumstances had been to us of late years, that we could afford to please the eye sometimes with trifles of this sort—when a passing sentiment seemed to overshade the brows of my companion. I am quick at detecting these summer clouds in Bridget

"I wish the good old times would come again," she said, "when we were not quite so rich. I do not mean that I want to be poor; but there was a middle state"—so she was pleased to ramble on,—"in which I am sure we were a great deal happier. A purchase is but a purchase, now that you have money enough and to spare.   Formerly it used to be a triumph. When we coveted a cheap luxury (and, O! how much ado I had to get you to consent in those times!)—we were used to have a debate two or three days before, and to weigh the *for* and *against*, and think what we might spare it out of, and what saving we could hit upon, that should be an equivalent. A thing was worth buying then, when we felt the money that we paid for it.

"Do you remember the brown suit, which you made to hang upon you, till all your friends cried shame upon you, it grew so threadbare—and all because of that folio Beaumont and Fletcher, which you dragged home late at night from Barker's in Covent Garden? Do you remember how we eyed it for weeks before we could make up our minds to the purchase, and had not come to a determination till it was near ten o'clock of the Saturday night, when you set off from Islington, fearing you should be too late—and when the old bookseller with some grumbling opened his shop, and by the twinkling taper (for he was setting bedwards) lighted out the relic from his dusty trea-sures—and when you lugged it home, wishing it were twice as cumbersome—and when you presented it to me—and when we were exploring the perfectness of it (*collating*, you called it)—and while I was repairing some of the loose leaves with paste, which your impatience would not suffer to be left till day-break—was there no pleasure in being a poor man? or can those neat black clothes which you wear now, and are so careful to keep brushed, since we have become rich and finical—give you half the honest vanity with which you flaunted it about in that overworn suit—your old corbeau—for four or five weeks longer than you should have done, to pacify your conscience for the mighty sum of fifteen—or sixteen shillings was it?—a great affair we thought it then—which you had lavished on the old folio. Now you can afford to buy any book that pleases you, but I do not see that you ever bring me home any nice old purchases now.

"When you came home with twenty apologies for laying out a less number of shillings upon that print after Lionardo, which we christened the 'Lady Blanch;' when you looked at the purchase, and thought of the money—and thought of the money, and looked again at the picture—was there no pleasure in being a poor man? Now, you have nothing to do but to walk into Colnaghi's, and buy a wilderness of Lionardos.   Yet do you?

"Then, do you remember our

pleasant walks to Enfield, and Potter's bar, and Waltham, when we had a holyday—holydays and all other fun are gone now we are rich—and the little hand-basket in which I used to deposit our day's fare of savoury cold lamb and salad—and how you would pry about at noon-tide for some decent house, where we might go in and produce our store—only paying for the ale that you must call for—and speculate upon the looks of the landlady, and whether she was likely to allow us a table-cloth—and wish for such another honest hostess as Izaak Walton has described many a one on the pleasant banks of the Lea, when he went a-fishing—and sometimes they would prove obliging enough, and sometimes they would look grudgingly upon us—but we had cheerful looks still for one another, and would eat our plain food savourily, scarcely grudging Piscator his Trout Hall? Now—when we go out a day's pleasuring, which is seldom, moreover, we *ride* part of the way, and go into a fine inn, and order the best of dinners, never debating the expense—which, after all, never has half the relish of those chance country snaps, when we were at the mercy of uncertain usage, and a precarious welcome.

"You are too proud to see a play anywhere now but in the pit. Do you remember where it was we used to sit, when we saw the battle of Hexham, and the Surrender of Calais, and Bannister and Mrs. Bland in the Children in the Wood—when we squeezed out our shillings a-piece to sit three or four times in a season in the one-shilling gallery—where you felt all the time that you ought not to have brought me—and more strongly I felt obligation to you for having brought me —and the pleasure was the better for a little shame—and when the curtain drew up, what cared wo for our place in the house, or what mattered it where we were sitting, when our thoughts were with Rosalind in Arden, or with Viola at the Court of Illyria? You used to say that the Gallery was the best place of all for enjoying a play socially—that the relish of such exhibitions must be in proportion to the infrequency of going—that the company we met there, not being in general readers of plays, were obliged to attend the more, and did attend, to what was going on, on the stage—because a word lost would have been a chasm, which it was impossible for them to fill up. With such reflections we consoled our pride then—and I appeal to you whether, as a woman, I met generally with less attention and accommodation than I have done since in more expensive situations in the house? The getting in, indeed, and the crowding up those inconvenient staircases, was bad enough—but there was still a law of civility to woman recognized to quite as great an extent as we ever found in the other passages—and how a little difficulty overcome heightened the snug seat and the play, afterwards! Now we can only pay our money and walk in. You cannot see, you say, in the galleries now. I am sure we saw, and heard too, well enough then—but sight, and all, I think, is gone with our poverty.

"There was pleasure in eating strawberries, before they became quite common—in the first dish of peas, while they were yet dear—to have them for a nice supper, a treat. What treat can we have now? If we were to treat ourselves now—that is, to have dainties a little above our means, it would be selfish and wicked. It is the very little more that we allow ourselves beyond what the actual poor can get at, that makes what I call a treat—when two people, living together as we have done, now and then indulge themselves in a cheap luxury, which both like; while each apologizes, and is willing to take both halves of the blame to his single share. I see no harm in people making much of themselves, in that sense of the word. It may give them a hint how to make much of others. But now—what I mean by the word—we never *do* make much of ourselves. None but the poor can do it. I do not mean the veriest poor of all, but persons as we were, just above poverty.

"I know what you were going to say, that it is mighty pleasant at the end of the year to make all meet,—and much ado we used to have every Thirty-first Night of December to account for our exceedings—many a long face did you make over your puzzled accounts, and in contriving to make it out how we had spent so much —or that we had not spent so much— or that it was impossible we should spend so much next year—and still we found our slender capital decreasing—but then,—betwixt ways, and projects, and compromises of one sort or another, and talk of curtailing this charge, and doing without that for the future—and the hope that youth brings, and laughing spirits (in which you were never poor till now), we pocketed up our loss, and in conclusion, with 'lusty brimmers' (as you used to quote it out of *hearty cheerful Mr. Cotton*, as you called him), we used to welcome in the 'coming guest.' Now we have no reckoning at all at the end of the old year —no flattering promises about the new year doing better for us."

Bridget is so sparing of her speech on most occasions, that when she gets into a rhetorical vein, I am careful how I interrupt it. I could not help, however, smiling at the phantom of wealth which her dear imagination had conjured up out of a clear income of poor —— hundred pounds a year. "It is true we were happier when we were poorer, but we were also younger, my cousin. I am afraid we must put up with the excess, for if we were to shake the superflux into the sea, we should not much mend ourselves. That we had much to struggle with, as we grew up together, we have reason to be most thankful. It strengthened and knit our compact closer. We could never have been what we have been to each other, if we had always had the sufficiency which you now complain of. The resisting power—those natural dilations of the youthful spirit, which circumstances cannot straiten—with us are long since passed away. Competence to age is supplementary youth, a sorry supplement indeed, but I fear the best that is to be had. We must ride where we formerly walked: live better and lie softer —and shall be wise to do so—than we had means to do in those good old days you speak of. Yet could those days return—could you and I once more walk our thirty miles a day—could Bannister and Mrs. Bland again be young, and you and I be young to see them— could the good old one-shilling gallery days return—they are dreams, my cousin, now—but could you and I at this moment, instead of this quiet argument, by our well-carpeted fireside, sitting on this luxurious sofa—be once more struggling up those inconvenient staircases, pushed about, and squeezed, and elbowed by the poorest rabble of poor gallery scramblers—could I once more hear those anxious shrieks of yours—and the delicious *Thank God, we are safe*, which always followed when the topmost stair, conquered, let in the first light of the whole cheerful theatre down beneath us—I know not the fathom line that ever touched a descent so deep as I would be willing to bury more wealth in than Crœsus had, or the great Jew R—— is supposed to have, to purchase it. And now do just look at that merry little Chinese waiter holding an umbrella, big enough for a bed-tester, over the head of that pretty insipid half Madonna-ish chit of a lady in that very blue summer-house."

THE CHILD ANGEL;
A DREAM.

I CHANCED upon the prettiest, oddest, fantastical thing of a dream the other night, that you shall hear of. I had been reading the "Loves of the Angels," and went to bed with my head full of speculations, suggested by that extraordinary legend. It had given birth to innumerable con; jectures; and, I remember the last waking thought, which I gave expression to on my pillow, was a sort of wonder, "what could come of it."

I was suddenly transported, how or whither I could scarcely make out—but to some celestial region. It was not the real heavens neither —not the downright Bible heaven —but a kind of fairy-land heaven, about which a poor human fancy may have leave to sport and air itself, I will hope, without presumption.

Methought—what wild things dreams are!—I was present—at what would you imagine?—at an angel's gossiping.

Whence it came, or how it

came, or who bid it come, or whether it came purely of its own head, neither you nor I know—but there lay, sure enough, wrapt in its little cloudy swaddling-bands—a Child Angel.

Sun-threads—filmy beams—ran through the celestial napery of what seemed its princely cradle. All the winged orders hovered round, watching when the new born should open its yet closed eyes; which, when it did, first one, and then the other—with a solicitude and apprehension, yet not such as, stained with fear, dim the expanding eyelids of mortal infants, but as if to explore its path in those its unhereditary palaces —what an inextinguishable titter that time spared not celestial visages! Nor wanted there to my seeming—O, the inexplicable simpleness of dreams!—bowls of that cheering nectar,

— which mortals *caudle* call below.

Nor were wanting faces of female ministrants,—stricken in years, as it might seem,—so dexterous were those heavenly attendants to counterfeit kindly similitudes of earth, to greet with terrestrial child-rites the young *present*, which earth had made to heaven.

Then were celestial harpings heard, not in full symphony, as those by which the spheres are tutored; but, as loudest instruments on earth speak oftentimes, muffled; so to accommodate their sound the better to the weak ears of the imperfect-born. And, with the noise of these subdued sound-ings, the Angelet sprang forth, fluttering its rudiments of pinions —but forthwith flagged and was recovered into the arms of those full-winged angels. And a wonder it was to see how, as years went round in heaven—a year in dreams is as a day—continually its white shoulders put forth buds of wings, but wanting the perfect angelic nutriment, anon was shorn of its aspiring, and fell fluttering—still caught by angel hands, for ever to put forth shoots, and to fall fluttering, because its birth was not of the unmixed vigour of heaven.

And a name was given to the Babe Angel; and it was to be called *Ge-Urania*, because its production was of earth and heaven.

And it could not taste of death, by reason of its adoption into immortal palaces; but it was to know weakness, and reliance, and the shadow of human imbecility; and it went with a lame gait; but in its goings it exceeded all mortal children in grace and swiftness. Then pity first sprang up in angelic bosoms; and yearnings (like the human) touched them at the sight of the immortal lame one.

And with pain did then first those Intuitive Essences, with pain and strife to their natures (not grief), put back their bright intelligences, and reduce their ethereal minds, schooling them to degrees and slower processes, so to adapt their lessons to the gradual illumination (as must needs be) of the half-earth-born; and what intuitive notices they could not repel (by reason that their nature is, to know all things at once) the half-heavenly novice, by the better part of its nature, aspired to receive into its understanding; so that Humility and Aspiration went on even-paced in the instruction of the glorious Amphibium.

But, by reason that Mature Humanity is too gross to breathe the air of that super-subtile region, its portion was, and is, to be a child for ever.

And because the human part of it might not press into the heart and inwards of the palace of its adoption, those full-natured angels tended it by turns in the purlieus of the palace, where were shady groves and rivulets, like this green earth from which it came; so Love, with Voluntary Humility, waited upon the entertainment of the new-adopted.

And myriads of years rolled round (in dreams Time is nothing), and still it kept, and is to keep, perpetual childhood, and is the Tutelar Genius of Childhood upon earth, and still goes lame and lovely.

By the banks of the river Pison is seen, lone sitting by the grave of the terrestrial Adah, whom the angel Nadir loved, a Child; but not the same which I saw in heaven. A mournful hue overcasts its lineaments; nevertheless, a correspondency is between the child by the grave, and that celestial orphan, whom I saw above; and the dimness of the grief upon the heavenly, is a shadow or emblem of that which stains the beauty of the terrestrial. And this correspondency is not to be understood but by dreams.

And in the archives of heaven I had grace to read, how that once the angel Nadir, being exiled from his place for mortal passion, upspringing on the wings of parental love (such power had parental love for a moment to suspend the else-irrevocable law) appeared for a brief instant in his station, and, depositing a wondrous Birth, straightway disappeared, and the palaces knew him no more. And this charge was the self-same Babe, who goeth lame and lovely—but Adah sleepeth by the river Pison.

CONFESSIONS OF A DRUNKARD.

Dehortations from the use of strong liquors have been the favourite topic of sober declaimers in all ages, and have been received with abundance of applause by water-drinking critics. But with the patient himself, the man that is to be cured, unfortunately their sound has seldom prevailed. Yet the evil is acknowledged, the remedy simple. Abstain. No force can oblige a man to raise the glass to his head against his will. 'Tis as easy as not to steal, not to tell lies.

Alas! the hand to pilfer, and the tongue to bear false witness, have no constitutional tendency. These are actions indifferent to them. At the first instance of the reformed will, they can be brought off without a murmur. The itching finger is but a figure in speech, and the tongue of the liar can with the same natural delight give forth useful truths with which it has been accustomed to scatter their pernicious contraries. But when a man has commenced sot——

O pause, thou sturdy moralist, thou person of stout nerves and a strong head, whose liver is happily untouched, and ere thy gorge riseth at the *name* which I had written, first learn what the *thing* is; how much of compassion, how much of human allowance, thou mayest virtuously mingle with thy disapprobation. Trample not on the ruins of a man. Exact not, under so terrible a penalty as infamy, a resuscitation from a state of death almost as real as that from which Lazarus rose not but by a miracle.

Begin a reformation, and custom will make it easy. But what if the beginning be dreadful, the first steps not like climbing a mountain but going through fire? what if the whole system must undergo a change violent as that which we conceive of the mutation of form in some insects? what if a process comparable to flaying alive be to be gone through? is the weakness that sinks under such struggles to be confounded with the pertinacity which clings to other vices, which have induced no constitutional necessity, no engagement of the whole victim, body and soul?

I have known one in that state, when he has tried to abstain but for one evening,—though the poisonous potion had long ceased to bring back its first enchantments, though he was sure it would rather deepen his gloom than brighten it,—in the violence of the struggle, and the necessity he had felt of getting rid of the present sensation at any rate, I have known him to scream out, to cry aloud, for the anguish and pain of the strife within him.

Why should I hesitate to declare, that the man of whom I speak is myself? I have no puling apology to make to mankind. I see them all in one way or another deviating from the pure reason. It is to my own nature alone I am accountable for the woe that I have brought upon it.

I believe that there are constitutions, robust heads and iron insides, whom scarce any excesses can hurt; whom brandy (I have seen them drink it like wine), at all events whom wine, taken in ever so plentiful a measure, can do no worse injury to than just to muddle their faculties, perhaps never very pellucid. On them this discourse is wasted. They would but laugh at a weak brother, who, trying his strength with them, and coming off foiled from the contest, would fain persuade them that such agonistic exercises are dangerous. It is to a very different description of persons I speak. It is to the weak—the nervous; to those who feel the want of some artificial aid to raise their spirits in society to what is no more than the ordinary pitch of all around them without it. This is the secret of our drinking. Such must fly the convivial board in the first instance, if they do not mean to sell themselves for term of life.

Twelve years ago I had completed my six-and-twentieth year. I had lived from the period of leaving school to that time pretty much in solitude. My companions were chiefly books, or at most one or two living ones of my own book-loving and sober stamp. I rose early, went to bed betimes, and the faculties which God had given me, I have reason to think, did not rust in me unused.

About that time I fell in with some companions of a different order. They were men of boisterous spirits, sitters up a-nights, disputants, drunken; yet seemed to have something noble about them. We dealt about the wit, or what passes for it after midnight, jovially. Of the quality called fancy I certainly possessed a larger share than my companions. Encouraged by their applause, I set up for a professed joker! I, who of all men am least fitted for such an occupation, having, in addition to the greatest difficulty which I experience at all times of finding words to express my meaning, a natural nervous impediment in my speech!

Reader, if you are gifted with nerves like mine, aspire to any character but that of a wit. When you find a tickling relish upon your tongue disposing you to that sort of conversation, especially if you find a preternatural flow of ideas setting in upon you at the sight of a bottle and fresh glasses, avoid giving way to it as you would fly your greatest destruction. If you cannot crush the power of fancy, or that within you which you mistake for such, divert it, give it some other play. Write an essay, pen a character or description,—but not as I do now, with tears trickling down your cheeks.

To be an object of compassion to friends, of derision to foes; to be suspected by strangers, stared at by fools; to be esteemed dull when you cannot be witty, to be applauded for witty when you know that you have been dull; to be called upon for the extemporaneous exercise of that faculty which no premeditation can give; to be spurred on to efforts which end in contempt; to be set on to provoke mirth which procures the procurer hatred; to give pleasure and be paid with squinting malice; to swallow draughts of life-destroying wine which are to be distilled into airy breath to tickle vain auditors; to mortgage miserable morrows for nights of madness; to waste whole seas of time upon those who pay it back in little inconsiderable drops of grudging applause,—are the wages of buffoonery and death.

Time, which has a sure stroke at dissolving all connections which have no solider fastening than this liquid cement, more kind to me than my own taste or penetration, at length opened my eyes to the supposed qualities of my first friends. No trace of them is left but in the vices which they introduced, and the habits they infixed. In them my friends survive still, and exercise ample retribution for any supposed infidelity that I may have been guilty of towards them.

My next more immediate companions were and are persons of such intrinsic and felt worth, that though accidentally their acquaintance has proved pernicious to me, I do not know that if the thing were to do over again, I should have the courage to eschew the mischief at the price of forfeiting the benefit. I came to them reeking from the steams of my late over-heated notions of companionship; and the slightest fuel which they unconsciously afforded, was sufficient to feed my own fires into a propensity.

They were no drinkers; but, one from professional habits, and another from a custom derived from his father, smoked tobacco. The devil could not have devised a more subtle trap to re-take a backsliding penitent. The transition, from gulping down draughts of liquid fire to puffing out innocuous blasts of dry smoke, was so like cheating him. But he is too hard for us when we hope to commute. He beats us at barter; and when we think to set off a new failing against an old infirmity, 'tis odds but he puts the trick upon us of two for one. That (comparatively) white devil of tobacco brought with him in the end seven worse than himself.

It were impertinent to carry the reader through all the processes by which, from smoking at first with malt liquor, I took my degrees through thin wines, through stronger wine and water, through small punch, to those juggling compositions, which, under the name of mixed liquours, slur a great deal of brandy or other poison under less and less water continually, until they come next to none, and so to none at all. But it is hateful to disclose the secrets of my Tartarus.

I should repel my readers, from a mere incapacity of believing me, were I to tell them what tobacco has been to me, the drudging service which I have paid, the slavery which I have vowed to it. How, when I have resolved to quit it, a feeling as of ingratitude has started up; how it has put on personal claims and made the demands of a friend upon me. How the reading of it casually in a book, as where Adams takes his whiff in the chimney-corner of some inn in Joseph Andrews, or Piscator in the Complete Angler breaks his fast upon a morning pipe in that delicate room *Piscatoribus Sacrum*, has in a moment broken down the resistance of weeks. How a pipe was ever in my midnight path before me, till the vision forced me to realise it,—how then its ascending vapours curled. its fragrance lulled, and the thousand delicious ministerings conversant about it, employing every faculty, extracted the sense of pain. How from illuminating it came to darken, from a quick solace it turned to a negative relief, thence to a restlessness and dissatisfaction, thence to a positive misery. How, even now, when the whole secret stands confessed in all its dreadful truth before me. I feel myself linked to it beyond the power of revocation. Bone of my bone——

Persons not accustomed to examine the motives of their actions, to reckon up the countless nails that rivet the chains of habit, or perhaps being bound by none so obdurate as those I have confessed to, may recoil from this as from an overcharged picture. But what short of such a bondage is it, which in spite of protesting friends, a weeping wife, and a reprobating world, chains down many a poor fellow, of no original indisposition to goodness, to his pipe and his pot?

I have seen a print after Correggio, in which three female figures are ministering to a man who sits fast bound at the root of a tree. Sensuality is soothing him, Evil Habit is nailing him to a branch, and Repugnance at the same instant of time is applying a snake to his side. In his face is feeble delight, the recollection of past rather than perception of present pleasures, languid enjoyment of evil with utter imbecility to good, a Sybaritic effeminacy, a submission to bondage, the springs of the will gone down like a broken clock, the sin and the suffering co-instantaneous, or the latter forerunning the former, remorse preceding action—all this represented in one point of time. —When I saw this, I admired the wonderful skill of the painter. But when I went away, I wept, because I thought of my own condition.

Of *that* there is no hope that it should ever change. The waters have gone over me. But out of the black depths, could I be heard, I would cry out to all those who have but set a foot in the perilous flood. Could the youth, to whom the flavour of his first wine is delicious as the opening scenes of life or the entering upon some newly-discovered paradise, look into my desolation, and be made to understand what a dreary thing it is when a man shall feel himself going down a precipice with open eyes and a passive will,—to see his destruction and have no power to stop it, and yet to feel it all the way emanating from himself; to perceive all goodness emptied out of him, and yet not to be able to forget a time when it was otherwise; to bear about the piteous spectacle of his own self-ruins:— could he see my fevered eye, feverish with last night's drinking, and feverishly looking for this night's repetition of the folly; could he feel the body of the death out of which I cry hourly with feebler and feebler outcry to be delivered,—it were enough to make him dash the sparkling beverage to the earth in all the pride of its mantling temptation; to make him clasp his teeth,

> and not undo 'em
> To suffer WET DAMNATION to run thro' 'em.

Yea, but (methinks I hear somebody object) if sobriety be that fine thing you would have us to understand, if the comforts of a cool brain are to be preferred to that state of heated excitement which you describe and deplore, what hinders in your instance that you do not return to those habits from which you would induce others never to swerve? if the blessing be worth preserving, is it not worth recovering?

Recovering!—O if a wish could transport me back to those days of youth, when a draught from the next clear spring could slake any heats which summer suns and youthful exercise had power to stir up in the blood, how gladly would I return to thee, pure element, the drink of children and of child-like holy hermit! In my dreams I can sometimes fancy thy cool refreshment purling over my burning tongue. But my waking stomach rejects it. That which refreshes innocence only makes me sick and faint.

But is there no middle way betwixt total abstinence and the excess which kills you?—For your sake, reader, and that you may never attain to my experience, with pain I must utter the dreadful truth, that there is none, none that I can find. In my stage of habit, (I speak not of habits less confirmed—for some of them I believe the advice to be most prudential) in the stage which I have reached, to stop short of that measure which is sufficient to draw on torpor and sleep, the benumbing apoplectic sleep of the drunkard, is to have taken none at all. The pain of the self-denial is all one. And what that is, I had rather the reader should believe on my credit, than know from his own trial. He will come to know it, whenever he shall arrive in that state in which, paradoxical as it may appear, *reason shall only visit him through intoxication;* for it is a fearful truth, that the intellectual faculties by repeated acts of intemperance may be driven from their orderly sphere of action, their clear daylight ministeries, until they shall be brought at last to depend, for the faint manifestation of their departing energies, upon the returning periods of the fatal madness to which they owe their devastation. The drinking man is never less himself than during his sober intervals. Evil is so far his good.[*]

Behold me then, in the robust period of life, reduced to imbecility and decay. Hear me count my gains, and the profits which I

---

[*] When poor M—— painted his last picture, with a pencil in one trembling hand, and a glass of brandy and water in the other, his fingers owed the comparative steadiness with which they were enabled to go through their task in an imperfect manner, to a temporary firmness derived from a repetition of practices, the general effect of which had shaken both them and him so terribly.

have derived from the midnight cup.

Twelve years ago, I was possessed of a healthy frame of mind and body. I was never strong, but I think my constitution (for a weak one) was as happily exempt from the tendency to any malady as it was possible to be. I scarce knew what it was to ail anything. Now, except when I am losing myself in a sea of drink, I am never free from those uneasy sensations in head and stomach, which are so much worse to bear than any definite pains or aches.

At that time I was seldom in bed after six in the morning, summer and winter. I awoke refreshed, and seldom without some merry thoughts in my head, or some piece of a song to welcome the new-born day. Now, the first feeling which besets me, after stretching out the hours of recumbence to their last possible extent, is a forecast of the wearisome day that lies before me, with a secret wish that I could have lain on still, or never awaked.

Life itself, my waking life, has much of the confusion, the trouble, and obscure perplexity, of an ill dream. In the day-time I stumble upon dark mountains.

Business, which, though never very particularly adapted to my nature, yet as something of necessity to be gone through, and therefore best undertaken with cheerfulness, I used to enter upon with some degree of alacrity, now wearies, affrights, perplexes me. I fancy all sorts of discourage-ments, and am ready to give up an occupation which gives me bread, from a harassing conceit of incapacity. The slightest commission given me by a friend, or any small duty which I have to perform for myself, as giving orders to a tradesman, &c., haunts me as a labour impossible to be got through. So much the springs of action are broken.

The same cowardice attends me in all my intercourse with mankind. I dare not promise that a friend's honour, or his cause, would be safe in my keeping, if I were put to the expense of any manly resolution in defending it. So much the springs of moral action are deadened within me.

My favourite occupations in times past now cease to entertain, I can do nothing readily. Application for ever so short a time kills me. This poor abstract of my condition was penned at long intervals, with scarcely an attempt at connexion of thought, which is now difficult to me.

The noble passages which formerly delighted me in history or poetic fiction now only draw a few tears, allied to dotage. My broken and dispirited nature seems to sink before anything great and admirable.

I perpetually catch myself in tears, for any cause, or none. It is inexpressible how much this infirmity adds to a sense of shame, and a general feeling of deterioration.

These are some of the instances, concerning which I can say with truth, that it was not always so with me.

Shall I lift up the veil of my weakness any further?—or is this disclosure sufficient?

I am a poor nameless egotist, who have no vanity to consult by these Confessions. I know not whether I shall be laughed at, or heard seriously. Such as they are, I commend them to the reader's attention, if he find his own case any way touched. I have told him what I am come to. Let him stop in time.

POPULAR FALLACIES.

I. — THAT A BULLY IS ALWAYS A COWARD.

This axiom contains a principle of compensation, which disposes us to admit the truth of it. But there is no safe trusting to dictionaries and definitions. We should more willingly fall in with this popular language, if we did not find *brutality* sometimes awkwardly coupled with *valour* in the same vocabulary. The comic writers, with their poetical justice, have contributed not a little to mislead us upon this point. To see a hectoring fellow exposed and beaten upon the stage, has something in it wonderfully diverting. Some people's share of animal spirits is notoriously low and defective. It has not strength to raise a vapour, or furnish out the wind of a tolerable bluster. These love to be told that huffing is no part of valour. The truest courage with them is that which is the least noisy and obtrusive. But confront one of these silent heroes with the swaggerer of real life, and his confidence in the theory quickly vanishes. Pretension do not uniformly bespeak non-performance. A modest, inoffensive deportment does not necessarily imply valour; neither does the absence of it justify us in denying that quality. Hickman wanted modesty—we do not mean *him* of Clarissa—but who ever doubted his courage? Even the poets—upon whom this equitable distribution of qualities should be most binding—have thought it agreeable to nature to depart from the rule upon occasion. Harapha, in the "Agonistes," is indeed a bully upon the received notions. Milton has made him at once a blusterer, a giant, and a dastard. But Almanzor, in Dryden, talks of driving armies singly before him—and does it. Tom Brown had a shrewder insight into this kind of character than either of his predecessors. He divides the palm more equably, and allows his hero a sort of dimidiate preeminence:—"Bully Dawson kicked by half the town, and half the town kicked by Bully Dawson." This was true distributive justice.

II.—THAT ILL-GOTTEN GAIN NEVER PROSPERS.

The weakest part of mankind have this saying commonest in their mouth. It is the trite consolation administered to the easy dupe, when he has been tricked out of his money or estate, that the acquisition of it will do the owner *no good*. But the rogues of this world—the prudenter part of them at least,—know better; and if the observation had been as true as it is old, would not have failed by this time to have discovered it. They have pretty sharp distinctions of the fluctuating and the permanent. "Lightly come, lightly go," is a proverb which they can very well afford to leave, when they leave little else, to the losers. They do not always find manors, got by rapine or chicanery, insensibly to melt away as the poets will have it; or that all gold glides, like thawing snow, from the thief's hand that grasps it. Church land, alienated to lay uses, was formerly denounced to have this slippery quality. But some portions of it somehow always stuck so fast, that the denunciators have been fain to postpone the prophecy of refundment to a late posterity.

III.—THAT A MAN MUST NOT LAUGH AT HIS OWN JEST.

THE severest exaction surely ever invented upon the self-denial of poor human nature! This is to expect a gentleman to give a treat without partaking of it; to sit esurient at his own table, and commend the flavour of his venison upon the absurd strength of his never touching it himself. On the contrary, we love to see a wag *taste* his own joke to his party; to watch a quirk or a merry conceit flickering upon the lips some seconds before the tongue is delivered of it. If it be good, fresh, and racy—begotten of the occasion; if he that utters it never thought it before, he is naturally the first to be tickled with it, and any suppression of such complacence we hold to be churlish and insulting. What does it seem to imply but that your company is weak or foolish to be moved by an image or a fancy, that shall stir you not at all, or but faintly? This is exactly the humour of the fine gentleman in Mandeville, who, while he dazzles his guests with the display of some costly toy, affects himself to "see nothing considerable in it."

IV.—THAT SUCH A ONE SHOWS HIS BREEDING.—THAT IT IS EASY TO PERCEIVE HE IS NO GENTLEMAN.

A SPEECH from the poorest sort of people, which always indicates that the party vituperated is a gentleman. The very fact which they deny, is that which galls and exasperates them to use this language. The forbearance with which it is usually received is a proof what interpretation the by-stander sets upon it. Of a kin to this, and still less politic, are the phrases with which, in their street rhetoric, they ply one another more grossly;—*He is a poor creature.— He has not a rag to cover——&c.;* though this last, we confess, is more frequently applied by females to females. They do not perceive that the satire glances upon themselves. A poor man, of all

things in the world, should not upbraid an antagonist with poverty.
Are there no other topics—as, to
tell him his father was hanged—
his sister, &c.—without exposing a
secret which should be kept snug
between them; and doing an
affront to the order to which they
have the honour equally to belong? All this while they do not
see how the wealthier man stands
by and laughs in his sleeve at
both.

V.—THAT THE POOR COPY THE VICES OF THE RICH.

A SMOOTH text to the letter; and,
preached from the pulpit, is sure
of a docile audience from the pews
lined with satin. It is twice sitting upon velvet to a foolish squire
to be told that *he*—and not *perverse nature*, as the homilies would
make us imagine, is the true cause
of all the irregularities in his
parish. This is striking at the
root of free-will indeed, and denying the originality of sin in any
sense. But men are not such implicit sheep as this comes to. If
the abstinence from evil on the
part of the upper classes is to
derive itself from no higher principle than the apprehension of
setting ill patterns to the lower,
we beg leave to discharge them
from all squeamishness on that
score: they may even take their
fill of pleasures, where they can
find them. The Genius of Poverty,
hampered and straitened as it is,
is not so barren of invention but
it can trade upon the staple of its
own vice, without drawing upon
their capital. The poor are not
quite such servile imitators as
they take them for. Some of
them are very clever artists in
their way. Here and there, we
find an original. Who taught the
poor to steal—to pilfer? They
did not go to the great for school-
masters in these faculties, surely.
It is well if in some vices they
allow us to be—no copyists. In
no other sense is it true that the
poor copy them, than as servants
may be said to *take after* their
masters and mistresses, when they
succeed to their reversionary cold
meats. If the master, from indisposition, or some other cause,
neglect his food, the servant dines
notwithstanding.

"O, but (some will say) the
force of example is great." We
knew a lady who was so scrupulous on this head, that she would
put up with the calls of the most
impertinent visitor, rather than
let her servant say she was not
at home, for fear of teaching her
maid to tell an untruth; and this
in the very face of the fact, which
she knew well enough, that the
wench was one of the greatest
liars upon the earth without teaching; so much so, that her mistress
possibly never heard two words
of consecutive truth from her in
her life. But nature must go for
nothing; example must be everything. This liar in grain, who
never opened her mouth without
a lie, must be guarded against a
remote inference, which she
(pretty casuist!) might possibly
draw from a form of words—liter-

ally false, but essentially deceiving no one—that under some circumstances a fib might not be so exceedingly sinful—a fiction, too, not at all in her own way, or one that she could be suspected of adopting, for few servant-wenches care to be denied to visitors.

This word *example* reminds us of another fine word which is in use upon these occasions—*encouragement*. "People in our sphere must not be thought to give encouragement to such proceedings." To such a frantic height is this principle capable of being carried, that we have known individuals who have thought it within the scope of their influence to sanction despair, and give *éclat* to—suicide. A domestic in the family of a county member lately deceased, from love, or some unknown cause, cut his throat, but not successfully. The poor fellow was otherwise much loved and respected; and great interest was used in his behalf, upon his recovery, that he might be permitted to retain his place; his word being first pledged, not without some substantial sponsors to promise for him, that the like should never happen again. His master was inclinable to keep him, but his mistress thought otherwise; and John in the end was dismissed, her ladyship declaring that she "could not think of encouraging any such doings in the county."

VI.—THAT ENOUGH IS AS GOOD AS A FEAST.

Not a man, woman, or child, in ten miles round Guildhall, who really believes this saying. The inventor of it did not believe it himself. It was made in revenge by somebody, who was disappointed of a regale. It is a vile cold-scrag-of-mutton sophism; a lie palmed upon the palate, which knows better things. If nothing else could be said for a feast, this is sufficient—that from the superflux there is usually something left for the next day. Morally interpreted, it belongs to a class of proverbs which have a tendency to make us undervalue *money*. Of this cast are those notable observations, that money is not health; riches cannot purchase everything: the metaphor which makes gold to be mere muck, with the morality which traces fine clothing to the sheep's back, and denounces pearl as the unhandsome excretion of an oyster. Hence, too, the phrase which imputes dirt to acres—a sophistry so barefaced, that even the literal sense of it is true only in a wet season. This, and abundance of similar sage saws assuming to inculcate *content*, we verily believe to have been the invention of some cunning borrower, who had designs upon the purse of his wealthier neighbour, which he could only hope to carry by force of these verbal jugglings. Translate any one of these sayings out of the artful metonymy which envelopes it, and the trick is apparent. Goodly legs and shoulders of mutton, exhilarating cordials, books, pictures, the opportunities of seeing foreign countries, independence, heart's ease, a man's own time to himself, are not *muck*—however we may be pleased to scandalise with that appellation the faithful metal that provides them for us.

VII.—OF TWO DISPUTANTS, THE WARMEST IS GENERALLY IN THE WRONG.

OUR experience would lead us to quite an opposite conclusion. Temper, indeed, is no test of truth; but warmth and earnestness are a proof at least of a man's own conviction of the rectitude of that which he maintains. Coolness is as often the result of an unprincipled indifference to truth or falsehood, as of a sober confidence in a man's own side in a dispute. Nothing is more insulting sometimes than the appearance of this philosophic temper. There is little Titubus, the stammering law-stationer in Lincoln's Inn—we have seldom known this shrewd little fellow engaged in an argument where we were not convinced he had the best of it, if his tongue would but fairly have seconded him. When he has been spluttering excellent broken sense for an hour together, writhing and labouring to be delivered of the point of dispute—the very gist of the controversy knocking at his teeth, which like some obstinate iron-grating still obstructed its deliverance—his puny frame convulsed, and face reddening all over at an unfairness in the logic which he wanted articulation to expose, it has moved our gall to see a smooth portly fellow of an adversary, that cared not a button for the merits of the question, by merely laying his hand upon the head of the stationer, and desiring him to be *calm* (your tall disputants have always the advantage), with a provoking sneer carry the argument clean from him in the opinion of all the bystanders, who have gone away clearly convinced that Titubus must have been in the wrong, because he was in a passion; and that Mr.——, meaning his opponent, is one of the fairest and at the same time one of the most dispassionate arguers breathing.

VIII.—THAT VERBAL ALLUSIONS ARE NOT WIT, BECAUSE THEY WILL NOT BEAR A TRANSLATION.

THE same might be said of the wittiest local allusions. A custom is sometimes as difficult to explain to a foreigner as a pun. What would become of a great part of the wit of the last age, if it were tried by this test? How would certain topics, as aldermanity, cuckoldry, have sounded to a Terentian auditory, though Terence himself had been alive to translate them? *Senator urbanus* with *Curruca* to boot for a synonym, would but faintly have done the business. Words, involving notions, are hard enough to render; it is too much to expect us to translate a sound, and give an elegant version to a jingle. The Virgilian harmony is not translatable, but by substituting harmonious sounds in another language for it. To Latinise a pun, we must seek a pun in Latin that will answer to it; as, to give an idea of the double endings in Hudibras, we must have recourse to a similar practice in old monkish doggrel. Dennis, the fiercest oppugner of puns in ancient or modern times, professes himself highly tickled with the "a stick," chiming to "ecclesiastic." Yet what is this but a species of pun, a verbal consonance?

IX.—THAT THE WORST PUNS ARE THE BEST.

If by worst be only meant the most far-fetched and startling, we agree to it. A pun is not bound by the laws which limit nicer wit. It is a pistol let off at the ear; not a feather to tickle the intellect. It is an antic which does not stand upon manners, but comes bounding into the presence, and does not show the less comic for being dragged in sometimes by the head and shoulders. What though it limp a little, or prove defective in one leg?—all the better. A pun may easily be too curious and artificial. Who has not at one time or other been at a party of professors (himself perhaps an old offender in that line), where, after ringing a round of the most ingenious conceits, every man contributing his shot, and some there the most expert shooters of the day; after making a poor *word* run the gauntlet till it is ready to drop; after hunting and winding it through all the possible ambages of similar sounds; after squeezing, and hauling, and tugging at it, till the very milk of it will not yield a drop further,—suddenly some obscure, unthought-of fellow in a corner, who was never 'prentice to the trade, whom the company for very pity passed over, as we do by a known poor man when a money-subscription is going round, no one calling upon him for his quota—has all at once come out with something so whimsical, yet so pertinent; so brazen in its pretensions, yet so impossible to be denied; so exquisitely good, and so deplorably bad, at the same time,—that it has proved a Robin Hood's shot; anything ulterior to that is despaired of; and the party breaks up, unanimously voting it to be the very worst (that is, best) pun of the evening. This species of wit is the better for not being perfect in all its parts. What it gains in completeness, it loses in naturalness. The more exactly it satisfies the critical, the less hold it has upon some other faculties. The puns which are most entertaining are those which will least bear an analysis. Of this kind is the following, recorded with a sort of stigma, in one of Swift's Miscellanies.

An Oxford scholar, meeting a porter who was carrying a hare through the streets, accosts him with this extraordinary question:

"Prithee, friend, is that thy own hair or a wig?"

There is no excusing this, and no resisting it. A man might blur ten sides of paper in attempting a defence of it against a critic who should be laughter-proof. The quibble in itself is not considerable. It is only a new turn given by a little false pronunciation to a very common though not very courteous inquiry. Put by one gentleman to another at a dinner-party, it would have been vapid; to the mistress of the house, it would have shown much less wit than rudeness. We must take in the totality of time, place, and person; the pert look of the inquiring scholar, the desponding looks of the puzzled porter: the one stopping at leisure, the other hurrying on with his burden; the innocent though rather abrupt tendency of the first member of the question, with the utter and inextricable irrelevancy of the second; the place—a public street, not favourable to frivolous investigations; the affrontive quality of the primitive inquiry (the common question) invidiously transferred to the derivative (the new turn given to it) in the implied satire; namely, that few of that tribe are expected to eat of the good things which they carry, they being in most countries considered rather as the temporary trustees than owners of such dainties,—which the fellow was beginning to understand; but then tho *wig* again comes in, and he can make nothing of it; all put together constitute a picture: Hogarth could have made it intelligible on canvas.

Yet nine out of ten critics will pronounce this a very bad pun, because of the defectiveness in the concluding member, which is its very beauty, and constitutes the surprise. The same person shall cry up for admirable the cold quibble from Virgil about the broken Cremona;* because it is made out in all its parts, and leaves nothing to the imagination. We venture to call it cold; because, of thousands who have admired it, it would be difficult to find one who has heartily chuckled at it. As appealing to the judgment merely (setting the risible faculty aside), we must pronounce it a monument of curious felicity. But as some stories are said to be too good to be true, it may with equal truth be asserted of this biverbal allusion, that it is too good to be natural. One cannot help suspecting that the incident was invented to fit the line. It would have been better had it been less perfect. Like some Virgilian hemistichs, it has suffered by filling up. The *nimium Vicina* was enough in conscience; the *Cremonæ* afterwards loads it. It is, in fact, a double pun; and we have always observed that a superfœtation in this sort of wit is dangerous. When a man has said a good thing, it is seldom politic to follow it up. We do not care to be cheated a second

* Swift.

time; or, perhaps the mind of man (with reverence be it spoken) is not capacious enough to lodge two puns at a time. The impression, to be forcible, must be simultaneous and undivided.

X.—THAT HANDSOME IS THAT HANDSOME DOES.

THOSE who use this proverb can never have seen Mrs. Conrady.

The soul, if we may believe Plotinus, is a ray from the celestial beauty. As she partakes more or less of this heavenly light, she informs, with corresponding characters, the fleshly tenement which she chooses, and frames to herself a suitable mansion.

All which only proves that the soul of Mrs. Conrady, in her preexistent state, was no great judge of architecture.

To the same effect, in a Hymn in honour of Beauty, divine Spenser *platonising* sings:—

——— Every spirit as it is more pure,
And hath in it the more of heavenly
     light,
So it the fairer body doth procure
To habit in, and it more fairly dight
With cheerful face and amiable sight.
For of the soul the body form doth take:
For soul is form, and doth the body
     make.

But Spenser, it is clear, never saw Mrs. Conrady.

These poets, we find, are no safe guides in philosophy; for here, in his very next stanza but one, is a saving clause, which throws us all out again, and leaves us as much to seek as ever:—

Yet oft it falls, that many a gentle mind
Dwells in deformed tabernacle drown'd,

Either by chance, against the course of
     kind,
Or through unaptness in the substance
     found,
Which it assumed of some stubborn
     ground,
That will not yield unto her form's direction,
But is performed with some foul imperfection.

From which it would follow, that Spenser had seen somebody like Mrs. Conrady.

The spirit of this good lady— her previous *anima*—must have stumbled upon one of these untoward tabernacles which he speaks of. A more rebellious commodity of clay for a ground, as the poet calls it, no gentle mind—and sure hers is one of the gentlest—ever had to deal with.

Pondering upon her inexplicable visage—inexplicable, we mean, but by this modification of the theory—we have come to a conclusion that, if one must be plain, it is better to be plain all over, than amidst a tolerable residue of features to hang out one that shall be exceptionable. No one can say of Mrs. Conrady's countenance that it would be better if she had but a nose. It is impossible to pull her to pieces in this manner. We have seen the most malicious beauties of her own sex baffled in the attempt at a selection. The *tout-ensemble* defies particularizing. It is too complete—too consistent, as we may say—to admit of these invidious reservations. It is not as if some Apelles had picked out here a lip—and there a chin—out of the collected ugliness of Greece, to frame a model by. It is a symmetrical whole. We challenge the minutest connoisseur to cavil at any part or parcel of the countenance in question; to say that this, or that, is improperly placed. We are convinced that true ugliness, no less than is affirmed of true beauty, is the result of harmony. Like that, too, it reigns without a competitor. No one ever saw Mrs. Conrady without pronouncing her to be the plainest woman that he ever met with in the course of his life. The first time that you are indulged with a sight of her face, is an era in your existence ever after. You are glad to have seen it—like Stonehenge. No one can pretend to forget it. No one ever apologised to her for meeting her in the street on such a day and not knowing her: the pretext would be too bare. Nobody can mistake her for another. Nobody can say of her, "I think I have seen that face somewhere, but I cannot call to mind where." You must remember that in such a parlour it first struck you—like a bust. You wondered where the owner of the house had picked it up. You wondered more when it began to move its lips—so mildly too! No one ever thought of asking her to sit for her picture. Lockets are for remembrance; and it would be clearly superfluous to hang an image at your heart, which, once seen, can never be out of it. It is not a mean face either; its entire originality precludes that. Neither is it of that order of plain faces which improve upon acquaintance. Some very good but ordinary people, by an unwearied perseverance in good offices, put a cheat upon our eyes; juggle our senses out of their natural impressions; and set us upon discovering good indications in a countenance, which at first sight promised nothing less. We detect gentleness, which had escaped us, lurking about an under lip. But when Mrs. Conrady has done you a service, her face remains the same; when she has done you a thousand, and you know that she is ready to double the number, still it is that individual face. Neither can you say of it, that it would be a good face if it were not marked by the small-pox—a compliment which is always more admissive than excusatory—for either Mrs. Conrady never had the small-pox; or, as we say, took it kindly. No, it stands upon its own merits fairly. There it is. It is her mark, her token; that which she is known by.

XI.—THAT WE MUST NOT LOOK A GIFT HORSE IN THE MOUTH:

Nor a lady's age in the parish register. We hope we have more delicacy than to do either; but some faces spare us the trouble of these *dental* inquiries. And what if the beast, which my friend would force upon my acceptance, prove, upon the face of it, a sorry Rosinante, a lean, ill-favoured jade, whom no gentleman could think of setting up in his stables? Must I, rather than not be obliged to my friend, make her a companion to Eclipse or Lightfoot? A horse-giver, no more than a horse-seller, has a right to palm his spavined article upon us for good ware An equivalent is expected in either case; and, with my own good-will, I could no more be cheated out of my thanks than out of my money. Some people have a knack of putting upon you gifts of no real value, to engage you to substantial gratitude We thank them for nothing Our friend Mitis carries this humour of never refusing a present to the very point of absurdity—if it were possible to couple the ridiculous with so much mistaken delicacy and real good-nature. Not an apartment in his fine house (and he has a true taste in household decorations), but is stuffed up with some preposterous print or mirror—the worst adapted to his panels that may be—the presents of his friends that know his weakness; while his noble Vandykes are displaced to make room for a set of daubs, the work of some wretched artist of his acquaintance, who, having had them returned upon his hands for bad likenesses, finds his account in bestowing them here gratis. The good creature has not the heart to mortify the painter at the expense of an honest refusal. It is pleasant (if it did not vex one at the same time) to see him sitting in his dining parlour, surrounded with obscure aunts and cousins to God knows whom, while the true Lady Marys and Lady Bettys of his own honourable family, in favour to these adopted frights, are consigned to the staircase and the lumber-room. In like manner, his goodly shelves are one by one stripped of his favourite old authors, to give place to a collection of presentation copies—the flour and bran of modern poetry. A presentation copy, reader—if haply you are yet innocent of such favours—is a copy of a book which does not sell, sent you by the author, with his foolish autograph at the beginning of it; for which, if a stranger, he only demands your friendship; if a brother author, he expects from you a book of yours, which does sell, in return. We can speak to experience, having by us a tolerable assortment of these gift-horses. Not to ride a metaphor to death—we are willing to acknowledge, that in some gifts there is sense. A duplicate out of a friend's library (where he has more than one copy of a rare author) is intelligible. There are favours, short of the pecuniary—a thing not fit to be hinted at among gentlemen—which confer as much grace upon the acceptor as the offerer; the kind, we confess, which is most to our palate, is of those little conciliatory missives, which for their vehicle generally choose a hamper—little odd presents of game, fruit, perhaps wine—though it is essential to the delicacy of the latter, that it be home-made. We love to have our friend in the country sitting thus at our table by proxy; to apprehend his presence (though a hundred miles may be between us) by a turkey, whose goodly aspect reflects to us his "plump corpusculum;" to taste him in grouse or woodcock; to feel him gliding down in the toast peculiar to the latter; to concorporate him in a slice of Canterbury brawn. This is indeed to have him within ourselves; to know him intimately: such participation is methinks unitive, as the old theologians phrase it. For these considerations we should be sorry if certain restrictive regulations, which are thought to bear hard upon the peasantry of this country, were entirely done away with. A hare, as the law now stands, makes many friends. Caius conciliates Titius (knowing his *goût*) with a leash of partridges. Titius (suspecting his partiality for them) passes them to Lucius; who, in his turn, preferring his friend's relish to his own, makes them over to Marcius; till in their ever-widening progress, and round of unconscious circummigration, they distribute the seeds of harmony over half a parish. We are well-disposed to this kind of sensible remembrances; and are the less apt to be taken by those little airy tokens—impalpable to the palate—which, under the names of rings, lockets, keep-sakes, amuse some people's fancy mightily. We could never away with these indigestible trifles. They are the very kickshaws and foppery of friendship.

XII.—THAT HOME IS HOME THOUGH IT IS NEVER SO HOMELY.

Homes there are, we are sure, that are no homes; the home of the very poor man, and another which we shall speak to presently. Crowded places of cheap entertainment, and the benches of alehouses, if they could speak, might bear mournful testimony to the first. To them the very poor man resorts for an image of the home which he cannot find at home. For a starved grate, and a scanty firing, that is not enough to keep alive the natural heat in the fingers of so many shivering children with their mother, he finds in the depths of winter always a blazing hearth, and a hob to warm his pittance of beer by. Instead of the clamours of a wife, made gaunt by famishing, he meets with a cheerful attendance beyond the merits of the trifle which he can afford to spend. He has companions which his home denies him, for the very poor man has no visitors. He can look into the goings on of the world, and speak a little to politics. At home there are no politics stirring, but the domestic. All interests, real or imaginary, all topics that should expand the mind of man, and connect him to a sympathy with general existence, are crushed in the absorbing consideration of food to be obtained for th family. Beyond the price of bread, news is senseless and impertinent. At home there is no larder. Here there is at least a show of plenty;

and while he cooks his lean scrap of butcher's meat before the common bars, or munches his humbler cold viands, his relishing bread and cheese with an onion, in a corner, where no one reflects upon his poverty, he has a sight of the substantial joint providing for the landlord and his family. He takes an interest in the dressing of it; and while he assists in removing the trivet from the fire, he feels that there is such a thing as beef and cabbage, which he was beginning to forget at home. All this while he deserts his wife and children. But what wife, and what children! Prosperous men, who object to this desertion, image to themselves some clean contented family like that which they go home to. But look at the countenance of the poor wives who follow and persecute their good-man to the door of the public-house, which he is about to enter, when something like shame would restrain him, if stronger misery did not induce him to pass the threshold. That face, ground by want, in which every cheerful, every conversable lineament has been long effaced by misery,—is that a face to stay at home with? is it more a woman, or a wild cat? alas! it is the face of the wife of his youth, that once smiled upon him. It can smile no longer. What comforts can it share? what burthens can it lighten? Oh, 'tis a fine thing to talk of the humble meal shared together! But what if there be no bread in the cupboard? The innocent prattle of his children takes out the sting of a man's poverty. But the children of the very poor do not prattle. It is none of the least frightful features in that condition, that there is no childishness in its dwellings. Poor people, said a sensible old nurse to us once, do not bring up their children; they drag them up.

The little careless darling of the wealthier nursery, in their hovel is transformed betimes into a premature reflecting person. No one has time to dandle it, no one thinks it worth while to coax it, to soothe it, to toss it up and down, to humour it. There is none to kiss away its tears. If it cries, it can only be beaten. It has been prettily said, that "a babe is fed with milk and praise." But the aliment of this poor babe was thin, unnourishing; the return to its little baby-tricks, and efforts to engage attention, bitter ceaseless objurgation. It never had a toy, or knew what a coral meant. It grew up without the lullaby of nurses, it was a stranger to the patient fondle, the hushing caress, the attracting novelty, the costlier plaything, or the cheaper off-hand contrivance to divert the child; the prattled nonsense (best sense to it), the wise impertinences, the wholesome lies, the apt story interposed, that puts a stop to present sufferings, and awakens the passions of young wonder. It was never sung to—no one ever told to it a tale of the nursery. It was dragged up, to live or to die as it happened. It had no young dreams. It broke at once into the iron realities of life. A child exists not for the very poor as any object of dalliance; it is only another mouth to be fed, a pair of little hands to be betimes inured to labour. It is the rival, till it can be the co-operator, for food with the parent. It is never his mirth, his diversion, his solace: it never makes him young again, with recalling his young times. The children of the very poor have no young times. It makes the very heart to bleed to over-hear the casual street-talk between a poor woman and her little girl, a woman of the better sort of poor, in a condition rather above the squalid beings which we have been contemplating. It is not of toys, of nursery books, of summer holidays (fitting that age); of the promised sight, or play; of praised sufficiency at school. It is of mangling and clear-starching, of the price of coals, or of potatoes. The questions of the child, that should be the very outpourings of curiosity in idleness, are marked with forecast and melancholy providence. It has come to be a woman,—before it was a child. It has learned to go to market; it chaffers, it haggles, it envies, it murmurs; it is knowing, acute, sharpened; it never prattles. Had we not reason to say that the home of the very poor is no home?

There is yet another home, which we are constrained to deny to be one. It has a larder, which the home of the poor man wants; its fireside conveniences, of which the poor dream not. But with all this, it is no home. It is—the house of a man that is infested with many visitors. May we be branded for the veriest churl, if we deny our heart to the many noble-hearted friends that at times exchange their dwelling for our poor roof! It is not of guests that we complain, but of endless, purposeless visitants; droppers-in, as they are called. We sometimes wonder from what sky they fall. It is the very error of the position of our lodging; its horoscopy was ill calculated, being just situate in a medium—a plaguy suburban mid-space—fitted to catch idlers from town or country. We are older than we were, and age is easily put out of its way. We have fewer sands in our glass to reckon upon, and we cannot brook to see them drop in endlessly succeeding impertinences. At our time of life, to be alone sometimes is as needful as sleep. It is the refreshing sleep of the day. The growing infirmities of age manifest themselves in nothing more strongly than in an inveterate dislike of interruption. The thing which we are doing, we wish to be permitted to do. We have neither much knowledge nor devices; but there are fewer in the place to which we hasten. We are not willingly put out of our way, even at a game of nine-pins. While youth was, we had vast reversions in time future; we are reduced to a present pittance, and obliged to economise in that article. We bleed away our moments now as hardly as our ducats. We cannot bear to have our thin wardrobe eaten and fretted into by moths. We are willing to barter our good time with a friend, who gives us in exchange his own. Herein is the distinction between the genuine guest and the visitant. This latter takes your good time, and gives you his bad in exchange. The guest is domestic to you as your good cat, or household bird; the visitant is your fly, that flaps in at your window and out again, leaving nothing but a sense of disturbance, and victuals spoiled. The inferior functions of life begin to move heavily. We cannot concoct our food with interruptions. Our chief meal, to be nutritive, must be solitary. With difficulty we can eat before a guest; and never understood what the relish of public feasting meant. Meats have no sapor, nor digestion fair play, in a crowd. The unexpected coming in of a visitant stops the machine. There is a punctual generation who time their calls to the precise commencement of your dining-hour—not to eat—but to see you eat. Our knife and fork drop instinctively, and we feel that we have swallowed our latest morsel. Others again show their genius, as we have said, in knocking the moment you have just sat down to a book. They have a peculiar compassionate sneer, with which they "hope that they do not interrupt your studies." Though they flutter off the next moment, to carry their impertinences to the nearest student that they can call their friend, the tone of the book is spoiled; we shut the leaves, and with Dante's lovers, read no more that day. It were well if the effect of intrusion were simply co-extensive with its presence, but it mars all the good hours afterwards. These scratches in appearance leave an orifice that closes not hastily. "It is a prostitution of the bravery of friendship," says worthy Bishop Taylor, "to spend it upon impertinent people, who are, it may be, loads to their families, but can never ease my loads." This is the secret of their gaddings, their visits, and morning calls. They too have homes, which are—no homes.

XIII.—THAT YOU MUST LOVE ME AND LOVE MY DOG.

"GOOD sir, or madam—as it may be—we most willingly embrace the offer of your friendship. We have long known your excellent qualities. We have wished to have you nearer to us; to hold you within the very innermost fold of our heart. We can have no reserve towards a person of your open and noble nature. The frankness of your humour suits us exactly. We have been long looking for such a friend. Quick—let us disburthen our troubles into each other's bosom—let us make our single joys shine by reduplication.—But *yap, yap, yap!* what is this confounded cur? he has fastened his tooth, which is none of the bluntest, just in the fleshy part of my leg."

"It is my dog, sir. You must love him for my sake. Here, Test—Test—Test!"

"But he has bitten me."

"Ay, that he is apt to do, till you are better acquainted with him. I have had him three years. He never bites me."

Yap, yap, yap!—"He is at it again."

"Oh, sir, you must not kick him. He does not like to be kicked. I expect my dog to be treated with all the respect due to myself."

"But do you always take him out with you, when you go a friendship-hunting?"

"Invariably. 'Tis the sweetest, prettiest, best-conditioned animal. I call him my *test*—the touchstone by which to try a friend. No one can properly be said to love me, who does not love him."

"Excuse us, dear sir—or madam, aforesaid—if upon further consideration we are obliged to decline the otherwise invaluable offer of your friendship. We do not like dogs."

"Mighty well, sir,—you know the conditions—you may have worse offers. Come along, Test."

The above dialogue is not so imaginary, but that, in the intercourse of life, we have had frequent occasions of breaking off an agreeable intimacy by reason of these canine appendages. They do not always come in the shape of dogs; they sometimes wear the more plausible and human character of kinsfolk, near acquaintances, my friend's friend, his partner, his wife, or his children. We could never yet form a friendship—not to speak of more delicate correspondence—however much to our taste, without the intervention of some third anomaly, some impertinent clog affixed to the relation—the understood *dog* in the proverb. The good things of life are not to be had singly, but come to us with a mixture; like a school-boy's holiday, with a task affixed to the tail of it. What a delightful companion is * * * *, if he did not always bring his tall cousin with him! He seems to grow with him; like some of those double births which we remember to have read of with such wonder and delight in the old "Athenian Oracle," where Swift commenced author by writing Pindaric Odes (what a beginning for him!) upon Sir William Temple. There is the picture of the brother, with the little brother peeping out at his shoulder; a species of fraternity, which we have no name of kin close enough to comprehend. When * * * * comes, poking in his head and shoulder into your room, as if to feel his entry, you think, surely you have now got him to yourself—what a three hours' chat we shall have!—but ever in the haunch of him, and before his diffident body is well disclosed in your apartment, appears the haunting shadow of the cousin, overpeering his modest kinsman, and sure to overlay the expected good talk with his insufferable procerity of stature, and uncorresponding dwarfishness of observation. Misfortunes seldom come alone. 'Tis hard when a blessing comes accompanied. Cannot we like Sempronia, without sitting down to chess with her eternal brother; or know Sulpicia, without knowing all the round of her card-playing relations?—must my friend's brethren of necessity be mine also? must we be hand and glove with Dick Selby the parson, or Jack Selby the calico-printer, because W. S., who is neither, but a ripe wit and a critic, has the misfortune to claim a common parentage with them? Let him lay down his brothers; and 'tis odds but we will cast him in a pair of ours (we have a superflux) to balance the concession. Let F. H. lay down his garrulous uncle; and Honorius dismiss his vapid wife, and superfluous establishment of six boys: things between boy and manhood—too ripe for play, too raw for conversation —that come in, impudently staring his father's old friend out of countenance; and will neither aid nor let alone, the conference; that we may once more meet upon equal terms, as we were wont to do in the disengaged state of bachelorhood.

It is well if your friend, or mistress, be content with these canicular probations. Few young ladies but in this sense keep a dog. But when Rutilia hounds at you her tiger aunt; or Ruspina expects you to cherish and fondle her viper sister, whom she has preposterously taken into her bosom, to try stinging conclusions upon your constancy; they must not complain if the house be rather thin of suitors. Scylla must have broken off many excellent matches in her time, if she insisted upon all that loved her loving her dogs also.

An excellent story to this moral is told of Merry, of Della Cruscan memory. In tender youth he loved and courted a modest appanage to the Opera—in truth, a dancer —who had won him by the artless contrast between her manners and situation. She seemed to him a native violet, that had been transplanted by some rude accident into that exotic and artificial hotbed. Nor, in truth, was she less genuine and sincere than she appeared to him. He wooed and won this flower. Only for appearance sake, and for due honour to the bride's relations, she craved that she might have the attendance of her friends and kindred at the approaching solemnity. The request was too amiable not to be conceded; and in this solicitude for conciliating the good-will of mere relations, he found a presage of her superior attentions to himself, when the golden shaft should have "killed the flock of all affections else." The morning came: and at the Star and Garter, Richmond—the place appointed for the breakfasting—accompanied with one English friend, he impatiently awaited what reinforcements the bride should bring to grace the ceremony. A rich muster she had made. They came in six coaches—the whole corps du ballet—French, Italian, men and women. Monsieur de B., the famous *pirouetter* of the day, led his fair spouse, but craggy, from the banks of the Seine. The Prima Donna had sent her excuse. But the first and second Buffa were there; and Signor Sc—, and Signora Ch—, and Madame V—, with a countless cavalcade besides of choruser, figurantes! at the sight of whom Merry afterwards declared, that "then for the first time it struck him seriously, that he was about to marry—a dancer." But there was no help for it. Besides, it was her day; these were, in fact, her friends and kinsfolk. The assemblage, though whimsical, was all very natural. But when the bride —handing out of the last coach a still more extraordinary figure than the rest—presented to him as her *father*—the gentleman that was to *give her away*—no less a person than Signor Delpini himself—with a sort of pride, as much as to say, See what I have brought to do us honour!—the thought of so extraordinary a paternity quite overcame him; and slipping away under some pretence from the bride and her motley adherents, poor Merry took horse from the back yard to the nearest seacoast, from which, shipping himself to America, he shortly after consoled himself with a more congenial match in the person of Miss Brunton; relieved from his intended clown father, and a bevy of painted buffas for bridemaids.

At what precise minute that little airy musician doffs his night gear, and prepares to tune up his unseasonable matins, we are not naturalist enough to determine. But for a mere human gentleman —that has no orchestra business to call him from his warm bed to such preposterous exercises—we take ten, or half after ten (eleven, of course, during this Christmas solstice), to be the very earliest hour at which he can begin to think of abandoning his pillow. To think of it, we say; for to do it in earnest requires another half hour's good consideration. Not but there are pretty sun-risings, as we are told, and such like gawds, abroad in the world, in summer-time especially, some hours before what we have assigned; which a gentleman may see, as they say, only for getting up. But having been tempted once or twice, in earlier life, to assist at those ceremonies, we confess our curiosity abated. We are no longer ambitious of being the sun's courtiers, to attend at his morning levees. We hold the good hours of the dawn too sacred to waste them upon such observances; which have in them, besides, something Pagan and Persic. To say truth, we never anticipated our usual hour, or got up with the sun (as 'tis called), to go a journey, or upon a foolish whole day's pleasuring, but we suffered for it all the long hours after in listlessness and headaches; Nature herself sufficiently declaring her sense of our presumption in aspiring to regulate our frail waking courses by the measures of that celestial and sleepless traveller. We deny not that there is something sprightly and vigorous, at the outset especially, in these break-of-day excursions. It is flattering to get the start of a lazy world; to conquer Death by proxy in his image. But the seeds of sleep and mortality are in us; and we pay usually, in strange qualms before night falls, the penalty of the unnatural inversion. Therefore, while the busy part of mankind are fast huddling on their clothes, are already up and about their occupations, content to have swallowed their sleep by wholesale; we choose to linger a-bed and digest our dreams. It is the very time to recombine the wandering images, which night in a confused mass presented; to snatch them from forgetfulness; to shape, and mould them. Some people have no good of their dreams. Like fast feeders, they gulp them too grossly, to taste them curiously. We love to chew the cud of a foregone vision; to collect the scattered rays of a brighter phantasm, or act over again, with firmer nerves, the sadder nocturnal tragedies; to drag into day-light a struggling and half-vanishing night-mare; to handle and examine the terrors, or the airy solaces. We have too much respect for these spiritual communications, to let them go so lightly. We are not so stupid, or so careless as that Imperial forgetter of his dreams, that we should need a seer to remind us of the form of them. They seem to us to have as much significance as our waking concerns; or rather to import us more nearly, as more nearly we approach by years to the shadowy world, whither we are hastening. We have shaken hands with the world's business; we have done with it; we have discharged ourself of it. Why should we get up? we have neither suit to solicit, nor affairs to manage. The drama has shut upon us at the fourth act. We have nothing here to expect, but in a short time a sick-bed, and a dismissal. We delight to anticipate death by such shadows as night affords. We are already half acquainted with ghosts. We were never much in the world. Disappointment early struck a dark veil between us and its dazzling illusions. Our spirits showed grey before our hairs. The mighty changes of the world already appear as but the vain stuff out of which dramas are composed. We have asked no more of life than what the mimic images in play-houses present us with. Even those types have waxed fainter. Our clock appears to have struck. We are SUPERANNUATED. In this dearth of mundane satisfaction, we contract politic alliances with shadows. It is good to have friends at court. The extracted media of dreams seem no ill introduction to that spiritual presence, upon which, in no long time, we expect to be thrown. We are trying to know a little of the usages of that colony; to learn the language and the faces we shall meet with there, that we may be the less awkward at our first coming among them. We willingly call a phantom our fellow, as knowing we shall soon be of their dark companionship. Therefore we cherish dreams. We try to spell in them the alphabet of the invisible world; and think we know already how it shall be with us. Those uncouth shapes which, while we clung to flesh and blood, affrighted us, have become familiar. We feel attenuated into their meagre essences, and have given the hand of half-way approach to incorporeal being. We once thought life to be something; but it has unaccountably fallen from us before its time. Therefore we choose to dally with visions. The sun has no purposes of ours to light us to. Why should we get up?

IV.—THAT WE SHOULD LIE DOWN WITH THE LAMB.

We could never quite understand the philosophy of this arrangement, or the wisdom of our ancestors in sending us for instruction to these woolly bedfellows. A sheep, when it is dark, has nothing to do but to shut his silly eyes, and sleep if he can. Man found out long sixes—Hail, candle-light! without disparagement to sun or moon, the kindliest luminary of the three—if we may not rather style thee their radiant deputy, mild viceroy of the moon! —We love to read, talk, sit silent, eat, drink, sleep, by candle-light. They are everybody's sun and moon. This is our peculiar and household planet. Wanting it, what savage unsocial nights must our ancestors have spent, winter in caves and unillumined fastnesses! They must have lain about and grumbled at one another in the dark. What repartees could have passed, when you must have felt about for a smile, and handled a neighbour's cheek to be sure that he understood it? This accounts for the seriousness of the elder poetry. It has a sombre cast (try Hesiod or Ossian), derived from the tradition of those unlantern'd nights. Jokes came in with candles. We wonder how they saw to pick up a pin, if they had any. How did they sup? what a mélange of chance carving they must have made of it?—here one had got a leg of a goat when he wanted a horse's shoulder—there another had dipped his scooped palm in a kid-skin of wild honey, when he meditated right mare's milk. There is neither good eating nor drinking in fresco. Who, even in these civilized times, has never experienced this, when at some economic table he has commenced dining after dusk, and waited for the flavour till the lights came? The senses absolutely give and take reciprocally. Can you tell pork from veal in the dark? or distinguish Sherris from pure Malaga? Take away the candle from the smoking man; by the glimmering of the left ashes, he knows that he is still smoking, but he knows it only by an inference; till the restored light, coming in aid of the olfactories, reveals to both senses the full aroma. Then how he redoubles his puffs! how he burnishes!—there is absolutely no such thing as reading but by a candle. We have tried the affectation of a book at noon-day in gardens, and in sultry arbours; but it was labour thrown away. Those gay motes in the beam come about you, hovering and teasing, like so many coquettes, that will have you all to their self and are jealous of your abstractions. By the midnight taper, the writer digests his meditations. By the same light we must approach to their perusal, if we would catch the flame, the odour. It is a mockery, all that is reported of the influential Phoebus. No true poem ever owed its birth to the sun's light. They are abstracted works—

Things that were born, when none but the stiff night,
And his dumb candle, saw his pinching throes.

Marry, daylight—daylight might furnish the images, the crude material; but for the fine shapings, the true turning and filing (as mine author hath it), they must be content to hold their inspiration of the candle.—The mild internal light, that reveals them, like fires on the domestic hearth, goes out in the sun-shine. Night and silence call out the starry fancies. Milton's Morning Hymn in Paradise, we would hold a good wager, was penned at midnight; and Taylor's rich description of a sun-rise smells decidedly of the taper. Even ourself, in these our humbler lucubrations tune our best-measured cadences (Prose has her cadences) not unfrequently to the charm of the drowsier watchman, "blessing the doors;" or the wild sweep of winds at midnight. Even now a loftier speculation than we have yet attempted, courts our endeavours. We would indite something about the Solar System.—*Betty, bring the candles.*

XVI.—THAT A SULKY TEMPER IS A MISFORTUNE.

We grant that it is, and a very serious one—to a man's friends, and to all that have to do with him; but whether the condition of the man himself is so much to be deplored, may admit of a question. We can speak a little to it, being ourselves but lately recovered—we whisper it in confidence, reader—out of a long and desperate fit of the sullens. Was the cure a blessing? The conviction which wrought it, came too clearly to leave a scruple of the fanciful injuries—for they were mere fancies—which had provoked the humour. But the humour itself was too self-pleasing while it lasted—we know how bare we lay ourself in the confession—to be abandoned all at once with the grounds of it. We still brood over wrongs which we know to have been imaginary; and for our old acquaintance N——, whom we find to have been a truer friend than we took him for, we substitute some phantom —a Caius or a Titius—as like him as we dare to form it, to wreak our yet unsatisfied resentments on. It is mortifying to fall at once from the pinnacle of neglect; to forego the idea of having been ill-used and contumaciously treated by an old friend. The first thing to aggrandize a man in his own conceit, is to conceive of himself as neglected. There let him fix if he can. To undeceive him is to deprive him of the most tickling morsel within the range of self-complacency. No flattery can come near it. Happy is he who suspects his friend of an injustice; but supremely blest, who thinks all his friends in a conspiracy to depress and undervalue him. There is a pleasure (we sing not to the profane) far beyond the reach of all that the world calls joy—a deep, enduring satisfaction in the depths, where the superficial seek it not, of discontent. Were we to recite one half of this mystery—which we were let into by our late dissatisfaction, all the world would be in love with disrespect; we should wear a slight for a bracelet, and neglects and contumacies would be the only matter for courtship. Unlike to that mysterious book in the Apocalypse, the study of this mystery is unpalatable only in the commencement. The first sting of a suspicion is grievous; but wait—out of that wound, which to flesh and blood seemed so difficult, there is balm and honey to be extracted. Your friend passed you on such or such a day,—having in his company one that you conceived worse than ambiguously disposed towards you,—passed you in the street without notice. To be sure, he is something short-sighted; and it was in your power to have accosted *him*. But facts and sane inferences are trifles to a true adept in the science of dissatisfaction. He must have seen you; and S——, who was with him, must have been the cause of the contempt. It galls you, and well it may. But have patience. Go home, and make the worst of it, and you are a made man from this time. Shut yourself up, and —rejecting, as an enemy to your peace, every whispering suggestion that but insinuates there may be a mistake—reflect seriously upon the many lesser instances which you had begun to perceive, in proof of your friend's disaffection towards you. None of them singly was much to the purpose, but the aggregate weight is positive; and you have this last affront to clench them. Thus far the process is anything but agreeable. But now to your relief comes the comparative faculty. You conjure up all the kind feelings you have had for your friend; what you have been to him, and what you would have been to him, if he would have suffered you; how you defended him in this or that place; and his good name—his literary reputation, and so forth, was always dearer to you than your own! Your heart, spite of itself, yearns towards him. You could weep tears of blood but for a restraining pride. How say you? do you not yet begin to apprehend a comfort?—some allay of sweetness in the bitter waters? Stop not here, nor penuriously cheat yourself of your reversions. You are on vantage ground. Enlarge your speculations, and take in the rest of your friends, as a spark kindles more sparks. Was there one among them who has not to you proved hollow, false, slippery as water? Begin to think that the relation itself is inconsistent with mortality. That the very idea of friendship, with its component parts, as honour, fidelity, steadiness, exists but in your single bosom. Image yourself to yourself as the only possible friend in a world incapable of that communion. Now the gloom thickens. The little star of self-love twinkles, that is to encourage you through deeper glooms than this. You are not yet at the half point of your elevation. You are not yet, believe me, half sulky enough. Adverting to the world in general (as these circles in the mind will spread to infinity), reflect with what strange injustice you have been treated in quarters where (setting gratitude and the expectation of friendly returns aside as chimeras) you pretended no claim beyond justice, the naked due of all men. Think the very idea of right and fit fled from the earth, or your breast the solitary receptacle of it till you have swelled yourself into at least one hemi-sphere; the other being the vast Arabia Stony of your friends and the world aforesaid. To grow bigger every moment in your own conceit, and the world to lessen; to deify yourself at the expense of your species; to judge the world —this is the acme and supreme point of your mystery—these the true PLEASURES OF SULKINESS. We profess no more of this grand secret than what ourself experimented on one rainy afternoon in the last week, sulking in our study. We had proceeded to the penultimate point, at which the true adept seldom stops, where the consideration of benefit forgot is about to merge in the meditation of general injustice—when a knock at the door was followed by the entrance of the very friend whose not seeing of us in the morning (for we will now confess the case our own), an accidental oversight, had given rise to so much agreeable generalization! To mortify us still more, and take down the whole flattering superstructure which pride had piled upon neglect, he had brought in his hand the identical S——, in whose favour we had suspected him of the contumacy. Asseverations were needless, where the frank manner of them both was convictive of the injurious nature of the suspicion. We fancied that they perceived our embarrassment; but were too proud, or something else, to confess to the secret of it. We had been but too lately in the condition of the noble patient in Argos:—

Qui se credebat miros audire tragœdos,
In vacuo lætus sessor plausorque theatro—

and could have exclaimed with equal reason against the friendly hands that cured us—

Pol, me occidistis, amici,
Non servastis, ait; cui sic extorta vo-
luptas,
Et demptus per vim mentis gratissimus
error.

ELIANA.

THE GENTLE GIANTESS.

THE Widow Blacket, of Oxford, is the largest female I ever had the pleasure of beholding. There may be her parallel upon the earth; but surely I never saw it. I take her to be lineally descended from the maid's aunt of Brainford, who caused Master Ford such uneasiness. She hath Atlantean shoulders; and, as she stoopeth in her gait,—with as few offences to answer for in her own particular as any of Eve's daughter's—her back seems broad enough to bear the blame of all the peccadilloes that have been committed since Adam. She girdeth her waist—or what she is pleased to esteem as such—nearly up to her shoulders; from beneath which that huge dorsal expanse, in mountainous declivity, emergeth. Respect for her alone preventeth the idle boys, who follow her about in shoals, whenever she cometh abroad, from getting up, and riding. But her presence infallibly commands a reverence. She is indeed, as the Americans would express it, something awful. Her person is a burden to herself no less than to the ground which bears her. To her mighty bone, she hath a pinguitude withal, which makes the depth of winter to her the most desirable season. Her distress in the warmer solstice is pitiable. During the months of July and August, she usually renteth a cool cellar, where ices are kept, whereinto she descendeth when Sirius rageth. She dates from a hot Thursday,—some twenty-five years ago. Her apartment in summer is pervious to the four winds. Two doors, in north and south direction, and two windows, fronting the rising and the setting sun, never closed, from every cardinal point catch the contributory breezes. She loves to enjoy what she calls a quadruple draught. That must be a shrewd zephyr that can escape her. I owe a painful face-ache, which oppresses me at this moment, to a cold caught, sitting by her, one day in last July, at this receipt of coolness. Her fan, in ordinary, resembleth a banner spread, which she keepeth continually on the alert to detect the least breeze. She possesseth an active and gadding mind, totally incommensurate with her person. No one delighteth more than herself in country exercises and pastimes I have passed many an agreeable holy-day with her in her favourite park at Woodstock. She performs her part in these delightful ambulatory excursions by the aid of a portable garden-chair. She setteth out with you at a fair footgallop, which she keepeth up till you are both well breathed, and then reposeth she for a few seconds. Then she is up again for a hundred paces or so, and again resteth; her movement, on these sprightly occasions, being something between walking and flying. Her great weight seemeth to propel her forward, ostrich-fashion. In this kind of relieved marching, I have traversed with her many scores of acres on those well-wooded and well-watered domains. Her delight at Oxford is in the public walks and gardens, where, when the weather is not too oppressive, she passeth much of her valuable time. There is a bench at Maudlin, or rather situated between the frontiers of that and ——'s College (some litigation, latterly, about repairs, has vested the property of it finally in——'s), where, at the hour of noon, she is ordinarily to be found sitting,— so she calls it by courtesy,—but, in fact, pressing and breaking of it down with her enormous settlement; as both those foundations, —who, however, are good-natured enough to wink at it,—have found, I believe, to their cost. Here she taketh the fresh air, principally at vacation-times, when the walks are freest from interruption of the younger fry of students. Here she passeth her idle hours, not idly, but generally accompanied with a book,—blessed if she can but intercept some resident Fellow (as usually there are some of that brood left behind at these periods), or stray Master of Arts (to most of whom she is better known than their dinner-bell), with whom she may confer upon any curious topic of literature. I have seen these shy gownsmen, who truly set but a very slight value upon female conversation, cast a hawk's eye upon her from the length of Maudlin Grove, and warily glide off into another walk,—true monks as they are; and ungently neglecting the delicacies of her polished converse for their own perverse and uncommunicating solitariness! Within-doors, her principal diversion is music, vocal and instrumental; in both which she is no mean professor. Her voice is wonderfully fine; but, till I got used to it, I confess it staggered me. It is, for all the world, like that of a piping bullfinch; while, from her size and stature, you would expect notes to drown the deep organ. The shake, which most fine singers reserve for the close or cadence, by some unaccountable flexibility or tremulousness of pipe, she carrieth quite through the composition: so that her time, to a common air or ballad, keeps double motion, like the earth,—running the primary circuit of the tune, and still revolving upon its own axis. The effect, as I said before, when you are used to it, is as agreeable as it is altogether new and surprising. The spacious apartment of her outward frame lodgeth a soul in all respects disproportionate. Of more than mortal make, she evinceth withal a trembling sensibility, a yielding infirmity of purpose, a quick susceptibility to reproach, and all the train of diffident and blushing virtues, which for their habitation usually seek out a feeble frame, an attenuated and meagre constitution. With more than man's bulk, her humours and occupations are eminently feminine. She sighs,—being six foot high. She languisheth,—being two feet wide. She worketh slender sprigs upon the delicate muslin,—her fingers being capable of moulding a Colossus. She sippeth her wine out of her glass daintily,—her capacity being that of a tun of Heidelberg. She goeth mincingly with those feet of hers, whose solidity need not fear the black ox's pressure. Softest and largest of thy sex, adieu! By what parting attribute may I salute thee, last and best of the Titanesses,—Ogress, fed with milk instead of blood; not least, or least handsome, among Oxford's stately structures,—Oxford, who, in its deadest time of vacation, can never properly be said to be empty, having thee to fill it.

———

THE REYNOLDS GALLERY.

The Reynolds Gallery has, upon the whole, disappointed me. Some of the portraits are interesting. They are faces of characters whom we (middle-aged gentlemen) were born a little too late to remember, but about whom we have heard our fathers tell stories till we almost fancy to have seen them. There is a charm in the portrait of a Rodney or a Keppel, which even a picture of Nelson must want for me. I should turn away after a slight inspection from the best likeness that could be made of Mrs. Anne Clarke; but Kitty Fisher is a considerable personage. Then the dresses of some of the women so exactly remind us of modes which we can just recall; of the forms under which the venerable relationship of aunt or mother first presented themselves to our young eyes; the aprons, the coifs, the lappets, the hoods. Mercy on us! what a load of head-ornaments seem to have conspired to bury a pretty face in the picture of Mrs. Long, *yet could not!* Beauty must have some "charmed life" to have been able to surmount the conspiracy of fashion in those days to destroy it.

The portraits which least pleased me were those of boys, as Infant Bacchuses, Jupiters, &c. But the artist is not to be blamed for the disguise. No doubt, the parents wished to see their children deified in their lifetime. It was but putting a thunderbolt (instead of a squib) into young master's hands; and a whey-faced chit was transformed into the infant ruler of Olympus,—him who was afterward to shake heaven and earth with his black brow. Another good boy pleased his grandmamma with saying his prayers so well, and the blameless dotage of the good old woman imagined in him an adequate representative of the infancy of the awful Prophet Samuel. *But the great historical compositions, where the artist was at liberty* to paint from *his own idea,* —the *Beaufort and the Ugolino:* why, then, I must confess, pleading the liberty of table-talk for my presumption, that they have not left any very elevating impressions on my mind. Pardon a ludicrous comparison. I know, madam, you admire them both; but placed opposite to each other, as they are at the Gallery, as if to set the one work in competition with the other, they did remind me of the famous contention for the prize of deformity, mentioned in the 173rd number of the "Spectator." The one stares, and the other grins; but is there common dignity in their countenances? Does anything of the history of their life gone by peep through the ruins of the mind in the face, like the unconquerable grandeur that surmounts the distortions of the Laocoön? The figures which stand by the bed of Beaufort are indeed happy representations of the plain unmannered old nobility of the English historical plays of Shakspeare; but, for anything else, give me leave to recommend those macaroons.

After leaving the Reynolds Gallery (where, upon the whole, I received a good deal of pleasure), and feeling that I had quite had my fill of paintings, I stumbled upon a picture in Piccadilly (No. 22, I think), which purports to be a portrait of Francis the First by Leonardo da Vinci. Heavens, what a difference! It is but a portrait, as most of those I had been seeing; but, placed by them, it would kill them, swallow them up as Moses' rod the other rods. Where did these old painters get their models? I see no such figures, not in my dreams, as this Francis, in the character, or rather with the attributes of John the Baptist. A more than martial majesty in the brow and upon the eyelid; an arm muscular, beautifully formed; the long, graceful, massy fingers compressing, yet so as not to hurt, a lamb more lovely, more sweetly shrinking, than we can conceive that milk-white one which followed Una; the picture altogether looking as if it were eternal,—combining the truth of flesh with a promise of permanence like marble.

Leonardo, from the one or two specimens we have of him in England, must have been a stupendous genius. I scarce can think he has had his full fame,—he who could paint that wonderful personification of the Logos, or third person of the Trinity, grasping a globe, late in the possession of Mr. Troward of Pall Mall, where the hand was, by the boldest license, twice as big as the truth of drawing warranted; yet the effect, to every one that saw it, by some magic of his genius was confessed to be not *monstrous*, but *miraculous* and *silencing*. It could not be gainsaid.

———

GUY FAUX.

A VERY ingenious and subtle writer, whom there is good reason for suspecting to be an ex-Jesuit, not unknown at Douay some five-and-twenty years since (he will not obtrude himself at M——th again in a hurry), about a twelvemonth back set himself to prove the character of the Powder Plot conspirators to have been that of heroic self-devotedness and true Christian martyrdom. Under the mask of Protestant candour, he actually gained admission for his treatise into a London weekly paper not particularly distinguished for its zeal towards either religion. But, admitting Catholic principles, his arguments are shrewd and incontrovertible. He says:—

"Guy Faux was a fanatic; but he was no hypocrite. He ranks among *good haters*. He was cruel, bloody-minded, reckless of all considerations but those of an infuriated and bigoted faith; but he was a true son of the Catholic Church, a martyr, and a confessor, for all that. He who can prevail upon himself to devote his life for a cause, however we may condemn his opinions or abhor his actions, vouches at least for the honesty of his principles and the disinterestedness of his motives. He may be guilty of the worst practices; but he is capable of the greatest. He is no longer a slave, but free. The contempt of death is the beginning of virtue. The hero of the Gunpowder Plot was, if you will, a fool, a madman, an assassin; call him what names you please: still he was neither knave nor coward. He did not propose to blow up the parliament, and come off scotfree himself: he showed that he valued his own life no more than theirs in such a cause, where the integrity of the Catholic faith and the salvation of perhaps millions of souls was at stake. He did not call it a murder, but a sacrifice, which he was about to achieve: he was armed with the Holy Spirit and with fire: he was the Church's chosen servant and her blessed martyr. He comforted himself as 'the best of cut-throats.' How many wretches are there that would have undertaken to do what he intended, for a sum of money, if they could have got off with impunity! How few are there who would have put themselves in Guy Faux's situation to save the universe! Yet, in the latter case, we affect to be thrown into greater consternation than at the most unredeemed acts of villany; as if the absolute disinterestedness of the motive doubled the horror of the deed! The cowardice and selfishness of mankind are in fact shocked at the consequences to themselves (if such examples are held up for imitation); and they make a fearful outcry against the violation of every principle of morality, lest they, too, should be called on for any such tremendous sacrifices; lest they, in their turn, should have to go on the forlorn hope of extra-official duty. *Charity begins at home* is a maxim that prevails as well in the courts of conscience as in those of prudence. We would be thought to shudder at the consequences of crime to others, while we tremble for them to ourselves. We talk of the dark and cowardly assassin; and this is well, when an individual shrinks from the face of an enemy, and purchases his own safety by striking a blow in the dark: but how the charge of cowardly can be applied to the public assassin, who, in the very act of destroying another, lays down his life as the pledge and forfeit of his sincerity and boldness, I am at a loss to devise. There may be barbarous prejudice, rooted hatred, unprincipled treachery in such an act; but he who resolves to take all the danger and odium upon himself can no more be branded with cowardice, than Regulus devoting himself for his country, or Codrus leaping into the fiery gulf. A wily Father Inquisitor, coolly and with plenary authority condemning hundreds of helpless, unoffending victims to the flames, or the horrors of a living tomb, while he himself would not suffer a hair of his head to be hurt, is, to me, a character without any qualifying trait in it. Again: The Spanish conqueror and hero, the favourite of his monarch, who enticed thirty thousand poor Mexicans into a large open building under promise of strict faith and cordial good-will, and then set fire to it, making sport of the cries and agonies of these deluded creatures, is an instance of uniting the most hardened cruelty with the most heartless selfishness. His plea was, keeping no faith with heretics; this was Guy Faux's too: but I am sure at least that the latter kept faith with himself; he was in earnest in his professions. *His* was not gay, wanton, unfeeling depravity; he did not murder in sport: it was serious work that he had taken in hand. To see this arch-bigot, this heart-whole traitor, this pale miner in the infernal regions, skulking in his retreat with his cloak and dark lantern, moving cautiously about among his barrels of gunpowder loaded with death, but not yet ripe for destruction, regardless of the lives of others, and more than indifferent to his own, presents a picture of the strange infatuation of the human understanding, but not of the depravity of the human will, without an equal. There were thousands of pious Papists privy to and ready to applaud the deed when done: there was no one but our old fifth-of-November friend, who still flutters in rags and straw on the occasion, that had the courage to attempt it. In him stern duty and unshaken faith prevailed over natural frailty."

It is impossible, upon Catholic principles, not to admit the force of this reasoning: we can only not help smiling (with the writer) at the simplicity of the gulled editor, swallowing the dregs of Loyola for the very quintessence of sublimated reason in England at the commencement of the nineteenth century. We will just, as a contrast, show what we Protestants (who are a party concerned) thought upon the same subject at a period rather nearer to the heroic project in question.

The Gunpowder Treason was the subject which called forth the earliest specimen which is left us of the pulpit eloquence of Jeremy Taylor. When he preached the sermon on that anniversary, which is printed at the end of the folio edition of his Sermons, he was a young man, just commencing his ministry under the auspices of Archbishop Laud. From the learning and maturest oratory which it manifests, one should rather have conjectured it to have proceeded from the same person after he was ripened by time into a Bishop and Father of the Church. "And, really, these *Romano-barbari* could never pretend to any precedent for an act so barbarous as theirs. Adramelech, indeed, killed a king; but he spared the people. Haman would have killed the people, but spared the king; but that both king and people, princes and judges, branch and rush and root, should die at once (as if Caligula's wish were actuated, and all England upon one head), was never known till now, that all the malice of the world met in this as in a centre. The Sicilian evensong, the matins of St. Bartholomew, known for the pitiless and damned massacres, were but καπνου σκιας οναρ, the dream of the shadow of smoke, if compared with this great fire. *In tam occupato sæculo fabulas vulgares nequitia non invenit.* This was a busy age. Herostratus must have invented a more sublimed malice than the burning of one temple, or not have been so much as spoke of since the discovery of the powder treason. But I must make more haste; I shall not else climb the sublimity of this Impiety. Nero was sometimes the *populare odium*, was popularly hated, and deserved it too: for he slew his master, and his wife, and all his family, once or twice over; opened his mother's womb; fired the city, laughed at it, slandered the Christians for it: but yet all these were but *principia malorum*, the very first rudiments of evil. Add, then, to these, Herod's masterpiece at Ramah, as it was deciphered by the tears and sad threnes of the matrons in a universal mourning for the loss of their pretty infants; yet this of Herod will prove but an infant wickedness, and that of Nero the evil but of one city. I would willingly have found out an example, but see I cannot. Should I put into the scale the extract of the old tyrants famous in antique stories:—

Bistonii stabulum regis, Busiridis aras,
Antiphatæ mensas, et Taurica regna
    Thoantis;—

should I take for true story the highest cruelty as it was fancied by the most hieroglyphical Egyptian,—this alone would weigh them down, as if the Alps were put in scale against the dust of a balance. For, had this accursed treason prospered, we should have had the whole kingdom mourn for the inestimable loss of its chiefest glory, its life, its present joy, and all its very hopes for the future. For such was their destined malice, that they would not only have inflicted so cruel a blow, but have made it incurable, by cutting off our supplies of joy, the whole succession of the Line Royal. Not only the vine itself, but all the *gemmulæ*, and the tender olive branches, should either have been bent to their intentions, and made to grow crooked, or else been broken.

"And now, after such a sublimity of malice, I will not instance in the sacrilegious ruin of the neighbouring temples, which needs must have perished in the flame; nor in the disturbing the ashes of our entombed kings, devouring their dead ruins like sepulchral dogs: these are but minutes in respect of the ruin prepared for the living temples:—

Stragem sed istam non tulit
Christus cadentum Principum
Impune, ne forsan sui
Patris pariret fabricam.

Ergo quæ poterit lingua retexere
Laudes, Christe, tuas, qui domitum struis
Inædum populum cum Duce perfido!"

In such strains of eloquent indignation did Jeremy Taylor's young oratory inveigh against that stupendous attempt which he truly says had no parallel in ancient or modern times. A century and a half of European crimes has elapsed since he made the assertion, and his position remains in its strength. He wrote near the time in which the nefarious project had like to have been completed. Men's minds still were shuddering from the recentness of the escape. It must have been within his memory, or have been sounded in his ears so young by his parents, that he would seem, in his maturer years, to have remembered it. No wonder, then, that he describes it in words that burn. But to us, to whom the tradition has come slowly down, and has had time to cool, the story of Guido Vaux sounds rather like a tale, a fable, and an invention, than true history. It supposes such gigantic audacity of daring, combined with such more than infantile stupidity in the motive,—such a combination of the fiend and the monkey,—that credulity is almost swallowed up in contemplating the singularity of the attempt. It has accordingly, in some degree, shared the fate of fiction. It is familiarized to us in a kind of serio-ludicrous way, like the story of *Guy of Warwick*, or *Valentine and Orson*. The way which we take to perpetuate the memory of this deliverance is well adapted to keep up this fabular notion. Boys go about the streets annually with a beggarly scarecrow dressed up, which is to be burnt indeed, at night, with holy zeal; but, meantime, they beg a penny for *poor Guy:* this periodical petition, which we have heard from our infancy, combined with the dress and appearance of the effigy, so well calculated to move compassion, has the effect of quite removing from our fancy the horrid circumstances of the story which is thus commemorated; and in *poor Guy* vainly should we try to recognise any of the features of that tremendous madman in iniquity, Guido Vaux, with his horrid crew of accomplices, that sought to emulate earthquakes and bursting volcanoes in their more than mortal mischief.

Indeed, the whole ceremony of burning Guy Faux, or *the Pope*, as he is indifferently called, is a sort of *Treason Travestie*, and admirably adapted to lower our feelings upon this memorable subject. The printers of the little duodecimo *Prayer Book*, printed by T. Baskett,* in 1749, which has the effigy of his sacred majesty George II. piously prefixed, have illustrated the service (a very fine one in itself), which is appointed for the anniversary of this day, with a print, which it is not very easy to describe; but the contents appear to be these: The scene is a room, I conjecture, in the king's palace. Two persons—one of whom I take to be James himself, from his wearing his hat, while the other stands bare-headed—are intently surveying a sort of speculum, or magic mirror, which stands upon a pedestal in the midst of the room, in which a little figure of Guy Faux with his dark lantern, approaching the door of the Parliament House, is made discernible by the light proceeding from a *great eye* which shines in from the topmost corner of the apartment; by which eye the pious artist no doubt meant to designate Providence. On the other side of the mirror is a figure doing something, which puzzled me when a child, and continues to puzzle me now. The best I can make of it is, that it is a conspirator busy laying the train; but, then, why is he represented in the king's chamber? Conjecture upon so fantastical a design is vain; and I only notice the print as being one of the earliest graphic representations which woke my childhood into wonder, and doubtless combined, with the mummery before mentioned, to take off the edge of that horror which the naked historical mention of Guido's conspiracy could not have failed of exciting.

Now that so many years are past since that abominable machi-

* The same, I presume, upon whom the clergyman in the song of the "Vicar and Moses," not without judgment, passes this memorable censure:
"Here, Moses the king:
'Tis a scandalous thing
That this Baskett should print for the
        Crown."
Elia and Eliana.

nation was happily frustrated, it will not, I hope, be considered a profane sporting with the subject, if we take no very serious survey of the consequences that would have flowed from this plot if it had had a successful issue. The first thing that strikes us, in a selfish point of view, is the material change which it must have produced in the course of the nobility. All the ancient peerage being extinguished, as it was intended, at one blow, the *Red Book* must have been closed for ever, or a new race of peers must have been created to supply the deficiency. As the first part of this dilemma is a deal too shocking to think of, what a fund of mouth-watering reflections does this give rise to in the breast of us plebeians of A.D. 1823! Why, you or I, reader, might have been Duke of——, or Earl of——. I particularize no titles, to avoid the least suspicion of intention to usurp the dignities of the two noblemen whom I have in my eye; but a feeling more dignified than envy sometimes excites a sigh, when I think how the posterity of Guido's Legend of Honour (among whom you or I might have been) might have rolled down "dulcified," as Burke expresses it, "by an exposure to the influence of heaven in a long flow of generations, from the hard, acidulous, metallic tincture of the spring."* What new orders of merit, think you, this English Napoleon would have

chosen? Knights of the Barrel, or Lords of the Tub, Grand Almoners of the Cellar, or Ministers of Explosion? We should have given the train *conchant*, and the fire *rampant*, in our arms; we should have quartered the dozen white matches in our coats: the Shallows would have been nothing to us.

Turning away from these mortifying reflections, let us contemplate its effects upon the *other house;* for they were all to have gone together,—king, lords, commons.

To assist our imagination, let us take leave to suppose (and we do it in the harmless wantonness of fancy)—to suppose that the tremendous explosion had taken place in our days. We better know what a House of Commons is in our days, and can better estimate our loss. Let us imagine, then, to ourselves, the united members sitting in full conclave above; Faux just ready with his train and matches below,—in his hand a "reed tipt with fire." He applies the fatal engine.

To assist our notions still further, let us suppose some lucky dog of a reporter, who had escaped by miracle upon some plank of St. Stephen's benches, and came plump upon the roof of the adjacent Abbey; from whence descending, at some neighbouring coffee-house, first wiping his clothes and calling for a glass of lemonade, he sits down and reports what he had heard and seen (*quorum pars magna fuit*), for the

* Letter to a Noble Lord.

Morning Post or the *Courier*. We can scarcely imagine him describing the event in any other words but some such as these:—

"A *motion* was put and carried, that this House, do *adjourn;* that the speaker do *quit the chair.* The House rose amid clamours for order."

In some such way the event might most technically have been conveyed to the public. But a poetical mind, not content with this dry method of narration, cannot help pursuing the effects of this tremendous blowing up, this adjournment in the air, *sine die.* It seems the benches mount,—the chair first, and then the benches; and first the treasury bench, hurried up in this nitrous explosion, —the members, as it were, pairing off; Whigs and Tories taking their friendly apotheosis together (as they did their sandwiches below in Bellamy's room). Fancy, in her flight, keeps pace with the aspiring legislators: she sees the awful seat of order mounting, till it becomes finally fixed, a constellation, next to Cassiopeia's chair,—the wig of him that sat in it taking its place near Berenice's curls. St. Peter, at heaven's wicket,—no, not St. Peter,—St. Stephen, with open arms, receives his own.

While Fancy beholds these celestial appropriations, Reason, no less pleased, discerns the mighty benefit which so complete a renovation must produce below. Let the most determined foe to **corruption,** the most thorough-paced redresser of abuses, try to conceive a more absolute purification of the house than this was calculated to produce. Why, pride's purge was nothing to it. The whole borough-mongering system would have been got rid of, fairly *exploded;* with it the senseless distinctions of party must have disappeared, faction must have vanished, corruption have expired in air. From Hundred, Tything, and Wapentake, some new Alfred would have convened, in all its purity, the primitive Witenagemote,—fixed upon a basis of property or population permanent as the poles.

From this dream of universal restitution, Reason and Fancy with difficulty awake to view the real state of things. But, blessed be Heaven! St. Stephen's walls are yet standing, all her seats firmly secured; nay, some have doubted (since the Septennial Act) whether gunpowder itself, or anything short of a *committee* **above** *stairs,* would be able to shake any one member from his **seat.** That great and final improvement to the Abbey, which is all that seems wanting,—the removing Westminster Hall and its appendages, and letting in the view of the Thames,—must not be expected in our days. Dismissing, therefore, all such speculations as mere tales of a tub, it is the duty of every honest Englishman to endeavour, by means less wholesale than Guido's, to ameliorate, without extinguishing, parliaments; to hold the *lantern* to the dark places of corruption; to apply the *match* to the rotten parts of the system only; and to wrap himself up, not in the muffling mantle of conspiracy, but in the warm, honest *cloak* of integrity and patriotic intention.

A VISION OF HORNS.

My thoughts had been engaged last evening in solving the problem, why in all times and places the *horn* has been agreed upon as the symbol, or honourable badge, of married men. Moses' horn, the horn of Ammon, of Amalthea, and a cornucopia of legends besides, came to my recollection, but afforded no satisfactory solution, or rather involved the question in deeper obscurity. Tired with the fruitless chase of inexplicant analogies, I fell asleep, and dreamed in this fashion:—

Methought certain scales or films fell from my eyes, which had hitherto hindered these little tokens from being visible. I was somewhere in the Cornhill (as it might be termed) of some Utopia. Busy citizens jostled each other, as they may do in our streets, with care (the care of making a penny) written upon their foreheads; and *something else*, which is rather imagined than distinctly imaged, upon the brows of my own friends and fellow-townsmen.

In my first surprise, I supposed myself gotten into some forest,—Arden, to be sure, or Sherwood; but the dresses and deportment, all civic, forbade me to continue in that delusion. Then a scriptural thought crossed me (especially as there were nearly as many Jews as Christians among them), whether it might not be the children of Israel going up to besiege Jericho. I was undeceived of both errors by the sight of many faces which were familiar to me. I found myself strangely (as it will happen in dreams) at one and the same time in an unknown country with known companions. I met old friends, not with new faces, but with their old faces oddly adorned in front, with each man a certain corneous excrescence. Dick Mitis, the little cheesemonger in St. ——'s Passage, was the first that saluted me, with his hat off (you know Dick's way to a customer); and, I not being aware of him, he thrust a strange beam into my left eye, which pained and grieved me exceedingly; but, instead of apology, he only grinned and fleered in my face, as much as to say, "It is the custom of the country," and passed on.

I had scarce time to send a civil message to his lady, whom I have always admired as a pattern of a wife, and do indeed take Dick and her to be a model of conjugal agreement and harmony, when I felt an ugly smart in my neck, as if something had gored it behind; and, turning round, it was my old friend and neighbour, Dulcet, the confectioner, who, meaning to be pleasant, had thrust his protuberance right into my nape, and seemed proud of his power of offending.

Now I was assailed right and left, till in my own defence I was obliged to walk sidling and wary, and look about me, as you guard your eyes in London streets; for the horns thickened, and came at me like the ends of umbrellas poking in one's face.

I soon found that these townsfolk were the civilest, best-mannered people in the world; and that, if they had offended at all, it was entirely owing to their blindness. They do not know what dangerous weapons they protrude in front, and will stick their best friends in the eye with provoking complacency. Yet the best of it is, they can see the beams on their neighbours' foreheads, if they are as small as motes; but their own beams they can in no wise discern.

There was little Mitis, that I told you I just encountered. He has simply (I speak of him at home in his own shop) the smoothest forehead in his own conceit. He will stand you a quarter of an hour together, contemplating the serenity of it in the glass, before he begins to shave himself in a morning; yet you saw what a desperate gash he gave me.

Desiring to be better informed of the ways of this extraordinary people, I applied myself to a fellow of some assurance, who (it appeared) acted as a sort of interpreter to strangers: he was dressed in a military uniform, and strongly resembled Col.——, of the Guards. And "Pray, sir," said I, "have all the inhabitants of your city these troublesome excrescences? I beg pardon: I see you have none. You perhaps are single."—"Truly, sir," he replied with a smile, "for the most part we have, but not all alike. There are some, like Dick, that sport but one tumescence. Their ladies have been tolerably faithful,—have confined themselves to a single aberration or so: these we call Unicorns. Dick, you must know, is my Unicorn. [He spoke this with air of invincible assurance.] Then we have Bicorns, Tricorns, and so on up to Millecorns. [Here methought I crossed and blessed myself in my dream.] Some again we have,—there goes one: you see how happy the rogue looks,—how he walks smiling, and perking up his face, as if he thought himself the only man. He is not married yet; but on Monday next he leads to the altar the accomplished widow Dacres, relict of our late sheriff."

"I see, sir," said I, "and observe that he is happily free from the national *goitre* (let me call it) which distinguishes most of your countrymen."

"Look a little more narrowly," said my conductor.

I put on my spectacles; and, observing the man a little more diligently, above his forehead I could mark a thousand little twinkling shadows dancing the hornpipe; little hornlets, and rudiments of horn, of a soft and pappy consistence (for I handled some of them), but which, like coral out of water, my guide informed me, would infallibly stiffen and grow rigid within a week or two from the expiration of his bachelorhood.

Then I saw some horns strangely growing out behind; and my interpreter explained these to be married men, whose wives had conducted themselves with infinite propriety since the period of their marriage, but were thought to have antedated their good men's titles, by certain liberties they had indulged themselves in, prior to the ceremony. This kind of gentry wore their horns backwards, as has been said, in the fashion of the old pig-tails; and, as there was nothing obtrusive or ostentatious in them, nobody took any notice of it.

Some had pretty little budding antlers, like the first essays of a young fawn. These, he told me, had wives whose affairs were in a hopeful way, but not quite brought to a conclusion.

Others had nothing to show: only by certain red angry marks and swellings in their foreheads, which itched the more they kept rubbing and chafing them, it was to be hoped that something was brewing.

I took notice that every one jeered at the rest, only none took notice of the sea-captains; yet these were as well provided with their tokens as the best among them. This kind of people, it seems, taking their wives upon so contingent tenures, their lot was considered as nothing but natural: so they wore their marks without impeachment, as they might carry their cockades; and nobody respected them a whit the less for it.

I observed, that the more sprouts grew out of a man's head, the less weight they seemed to carry with them; whereas a single token would now and then appear to give the wearer some uneasiness. This shows that use is a great thing.

Some had their adornings gilt, which needs no explanation; while others, like musicians, went sounding theirs before them,—a sort of music which I thought might very well have been spared.

It was pleasant to see some of the citizens encounter between themselves; how they smiled in their sleeves at the shock they received from their neighbour, and none seemed conscious of the shock which their neighbour experienced in return.

Some had great corneous stumps, seemingly torn off and bleeding. These, the interpreter warned me, were husbands who had retaliated upon their wives, and the badge was in equity divided between them.

While I stood discerning these things, a slight tweak on my cheek unawares, which brought tears into my eyes, introduced to me my friend Placid, between whose lady and a certain male cousin some idle flirtations I remember to have heard talked of; but that was all. He saw he had somehow hurt me, and asked my pardon with that round, unconscious face of his; and looked so tristful and contrite for his no-offence, that I was ashamed for the man's penitence. Yet I protest it was but a scratch. It was the least little hornet of a horn that could be framed. "Shame on the man," I secretly exclaimed, "who could thrust so much as the value of a hair into a brow so unsuspecting and inoffensive! What, then, must they have to answer for, who plant great, monstrous, timber-like, projecting antlers upon the heads of those whom they call their friends, when a puncture of this atomical tenuity made my eyes to water at this rate! All the pincers at Surgeons' Hall cannot pull out for Placid that little hair."

I was curious to know what became of these frontal excrescences when the husbands died; and my guide informed me that the chemists in their country made a considerable profit by them, extracting from them certain subtile essences: and then I remembered that nothing was so efficacious in my own, for restoring swooning matrons, and wives troubled with the vapours, as a strong sniff or two at the composition appropriately called hartshorn,—far beyond *sal volatile*.

Then also I began to understand why a man, who is the jest of the company, is said to be the butt,—as much as to say, such a one butteth with the horn.

I inquired if by no operation these wens were ever extracted; and was told that there was indeed an order of dentists, whom they call canonists in their language, who undertook to restore the forehead to its pristine smoothness; but that ordinarily it was not done without much cost and trouble; and, when they succeeded in plucking out the offending part, it left a painful void, which could not be filled up; and that many patients who had submitted to the excision were eager to marry again, to supply with a good second antler the baldness and deformed gap left by the extraction of the former, as men losing their natural hair substitute for it a less becoming periwig.

Some horns I observed beautifully taper, smooth, and (as it were) flowering. These I understand were the portions brought by handsome women to their spouses; and I pitied the rough, homely, unsightly deformities on the brows of others, who had been deceived by plain and ordinary partners. Yet the latter I observed to be by far the most common; the solution of which I leave to the natural philosopher.

One tribe of married men I particularly admired at, who, instead of horns, wore ingrafted on their forehead a sort of horn-book. "This," quoth my guide, "is the greatest mystery in our country, and well worth an explanation. You must know that all infidelity is not of the senses. We have as well intellectual as material wittols. These, whom you see decorated with the order of the book, are triflers, who encourage about their wives' presence the society of your men of genius (their good friends, as they call them),—literary disputants, who ten to one out-talk the poor husband, and commit upon the understanding of the woman a violence and estrangement in the end, little less painful than the coarser sort of alienation. Whip me these knaves—[my conductor here expressed himself with a becoming warmth],—whip me them, I say, who, with no excuse from the passions, in cold blood seduce the minds, rather than the persons, of their friends' wives; who, for the tickling pleasure of hearing themselves prate, dehonestate the intellects of married women, dishonouring the husband in what should be his most sensible part. If I must be——[here he used a plain word] let it be by some honest sinner like myself, and not by one of these gad-flies, these debauchers of the understanding, these flattery-buzzers." He was going on in this manner, and I was getting insensibly pleased with my friend's manner (I had been a little shy of him at first), when the dream suddenly left me, vanishing, as Virgil speaks, through the gate of Horn.

———

THE GOOD CLERK, A CHARACTER.

WITH SOME ACCOUNT OF "THE COMPLETE ENGLISH TRADESMAN."

THE GOOD CLERK.—He writeth a fair and swift hand, and is competently versed in the four first rules of arithmetic, in the Rule of Three (which is sometimes called the Golden Rule), and in Practice. We mention these things that we may leave no room for cavillers to say that anything essential hath been omitted in our definition; else, to speak the truth, these are but ordinary accomplishments, and such as every understrapper at a desk is commonly furnished with. The character we treat of soareth higher.

He is clean and neat in his person, not from a vain-glorious desire of setting himself forth to advantage in the eyes of the other sex, with which vanity too many of our young sparks now-a-days are infected; but to do credit, as we say, to the office. For this reason, he evermore taketh care that his desk or his books receive no soil; the which things he is commonly as solicitous to have fair and unblemished, as the owner of a fine horse is to have him appear in good keep.

He riseth early in the morning; not because early rising conduceth to health (though he doth not altogether despise that consideration), but chiefly to the intent that he may be first at the desk. There is his post,—there he delighteth to be, unless when his meals or necessity calleth him away; which time he always esteemeth as lost, and maketh as short as possible.

He is temperate in eating and drinking, that he may preserve a clear head and steady hand for his master's service. He is also partly induced to this observation of the rules of temperance by his respect for religion and the laws of his country; which things, it may once for all be noted, do add special assistances to his actions, but do not and cannot furnish the main spring or motive thereto. His first ambition, as appeareth all along, is to be a good clerk; his next, a good Christian, a good patriot, &c.

Correspondent to this, he keepeth himself honest, not for fear of the laws, but because he hath observed how unseemly an article it maketh in the day-book or ledger when a sum is set down lost or missing; it being his pride to make these books to agree and to tally, the one side with the other, with a sort of architectural symmetry and correspondence.

He marrieth, or marrieth not, as best suiteth with his employer's views. Some merchants do the rather desire to have married men in their counting-houses, because they think the married state a pledge for their servants' integrity, and an incitement to them to be industrious; and it was an observation of a late Lord Mayor of London, that the sons of clerks do generally prove clerks themselves, and that merchants en-couraging persons in their employ to marry, and to have families, was the best method of securing a breed of sober, industrious young men attached to the mercantile interest. Be this as it may, such a character as we have been describing will wait till the pleasure of his employer is known on this point; and regulateth his desires by the custom of the house or firm to which he belongeth.

He avoideth profane oaths and jesting, as so much time lost from his employ. What spare time he hath for conversation, which, in a counting-house such as we have been supposing, can be but small, he spendeth in putting seasonable questions to such of his fellows (and sometimes *respectfully* to the master himself) who can give him information respecting the price and quality of goods, the state of exchange, or the latest improvements in book-keeping; thus making the motion of his lips, as well as of his fingers, subservient to his master's interest. Not that he refuseth a brisk saying, or a cheerful sally of wit, when it comes unforced, is free of offence, and hath a convenient brevity. For this reason, he hath commonly some such phrase as this in his mouth:—

> It's a slovenly look
> To blot your book.

Or,

> Red ink for ornament, black for use:
> The best of things are open to abuse.

So upon the eve of any great

holy-day, of which he keepeth one or two at least every year, he will merrily say, in the hearing of a confidential friend, but to none other,—

All work and no play
Makes Jack a dull boy.

Or,

A bow always bent must crack at last.

But then this must always be understood to be spoken confidentially, and, as we say, *under the rose*.

Lastly, his dress is plain, without singularity; with no other ornament than the quill, which is the badge of his function, stuck behind the dexter ear, and this rather for convenience of having it at hand, when he hath been called away from his desk, and expecteth to resume his seat there again shortly, than from any delight which he taketh in foppery or ostentation. The colour of his clothes is generally noted to be black rather than brown, brown rather than blue or green. His whole deportment is staid, modest, and civil. His motto is "Regularity."

This character was sketched in an interval of business, to divert some of the melancholy hours of a counting-house. It is so little a creature of fancy, that it is scarce anything more than a recollection of some of those frugal and economical maxims, which, about the beginning of the last century (England's meanest period), were endeavoured to be inculcated and instilled into the breasts of the London Apprentices* by a class of instructors who might not inaptly be termed "The Masters of Mean Morals." The astonishing narrowness and illiberality of the lessons contained in some of those books is inconceivable by those whose studies have not led them that way, and would almost induce one to subscribe to the hard censure which Drayton has passed upon the mercantile spirit:—

The gripple merchant, born to be the
curse
Of this brave isle.

I have now lying before me that curious book by Daniel Defoe, "The Complete English Tradesman." The pompous detail, the studied analysis of every little mean art, every sneaking address, every trick and subterfuge, short of larceny, that is necessary to the tradesman's occupation, with the hundreds of anecdotes, dialogues (in Defoe's liveliest manner) interspersed, all tending to the same amiable purpose,—namely, the sacrificing of every honest emotion of the soul to what he calls the main chance,—if you read it in an *ironical sense*, and as a piece of *covered satire*, make it one of the most amusing books which Defoe ever writ, as much so as any of his best novels. It is difficult to say what his intention was in writing it. It is almost impossible to suppose him

* This term designated a larger class of young men than that to which it is now confined. It took in the articled clerks of merchants and bankers, the George Barnwells of the day.

in earnest. Yet such is the bent of the book to narrow and to degrade the heart, that if such maxims were as catching and infectious as those of a licentious cast, which happily is not the case, had I been living at that time, I certainly should have recommended to the Grand Jury of Middlesex, who presented "The Fable of the Bees," to have presented this book of Defoe's in preference, as of a far more vile and debasing tendency. I will give one specimen of his advice to the young tradesman on the *government of his temper:* "The retail tradesman in especial, and even every tradesman in his station, must furnish himself with a competent stock of patience. I mean that sort of patience which is needful to bear with all sorts of impertinence, and the most provoking curiosity that it is possible to imagine the buyers, even the worst of them, are, or can be, guilty of. *A tradesman behind his counter must have no flesh and blood about him, no passions, no resentment;* he must never be angry,—no, not so much as seem to be so, if a customer tumbles him five hundred pounds' worth of goods, and scarce bids money for anything; nay, though they really come to his shop with no intent to buy, as many do, only to see what is to be sold, and though he knows they cannot be better pleased than they are at some other shop where they intend to buy, 'tis all one; the tradesman must take it; he must place it to the account of his calling, that *'tis his business to be ill used, and resent nothing;* and so must answer as obligingly to those that give him an hour or two's trouble, and buy nothing, as he does to those who, in half the time, lay out ten or twenty pounds. The case is plain; and if some do give him trouble, and do not buy, others make amends, and do buy; and as for the trouble, 'tis the business of the shop."

Here follows a most admirable story of a mercer, who by his indefatigable meanness, and more than Socratic patience under affronts, overcame and reconciled a lady, who, upon the report of another lady that he had behaved saucily to some third lady, had determined to shun his shop, but, by the over-persuasions of a fourth lady, was induced to go to it; which she does, declaring beforehand that she will buy nothing, but give him all the trouble she can. Her attack and his defence, her insolence and his persevering patience, are described in colours worthy of a Mandeville; but it is too long to recite. "The short inference from this long discourse," says he, "is this,—that here you see, and I could give you many examples like this, how and in what manner a shopkeeper is to behave himself in the way of his business; what impertinences, what taunts, flouts, and ridiculous things, he must bear in his trade; and must not show the least return, or the least signal of disgust: he must have no passions, no fire in his temper; he must be all soft and smooth; nay, if his real temper be naturally fiery and hot, he must show none of it in his shop; he must be a perfect *complete hypocrite*, if he will be a *complete tradesman.*[*] It is true, natural tempers are not to be always counterfeited: the man cannot easily be a lamb in his shop, and a lion in himself; but, let it be easy or hard, it must be done, and is done. There are men who have by custom and usage brought themselves to it, that nothing could be meeker and milder than they when behind the counter, and yet nothing be more furious and raging in every other part of life: nay, the provocations they have met with in their shops have so irritated their rage, that they would go upstairs from their shop, and fall into frenzies, and a kind of madness, and beat their heads against the wall, and perhaps mischief themselves, if not prevented, till the violence of it had gotten vent, and the passions abate and cool. I heard once of a shopkeeper that behaved himself thus to such an extreme, that, when he was provoked by the impertinence of the customers beyond what his temper could bear, he would go upstairs and beat his wife, kick his children about like dogs, and be as furious for two or three minutes as a man chained down in Bedlam; and again, when that heat was over, would sit

down, and cry faster than the children he had abused; and, after the fit, he would go down into the shop again, and be as humble, courteous, and as calm, as any man whatever; so absolute a government of his passions had he in the shop, and so little out of it: in the shop, a soulless animal that would resent nothing; and in the family, a madman: in the shop, meek like a lamb; but in the family outrageous, like a Lybian lion. The sum of the matter is, it is necessary for a tradesman to subject himself, by all the ways possible, to his business; *his customers are to be his idols: so far as he may worship idols by allowance, he is to bow down to them, and worship them;* at least, he is not in any way to displease them, or show any disgust or distaste, whatsoever they may say or do. The bottom of all is, that he is intending to get money by them; and it is not for him that gets money to offer the least inconvenience to them by whom he gets it: he is to consider, that, as Solomon says, "the borrower is servant to the lender;" so the seller is servant to the buyer. What he says on the head of "Pleasures and Recreations" is not less amusing: "The tradesman's pleasure should be in his business; his companions should be his books (he means his ledger, waste-book, &c.); and, if he has a family, he makes *his excursions upstairs, and no further.* None of my cautions aim at restraining a tradesman from divert-

[*] As no qualification accompanies this maxim, it must be understood as the genuine sentiment of the author!

ing himself, as we call it, with his fireside, or keeping company with his wife and children." Liberal allowance! nay, almost licentious and criminal indulgence! But it is time to dismiss this Philosopher of Meanness. More of this stuff would illiberalize the pages of the "Reflector." Was the man in earnest, when he could bring such powers of description, and all the charms of natural eloquence, in commendation of the meanest, vilest, wretchedest degradations of the human character? or did he not rather laugh in his sleeve at the doctrines which he inculcated; and, retorting upon the grave citizens of London their own arts, palm upon them a sample of disguised satire under the name of wholesome instruction?

REMINISCENCE OF SIR JEFFERY DUNSTAN.

To your account of Sir Jeffery Dunstan, in columns 829-30 (where, by an unfortunate erratum, the effigies of *two Sir Jefferys* appear, when the uppermost figure is clearly meant for Sir Harry Dimsdale), you may add that the writer of this has frequently met him in his latter days, about 1790 or 1791, returning in an evening, after his long day's itineracy, to his domicile,—a wretched shed in the most beggarly purlieu of Bethnal Green, a little on this side the Mile-end Turnpike. The lower figure in that leaf most correctly describes his then appearance, except that no graphic art can convey an idea of the general squalor of it, and of his bag (his constant concomitant) in particular. Whether it contained "old wigs" at that time, I know not; but it seemed a fitter repository for bones snatched out of kennels than for any part of a gentleman's dress, even at second-hand.

The ex-member for Garrat was a melancholy instance of a great man whose popularity is worn out. He still carried his sack; but it seemed a part of his identity rather than an implement of his profession; a badge of past grandeur: could anything have divested him of *that*, he would have shown a "poor forked animal" indeed. My life upon it, it contained no curls at the time I speak of. The most decayed and spiritless remnants of what was once a peruke would have scorned the filthy case; would absolutely have "burst its cerements." No: it was empty, or brought home bones, or a few cinders, possibly. A strong odour of burnt bones, I remember, blended with the scent of horse-flesh seething into dog's meat, and, only relieved a little by the breathings of a few brick-kilns, made up the atmosphere of the delicate suburban spot which this great man had chosen for the last scene of his earthly vanities. The cry of "old wigs" had ceased with the possession of any such fripperies: his sack might have contained not unaptly a little mould to scatter upon that grave to which he was now advancing; but it told of vacancy and desolation. His quips were silent too, and his brain was empty as his sack: he slank along, and seemed to decline popular observation. If a few boys followed him, it seemed rather from habit than any expectation of fun.

> Alas! how changed from *him*,
> The life of humour, and the soul of
> whim,
> Gallant and gay on Garrat's hustings
> proud!

But it is thus that the world rewards its favourites in decay. What faults he had, I know not. I have heard something of a peccadillo or so. But some little deviation from the precise line of rectitude might have been winked at in so tortuous and stigmatic a frame. Poor Sir Jeffery! it were well if some M.P.s in earnest have passed their parliamentary existence with no more offences against integrity than could be laid to thy charge! A fair dismissal was thy due, not so unkind a degradation; some little snug retreat, with a bit of green before thine eyes, and not a burial alive in the fetid beggaries of Bethnal. Thou wouldst have ended thy days in a manner more appropriate to thy pristine dignity, installed in munificent mockery (as in mock honours you had lived), —a poor knight of Windsor!

Every distinct place of public speaking demands an oratory peculiar to itself. The forensic fails within the walls of St. Stephen. Sir Jeffery was a living instance of this; for, in the flower of his popularity, an attempt was made to bring him out upon the stage (at which of the winter theatres I forget, but I well remember the anecdote) in the part of *Doctor Last.** The announcement drew a crowded house; but, notwithstanding infinite tutoring,—by Foote or Garrick, I forget which, —when the curtain drew up, the heart of Sir Jeffery failed, and he faltered on, and made nothing of his part, till the hisses of the house at last, in very kindness, dismissed him from the boards. Great as his parliamentary eloquence had shown itself, brilliantly as his off-hand sallies had sparkled on a hustings, they here totally failed him. Perhaps he had an aversion to borrowed wit, and, like my Lord Foppington, disdained to entertain himself (or others) with the forced products of another man's brain. Your man of quality is more diverted with the natural sprouts of his own.

ON A PASSAGE IN "THE TEMPEST."

As long as I can remember the play of "The Tempest," one passage in it has always set me upon wondering. It has puzzled me beyond measure. In vain I strove to find the meaning of it. I seemed

* It was at the Haymarket Theatre.

doomed to cherish infinite, hopeless curiosity.

It is where Prospero, relating the banishment of Sycorax from Argier, adds:—

> For one thing that she did,
> They would not take her life.

How have I pondered over this when a boy! How have I longed for some authentic memoir of the witch to clear up the obscurity! Was the story extant in the chronicles of Algiers? Could I get at it by some fortunate introduction to the Algerine ambassador? Was a voyage thither practicable? The Spectator, I knew, went to Grand Cairo only to measure the pyramid. Was not the object of my quest of at least as much importance? The blue-eyed hag! could *she* have done anything good or meritorious? might that succubus relent? then might there be hope for the Devil. I have often admired since that none of the commentators have boggled at this passage; how they could swallow this camel,—such a tantalizing piece of obscurity such an abortion of an anecdote.

At length, I think I have lighted upon a clue which may lead to show what was passing in the mind of Shakspeare when he dropped this imperfect rumour. In the "Accurate Description of Africa, by John Ogilby (folio), 1670," page 230, I find written as follows. The marginal title to the narrative is, "Charles the Fifth besieges Algier:"—

"In the last place, we will briefly give an account of the emperour, Charles the Fifth, when he besieg'd this city; and of the great loss he suffer'd therein.

"This prince, in the year one thousand five hundred forty-one, having embarqued upon the sea an army of twenty-two thousand men aboard eighteen gallies, and an hundred tall ships, not counting the barques and shallops, and other small boats, in which he had engaged the principal of the Spanish and Italian nobility, with a good number of the Knights of Malta; he was to land on the coasts of Barbary, at a cape call'd Matifou. From this place unto the city of Algier, a flat shore or strand extends itself for about four leagues, the which is exceeding favourable to gallies. There he put ashore with his army, and in a few days caused a fortress to be built, which unto this day is call'd the castle of the Emperour.

"In the meantime the city of Algier took the alarm, having in it at that time but eight hundred Turks, and six thousand Moors, poor-spirited men, and unexercised in martial affairs; besides it was at that time fortifi'd only with walls, and had no outworks: insomuch that by reason of its weakness, and the great forces of the Emperour, it could not in appearance escape taking. In fine, it was attempted with such order, that the army came up to the very gates, where the Chevalier de Sauignac, a Frenchman by nation, made himself remarkable above all the rest, by the miracles of his valour. For having repulsed the Turks, who, having made a sally at the gate call'd Babason, and there desiring to enter along with them, when he saw that they shut the gate upon him, he ran his ponyard into the same, and left it sticking deep therein. They next fell to battering the city by the force of cannon; which the assailants so weakened, that in that great extremity the defendants lost their courage, and resolved to surrender.

"But as they were thus intending, there was a witch of the town, whom the history does not name, which went to seek out Assam Aga, that commanded within, and pray'd him to make it good yet nine days longer, with assurance, that within that time he should infallibly see Algier delivered from that siege, and the whole army of the enemy dispersed, so that Christians should be as cheap as birds. In a word, the thing did happen in the manner as foretold; for upon the twenty-first day of October, in the same year, there fell a continual rain upon the land, and so furious a storm at sea, that one might have seen ships hoisted into the clouds, and in one instant again precipitated into the bottom of the water: insomuch that that same dreadful tempest was followed with the loss of fifteen gallies, and above an hundred other vessels; which was the cause why the Emperour, seeing his army wasted by the bad weather, pursued by a famine, occasioned by wrack of his ships, in which was the greatest part of his victuals and amunition, he was constrain'd to raise the siege, and set sail for Sicily, whither he retreated with the miserable reliques of his fleet.

"In the meantime that witch being acknowledged the deliverer of Algier, was richly remunerated, and the credit of her charms authorized. So that ever since, witchcraft hath been very freely tolerated; of which the chief of the town, and even those who are esteem'd to be of greatest sanctity among them, such as are the Marabous, a religious order of their sect, do for the most part make profession of it, under a goodly pretext of certain revelations which they say they have had from their prophet, Mahomet.

"And hereupon those of Algier, to palliate the shame and the reproaches that are thrown upon them for making use of a witch in the danger of this siege, do say that the loss of the forces of Charles V. was caused by a prayer of one of their Marabous, named Cidy Utica, which was at that time in great credit, not under the notion of a magician, but for a person of a holy life. Afterwards in remembrance of their success, they have erected unto him a small mosque without the Babason gate, where he is buried, and in which they keep sundry lamps burning in honour of him: nay, they sometimes repair thither to make their *sala*, for a testimony of greater veneration."

Can it be doubted, for a moment, that the dramatist had come fresh from reading some *older narrative* of this deliverance of Algier by a witch, and transferred the merit of the deed to his Sycorax, exchanging only the "rich remuneration," which did not suit his purpose, to the simple pardon of her life? Ogilby wrote in 1670; but the authorities to which he refers for his account of Barbary are Johannes de Leo or Africanus, Louis Marmol, Diego de Haedo, Johannes Gramaye, Braeves, Cel. Curio, and Diego de Torres, names totally unknown to me, and to which I beg leave to refer the curious reader for his fuller satisfaction.

THE MONTHS.

Rummaging over the contents of an old stall at a half *book*, half *old-iron shop*, in an alley leading from Wardour Street to Soho Square, yesterday, I lit upon a ragged duodecimo which had been the strange delight of my infancy, and which I had lost sight of for more than forty years, —the "Queen-like Closet, or Rich Cabinet;" written by Hannah Woolly, and printed for R. C. and T. S., 1681; being an abstract of receipts in cookery, confectionery, cosmetics, needlework, morality, and all such branches of what were then considered as female accomplishments. The price demanded was sixpence, which the owner (a little squab duodecimo character himself) enforced with the assurance that his "own mother should not have it for a farthing less." On my demurring at this extraordinary assertion, the dirty little vendor reinforced his assertion with a sort of oath, which seemed more than the occasion demanded: "And now," said he, "I have put my soul to it." Pressed by so solemn an asseveration, I could no longer resist a demand which seemed to set me, however unworthy, upon a level with his dearest relations; and, depositing a tester, I bore away the tattered prize in triumph. I remembered a gorgeous description of the twelve months of the year, which I thought would be a fine substitute for those poetical descriptions of them which your "Every-day-Book" had nearly exhausted out of Spenser. "This will be a treat," thought I, "for friend Hone." To memory they seemed no less fantastic and splendid than the other. But what are the mistakes of childhood! On reviewing them, they turned out to be only a set of commonplace receipts for working the seasons, months, heathen gods and goddesses, &c., in *samplers!* Yet, as an instance of the homely occupation of our great-grandmothers, they may be amusing to some readers. "I have seen," says the notable Hannah Woolly, "such ridiculous things done in work, as it is an abomination to any artist to behold. As for example: You may find, in some pieces, *Abraham* and *Sarah,* and many other persons of old time, clothed as they go now-a-days, and truly sometimes worse; for they most resemble the pictures on ballads. Let all ingenious women have regard, that when they work any image, to represent it aright. First, let it be drawn well, and then observe the directions which are given by knowing men. I do assure you, I never durst work any Scripture story without informing myself from the ground of it; nor any other story, or single person, without informing myself both of the visage and habit; as followeth:—

"If you work *Jupiter, the imperial feigned God,* he must have long, black, curled hair, a purple garment trimmed with gold, and sitting upon a golden throne, with bright yellow clouds about him."

THE TWELVE MONTHS OF THE YEAR.

March. Is drawn in tawny, with a fierce aspect: a helmet upon his head, and leaning on a spade; and a basket of garden-seeds in his left hand, and in his right hand the sign of *Aries;* and winged.

April. A young man in green, with a garland of myrtle and hawthorn-buds; winged; in one hand primroses and violets, in the other the sign *Taurus.*

May. With a sweet and lovely countenance; clad in a robe of white and green, embroidered with several flowers; upon his head a garden of all manner of roses; on the one hand a nightingale, in the other a lute. His sign must be *Gemini.*

June. In a mantle of dark grass-green; upon his head a garland of bents, kings-cups, and maiden-hair; in his left hand an angle, with a box of cantharides; in his right, the sign *Cancer;* and upon his arms a basket of seasonable fruits.

July. In a jacket of light yellow, eating cherries; with his face and bosom sun-burnt; on his head a wreath of centaury and wild thyme; a scythe on his shoulder, and a bottle at his girdle; carrying the sign *Leo.*

August. A young man of fierce and choleric aspect, in a flame-coloured garment; upon his head a garland of wheat and rye; upon his arm a basket of all manner of ripe fruits; at his belt a sickle: his sign *Virgo.*

September. A merry and cheerful countenance, in a purple robe; upon his head a wreath of red and white grapes; in his left hand a handful of oats; withal carrying a horn of plenty, full of all manner of ripe fruits; in his right hand the sign *Libra.*

October. In a garment of yellow and carnation; upon his head a garland of oak-leaves with acorns; in his right hand the sign *Scorpio;* in his left hand a basket of medlars, services, and chestnuts, and any other fruits then in season.

November. In a garment of changeable green and black; upon his head a garland of olives, with the fruit in his left hand bunches of parsnips and turnips in his right: his sign *Sagittarius*.

December. A horrid and fearful aspect, clad in Irish rags, or coarse frieze girt unto him; upon his head three or four night-caps, and over them a Turkish turban; his nose red, his mouth and beard clogged with icicles; at his back a bundle of holly, ivy, or mistletoe; holding in furred mittens the sign of *Capricornus.*

January. Clad all in white, as the earth looks with the snow, blowing his nails; in his left arm a billet; the sign *Aquarius* standing by his side.

February. Clothed in a dark sky-colour, carrying in his right hand the sign *Pisces.*

The following receipt "To dress up a chimney very fine for the summer-time, as I have done many, and they have been liked very well," may not be unprofitable to the housewives of this century:—

"First, take a pack-thread, and fasten it even to the inner part of the chimney, so high as that you can see no higher as you walk up and down the house. You must drive in several nails to hold up all your work. Then get good store of old green moss from trees, and melt an equal proportion of beeswax and rosin together; and, while it is hot, dip the wrong ends of the moss in it, and presently clap it upon your pack-thread, and press it down hard with your hand. You must make haste, else it will cool before you can fasten it, and then it will fall down. Do so all around where the pack-thread goes; and the next row you must join to that, so that it may seem all in one: thus do till you have finished it down to the bottom. Then take some other kind of moss, of a whitish colour and stiff, and of several sorts or kinds, and place that upon the other, here and there carelessly, and in some places put a good deal, and some a little; then any kind of fine snail-shells, in which the snails are dead, and little toad-stools, which are very old, and look like velvet, or *any other thing that was old and pretty:* place it here and there as your fancy serves, and fasten all with wax and rosin. Then, for the hearth of your chimney, you may lay some orpan-sprigs in order all over, and it will grow as it lies; and, according to the season, get what flowers you can, and stick in as if they grew, and a few sprigs of sweet-briar: the flowers you must renew every week; but the moss will last all the summer, till it will be time to make a fire; and the orpan will last near two months. A chimney thus done doth grace a room exceedingly."

One phrase in the above should particularly recommend it to such of your female readers as, in the nice language of the day, have done growing some time,—"little toad-stools, &c., and anything that is *old and pretty.*" Was ever antiquity so smoothed over? The culinary recipes have nothing remarkable in them, except the costliness of them. Every thing (to the meanest meats) is sopped in claret, steeped in claret, basted with claret, as if claret were as cheap as ditch-water. I remember Bacon recommends opening a turf or two in your garden walks, and pouring into each a bottle of claret, to recreate the sense of smelling, being no less grateful than beneficial. We hope the Chancellor of the Exchequer will attend to this in his next reduction of French wines, that we may once more water our gardens with right Bourdeaux. The medical recipes are as whimsical as they are cruel. Our ancestors were not at all effeminate on this head. Modern sentimentalists would shrink at a cock plucked and bruised in a mortar alive to make a cullis, or a live mole baked in an oven (*be sure it be alive*) to make a powder for consumption. But the whimsicalest of all are the directions to servants (for this little book is a compendium of all duties): the footman is seriously admonished not to stand lolling against his master's chair while he waits at table; for "to lean on a chair when they wait is a particular favour shown to any superior servant, as the chief gentleman, or the waiting-woman when she rises from the table." Also he must not "hold the plates before his mouth to be defiled with his breath, nor touch them on the right [inner] side." Surely Swift must have seen this little treatise.

Hannah concludes with the following address, by which the self-estimate which she formed of her usefulness may be calculated:—

"*Ladies*, I hope you're pleas'd, and so
   shall I,
If what I've writ, you may be gainers by:
If not, it is your fault, it is not mine,
Your benefit in this I do design.
Much labour and much time it hath me
   cost,
Therefore, I beg, let none of it be lost.
'The money you shall pay for this my
   book,
You'll not repent of, when in it you
   look.
No more at present to you I shall say,
But wish you all the happiness I may."

BIOGRAPHICAL MEMOIR OF MR. LISTON.

THE subject of our Memoir is lineally descended from Johan de L.'Estoune (see "Domesday Book," where he is so written), who came in with the Conqueror, and had lands awarded him at Lupton Magna, in Kent. His particular merits or services, Fabian, whose authority I chiefly follow, has forgotten, or perhaps thought it immaterial, to specify. Fuller thinks that he was standard-bearer to Hugo de Agmondesham, a powerful Norman baron, who was slain by the hand of Harold himself at the fatal battle of Hastings. Be this as it may, we find a family of that name flourishing some centuries later in that county. John Delliston, knight, was High Sheriff for Kent, according to Fabian, *quinto Henrici Sexti;* and we trace the lineal branch flourishing downwards,—the orthography varying, according to the unsettled usage of the times, from

Delleston to Leston or Liston, between which it seems to have alternated, till, in the latter end of the reign of James I., it finally settled into the determinate and pleasing dissyllabic arrangement which it still retains. Aminadab Liston, the eldest male representative of the family of that day, was of the strictest order of Puritans. Mr. Foss, of Pall Mall, has obligingly communicated to me an undoubted tract of his, which bears the initials only, A. L., and is entitled, "The Grinning Glass, or Actor's Mirrour; where in the vituperative Visnomy of Vicious Players for the Scene is as virtuously reflected back upon their mimetic Monstrosities as it has viciously (hitherto) vitiated with its vile Vanities her Votarists." A strange title, but bearing the impress of those absurdities with which the title-pages of that pamphlet-spawning age abounded. The work bears date 1617. It preceded the "Histriomastix" by fifteen years; and, as it went before it in time, so it comes not far short of it in virulence. It is amusing to find an ancestor of Liston's thus bespattering the players at the commencement of the seventeenth century:—

"Thinketh He" (the actor), "with his costive countenances, to wry a sorrowing soul out of her anguish, or by defacing the divine denotement of destinate dignity (daignely described in the face humane and no other) to reinstamp the Paradice-plotted similitude with a novel and naughty approximation (not in the first intention) to those abhorred and ugly God-forbidden correspondences, with flouting Apes' jeering gibberings, and Babion babbling-like, to hoot out of countenance all modest measure, as if our sins were not sufficing to stoop out backs without He wresting and crooking his members to mistimed mirth (rather malice) in deformed fashion, leering when he should learn, prating for praying, goggling his eyes (better upturned for grace), whereas in Paradice (if we can go thus high for His profession) that develish Serpent appeareth his undoubted Predecessor, first induing a mask like some roguish roistering Roscius (I spit at them all) to beguile with Stage shows the gaping Woman, whose Sex hath still chiefly upheld these Mysteries, and are voiced to be the chief Stage-haunters, where, as I am told, the custom is commonly to mumble (between acts) apples, not ambiguously derived from that pernicious Pippin (worse in effect than the Apples of Discord), whereas sometimes the hissing sounds of displeasure, as I hear, do lively reintonate that snake-taking-leave, and diabolical goings off, in Paradice."

The Puritanic effervescence of the early Presbyterians appears to have abated with time, and the opinions of the more immediate ancestors of our subject to have subsided at length into a strain of moderate Calvinism. Still a tincture of the old leaven was to be expected among the posterity of A. L.

Our hero was an only son of Habakkuk Liston, settled as an Anabaptist minister upon the patrimonial soil of his ancestors. A regular certificate appears, thus entered in the Church-book at Lupton Magna:—"*Johannes, filius Habakkuk et Rebeccæ Liston, Dissentientium, natus quinto Decembri, 1780, baptizatus sexto Februarii sequentis; Sponsoribus J. et W. Woollaston, und cum Maria Merryweather.*" The singularity of an Anabaptist minister conforming to the child-rites of the Church would have tempted me to doubt the authenticity of this entry, had I not been obliged with the actual sight of it by the favour of Mr. Minns, the intelligent and worthy parish clerk of Lupton. Possibly some expectation in point of worldly advantages from some of the sponsors might have induced this unseemly deviation, as it must have appeared, from the practice and principles of that generally rigid sect. The term *Dissentientium* was possibly intended by the orthodox clergyman as a slur upon the supposed inconsistency. What, or of what nature, the expectations we have hinted at may have been, we have now no means of ascertaining. Of the Woollastons no trace is now discoverable in the village. The name of Merryweather occurs over the front of a grocer's shop at the western extremity of Lupton.

Of the infant Liston we find no events recorded before his fourth year, in which a severe attack of the measles bid fair to have robbed the rising generation of a fund of innocent entertainment. He had it of the confluent kind, as it is called; and the child's life was for a week or two despaired of. His recovery he always attributes (under Heaven) to the humane interference of one Dr. Wilhelm Richter, a German empiric, who, in this extremity, prescribed a copious diet of *sauerkraut*, which the child was observed to reach at with avidity, when other food repelled him; and from this change of diet his restoration was rapid and complete. We have often heard him name the circumstance with gratitude; and it is not altogether surprising that a relish for this kind of aliment, so abhorrent and harsh to common English palates, has accompanied him through life. When any of Mr. Liston's intimates invite him to supper, he never fails of finding, nearest to his knife and fork, a dish of *sauerkraut*.

At the age of nine, we find our subject under the tuition of the Rev. Mr. Goodenough (his father's health not permitting him probably to instruct him himself), by whom he was inducted into a competent portion of Latin and Greek, with some mathematics, till the death of Mr. Goodenough, in his own seventieth, and Master Liston's eleventh year, put a stop for the present to his classical progress.

We have heard our hero, with emotions which do his heart honour, describe the awful circumstances attending the decease of this worthy old gentleman. It seems they had been walking out together, master and pupil, in a fine sunset, to the distance of three-quarters of a mile west of Lupton, when a sudden curiosity took Mr. Goodenough to look down upon a chasm, where a shaft had been lately sunk in a mining speculation (then projecting, but abandoned soon after, as not answering the promised success, by Sir Ralph Shepperton, knight, and member for the county). The old clergyman leaning over, either with incaution or sudden giddiness (probably a mixture of both), suddenly lost his footing, and, to use Mr. Liston's phrase, disappeared, and was doubtless broken into a thousand pieces. The sound of his head, &c., dashing successively upon the projecting masses of the chasm, had such an effect upon the child, that a serious sickness ensued; and, even for many years after his recovery, he was not once seen so much as to smile.

The joint death of both his parents, which happened not many months after this disastrous accident, and were probably (one or both of them) accelerated by it, threw our youth upon the protection of his maternal great-aunt, Mrs. Sittingbourn. Of this aunt we have never heard him speak but with expressions amounting almost to reverence. To the influence of her early counsels and manners he has always attributed the firmness with which, in maturer years, thrown upon a way of life commonly not the best adapted to gravity and self-retirement, he has been able to maintain a serious character, untinctured with the levities incident to his profession. Ann Sittingbourn (we have seen her portrait by Hudson) was stately, stiff, tall, with a cast of features strikingly resembling the subject of this memoir. Her estate in Kent was spacious and well wooded; the house one of those venerable old mansions which are so impressive in childhood, and so hardly forgotten in succeeding years. In the venerable solitudes of Charnwood, among thick shades of the oak and beech (this last his favourite tree), the young Liston cultivated those contemplative habits which have never entirely deserted him in after years. Here he was commonly in the summer months to be met with, with a book in his hand,—not a play-book,—meditating. Boyle's "Reflections" was at one time the darling volume; which, in its turn, was superseded by Young's "Night Thoughts," which has continued its hold upon him through life. He carries i always about him; and it is no uncommon thing for him to be seen, in the refreshing intervals of his occupation, leaning against a side-scene, in a sort of Herbert-of-Cherbury posture, turning over a pocket-edition of his favourite author.

But the solitudes of Charnwood

were not destined always to obscure the path of our young hero. The premature death of Mrs. Sittingbourn, at the age of seventy, occasioned by incautious burning of a pot of charcoal in her sleeping-chamber, left him in his nineteenth year nearly without resources. That the stage at all should have presented itself as an eligible scope for his talents, and, in particular, that he should have chosen a line so foreign to what appears to have been his turn of mind, may require some explanation.

At Charnwood, then, we behold him thoughtful, grave, ascetic. From his cradle averse to flesh-meats and strong drink; abstemious even beyond the genius of the place, and almost in spite of the remonstrances of his great-aunt, who, though strict, was not rigid, —water was his habitual drink, and his food little beyond the remast and beech-nuts of his favourite groves. It is a medical fact, that this kind of diet, however favourable to the contemplative powers of the primitive hermits, &c., is but ill adapted to the less robust minds and bodies of a later generation. Hypochondria almost constantly ensues. It was so in the case of the young Liston. He was subject to sights, and had visions. Those arid beech-nuts, distilled by a complexion naturally adust, mounted into an occiput already prepared to kindle by long seclusion and the fervour of strict Calvinistic notions. In the glooms of Charn-

wood, he was assailed by illusions similar in kind to those which are related of the famous Anthony of Padua. Wild antic faces would ever and anon protrude themselves upon his sensorium. Whether he shut his eyes, or kept them open, the same illusions operated. The darker and more profound were his cogitations, the droller and more whimsical became the apparitions. They buzzed about him thick as flies, flapping at him, flouting him, hooting in his ear, yet with such comic appendages, that what at first was his bane became at length his solace; and he desired no better society than that of his merry phantasmata. We shall presently find in what way this remarkable phenomenon influenced his future destiny.

On the death of Mrs. Sittingbourn, we find him received into the family of Mr. Willoughby, an eminent Turkey merchant, resident in Birchin Lane, London. We lose a little while here the chain of his history,—by what inducements this gentleman was determined to make him an inmate of his house. Probably he had had some personal kindness for Mrs. Sittingbourn formerly; but, however it was, the young man was here treated more like a son than a clerk, though he was nominally but the latter. Different avocations, the change of scene, with that alternation of business and recreation which in its greatest perfection is to be had only in London, appear to have weaned him in a short time from the hypochondriacal affections which had beset him at Charnwood.

In the three years which followed his removal to Birchin Lane, we find him making more than one voyage to the Levant, as chief factor for Mr. Willoughby at the Porte. We could easily fill our biography with the pleasant passages which we have heard him relate as having happened to him at Constantinople; such as his having been taken up on suspicion of a design of penetrating the seraglio, &c.; but, with the deepest convincement of this gentleman's own veracity, we think that some of the stories are of that whimsical, and others of that romantic nature, which, however diverting, would be out of place in a narrative of this kind, which aims not only at strict truth, but at avoiding the very appearance of the contrary.

We will now bring him over the seas again, and suppose him in the counting-house in Birchin Lane, his protector satisfied with the returns of his factorage, and all going on so smoothly, that we may expect to find Mr. Liston at last an opulent merchant upon 'Change, as it is called. But see the turns of destiny! Upon a summer's excursion into Norfolk, in the year 1801, the accidental sight of pretty Sally Parker, as she was called (then in the Norwich company), diverted his inclinations at once from commerce; and he became, in the language of commonplace biography, stage-struck. Happy for the lovers of mirth was it that our hero took this turn; he might else have been to this hour that unentertaining character, a plodding London merchant.

We accordingly find him shortly after making his *début*, as it is called, upon the Norwich boards, in the season of that year, being then in the twenty-second year of his age. Having a natural bent to tragedy, he chose the part of Pyrrhus, in the "Distressed Mother," to Sally Parker's Hermione. We find him afterwards as Barnwell, Altamont, Chamont, &c.; but, as if Nature had destined him to the sock, an unavoidable infirmity absolutely discapacitated him for tragedy. His person, at this latter period of which I have been speaking, was graceful, and even commanding; his countenance set to gravity: he had the power of arresting the attention of an audience at first sight almost beyond any other tragic actor. But he could not hold it. To understand this obstacle, we must go back a few years to those appalling reveries at Charnwood. Those illusions, which had vanished before the dissipation of a less recluse life and more free society, now in his solitary tragic studies, and amid the intense calls upon feeling incident to tragic acting, came back upon him with tenfold vividness. In the midst of some most pathetic passage (the parting of Jaffier with his dying friend, for instance), he would suddenly be surprised with a fit of violent horse-laughter.

While the spectators were all sob-bing before him with emotion, suddenly one of those grotesque faces would peep out upon him, and he could not resist the impulse. A timely excuse once or twice served his purpose; but no audiences could be expected to bear repeatedly this violation of the continuity of feeling. He describes them (the illusions) as so many demons haunting him, and paralyzing every effect. Even now, I am told, he cannot recite the famous soliloquy in "Hamlet," even in private, without immoderate bursts of laughter. However, what he had not force of reason sufficient to overcome, he had good sense enough to turn into emolument, and determined to make a commodity of his distemper. He prudently exchanged the buskin for the sock, and the illusions instantly ceased; or, if they occurred for a short season, by their very co-operation added a zest to his comic vein,—some of his most catching faces being (as he expresses it) little more than transcripts and copies of those extraordinary phantasmata.

We have now drawn out our hero's existence to the period when he was about to meet, for the first time, the sympathies of a London audience. The particulars of his success since have been too much before our eyes to render a circumstantial detail of them expedient. I shall only mention, that Mr. Willoughby, his resentments having had time to subside, is at present one of the fastest friends of his old renegado factor; and that Mr. Liston's hopes of Miss Parker vanishing along with his unsuccessful suit to Melpomene, in the autumn of 1811 he married his present lady, by whom he has been blessed with one son, Philip, and two daughters, Ann and Augustina.

AUTOBIOGRAPHY OF MR. MUNDEN.

IN A LETTER TO THE EDITOR OF THE "LONDON MAGAZINE."

HARK'EE, Mr. Editor. A word in your ear. They tell me you are going to put me in print,—in print, sir; to publish my life. What is my life to you, sir? What is it to you whether I ever lived at all? My life is a very good life, sir. I am insured at the Pelican, sir. I am three-score years and six,—six; mark me, sir; but I can play Polonius, which, I believe, few of your corre—correspondents can do, sir. I suspect tricks, sir: I smell a rat; I do, I do. You would cog the die upon us; you would, you would, sir. But I will forestall you, sir. You would be deriving me from William the Conqueror, with a murrain to you. It is no such thing, sir. The town shall know better, sir. They begin to smoke your flams, sir. Mr. Liston may be born where he pleases, sir; but I will not be born at Lup—Lupton Magna for anybody's pleasure, sir. My son and I have looked over the great map of Kent together, and we can find no such place as you would palm upon us, sir; palm upon us, I say. Neither Magna nor Parva, as my son says, and he knows Latin, sir; Latin. If you write my life true, sir, you must set down, that I, Joseph Munden, comedian, came into the world upon Allhallows Day, Anno Domini, 1759—1759; no sooner nor later, sir; and I saw the first light—the first light, remember, sir, at Stoke Pogis—Stoke Pogis, *comitatu* Bucks, and not at Lup— Lup Magna, which I believe to be no better than moonshine—moonshine; do you mark me, sir? I wonder you can put such flimflams upon us, sir; I do, I do. It does not become you, sir; I say it,—I say it. And my father was an honest tradesman, sir: he dealt in malt and hops, sir; and was a corporation-man, sir; and of the Church of England, sir, and no Presbyterian; nor Ana—Anabaptist, sir; however you may be disposed to make honest people believe to the contrary, sir. Your bams are found out, sir. The town will be your stale-puts no longer, sir; and you must not send us jolly fellows, sir,—we that are comedians, sir,—you must not send us into groves and char— charnwoods a moping, sir. Neither charns, nor charnel-houses, sir. It is not our constitution, sir: I tell it you—I tell it you. I was a droll dog from my cradle. I came into the world tittering, and the midwife tittered, and the gossips spilt their caudle with tittering; and,

when I was brought to the font, the parson could not christen me for tittering. So I was never more than half baptized. And, when I was little Joey, I made 'em all titter; there was not a melancholy face to be seen in Pogis. Pure nature, sir. I was born a comedian. Old Screwup, the undertaker, could tell you, sir, if he were living. Why, I was obliged to be locked up every time there was to be a funeral at Pogis. I was—I was, sir. I used to *grimace* at the mutes, as he called it, and put 'em out with my mops and my mows, till they couldn't stand at a door for me. And when I was locked up, with nothing but a cat in my company, I followed my bent with trying to make her laugh; and sometimes she would, and sometimes she would not. And my schoolmaster could make nothing of me: I had only to thrust my tongue in my cheek— in my cheek, sir, and the rod dropped from his fingers; and so my education was limited, sir. And I grew up a young fellow, and it was thought convenient to enter me upon some course of life that should make me serious; but it wouldn't do, sir. And I was articled to a dry-salter. My father gave forty pounds premium with me, sir. I can show the indent— dent—dentures, sir. But I was born to be a comedian, sir: so I ran away, and listed with the players, sir: and I topt my parts at Amersham and Gerrard's Cross, and played my own father to his face, in his own town of Pogis, in the part of Gripe, when I was not full seventeen years of age; and he did not know me again, but he knew me afterwards; and then he laughed, and I laughed, and, what is better, the dry-salter laughed, and gave me up my articles for the joke's sake: so that I came into court afterwards with clean hands—with clean hands—do you see, sir?

[Here the manuscript becomes illegible for two or three sheets onwards, which we presume to be occasioned by the absence of Mr. Munden, jun., who clearly transcribed it for the press thus far. The rest (with the exception of the concluding paragraph, which is seemingly resumed in the first handwriting) appears to contain a confused account of some lawsuit, in which the elder Munden was engaged; with a circumstantial history of the proceedings of a case of breach of promise of marriage, made to or by (we cannot pick out which) Jemima Munden, spinster; probably the comedian's cousin, for it does not appear he had any sister; with a few dates, rather better preserved, of this great actor's engagements, —as "Cheltenham (spelt Cheltnam), 1776;" "Bath, 1779;" "London, 1789;" together with stage anecdotes of Messrs. Edwin, Wilson, Lee, Lewis, &c.; over which we have strained our eyes to no purpose, in the hope of presenting something amusing to the public. Towards the end, the manuscript brightens up a little, as we said, and concludes in the following manner:]

—— stood before them for six and thirty years [we suspect that Mr. Munden is here speaking of his final leave-taking of the stage], and to be dismissed at last. But I was heart-whole to the last, sir. What though a few drops did course themselves down the old veteran's cheeks: who could help it, sir? I was a giant that night, sir; and could have played fifty parts, each as arduous as Dozy. My faculties were never better, sir. But I was to be laid upon the shelf. It did not suit the public to laugh with their old servant any longer, sir. [Here some moisture has blotted a sentence or two.] But I can play Polonius still, sir; I can, I can.

Your servant, sir,
JOSEPH MUNDEN.

THE ILLUSTRIOUS DEFUNCT.*

Nought but a blank remains, a dead void space,
A step of life that promised such a race.—
DRYDEN.

NAPOLEON has now sent us back from the grave sufficient echoes

* Since writing this article, we have been informed that the object of our funeral oration is not definitively dead, but only moribund. So much the better: we shall have an opportunity of granting the request made to Walter by one of the children in the wood, and "kill him two times." The Abbé de Vertot having a siege to write, and not receiving the materials in time, composed the whole from his invention. Shortly after its

of his living renown: the twilight of posthumous fame has lingered long enough over the spot where the sun of his glory set; and his name must at length repose in the silence, if not in the darkness, of night. In this busy and evanescent scene, other spirits of the age are rapidly snatched away, claiming our undivided sympathies and regrets, until in turn they yield to some newer and more absorbing grief. Another name is now added to the list of the mighty departed,—a name whose influence upon the hopes and fears, the fates and fortunes, of our countrymen, has rivalled, and perhaps eclipsed, that of the defunct "child and champion of Jacobinism," while it is associated with all the sanctions of legitimate government, all the sacred authorities of social order and our most holy religion. We speak of one, indeed, under whose warrant heavy and incessant contributions were imposed upon our fellow-citizens, but who exacted nothing without the signet and the sign-manual of most devout Chancellors of the Exchequer. Not to dally longer with the sympathies of our readers, we think it right to premonish them that we are composing an epicedium upon no less distinguished a personage than the Lottery, whose last breath, after many penultimate puffs, has been sobbed forth by sorrowing con-

tractors, as if the world itself were about to be converted into a blank. There is a fashion of eulogy, as well as of vituperation; and, though the Lottery stood for some time in the latter predicament, we hesitate not to assert that *multis ille bonis flebilis occidit.* Never have we joined in the senseless clamour which condemned the only tax whereto we became voluntary contributors,— the only resource which gave the stimulus without the danger or infatuation of gambling; the only alembic which in these plodding days sublimized our imaginations, and filled them with more delicious dreams than ever flitted athwart the sensorium of Alnaschar.

Never can the writer forget, when, as a child, he was hoisted upon a servant's shoulder in Guildhall, and looked down upon the installed and solemn pomp of the then drawing Lottery. The two awful cabinets of iron, upon whose massy and mysterious portals the royal initials were gorgeously emblazoned, as if, after having deposited the unfulfilled prophecies within, the king himself had turned the lock, and still retained the key in his pocket; the bluecoat boy, with his naked arm, first converting the invisible wheel, and then diving into the dark recess for a ticket; the grave and reverend faces of the commissioners eyeing the announced number; the scribes below calmly committing it to their huge books; the anxious countenances of the

completion, the expected documents arrived, when he threw them aside, exclaiming, "You are of no use to me now; I have carried the town."

surrounding populace; while the giant figures of Gog and Magog, like presiding deities, looked down with a grim silence upon the whole proceeding,—constituted altogether a scene, which, combined with the sudden wealth supposed to be lavished from those inscrutable wheels, was well calculated to impress the imagination of a boy with reverence and amazement. Jupiter, seated between the two fatal urns of good and evil, the blind goddess with her cornucopia, the Parcæ wielding the distaff, the thread of life, and the abhorred shears, seemed but dim and shadowy abstractions of mythology, when I had gazed upon an assemblage exercising, as I dreamt, a not less eventful power, and all presented to me in palpable and living operation. Reason and experience, ever at their old spiteful work of catching and destroying the bubbles which youth delighted to follow, have indeed dissipated much of this illusion; but my mind so far retained the influence of that early impression, that I have ever since continued to deposit my humble offerings at its shrine, whenever the ministers of the Lottery went forth with type and trumpet to announce its periodical dispensations; and though nothing has been doled out to me from its undiscerning coffers but blanks, or those more vexatious tantalizers of the spirit denominated small prizes, yet do I hold myself largely indebted to this most generous diffuser of universal happiness. Ingrates that we are! are we to be thankful for no benefits that are not palpable to sense, to recognize no favours that are not of marketable value, to acknowledge no wealth unless it can be counted with the five fingers? If we admit the mind to be the sole depository of genuine joy, where is the bosom that has not been elevated into a temporary Elysium by the magic of the Lottery? Which of us has not converted his ticket, or even his sixteenth share of one, into a nest-egg of Hope, upon which he has sate brooding in the secret roosting-places of his heart, and hatched it into a thousand fantastical apparitions?

What a startling revelation of the passions if all the aspirations engendered by the Lottery could be made manifest! Many an impecuniary epicure has gloated over his locked-up warrant for future wealth, as a means of realizing the dream of his namesake in the "Alchemist:"—

"My meat shall all come in in Indian shells—
Dishes of agate set in gold, and studded
With emeralds, sapphires, hyacinths, and rubies;
The tongues of carps, dormice, and camels' heels,
Boiled i' the spirit of Sol, and dissolved in pearl
(Apicius' diet 'gainst the epilepsy).
And I will eat these broths with spoons of amber,
Headed with diamant and carbuncle.
My footboy shall eat pheasants, calvered salmons,
Knots, godwits, lampreys: I myself will have
The beards of barbels served, instead of salads;
Oiled mushrooms, and the swelling unctuous paps

Of a fat pregnant sow, newly cut off,
Dressed with an exquisite and poignant
    sauce,
For which I'll say unto my cook,
    'There's gold:
Go forth, and be a knight!'"

Many a doting lover has kissed the scrap of paper whose promissory shower of gold was to give up to him his otherwise unattainable Danaë; Nimrods have transformed the same narrow symbol into a saddle, by which they have been enabled to bestride the backs of peerless hunters; while nymphs have metamorphosed its Protean form into—

"Rings, gauds, conceits,
Knacks, trifles, nosegays, sweetmeats,"

and all the braveries of dress, to say nothing of the obsequious husband, the two-footmann'd carriage, and the opera-box. By the simple charm of this numbered and printed rag, gamesters have, for a time at least, recovered their losses; spendthrifts have cleared off mortgages from their estates; the imprisoned debtor has leapt over his lofty boundary of circumscription and restraint, and revelled in all the joys of liberty and fortune; the cottage-walls have swelled out into more goodly proportion than those of Baucis and Philemon; poverty has tasted the luxuries of competence; labour has lolled at ease in a perpetual arm-chair of idleness; sickness has been bribed into banishment; life has been invested with new charms; and death deprived of its former terrors. Nor have the affections been less gratified than the wants, appetites, and ambitions of mankind. By the conjurations of the same potent spell, kindred have lavished anticipated benefits upon one another, and charity upon all. Let it be termed a delusion,—a fool's paradise is better than the wise man's Tartarus; be it branded as an ignisfatuus,—it was at least a benevolent one, which, instead of beguiling its followers into swamps, caverns, and pitfalls, allured them on with all the blandishments of enchantment to a garden of Eden, —an ever-blooming Elysium of delight. True, the pleasures it bestowed were evanescent: but which of our joys are permanent? and who so inexperienced as not to know that anticipation is always of higher relish than reality, which strikes a balance both in our sufferings and enjoyments? "The fear of ill exceeds the ill we fear;" and fruition, in the same proportion, invariably falls short of hope. "Men are but children of a larger growth," who may amuse themselves for a long time in gazing at the reflection of the moon in the water; but, if they jump in to grasp it, they may grope for ever, and only get the farther from their object. He is the wisest who keeps feeding upon the future, and refrains as long as possible from undeceiving himself by converting his pleasant speculations into disagreeable certainties.

The true mental epicure always purchased his ticket early, and postponed inquiry into its fate to the last possible moment, during the whole of which intervening period he had an imaginary twenty thousand locked up in his desk; and was not this well worth all the money? Who would scruple to give twenty pounds interest for even the ideal enjoyment of as many thousands during two or three months? *Crede quod habes, et habes;* and the usufruct of such a capital is surely not dear at such a price. Some years ago, a gentleman in passing along Cheapside saw the figures 1,069, of which number he was the sole proprietor, flaming on the window of a lottery-office as a capital prize. Somewhat flurried by this discovery, not less welcome than unexpected, he resolved to walk round St. Paul's that he might consider in what way to communicate the happy tidings to his wife and family; but, upon re-passing the shop, he observed that the number was altered to 10,069, and, upon inquiry, had the mortification to learn that his ticket was a blank, and had only been stuck up in the window by a mistake of the clerk. This effectually calmed his agitation; but he always speaks of himself as having once possessed twenty thousand pounds, and maintains that his ten-minutes' walk round St. Paul's was worth ten times the purchase-money of the ticket. A prize thus obtained has, moreover, this special advantage,—it is beyond the reach of fate; it cannot be squandered; bankruptcy cannot lay siege to it; friends cannot pull it down, nor enemies blow it up; it bears a charmed life, and none of woman born can break its integrity, even by the dissipation, of a single fraction. Show me the property in these perilous times, that is equally compact and impregnable. We can no longer become enriched for a quarter of an hour; we can no longer succeed in such splendid failures: all our chances of making such a miss have vanished with the last of the Lotteries.

Life will now become a flat, prosaic routine of matter-of-fact; and sleep itself, erst so prolific of numerical configurations and mysterious stimulants to lottery adventure, will be disfurnished of its figures and figments. People will cease to harp upon the one lucky number suggested in a dream, and which forms the exception, while they are scrupulously silent upon the ten thousand falsified dreams which constitute the rule. Morpheus will stifle Cocker with a handful of poppies, and our pillows will be no longer haunted by the book of numbers. And who, too, shall maintain the art and mystery of puffing, in all its pristine glory, when the lottery professors shall have abandoned its cultivation? They were the first, as they will assuredly be the last, who fully developed the resources of that ingenious art; who cajoled and decoyed the most suspicious and wary reader into a perusal of their advertisements by devices of endless variety and cunning; who baited their lurking schemes with midnight murders, ghost-stories, crim-cons, bon-mots, balloons, dreadful catastrophes, and every diversity of joy and sorrow, to catch newspaper-gudgeons. Ought not such talents to be encouraged? Verily the abolitionists have much to answer for!

And now, having established the felicity of all those who gained imaginary prizes, let us proceed to show that the equally numerous class who were presented with real blanks have not less reason to consider themselves happy. Most of us have cause to be thankful for that which is bestowed; but we have all, probably, reason to be still more grateful for that which is withheld, and more especially for our being denied the sudden possession of riches. In the Litany, indeed, we call upon the Lord to deliver us "in all time of our wealth;" but how few of us are sincere in deprecating such a calamity! Massinger's Luke, and Ben Jonson's Sir Epicure Mammon, and Pope's Sir Balaam, and our own daily observation, might convince us that the Devil "now tempts by making rich, not making poor." We may read in the "Guardian" a circumstantial account of a man who was utterly ruined by gaining a capital prize; we may recollect what Dr. Johnson said to Garrick, when the latter was making a display of his wealth at Hampton Court,—"Ah, David, David! these are the things that make a death-bed terrible;" we may recall the Scripture declaration, as to the difficulty a rich man finds in entering into the kingdom of Heaven; and, combining all these denunciations against opulence, let us heartily congratulate one another upon our lucky escape from the calamity of a twenty or thirty thousand pound prize! The fox in the fable, who accused the unattainable grapes of sourness, was more of a philosopher than we are generally willing to allow. He was an adept in that species of moral alchemy which turns everything to gold, and converts disappointment itself into a ground of resignation and content. Such we have shown to be the great lesson inculcated by the Lottery, when rightly contemplated; and, if we might parody M. de Chateaubriand's jingling expression,— "*le Roi est mort: vive le Roi!*"—wo should be tempted to exclaim, "The Lottery is no more: long live the Lottery!"

THE ASS.

Mr. Collier, in his "Poetical Decameron" (Third Conversation), notices a tract printed in 1595, with the author's initials only, A. B., entitled "The Noblenesse of the Asse; a work rare, learned, and excellent." He has selected the following pretty passage from it: "He (the ass) refuseth no burden: he goes whither he is sent, without any contradiction. He lifts not his foote against any one; he bytes not; he is no fugitive, nor malicious affected. He doth all things in good sort, and to his liking that hath cause to employ him. If strokes be given him, he cares not for them; and, as our modern poet singeth,—

" 'Thou wouldst (perhaps) he should be-
        come thy foe,
And to that end dost beat him many
        times!
    He cares not for himselfe, much less
        thy blow.'"

Certainly Nature, foreseeing the cruel usage which this useful servant to man should receive at man's hand, did prudently in furnishing him with a tegument impervious to ordinary stripes. The malice of a child or a weak hand can make feeble impressions on him. His back offers no mark to a puny foeman. To a common whip or switch his hide presents an absolute insensibility. You might as well pretend to scourge a schoolboy with a tough pair of leather breeches on. His jerkin is well fortified; and therefore the costermongers, "between the years 1790 and 1800," did more politicly than piously in lifting up a part of his upper garment. I well remember that beastly and bloody custom. I have often longed to see one of those refiners in discipline himself at the cart's tail, with just such a convenient spot laid bare to the tender mercies of the whipster. But, since Nature has resumed her rights, it is to be hoped that this patient creature does not suffer to extremities; and that, to the savages who still belabour his poor carcase with their blows (considering the sort of anvil they are laid upon), he might in some sort, if he could speak, exclaim with the philosopher, "Lay on: you beat but upon the case of Anaxarchus."

Contemplating this natural safeguard, this fortified exterior, it is with pain I view the sleek, foppish, combed, and curried person of this animal as he is disnaturalized at watering-places, &c.. where they affect to make a palfry of him. Fie on all such sophistications! It will never do, master groom. Something of his honest, shaggy exterior will still peep up in spite of you,—his good, rough, native, pine-apple coating. You cannot "refine a scorpion into a fish, though you rinse it and scour it with ever so cleanly cookery."*

The modern poet quoted by A B. proceeds to celebrate a virtue for which no one to this day had been aware that the ass was remarkable:—

"One other gift this beast hath as his
        owne,
    Wherewith the rest could not be fur-
        nished;
    On man himself the same was not be-
        stowne:
    To wit, on him is ne'er engenderèd
    The hateful vermine that doth tearo
        the skin,
    And to the bode [body] doth make his
        passage in."

And truly, when one thinks on the suit of impenetrable armour with which Nature (like Vulcan to another Achilles) has provided him, these subtile enemies to *our* repose would have shown some dexterity in getting into *his* quar-

---

* Milton, *from memory.*

ters. As the bogs of Ireland by tradition expel toads and reptiles, he may well defy these small deer in his fastnesses. It seems the latter had not arrived at the exquisite policy adopted by the human vermin "between 1790 and 1800."

But the most singular and delightful gift of the ass, according to the writer of this pamphlet, is his *voice*, the "goodly, sweet, and continual brayings" of which, "whereof they forme a melodious and proportionable kinde of musicke," seem to have affected him with no ordinary pleasure. "Nor thinke I," he adds, "that any of our immoderate musitians can deny but that their song is full of exceeding pleasure to be heard; because therein is to be discerned both concord, discord, singing in the meane, the beginning to sing in large compasse, then following into rise and fall, the halfe-note, whole note, musicke of five voices, firme singing by four voices, three together, or one voice and a halfe. Then their variable contrarieties amongst them, when one delivers forth a long tenor or a short, the pausing for time, breathing in measure, breaking the minim or very least moment of time. Last of all, to heare the musicke of five or six voices chaunged to so many of asses is amongst them to heare a song of world without end."

There is no accounting for ears, or for that laudable enthusiasm with which an author is tempted to invest a favourite subject with the most incompatible perfections: I should otherwise, for my own taste, have been inclined rather to have given a place to these extraordinary musicians at that banquet of nothing-less-than-sweet-sounds, imagined by old Jeremy Collier (Essays, 1698, part ii. on Music), where, after describing the inspiriting effects of martial music in a battle, he hazards an ingenious conjecture, whether a sort of *anti-music* might not be invented, which should have quite the contrary effect of "sinking the spirits, shaking the nerves, curdling the blood, and inspiring despair and cowardice and consternation. 'Tis probable," he says, "the roaring of lions, the warbling of cats and screech-owls, together with a mixture of the howling of dogs, judiciously imitated and compounded, might go a great way in this invention." The dose, we confess, is pretty potent, and skilfully enough prepared. But what shall we say to the Ass of Silenus, who, if we may trust to classic lore, by his own proper sounds, without thanks to cat or screech-owl, dismayed and put to rout a whole army of giants? Here was *anti-music* with a vengeance; a whole *Pan-Dis-Harmonicon* in a single lungs of leather!

But I keep you trifling too long on this asinine subject. I have already passed the *Pons Asinorum*, and will desist, remembering the old pedantic pun of Jem Boyer, my schoolmaster,—

21*

"As *in præsenti* seldom makes
a WISE MAN *in futuro.*"

——

IN RE SQUIRRELS.

WHAT is gone with the cages
with the climbing squirrel, and
bells to them, which were formerly
the indispensable appendage to
the outside of a tinman's shop,
and were, in fact, the only live
signs? One, we believe, still
hangs out on Holborn; but they
are fast vanishing with the good
old modes of our ancestors. They
seem to have been superseded by
that still more ingenious refinement of modern humanity,—the
tread-mill; in which *human* squirrels still perform a similar round
of ceaseless, improgressive clambering, which must be nuts to
them.

We almost doubt the fact of the
teeth of this creature being so
purely orange-coloured as Mr.
Urban's correspondent gives out.
One of our old poets—and they
were pretty sharp observers of
Nature—describes them as brown.
But perhaps the naturalist referred to meant "of the colour
of a Maltese orange,"* which is
rather more obfuscated than your
fruit of Seville or St. Michael's,
and may help to reconcile the
difference. We cannot speak from

* Fletcher in the "Faithful Shep-
herdess." The satyr offers to Clorin—
"Grapes whose lusty blood
Is the learned poet's good,—
Sweeter yet did never crown
The head of Bacchus; nuts more brown
Than the *squirrels'* teeth that crack them."

observation; but we remember at
school getting our fingers into the
orangery of one of these little
gentry (not having a due caution
of the traps set there), and the result proved sourer than lemons.
The author of the "Task" somewhere speaks of their anger as
being "insignificantly fierce;" but
we found the demonstration of it
on this occasion quite as significant as we desired, and have not
been disposed since to look any
of these "gift horses" in the
mouth. Maiden aunts keep these
"small deer," as they do parrots,
to bite people's fingers, on purpose
to give them good advice "not to
adventure so near the cage another time." As for their "six
quavers divided into three quavers
and a dotted crotchet," I suppose
they may go into Jeremy Bent-
ham's next budget of fallacies,
along with the "melodious and
proportionable kinde of musicke"
recorded, in your last number, of
an highly-gifted animal.

——

ESTIMATE OF DE FOE'S
SECONDARY NOVELS.

IT has happened not seldom
that one work of some author has
so transcendently surpassed in
execution the rest of his compositions, that the world has agreed
to pass a sentence of dismissal
upon the latter, and to consign
them to total neglect and oblivion.
It has done wisely in this not to
suffer the contemplation of ex-
cellences of a lower standard to

abate or stand in the way of the pleasure it has agreed to receive from the masterpiece.

Again: it has happened, that from no inferior merit of execution in the rest, but from superior good fortune in the choice of its subject, some single work shall have been suffered to eclipse and cast into shade the deserts of its less fortunate brethren. This has been done with more or less injustice in the case of the popular allegory of Bunyan, in which the beautiful and scriptural image of a pilgrim or wayfarer (we are all such upon earth), addressing itself intelligibly and feelingly to the bosoms of all, has silenced, and made almost to be forgotten, the more awful and scarcely less tender beauties of the "Holy War made by Shaddai upon Diabolus," of the same author,—a romance less happy in its subject, but surely well worthy of a secondary immortality. But in no instance has this excluding partiality been exerted with more unfairness than against what may be termed the secondary novels or romances of De Foe.

While all ages and descriptions of people hang delighted over the "Adventures of Robinson Crusoe," and shall continue to do so, we trust, while the world lasts, how few comparatively will bear to be told that there exist other fictitious narratives by the same writer,—four of them at least of no inferior interest, except what results from a less felicitous choice of situation! "Roxana," "Singleton," "Moll Flanders," "Colonel Jack," are all genuine offspring of the same father. They bear the veritable impress of De Foe. An unpractised midwife that would not swear to the nose, lip, forehead, and eye of every one of them! They are, in their way, as full of incident and some of them every bit as romantic; only they want the uninhabited island, and the charm that has bewitched the world, of the striking solitary situation.

But are there no solitudes out of the cave and the desert? or cannot the heart in the midst of crowds feel frightfully alone? Singleton on the world of waters, prowling about with pirates less merciful than the creatures of any howling wilderness,—is he not alone, with the faces of men about him, but without a guide that can conduct him through the mists of educational and habitual ignorance, or a fellow-heart that can interpret to him the new-born yearnings and aspirations of unpractised penitence? Or when the boy Colonel Jack, in the loneliness of the heart (the worst solitude), goes to hide his ill-purchased treasure in the hollow tree by night, and miraculously loses, and miraculously finds it again,—whom hath he there to sympathize with him? or of what sort are his associates?

The narrative manner of De Foe has a naturalness about it beyond that of any other novel or romance writer. His fictions have all the air of true stories. It is impossible to believe, while you are reading them, that a real person is not narrating to you everywhere nothing but what really happened to himself. To this the extreme *homeliness* of their style mainly contributes. We use the word in its best and heartiest sense,—that which comes *home* to the reader. The narrators everywhere are chosen from low life, or have had their origin in it: therefore they tell their own tales (Mr. Coleridge has anticipated us in this remark), as persons in their degree are observed to do, with infinite repetition, and an over-acted exactness, lest the hearer should not have minded, or have forgotten, some things that had been told before. Hence the emphatic sentences marked in the good old (but deserted) Italic type; and hence, too, the frequent interposition of the reminding old colloquial parenthesis, "I say," "Mind," and the like, when the story-teller repeats what, to a practised reader, might appear to have been sufficiently insisted upon before: which made an ingenious critic observe, that his works, in this kind, were excellent reading for the kitchen. And, in truth, the heroes and heroines of De Foe can never again hope to be popular with a much higher class of readers than that of the servant-maid or the sailor. Crusoe keeps its rank only by tough prescription. Singleton, the pirate; Colonel Jack, the thief; Moll Flanders, both thief and harlot; Roxana, harlot and something worse,—would be startling in-gredients in the bill of fare of modern literary delicacies. But, then, what pirates, what thieves, and what harlots, is *the thief*, *the harlot*, and *the pirate* of De Foe! We would not hesitate to say, that in no other book of fiction, where the lives of such characters are described, is guilt and delinquency made less seductive, or the suffering made more closely to follow the commission, or the penitence more earnest or more bleeding, or the intervening flashes of religious visitation upon the rude and uninstructed soul more meltingly and fearfully painted. They, in this, come near to the tenderness of Bunyan; while the livelier pictures and incidents in them, as in Hogarth or in Fielding, tend to diminish that fastidiousness to the concerns and pursuits of common life which an unrestrained passion for the ideal and the sentimental is in danger of producing.

POSTSCRIPT TO THE "CHAPTER ON EARS."

A WRITER, whose real name, it seems, is *Boldero*, but who has been entertaining the town for the last twelve months with some very pleasant lucubrations under the assumed signature of *Leigh Hunt*,[*] in his "Indicator" of the 31st January last has thought fit to in-

[*] Clearly a fictitious appellation; for, if we admit the latter of these names to be in a manner English, what is *Leigh*? Christian nomenclature knows no such.

sinuate that I, *Elia*, do not write the little sketches which bear my signature in this magazine, but that the true author of them is a Mr. L——b. Observe the critical period at which he has chosen to impute the calumny,—on the very eve of the publication of our last number,—affording no scope for explanation for a full month; during which time I must needs lie writhing and tossing under the cruel imputation of nonentity. Good Heavens! that a plain man must not be allowed *to be*——

They call this an age of personality; but surely this spirit of anti-personality (if I may so express it) is something worse.

Take away my moral reputation,—I may live to discredit that calumny; injure my literary fame,—I may write that up again; but, when a gentleman is robbed of his identity, where is he?

Other murderers stab but at our existence, a frail and perishing trifle at the best; but here is an assassin who aims at our very essence; who not only forbids us *to be* any longer, but *to have been* at all. Let our ancestors look to it.

Is the parish register nothing? Is the house in Princes Street, Cavendish Square, where we saw the light six and forty years ago, nothing? Were our progenitors from stately Genoa, where we flourished four centuries back, before the barbarous name of Boldero * was known to a European

mouth, nothing? Was the goodly scion of our name, transplanted into England in the reign of the seventh Henry, nothing? Are the archives of the steelyard, in succeeding reigns (if haply they survive the fury of our envious enemies), showing that we flourished in prime repute, as merchants, down to the period of the Commonwealth, nothing?

"Why, then the world, and all that's in't, is nothing;
The covering sky is nothing; Bohemia nothing."

I am ashamed that this trifling writer should have power to move me so

———

ELIA TO HIS CORRESPONDENTS.

A CORRESPONDENT, who writes himself Peter Ball, or Bell, for his handwriting is as ragged as his manners, - admonishes me of the old saying, that some people (under a courteous periphrasis, I slur his less ceremonious epithet) had need have good memories. In my "Old Benchers of the Inner Temple," I have delivered myself, and truly, a Templar born. Bell clamours upon this, and thinketh that he hath caught a fox. It seems that in a former paper, retorting upon a weekly scribbler who had called my good identity in question (see Postscript to my "Chapter on Ears"), I profess myself a native of some spot near Cavendish Square, deducing my remoter origin from Italy. But

* It is clearly of transatlantic origin.

who does not see, except this tinkling cymbal, that, in the idle fiction of Genoese ancestry, I was answering a fool according to his folly,—that Elia there expresseth himself ironically as to an approved slanderer, who hath no right to the truth, and can be no fit recipient of it? Such a one it is usual to leave to his delusions; or, leading him from error still to contradictory error, to plunge him (as we say) deeper in the mire, and give him line till he suspend himself. No understanding reader could be imposed upon by such obvious rhodomontade to suspect me for an alien, or believe me other than English.

To a second correspondent, who signs himself "A Wiltshire Man," and claims me for a countryman upon the strength of an equivocal phrase in my "Christ's Hospital," a more mannerly reply is due. Passing over the Genoese fable, which Bell makes such a ring about, he nicely detects a more subtle discrepancy, which Bell was too obtuse to strike upon. Referring to the passage, I must confess that the term "native town," applied to Calne, *primâ facie* seems to bear out the construction which my friendly correspondent is willing to put upon it. The context too, I am afraid, a little favours it. But where the words of an author, taken literally, compared with some other passage in his writings, admitted to be authentic, involve a palpable contradiction, it hath been the custom of the ingenuous commen-tator to smooth the difficulty by the supposition that in the one case an allegorical or tropical sense was chiefly intended. So, by the word "native," I may be supposed to mean a town where I might have been born, or where it might be desirable that I should have been born, as being situate in wholesome air, upon a dry, chalky soil, in which I delight; or a town with the inhabitants of which I passed some weeks, a summer or two ago, so agreeably that they and it became in a manner native to me. Without some such latitude of interpretation in the present case, I see not how we can avoid falling into a gross error in physics, as to conceive that a gentleman may be born in two places, from which all modern and ancient testimony is alike abhorrent. Bacchus cometh the nearest to it, whom I remember Ovid to have honoured with the epithet "twice born."[*] But, not to mention that he is so called (we conceive) in reference to the places *whence* rather than the places *where* he was delivered,—for, by either birth, he may probably be challenged for a Theban, —in a strict way of speaking, he was a *filius femoris* by no means in the same sense as he had been before a *filius alvi;* for that latter

---

[*] "Imperfectus adhuc Infans genetricis
  abalvo
 Eripitur, patrioque tener (si credere
  dignum)
 Insultar femori . . . . .
 Tutaque bis geniti sunt incunabula
  Bacchi."

     Metamorph., lib. III.

was but a secondary and tralatitious way of being born, and he but a denizen of the second house of his geniture. Thus much by way of explanation was thought due to the courteous "Wiltshire Man."

To "Indagator," "Investigator," "Incertus," and the rest of the pack, that are so importunate about the true localities of his birth,—as if, forsooth, Elia were presently about to be passed to his parish,—to all such churchwarden critics he answereth, that, any explanation here given notwithstanding, he hath not so fixed his nativity (like a rusty vane) to one dull spot, but that, if he seeth occasion, or the argument shall demand it, he will be born again, in future papers, in whatever place, and at whatever period, shall seem good unto him.

"Modò me Thebis, modò Athenis."

UNITARIAN PROTESTS;

IN A LETTER TO A FRIEND OF THAT PERSUASION NEWLY MARRIED.

DEAR M——,—Though none of your acquaintance can with greater sincerity congratulate you upon this happy conjuncture than myself, one of the oldest of them, it was with pain I found you, after the ceremony, depositing in the vestry-room what is called a Protest. I thought you superior to this little sophistry. What! after submitting to the service of the Church of England,—after consenting to receive a boon from her, in the person of your amiable consort,—was it consistent with sense, or common good manners, to turn round upon her, and flatly taunt her with false worship? This language is a little of the strongest in your books and from your pulpits, though there it may well enough be excused from religious zeal and the native warmth of nonconformity. But at the altar,—the Church-of-England altar,—adopting her forms, and complying with her requisitions to the letter,—to be consistent, together with the practice, I fear, you must drop the language of dissent. You are no longer sturdy non-cons: you are there occasional conformists. You submit to accept the privileges communicated by a form of words, exceptionable, and perhaps justly, in your view; but, so submitting, you have no right to quarrel with the ritual which you have just condescended to owe an obligation to. They do not force you into their churches. You come voluntarily, knowing the terms. You marry in the name of the Trinity. There is no evading this by pretending that you take the formula with your own interpretation: (and, so long as you can do this, where is the necessity of protesting?) for the meaning of a vow is to be settled by the sense of the imposer, not by any forced construction of the taker; else might all vows, and oaths too, be eluded with impunity. You marry, then, essentially as Trinitarians; and the altar no sooner satisfied than, hey, presto! with the celerity of a juggler, you shift habits, and proceed pure Unitarians again in the vestry. You cheat the church out of a wife, and go home smiling in your sleeves that you have so cunningly despoiled the Egyptians. In plain English, the Church has married you in the name of so and so, assuming that you took the words in her sense: but you outwitted her; you assented to them in your sense only, and took from her what, upon a right understanding, she would have declined giving you.

This is the fair construction to be put upon all Unitarian marriages, as at present contracted; and, so long as you Unitarians could salve your consciences with the *équivoque*, I do not see why the Established Church should have troubled herself at all about the matter. But the protesters necessarily see farther. They have some glimmerings of the deception; they apprehend a flaw somewhere; they would fain be honest, and yet they must marry notwithstanding; for honesty's sake, they are fain to dehonestate themselves a little. Let me try the very words of your own protest, to see what confessions we can pick out of them.

"As Unitarians, therefore, we" (you and your newly-espoused bride) "most solemnly protest against the service" (which yourselves have just demanded), "because we are thereby called upon not only tacitly to acquiesce, but to profess a belief in a doctrine which is a dogma, as we believe, totally unfounded." But do you profess that belief during the ceremony? or are you only called upon for the profession, but do not make it? If the latter, then you fall in with the rest of your more consistent brethren who waive the protest; if the former, then, I fear, your protest cannot save you.

Hard and grievous it is, that, in any case, an institution so broad and general as the union of man and wife should be so cramped and straitened by the bands of an imposing hierarchy, that, to plight troth to a lovely woman, a man must be necessitated to compromise his truth and faith to Heaven; but so it must be, so long as you choose to marry by the forms of the Church over which that hierarchy presides.

"Therefore," say you, "we protest." Oh, poor and much-fallen word, Protest! It was not so that the first heroic reformers protested. They departed out of Babylon once for good and all; they came not back for an occasional contact with her altars,—a dallying, and then a protesting against dalliance; they stood not shuffling in the porch, with a Popish foot within, and its lame Lutheran fellow without, halting betwixt. These were the true Protestants. You are—protesters.

Besides the inconsistency of this proceeding, I must think it a piece of impertinence, unseasonable at least, and out of place, to obtrude these papers upon the officiating clergyman; to offer to a public functionary an instrument which by the tenor of his function he is not obliged to accept, but rather he is called upon to reject. Is it done in his clerical capacity? He has no power of redressing the grievance. It is to take the benefit of his ministry, and then insult him. If in his capacity of fellow-Christian only, what are your scruples to him, so long as you yourselves are able to get over them, and do get over them by the very fact of coming to require his services? The thing you call a Protest might with just as good a reason be presented to the churchwarden for the time being, to the parish-clerk, or the pew-opener.

The Parliament alone can redress your grievance, if any. Yet I see not how with any grace your people can petition for relief, so long as, by the very fact of your coming to church to be married, they do *bonâ fide* and strictly relieve themselves. The Upper House, in particular, is not unused to these same things, called Protests, among themselves. But how would this honourable body stare to find a noble lord conceding a measure, and in the next breath, by a solemn protest, disowning it! A protest there is a reason given for non-compliance, not a subterfuge for an equivocal occasional compliance. It was reasonable in the primitive Christians to avert from their persons, by whatever lawful means, the compulsory eating of meats which had been offered unto idols. I dare say the Roman prefects and exarchates had plenty of petitioning in their days. But what would a Festus or Agrippa have replied to a petition to that effect, presented to him by some evasive Laodicean, with the very meat between his teeth, which he had been chewing voluntarily, rather than abide the penalty? Relief for tender consciences means nothing, where the conscience has previously relieved itself; that is, has complied with the injunctions which it seeks preposterously to be rid of. Relief for conscience there is properly none, but what by better information makes an act appear innocent and lawful with which the previous conscience was not satisfied to comply. All else is but relief from penalties, from scandal incurred by a complying practice, where the conscience itself is not fully satisfied.

"But," say you, "we have hard measure: the Quakers are indulged with the liberty denied to us." They are; and dearly have they earned it. You have come in (as a sect at least) in the cool of the evening,—at the eleventh hour. The Quaker character was hardened in the fires of persecution in the seventeenth century; not quite to the stake and faggot, but little short of that; they grew up and thrived against noisome prisons, cruel beatings, whippings, stockings.

They have since endured a century or two of scoffs, contempts; they have been a by-word and a nay-word; they have stood unmoved: and the consequence of long conscientious resistance on one part is invariably, in the end, remission on the other. The Legislature, that denied you the tolerance, which I do not know that at that time you even asked, gave them the liberty, which, without granting, they would have assumed. No penalties could have driven them into the churches. This is the consequence of entire measures. Had the early Quakers consented to take oaths, leaving a protest with the clerk of the court against them in the same breath with which they had taken them, do you in your conscience think that they would have been indulged at this day in their exclusive privilege of affirming? Let your people go on for a century or so, marrying in your own fashion, and I will warrant them, before the end of it, the Legislature will be willing to concede to them more than they at present demand.

Either the institution of marriage depends not for its validity upon hypocritical compliances with the ritual of an alien Church (and then I do not see why you cannot marry among yourselves, as the Quakers, without their indulgence, would have been doing to this day), or it does depend upon such ritual compliance; and then, in your protests, you offend against a divine ordinance. I have read in the Essex Street Liturgy a form for the celebration of marriage. Why is this become a dead letter? Oh! it has never been legalized; that is to say, in the law's eye, it is no marriage. But do you take upon you to say, in the view of the gospel it would be none? Would your own people, at least, look upon a couple so paired to be none? But the case of dowries, alimonies, inheritances, &c., which depend for their validity upon the ceremonial of the Church by law established,—are these nothing? That our children are not legally *Filii Nullius*,—is this nothing? I answer, Nothing; to the preservation of a good conscience, nothing; to a consistent Christianity, less than nothing. Sad worldly thorns they are indeed, and stumbling-blocks well worthy to be set out of the way by a Legislature calling itself Christian; but not likely to be removed in a hurry by any shrewd legislators who perceive that the petitioning complainants have not so much as bruised a shin in the resistance, but, prudently declining the briers and the prickles, nestle quietly down in the smooth two-sided velvet of a protesting occasional conformity.

I am, dear sir,
   With much respect,
     yours, &c.,

        ELIA.

———

ON THE CUSTOM OF HISSING AT THE THEATRES;

WITH SOME ACCOUNT OF A CLUB OF DAMNED AUTHORS.

MR. REFLECTOR,—I am one of those persons whom the world has thought proper to designate by the title of Damned Authors. In that memorable season of dramatic failures, 1806-7,—in which no fewer, I think, than two tragedies, four comedies, one opera, and three farces, suffered at Drury Lane Theatre,—I was found guilty of constructing an afterpiece, and was *damned*.

Against the decision of the public in such instances there can be no appeal. The clerk of Chatham might as well have protested against the decision of Cade and his followers, who were then *the public*. Like him, I was condemned because I could write.

Not but it did appear to some of us that the measures of the popular tribunal at that period savoured a little of harshness and of the *summum jus*. The public mouth was early in the season fleshed upon the "Vindictive Man," and some pieces of that nature; and it retained, through the remainder of it, a relish of blood. As Dr. Johnson would have said, "Sir, there was a habit of sibilation in the house."

Still less am I disposed to inquire into the reason of the comparative lenity, on the other hand, with which some pieces were treated, which, to indifferent judges, seemed at least as much deserving of condemnation as some of those which met with it. I am willing to put a favourable construction upon the votes that were given against us; I believe that there was no bribery or designed partiality in the case: only "our nonsense did not happen to suit their nonsense;" that was all.

But against the *manner* in which the public, on these occasions, think fit to deliver their disapprobation, I must and ever will protest.

Sir, imagine—but you have been present at the damning of a piece (those who never had that felicity, I beg them to imagine)— a vast theatre, like that which Drury Lane was before it was a heap of dust and ashes (I insult not over its fallen greatness; let it recover itself when it can for me, let it lift up its towering head once more, and take in poor authors to write for it; *hic cæstus artemque repono*),—a theatre like that, filled with all sorts of disgusting sounds,—shrieks, groans, hisses, but chiefly the last, like the noise of many waters, or that which Don Quixote heard from the fulling-mills, or that wilder combination of devilish sounds which St. Anthony listened to in the wilderness.

Oh! Mr. Reflector, is it not a pity that the sweet human voice, which was given man to speak with, to sing with, to whisper tones of love in, to express compliance, to convey a favour, or to grant a suit,—that voice, which in a Siddons or a Braham rouses us, in a siren Catalani charms and captivates us,—that the musical, expressive human voice should be converted into a rival of the noises of silly geese, and irrational, venomous snakes?

I never shall forget the sounds on *my night*. I never before that time fully felt the reception which the Author of All Ill, in the "Paradise Lost," meets with from the critics in the *pit*, at the final close of his "Tragedy upon the Human Race,"—though that, alas! met with too much success:—

"From innumerable tongues
A dismal universal *hiss*, the sound
Of public scorn. Dreadful was the din
Of *hissing* through the hall, thick swarm-
  ing now
With complicated monsters, head and
  tail,
Scorpion and asp, and Amphisbæna dire,
Cerastes horned, Hydrus, and Elops
  drear,
And Dipsas."

For *hall* substitute *theatre*, and you have the very image of what takes place at what is called the *damnation* of a piece,—and properly so called; for here you see its origin plainly, whence the custom was derived, and what the first piece was that so suffered. After this, none can doubt the propriety of the appellation.

But, sir, as to the justice of bestowing such appalling, heart-withering denunciations of the popular obloquy upon the venial mistake of a poor author, who thought to please us in the act of filling his pockets,—for the sum of his demerits amounts to no more than that,—it does, I own, seem to me a species of retributive justice far too severe for the offence. A culprit in the pillory (bate the eggs) meets with no severer exprobration.

Indeed, I have often wondered that some modest critic has not proposed that there should be a wooden machine to that effect erected in some convenient part of the *proscenium*, which an unsuccessful author should be required to mount, and stand his hour, exposed to the apples and oranges of the pit. This *amende honorable* would well suit with the meanness of some authors, who, in their prologues, fairly prostrate their skulls to the audience, and seem to invite a pelting.

Or why should they not have their pens publicly broke over their heads, as the swords of recreant knights in old times were, and an oath administered to them that they should never write again?

Seriously, *Messieurs the Public*, this outrageous way which you have got of expressing your displeasures is too much for the occasion. When I was deafening under the effects of it, I could not help asking what crime of great moral turpitude I had committed: for every man about me seemed to feel the offence as personal to himself; as something which public interest and private feelings alike called upon him, in the strongest possible manner, to stigmatize with infamy.

The Romans, it is well known to you, Mr. Reflector, took a gentler method of marking their disapprobation of an author's work. They were a humane and equitable nation. They left the *furca* and the *patibulum*, the axe and the rods, to great offenders: for these minor and (if I may so term them) extra-moral offences, *the bent thumb* was considered as a sufficient sign of disapprobation,—*vertere pollicem;* as *the pressed thumb, premere pollicem*, was a mark of approving.

And really there seems to have been a sort of fitness in this method, a correspondency of sign in the punishment to the offence. For, as the action of writing is performed by bending the thumb forward, the retroversion or bending back of that joint did not unaptly point to the opposite of that action; implying that it was the will of the audience that the author should *write no more:* a much more significant as well as more humane way of expressing that desire than our custom of hissing, which is altogether senseless and indefensible. Nor do we find that the Roman audiences deprived themselves, by this lenity, of any tittle of that supremacy which audiences in all ages have thought themselves bound to maintain over such as have been candidates for their applause. On the contrary, by this method they seem to have had the author, as we should ex-press it, completely *under finger and thumb.*

The provocations to which a dramatic genius is exposed from the public are so much the more vexatious as they are removed from any possibility of retaliation, the hope of which sweetens most other injuries; for the public *never writes itself.* Not but something very like it took place at the time of the O. P. differences. The placards which were nightly exhibited were, properly speaking, the composition of the public. The public wrote them, the public applauded them; and precious morceaux of wit and eloquence they were,—except some few, of a better quality, which it is well known were furnished by professed dramatic writers. After this specimen of what the public can do for itself, it should be a little slow in condemning what others do for it.

As the degrees of malignancy vary in people according as they have more or less of the Old Serpent (the father of hisses) in their composition, I have sometimes amused myself with analyzing this many-headed hydra, which calls itself the public, into the component parts of which it is "complicated, head and tail," and seeing how many varieties of the snake kind it can afford.

First, there is the Common English Snake.—This is that part of the auditory who are always the majority at damnations; but who, having no critical venom in themselves to sting them on, stay till they hear others hiss, and then join in for company.

The Blind Worm is a species very nearly allied to the foregoing. Some naturalists have doubted whether they are not the same.

The Rattlesnake.—These are your obstreperous talking critics,—the impertinent guides of the pit,—who will not give a plain man leave to enjoy an evening's entertainment; but, with their frothy jargon and incessant finding of faults, either drown his pleasure quite, or force him, in his own defence, to join in their clamours censure. The hiss always originates with these. When this creature springs his *rattle*, you would think, from the noise it makes, there was something in it; but you have only to examine the instrument from which the noise proceeds, and you will find it typical of a critic's tongue,—a shallow membrane, empty, voluble, and seated in the most contemptible part of the creature's body.

The Whipsnake.—This is he that lashes the poor author the next day in the newspapers.

The Deaf Adder, or *Surda Echidna* of Linnæus.—Under this head may be classed all that portion of the spectators (for audience they properly are not), who, not finding the first act of a piece answer to their preconceived notions of what a first act should be, like Obstinate in John Bunyan, positively thrust their fingers in their ears, that they may not hear a word of what is coming, though perhaps the very next act may be composed in a style as different as possible, and be written quite to their own tastes. These adders refuse to hear the voice of the charmer, because the tuning of his instrument gave them offence.

I should weary you, and myself too, if I were to go through all the classes of the serpent kind. Two qualities are common to them all. They are creatures of remarkably cold digestions, and chiefly haunt *pits* and low grounds

I proceed with more pleasure to give you an account of a club to which I have the honour to belong. There are fourteen of us, who are all authors that have been once in our lives what is called *damned*. We meet on the anniversaries of our respective nights, and make ourselves merry at the expense of the public. The chief tenets which distinguish our society, and which every man among us is bound to hold for gospel, are,—

That the public, or mob, in all ages, have been a set of blind, deaf, obstinate, senseless, illiterate savages. That no man of genius, in his senses, would be ambitious of pleasing such a capricious, ungrateful rabble. That the only legitimate end of writing for them is to pick their pockets; and, that failing, we are at full liberty to vilify and abuse them as much as ever we think fit.

That authors, by their affected pretences to humility, which they made use of as a cloak to insinuate their writings into the callous senses of the multitude, obtuse to everything but the grossest flattery, have by degrees made that great beast their master; as we may act submission to children till we are obliged to practise it in earnest. That authors are and ought to be considered the masters and preceptors of the public, and not *vice versâ*. That it was so in the days of Orpheus, Linus, and Musæus; and would be so again, if it were not that writers prove traitors to themselves. That, in particular, in the days of the first of those three great authors just mentioned, audiences appear to have been perfect models of what audiences should be; for though, along with the trees and the rocks and the wild creatures which he drew after him to listen to his strains, some serpents doubtless came to hear his music, it does not appear that any one among them ever lifted up *a dissentient voice*. They knew what was due to authors in those days. Now every stock and stone turns into a serpent, and has a voice.

That the terms "courteous reader" and "candid auditors," as having given rise to a false notion in those to whom they were applied, as if they conferred upon them some right, *which they cannot have*, of exercising their judgments, ought to be utterly banished and exploded.

These are our distinguishing tenets. To keep up the memory of the cause in which we suffered, as the ancients sacrificed a goat, a supposed unhealthy animal, to Æsculapius, on our feast-nights we cut up a goose, an animal typical of *the popular voice*, to the deities of Candour and Patient Hearing. A zealous member of the society once proposed that we should revive the obsolete luxury of viper-broth; but, the stomachs of some of the company rising at the proposition, we lost the benefit of that highly salutary and *antidotal dish*.

The privilege of admission to our club is strictly limited to such as have been fairly *damned*. A piece that has met with ever so little applause, that has but languished its night or two, and then gone out, will never entitle its author to a seat among us. An exception to our usual readiness in conferring this privilege is in the case of a writer, who, having been once condemned, writes again, and becomes candidate for a second martyrdom. Simple damnation we hold to be a merit; but to be twice damned we adjudge infamous. Such a one we utterly reject, and blackball without a hearing:—

"The common damned shun his society."

Hoping that your publication of our regulations may be a means of inviting some more members into our society, I conclude this long letter.

I am, sir, yours,
SEMEL-DAMNATUS.

———

CAPTAIN STARKEY.

DEAR SIR,—I read your account of this unfortunate being, and his forlorn piece of self-history,* with that smile of half-interest which the annals of insignificance excite, till I came to where he says, "I was bound apprentice to Mr. William Bird, an eminent writer, and teacher of languages and mathematics," &c.; when I started as one does in the recognition of an old acquaintance in a supposed stranger. This, then, was that Starkey of whom I have heard my sister relate so many pleasing anecdotes; and whom, never having seen, I yet seem almost to remember. For nearly fifty years, she had lost all sight of him; and, behold! the gentle usher of her youth, grown into an aged beggar, dubbed with an opprobrious title to which he had no pretensions; an object and a May-game! To what base purposes may we not return! What may not have been the meek creature's sufferings, what his wanderings, before he finally settled down in the comparative comfort of an old hospitaller of the almonry of Newcastle? And is poor Starkey dead?

I was a scholar of that "eminent writer" that he speaks of; but Starkey had quitted the school about a year before I came to it. Still the odour of his merits had left a fragrancy upon the recollection of the elder pupils. The schoolroom stands where it did, looking into a discoloured, dingy garden in the passage leading from Fetter Lane into Bartlett's Buildings. It is still a school, though the main prop, alas! has fallen so ingloriously; and bears a Latin inscription over the entrance in the lane, which was unknown in our humbler times. Heaven knows what "languages" were taught in it then! I am sure that neither my sister nor myself brought any out of it but a little of our native English. By "mathematics," reader, must be understood "ciphering." It was, in fact, a humble day-school, at which reading and writing were taught to us boys in the morning; and the same slender erudition was communicated to the girls, our sisters, &c., in the evening. Now, Starkey presided, under Bird, over both establishments. In my time, Mr. Cook, now or lately a respectable singer and performer at Drury Lane Theatre, and nephew to Mr. Bird, had succeeded to him. I well remember Bird. He was a squat, corpulent, middle-sized man, with something of the gentleman about him, and that peculiar mild tone—especially while he was inflicting punishment—which is so much more terrible to children than the angriest looks and gestures. Whippings were not frequent; but, when they took place, the

* "Memoirs of the Life of Benjamin Starkey, late of London, but now an inmate of the Freeman's Hospital in Newcastle. Written by himself. With a portrait of the author, and a fac-simile of his handwriting. Printed and sold by William Hall, Great Market, Newcastle." 1818. 12mo, p. 14.

correction was performed in a private room adjoining, where we could only hear the plaints, but saw nothing. This heightened the decorum and the solemnity. But the ordinary chastisement was the bastinado, a stroke or two on the palm with that almost obsolete weapon now,—the ferule. A ferule was a sort of flat ruler, widened, at the inflicting end, into a shape resembling a pear,—but nothing like so sweet,—with a delectable hole in the middle to raise blisters, like a cupping-glass. I have an intense recollection of that disused instrument of torture, and the malignancy, in proportion to the apparent mildness, with which its strokes were applied. The idea of a rod is accompanied with something ludicrous; but by no process can I look back upon this blister-raiser with anything but unmingled horror. To make him look more formidable,—if a pedagogue had need of these heightenings,—Bird wore one of those flowered Indian gowns formerly in use with school-masters, the strange figures upon which we used to interpret into hieroglyphics of pain and suffering. But, boyish fears apart, Bird, I believe, was, in the main, a humane and judicious master.

Oh, how I remember our legs wedged into those uncomfortable sloping desks, where we sat elbowing each other; and the injunctions to attain a free hand, unattainable in that position; the first copy I wrote after, with its moral lesson, "Art improves Nature;"

the still earlier pothooks and the hangers, some traces of which I fear may yet be apparent in this manuscript; the truant looks side-long to the garden, which seemed a mockery of our imprisonment; the prize for best spelling which had almost turned my head, and which, to this day, I cannot reflect upon without a vanity, which I ought to be ashamed of; our little leaden inkstands, not separately subsisting, but sunk into the desks; the bright, punctually-washed morning fingers, darkening gradually with another and another ink-spot! What a world of little associated circumstances, pains, and pleasures, mingling their quotas of pleasure, arise at the reading of those few simple words,—"Mr. William Bird, an eminent writer, and teacher of languages and mathematics, in Fetter Lane, Holborn!"

Poor Starkey, when young, had that peculiar stamp of old-fashionedness in his face which makes it impossible for a beholder to predicate any particular age in the object. You can scarce make a guess between seventeen and seven and thirty. This antique cast always seems to promise ill-luck and penury. Yet it seems he was not always the abject thing he came to. My sister, who well remembers him, can hardly forgive Mr. Thomas Ranson for making an etching so unlike her idea of him when he was a youthful teacher at Mr. Bird's school. Old age and poverty—a lifelong poverty, she thinks—could at no time have so effaced the marks of native gentility which were once so visible in a face otherwise strikingly ugly, thin, and care-worn. From her recollections of him, she thinks that he would have wanted bread before he would have begged or borrowed a halfpenny. "If any of the girls," she says, "who were my school-fellows, should be reading, through their aged spectacles, tidings, from the dead, of their youthful friend Starkey, they will feel a pang, as I do, at having teased his gentle spirit." They were big girls, it seems—too old to attend his instructions with the silence necessary; and, however old age and a long state of beggary seem to have reduced his writing fa-culties to a state of imbecility, in those days his language occasion-ally rose to the bold and figura-tive; for, when he was in despair to stop their chattering, his or-dinary phrase was, "Ladies, if you will not hold your peace, not all the powers in heaven can make you." Once he was missing for a day or two: he had run away. A little, old, unhappy-looking man brought him back,—it was his father,—and he did no busi-ness in the school that day, but sat moping in a corner, with his hands before his face; and the girls, his tormentors, in pity for his case, for the rest of that day forbore to annoy him. "I had been there but a few months," adds she, "when Starkey, who was the chief instructor of us girls, communicated to us a profound secret,—that the tragedy of 'Cato' was shortly to be acted by the elder boys, and that we were to be invited to the representation." That Starkey lent a helping hand in fashioning the actors, she re-members; and, but for his unfor-tunate person, he might have had some distinguished part in the scene to enact. As it was, he had the arduous task of prompter as-signed to him, and his feeble voice was heard clear and dis-tinct, repeating the text during the whole performance. She de-scribes her recollection of the cast of characters, even now, with a relish. Martia, by the handsome Edgar Hickman, who afterwards went to Africa, and of whom she never afterwards heard tidings; Lucia, by Master Walker, whose sister was her particular friend; Cato, by John Hunter, a masterly declaimer, but a plain boy, and shorter by the head than his two sons in the scene, &c. In con-clusion, Starkey appears to have been one of those mild spirits, which, not originally deficient in understanding, are crushed by penury into dejection and feeble-ness. He might have proved a useful adjunct, if not an orna-ment, to society, if Fortune had taken him into a very little foster-ing; but, wanting that, he became a captain,—a by-word,—and lived and died a broken bulrush.

———

A POPULAR FALLACY,

THAT A DEFORMED PERSON IS A LORD.

AFTER a careful perusal of the most approved works that treat of nobility, and of its origin in these realms in particular, we are left very much in the dark as to the original patent in which this branch of it is recognised. Neither Camden in his "Etymologie and Original of Barons," nor Dugdale in his "Baronage of England," nor Selden (a more exact and laborious inquirer than either) in his "Titles of Honour," afford a glimpse of satisfaction upon the subject. There is an heraldic term, indeed, which seems to imply gentility, and the right to coat armour (but nothing further), in persons thus qualified. But the *sinister bend* is more probably interpreted by the best writers on this science, of some irregularity of birth than of bodily conformation. Nobility is either hereditary or by creation, commonly called patent. Of the former kind, the title in question cannot be, seeing that the notion of it is limited to a personal distinction which does not necessarily follow in the blood. Honours of this nature, as Mr. Anstey very well observes, descend, moreover, in a *right line*. It must be by patent, then, if anything. But who can show it? How comes it to be dormant? Under what king's reign is it patented? Among the grounds of nobility cited by the learned Mr. Ashmole, after "Services in the Field or in the Council Chamber," he judiciously sets down "Honours conferred by the sovereign out of mere benevolence, or as favouring one subject rather than another for some likeness or conformity observed (or but supposed) in him to the royal nature;" and instances the graces showered upon Charles Brandon, who, "in his goodly person being thought not a little to favour the port and bearing of the king's own majesty, was by that sovereign, King Henry the Eighth, for some or one of these respects, highly promoted and preferred." Here, if anywhere, we thought we had discovered a clue to our researches. But after a painful investigation of the rolls and records under the reign of Richard the Third, or "Richard Crouchback," as he is more usually designated in the chronicles,—from a traditionary stoop or gibbosity in that part,—we do not find that that monarch conferred any such lordships as here pretended, upon any subject or subjects, on a simple plea of "conformity" in that respect to the "royal nature." The posture of affairs, in those tumultuous times preceding the battle of Bosworth, possibly left him at no leisure to attend to such niceties. Further than his reign, we have not extended our inquiries; the kings of England who preceded or followed him being generally described by historians to have been of straight and clean limbs, the "natural derivative," says Daniel,[*] "of high blood, if not its primitive recommendation to such ennoblement, as denoting strength and martial prowess,—the qualities set most by in that fighting age." Another motive, which inclines us to scruple the validity of this claim, is the remarkable fact, that none of the persons in whom the right is supposed to be vested do ever insist upon it themselves. There is no instance of any of them "suing his patent," as the law books call it; much less of his having actually stepped up into his proper seat, as, so qualified, we might expect that some of them would have had the spirit to do, in the House of Lords. On the contrary, it seems to be a distinction thrust upon them. "Their title of 'lord,'" says one of their own body, speaking of the common people, "I never much valued, and now I entirely despise; and yet they will force it upon me as an honour which they have a right to bestow, and which I have none to refuse."[**] Upon a dispassionate review of the subject, we are disposed to believe that there is no right to the peerage incident to mere bodily configuration; that the title in dispute is merely honorary, and depending upon the breath of the common people, which in these realms is so far from the power of conferring nobility, that the ablest constitutionalists have agreed in nothing more unanimously than in the maxim, that "the king is the sole fountain of honour."

* History of England, "Temporibus Edwardi Primi et sequentibus."
** Ray on Deformity.

LETTER TO AN OLD GENTLEMAN WHOSE EDUCATION HAS BEEN NEGLECTED.

Dear Sir,—I send you a bantering "Epistle to an Old Gentleman whose Education is supposed to have been neglected." Of course, it was *suggested* by some letters of your admirable Opium-Eater, the discontinuance of which has caused so much regret to myself in common with most of your readers. You will do me injustice by supposing that, in the remotest degree, it was my intention to ridicule those papers. The fact is, the most serious things may give rise to an innocent burlesque; and, the more serious they are, the fitter they become for that purpose. It is not to be supposed that Charles Cotton did not entertain a very high regard for Virgil, notwithstanding he travestied that poet. Yourself can testify the deep respect I have always held for the profound learning and penetrating genius of our friend. Nothing upon earth would give me greater pleasure than to find that he has not lost sight of his entertaining and instructive purpose.

I am, dear sir, yours and his sincerely,
ELIA.

My dear Sir,—The question which you have done me the honour to propose to me, through the medium of our common friend, Mr. Grierson, I shall endeavour to answer with as much exactness as a limited observation and experience can warrant.

You ask,—or rather Mr. Grierson, in his own interesting language, asks for you,—"Whether a person at the age of sixty-three, with no more proficiency than a tolerable knowledge of most of the characters of the English alphabet at first sight amounts to, by dint of persevering application and good masters,—a docile and ingenuous disposition on the part of the pupil always presupposed,—may hope to arrive, within a presumable number of years, at that degree of attainments which shall entitle the possessor to the character, which you are on so many accounts justly desirous of acquiring, of a *learned man*."

This is fairly and candidly stated,—only I could wish that on one point you had been a little more explicit. In the mean time, I will take it for granted, that by a "knowledge of the alphabetic characters" you confine your meaning to the single powers only, as you are silent on the subject of the diphthongs and harder combinations.

Why, truly, sir, when I consider the vast circle of sciences,—it is not here worth while to trouble you with the distinction between learning and science, which a man must be understood to have made the tour of in those days, before the world will be willing to concede to him the title which you aspire to,—I am almost disposed to reply to your inquiry by a direct answer in the negative.

However, where all cannot be compassed, a great deal that is truly valuable may be accomplished. I am unwilling to throw out any remarks that should have a tendency to damp a hopeful genius; but I must not, in fairness, conceal from you that you have much to do. The consciousness of difficulty is sometimes a spur to exertion. Rome—or rather, my dear sir, to borrow an illustration from a place as yet more familiar to you, Rumford—Rumford was not built in a day.

Your mind as yet, give me leave to tell you, is in the state of a sheet of white paper. We must not blot or blur it over too hastily. Or, to use an opposite simile, it is like a piece of parchment all bescrawled and bescribbled over with characters of no sense or import, which we must carefully erase and remove before we can make way for the authentic characters or impresses which are to be substituted in their stead by the corrective hand of science.

Your mind, my dear sir, again, resembles that same parchment, which we will suppose a little hardened by time and disuse. We may apply the characters; but are we sure that the ink will sink?

You are in the condition of a traveller that has all his journey to begin. And, again, you are worse off than the traveller which I have supposed; for you have already lost your way.

You have much to learn, which you have never been taught; and more, I fear, to unlearn, which you have been taught erroneously. You have hitherto, I dare say, imagined that the sun moves round the earth. When you shall have mastered the true solar system, you will have quite a different theory upon that point, I assure you. I mention but this instance. Your own experience, as knowledge advances, will furnish you with many parallels.

I can scarcely approve of the intention, which Mr. Grierson informs me you have contemplated, of entering yourself at a common seminary, and working your way up from the lower to the higher forms with the children. I see more to admire in the modesty than in the expediency of such a resolution. I own I cannot reconcile myself to the spectacle of a gentleman at your time of life, seated, as must be your case at first, below a tyro of four or five; for at that early age the rudiments of education usually commence in this country. I doubt whether more might not be lost in the point of fitness than would be gained in the advantages which you propose to yourself by this scheme.

You say you stand in need of emulation; that this incitement is nowhere to be had but at a public school; that you should be more sensible of your progress by comparing it with the daily progress of those around you. But have you considered the nature of emulation, and how it is sustained at these tender years which you would have to come in competition with? I am afraid you are dreaming of academic prizes and distinctions. Alas! in the university for which you are preparing, the highest medal would be a silver penny; and you must graduate in nuts and oranges.

I know that Peter, the Great Czar—or Emperor—of Muscovy, submitted himself to the discipline of a dockyard at Deptford, that he might learn, and convey to his countrymen, the noble art of ship-building. You are old enough to remember him, or at least the talk about him. I call to mind also other great princes, who, to instruct themselves in the theory and practice of war, and set an example of subordination to their subjects, have condescended to enrol themselves as private soldiers; and, passing through the successive ranks of corporal, quartermaster, and the rest, have served their way up to the station at which most princes are willing enough to set out,—of general and commander-in-chief over their own forces. But—besides that there is oftentimes great sham and pretence in their show mock humility—the competition which they stooped to was with their coevals, however inferior to them in birth. Between ages so very disparate as those which you contemplate, I fear there can no salutary emulation subsist.

Again: in the other alternative, could you submit to the ordinary reproofs and discipline of a day-school? Could you bear to be corrected for your faults? Or how would it look to see you put to stand, as must be the case sometimes, in a corner?

I am afraid the idea of a public school in your circumstances must be given up.

But is it impossible, my dear

sir, to find some person of your own age,—if of the other sex, the more agreeable, perhaps,—whose information, like your own, has rather lagged behind his years, who should be willing to set out from the same point with yourself; to undergo the same tasks? —thus at once inciting and sweetening each other's labours in a sort of friendly rivalry. Such a one, I think, it would not be difficult to find in some of the western parts of this island,—about Dartmoor, for instance.

Or what if, from your own estate, —that estate, which, unexpectedly acquired so late in life, has inspired into you this generous thirst after knowledge,—you were to select some elderly peasant, that might best be spared from the land, to come and begin his education with you, that you might till, as it were, your minds together,—one whose heavier progress might invite, without a fear of discouraging, your emulation? We might then see—starting from an equal post—the difference of the clownish and the gentle blood.

A private education, then, or such a one as I have been describing, being determined on, we must in the next place look out for a preceptor; for it will be some time before either of you, left to yourselves, will be able to assist the other to any great purpose in his studies.

And now, my dear sir, if, in describing such a tutor as I have imagined for you, I use a style a little above the familiar one in which I have hitherto chosen to address you, the nature of the subject must be my apology. *Difficile est de scientiis inscienter loqui;* which is as much as to say, that, "in treating of scientific matters, it is difficult to avoid the use of scientific terms." But I shall endeavour to be as plain as possible. I am not going to present you with the *ideal* of a pedagogue as it may exist in my fancy, or has possibly been realized in the persons of Buchanan and Busby. Something less than perfection will serve our turn. The scheme which I propose in this first or introductory letter has reference to the first four or five years of your education only; and in enumerating the qualifications of him that should undertake the direction of your studies, I shall rather point out the *minimum*, or *least*, that I shall require of him, than trouble you in the search of attainments neither common nor necessary to our immediate purpose.

He should be a man of deep and extensive knowledge. So much at least is indispensable. Something older than yourself, I could wish him, because years add reverence.

To his age and great learning, he should be blessed with a temper and a patience willing to accommodate itself to the imperfections of the slowest and meanest capacities. Such a one, in former days, Mr. Hartlib appears to have been; and such, in our days, I take Mr. Grierson to be: but our friend, you know, unhappily, has other engagements. I do not demand a consummate grammarian; but he must be a thorough master of vernacular orthography, with an insight into the accentualities and punctualities of modern Saxon, or English. He must be competently instructed (or how shall he instruct you?) in the tetralogy, or four first rules, upon which not only arithmetic, but geometry, and the pure mathematics themselves, are grounded. I do not require that he should have measured the globe with Cook or Ortelius; but it is desirable that he should have a general knowledge (I do not mean a very nice or pedantic one) of the great division of the earth into four parts, so as to teach you readily to name the quarters. He must have a genius capable in some degree of soaring to the upper element, to deduce from thence the not much dissimilar computation of the cardinal points, or hinges, upon which those invisible phenomena, which naturalists agree to term *winds*, do perpetually shift and turn. He must instruct you, in imitation of the old Orphic fragments (the mention of which has possibly escaped you), in numeric and harmonious responses, to deliver the number of solar revolutions within which each of the twelve periods, into which the *Annus Vulgaris*, or common year, is divided, doth usually complete and terminate itself. The intercalaries and other subtle problems he will do well to omit, till riper years and course of study shall have rendered you more capable thereof. He must be capable of embracing all history, so as, from the countless myriads of individual men who have peopled this globe of earth, —*for it is a globe*,—by comparison of their respective births, lives, deaths, fortunes, conduct, prowess, &c., to pronounce, and teach you to pronounce, dogmatically and catechetically, who was the richest, who was the strongest, who was the wisest, who was the meekest, man that ever lived; to the facilitation of which solution, you will readily conceive, a smattering of biography would in no inconsiderable degree conduce. Leaving the dialects of men (in one of which I shall take leave to suppose you by this time at least superficially instituted), you will learn to ascend with him to the contemplation of that unarticulated language which was before the written tongue; and, with the aid of the elder Phrygian or Æsopic key, to interpret the sounds by which the animal tribes communicate their minds, evolving moral instruction with delight from the dialogue of cocks, dogs, and foxes. Or, marrying theology with verse, from whose mixture a beautiful and healthy offspring may be expected, in your own native accents (but purified), you will keep time together to the profound harpings of the more modern or Wattsian hymnics.

Thus far I have ventured to conduct you to a "hill-side, whence you may discern the right path of a virtuous and noble education; laborious, indeed, at the first ascent, but else so smooth, so green, so full of goodly prospects and melodious sounds on every side, that the harp of Orpheus was not more charming."*

With my best respects to Mr. Grierson, when you see him,

I remain, dear sir, your obedient servant,

ELIA.

ON THE AMBIGUITIES ARISING FROM PROPER NAMES.

How oddly it happens that the same sound shall suggest to the minds of two persons hearing it ideas the most opposite! I was conversing, a few years since, with a young friend upon the subject of poetry, and particularly that species of it which is known by the name of the epithalamium. I ventured to assert that the most perfect specimen of it in our language was the "Epithalamium" of Spenser upon his own marriage.

My young gentleman, who has a smattering of taste, and would not willingly be thought ignorant of anything remotely connected with the *belles-lettres*, expressed a degree of surprise, mixed with mortification, that he should never have heard of this poem; Spenser being an author with

Milton's "Tractate on Education," addressed to Mr. Hartlib.

whose writings he thought himself peculiarly conversant.

I offered to show him the poem in the fine folio copy of the poet's works which I have at home. He seemed pleased with the offer, though the mention of the folio seemed again to puzzle him. But, presently after, assuming a grave look, he compassionately muttered to himself, "Poor Spencer!"

There was something in the tone with which he spoke these words that struck me not a little. It was more like the accent with which a man bemoans some recent calamity that has happened to a friend, than that tone of sober grief with which we lament the sorrows of a person, however excellent and however grievous his afflictions may have been, who has been dead more than two centuries. I had the curiosity to inquire into the reasons of so uncommon an ejaculation. My young gentleman, with a more solemn tone of pathos than before, repeated, "Poor Spencer!" and added, "He has lost his wife!"

My astonishment at this assertion rose to such a height, that I began to think the brain of my young friend must be cracked, or some unaccountable reverie had gotten possession of it. But, upon further explanation, it appeared that the word "Spenser" —which to you or me, reader, in a conversation upon poetry too, would naturally have called up the idea of an old poet in a ruff, one Edmund Spenser, that flourished in the days of Queen Elizabeth, and wrote a poem called "The Fairy Queen," with "The Shepherd's Calendar," and many more verses besides—did, in the mind of my young friend, excite a very different and quite modern idea; namely, that of the Honourable William Spencer, one of the living ornaments, if I am not misinformed, of this present poetical era, A. D. 1811.

ELIA ON HIS "CONFESSIONS OF A DRUNKARD."

MANY are the sayings of Elia, painful and frequent his lucubrations, set forth for the most part (such his modesty!) without a name; scattered about in obscure periodicals and forgotten miscellanies. From the dust of some of these it is our intention occasionally to revive a tract or two that shall seem worthy of a better fate, especially at a time like the present, when the pen of our industrious contributor, engaged in a laborious digest of his recent Continental tour, may haply want the leisure to expatiate in more miscellaneous speculations. We have been induced, in the first instance, to reprint a thing which he put forth in a friend's volume some years since, entitled "The Confessions of a Drunkard," seeing that Messieurs the Quarterly Reviewers have chosen to embellish their last dry pages with fruitful quotations therefrom; adding, from their peculiar brains, the gratuitous affirmation, that they have reason to believe that the describer (in his delineations of a drunkard, forsooth!) partly sat for his own picture. The truth is, that our friend had been reading among the essays of a contemporary, who has perversely been confounded with him, a paper, in which Edax (or the Great Eater) humorously complaineth of an inordinate appetite; and it struck him that a better paper—of deeper interest and wider usefulness—might be made out of the imagined experiences of a Great Drinker. Accordingly he set to work, and, with that mock fervour and counterfeit earnestness with which he is too apt to over-realize his descriptions, has given us — a frightful picture indeed, but no more resembling the man Elia than the fictitious Edax may be supposed to identify itself with Mr. L., its author. It is, indeed, a compound extracted out of his long observations of the effects of drinking upon all the world about him; and this accumulated mass of misery he hath centred (as the custom is with judicious essayists) in a single figure. We deny not that a portion of his own experiences may have passed into the picture (as who, that is not a washy fellow, but must at some times have felt the after-operation of a too-generous cup?); but then how heightened! how exaggerated! how little within the sense of the Review, where a part, in their slanderous usage, must be understood to stand for the whole. But it is useless to expostulate with this Quarterly slime, brood of Nilus, watery heads with hearts of jelly, spawned under the sign of Aquarius, incapable of Bacchus, and therefrom cold, washy, spiteful, bloodless. Elia shall string them up one day, and show their colours,—or, rather how colourless and vapid the whole fry,—when he putteth forth his long-promised, but unaccountably hitherto delayed, "Confessions of a Water-drinker.'

THE LAST PEACH.

I am the miserablest man living. Give me counsel, dear Editor. I was bred up in the strictest principles of honesty, and have passed my life in punctual adherence to them. Integrity might be said to be ingrained in our family. Yet I live in constant fear of one day coming to the gallows.

Till the latter end of last autumn, I never experienced these feelings of self-mistrust, which ever since have imbittered my existence. From the apprehension of that unfortunate man,* whose story began to make so great an impression upon the public about that time, I date my horrors. I never can get it out of my head that I shall some time or other commit a forgery, or do some

* Fauntleroy.

equally vile thing. To make matters worse, I am in a banking-house. I sit surrounded with a cluster of bank-notes. These were formerly no more to me than meat to a butcher's dog. They are now as toads and aspics. I feel all day like one situated amidst gins and pitfalls. Sovereigns, which I once took such pleasure in counting out, and scraping up with my little tin shovel (at which I was the most expert in the banking-house), now scald my hands. When I go to sign my name, I set down that of another person, or write my own in a counterfeit character. I am beset with temptations without motive. I want no more wealth than I possess. A more contented being than myself, as to money matters, exists not. What should I fear?

When a child, I was once let loose, by favour of a nobleman's gardener, into his lordship's magnificent fruit-garden with full leave to pull the currants and the gooseberries; only I was interdicted from touching the wall-fruit. Indeed, at that season (it was the end of autumn), there was little left. Only on the south wall (can I forget the hot feel of the brick-work?) lingered the one last peach. Now, peaches are a fruit which I always had, and still have, an almost utter aversion to. There is something to my palate singularly harsh and repulsive in the flavour of them. I know not by what demon of contradiction inspired, but I was haunted with an irresistible desire to pluck it. Tear myself as often as I would from the spot, I found myself still recurring to it; till, maddening with desire (desire I cannot call it), with wilfulness rather,—without appetite,—against appetite, I may call it,—in an evil hour I reached out my hand, and plucked it. Some few raindrops just then fell; the sky (from a bright day) became overcast; and I was a type of our first parents, after the eating of that fatal fruit. I felt myself naked and ashamed, stripped of my virtue, spiritless. The downy fruit, whose sight rather than savour had tempted me, dropped from my hand never to be tasted. All the commentators in the world cannot persuade me but that the Hebrew word, in the second chapter of Genesis, translated "apple," should be rendered "peach." Only this way can I reconcile that mysterious story.

Just such a child at thirty am I among the cash and valuables, longing to pluck, without an idea of enjoyment further. I cannot reason myself out of these fears: I dare not laugh at them. I was tenderly and lovingly brought up. What then? Who that in life's entrance had seen the babe F——, from the lap stretching out his little fond mouth to catch the maternal kiss, could have predicted, or as much as imagined, that life's very different exit? The sight of my own fingers torments me; they seem so admirably constructed for—pilfering.

Then that jugular vein which I have in common——; in an emphatic sense may I say with David, I am "fearfully made." All my mirth is poisoned by these unhappy suggestions. If, to dissipate reflection, I hum a tune, it changes to the "Lamentations of a Sinner." My very dreams are tainted. I awake with a shocking feeling of my hand in some pocket.

Advise me, dear Editor, on this painful heart-malady. Tell me, do you feel anything allied to it in yourself? Do you never feel an itching, as it were,—a *dactylomania*,—or am I alone? You have my honest confession. My next may appear from Bow Street.

SUSPENSURUS.

REFLECTIONS IN THE PILLORY

About the year 18—, one R——d, a respectable London merchant (since dead), stood in the pillory for some alleged fraud upon the revenue. Among his papers were found the following "Reflections," which we have obtained by favour of our friend Elia, who knew him well, and had heard him describe the train of his feelings, upon that trying occasion, almost in the words of the manuscript. Elia speaks of him as a man (with the exception of the peccadillo aforesaid) of singular integrity in all his private dealings, possessing great suavity of manner, with a certain turn for humour. As our object is to present human nature under every possible circumstance, we do not think that we shall sully our pages by inserting it.—

EDITOR.

SCENE,—Opposite the Royal Exchange.
TIME,—Twelve to One, Noon.

KETCH, my good fellow, you

have a neat hand. Prithee adjust this new collar to my neck gingerly. I am not used to these wooden cravats. There, softly, softly. That seems the exact point between ornament and strangulation. A thought looser on this side. Now it will do. And have a care, in turning me, that I present my aspect due vertically. I now face the orient. In a quarter of an hour I shift southward,—do you mind?—and so on till I face the east again, travelling with the sun. No half-points, I beseech you,—N. N. by W., or any such elaborate niceties. They become the shipman's card, but not this mystery. Now leave me a little to my own reflections.

Bless us, what a company is assembled in honour of me! How grand I stand here! I never felt so sensibly before the effect of solitude in a crowd. I muse in solemn silence upon that vast miscellaneous rabble in the pit there. From my private box I contemplate, with mingled pity and wonder, the gaping curiosity of those underlings. There are my Whitechapel supporters. Rosemary Lane has emptied herself of the very flower of her citizens to grace my show. Duke's Place sits desolate. What is there in my face, that strangers should come so far from the east to gaze upon it? [*Here an egg narrowly misses him.*] That offering was well meant, but not so cleanly executed. By the tricklings, it should not be either myrrh or frankincense. Spare your pre-sents, my friends: I am noways mercenary. I desire no missive tokens of your approbation. I am past those valentines. Bestow these coffins of untimely chickens upon mouths that water for them. Comfort your addle spouses with them at home, and stop the mouths of your brawling brats with such Olla Podridas: they have need of them. [*A brick is let fly.*] Disease not, I pray you, nor dismantle your rent and ragged tenements, to furnish me with architectural decorations, which I can excuse. This fragment might have stopped a flaw against snow comes. [*A coal flies.*] Cinders are dear, gentlemen. This nubbling might have helped the pot boil, when your dirty cuttings from the shambles at three-ha'pence a pound shall stand at a cold simmer. Now, south about, Ketch. I would enjoy Australian popularity.

What, my friends from over the water! Old benchers—flies of a day—ephemeral Romans—welcome! Doth the sight of me draw souls from limbo? Can it dis-people purgatory?—Ha!

What am I, or what was my father's house, that I should thus be set up a spectacle to gentlemen and others? Why are all faces, like Persians at the sunrise, bent singly on mine alone? It was wont to be esteemed an ordinary visnomy, a quotidian merely. Doubtless these assembled myriads discern some traits of nobleness, gentility, breeding, which hitherto have escaped the common observation,—some intimations, as it were, of wisdom, valour, piety, and so forth. My sight dazzles; and, if I am not deceived by the too-familiar pressure of this strange neckcloth that envelops it, my countenance gives out lambent glories. For some painter now to take me in the lucky point of expression!—the posture so convenient!—the head never shifting, but standing quiescent in a sort of natural frame. But these artisans require a westerly aspect. Ketch, turn me.

Something of St. James's air in these my new friends. How my prospects shift and brighten! Now, if Sir Thomas Lawrence be anywhere in that group, his fortune is made for ever. I think I see some one taking out a crayon. I will compose my whole face to a smile, which yet shall not so predominate but that gravity and gaiety shall contend, as it were, —you understand me? I will work up my thoughts to some mild rapture,—a gentle enthusiasm,— which the artist may transfer, in a manner, warm to the canvas. I will inwardly apostrophise my tabernacle.

Delectable mansion, hail! House not made of every wood! Lodging that pays no rent; airy and commodious; which, owing no window-tax, art yet all casement, out of which men have such pleasure in peering and overlooking, that they will sometimes stand an hour together to enjoy thy prospects! Cell, recluse from the vulgar! Quiet retirement from the great Babel, yet affording sufficient glimpses into it! Pulpit, that instructs without note or sermon-book; into which the preacher is inducted without tenth or first-fruit! Throne, unshared and single, that disdainest a Brentford competitor! Honour without co-rival! Or hearest thou, rather, magnificent theatre, in which the spectator comes to see and to be seen? From thy giddy heights I look down upon the common herd, who stand with eyes upturned, as if a winged messenger hovered over them; and mouths open, as if they expected manna. I feel, I feel, the true episcopal yearnings. Behold in me, my flock, your true overseer! What though I cannot lay hands, because my own are laid; yet I can mutter benedictions. True *otium cum dignitate!* Proud Pisgah eminence! pinnacle sublime! O Pillory! 'tis thee I sing! Thou younger bro-ther to the gallows, without his rough and Esau palms, that with ineffable contempt surveyest beneath thee the grovelling stocks, which claim presumptuously to be of thy great race! Let that low wood know that thou art far higher born. Let that domicile for groundling rogues and base earth-kissing varlets envy thy preferment, not seldom fated to be the wanton baiting-house, the temporary retreat, of poet and of patriot. Shades of Bastwick and of Prynne hover over thee,— Defoe is there, and more greatly daring Shebbeare,—from their (little more elevated) stations they look down with recognitions. Ketch, turn me.

I now veer to the north. Open your widest gates, thou proud Exchange of London, that I may look in as proudly! Gresham's wonder, hail! I stand upon a level with all your kings. They and I, from equal heights, with equal superciliousness, o'erlook the plodding money-hunting tribe below, who busied in their sordid speculations, scarce elevate their eyes to notice your ancient, or my recent, grandeur. The second Charles smiles on me from three pedestals!* He closed the Exchequer: I cheated the Excise. Equal our darings, equal be our lot.

Are those the quarters? 'tis their fatal chime. That the ever-winged hours would but stand still! but I must descend,—descend from this dream of greatness. Stay, stay, a little while, importunate hour-hand! A moment or two, and I shall walk on foot with the undistinguished many. The clock speaks one. I return to common life. Ketch, let me out.

* A statue of Charles II., by the elder Cibber, adorns the front of the Exchange. He stands also on high, in the train of his crowned ancestors, in his proper order, *within* that building. But the merchants of London, in a superfetation of loyalty, have, within a few years, caused to be erected another effigy of him on the ground in the centre of the interior. We do not hear that a fourth is in contemplation.

CUPID'S REVENGE.

Leontius, Duke of Lycia, who in times past had borne the character of a wise and just governor, and was endeared to all ranks of his subjects, in his latter days fell into a sort of dotage, which manifested itself in an extravagant fondness for his daughter Hidaspes. This young maiden, with the Prince Leucippus, her brother, were the only remembrances left to him of a deceased and beloved consort. For *her*, nothing was thought too precious. Existence was of no value to him but as it afforded opportunities of gratifying her wishes. To be instrumental in relieving her from the least little pain or grief, he would have lavished his treasures to the giving away of the one-half of his dukedom.

All this deference on the part of the parent had yet no power upon the mind of the daughter to move her at any time to solicit any unbecoming suit, or to disturb the even tenor of her thoughts. The humility and dutifulness of her carriage seemed to keep pace with his apparent willingness to release her from the obligations of either. She might have satisfied her wildest humours and caprices; but, in truth, no such troublesome guests found harbour in the bosom of the quiet and unaspiring maiden.

Thus far the prudence of the princess served to counteract any ill effects which this ungovernable partiality in a parent was cal-

culated to produce in a less virtuous nature than Hidaspes'; and
this foible of the duke's, so long
as no evil resulted from it, was
passed over by the courtiers as a
piece of harmless frenzy.

But upon a solemn day,—a sad
one, as it proved for Lycia,—
when the returning anniversary
of the princess's birth was kept
with extraordinary rejoicings, the
infatuated father set no bounds to
his folly, but would have his subjects to do homage to her for that
day, as to their natural sovereign;
as if he, indeed, had been dead,
and she, to the exclusion of the
male succession, was become the
rightful ruler of Lycia. He saluted her by the style of Duchess;
and with a terrible oath, in the
presence of his nobles, he confirmed to her the grant of all
things whatsoever that she should
demand on that day, and for the
six next following; and if she
should ask anything, the execution of which must be deferred
until after his death, he pronounced a dreadful curse upon
his son and successor, if he failed
to see to the performance of it.

Thus encouraged, the princess
stepped forth with a modest boldness; and, as if assured of no
denial, spake as follows.

But, before we acquaint you
with the purport of her speech,
we must premise, that in the land
of Lycia, which was at that time
pagan, above all their other gods
the inhabitants did in an especial
manner adore the deity who was
supposed to have influence in the
disposing of people's affections in
love. Him, by the name of God
Cupid, they feigned to be a *beautiful boy,* and *winged;* as indeed,
between young persons, these
frantic passions are usually least
under constraint; while the wings
might signify the haste with which
these ill-judged attachments are
commonly dissolved, and do indeed go away as lightly as they
come, flying away in an instant
to light upon some newer fancy.
They painted him *blindfolded,* because these silly affections of
lovers make them blind to the
defects of the beloved object,
which every one is quick-sighted
enough to discover but themselves; or because love is for the
most part led blindly, rather than
directed by the open eye of the
judgment, in the hasty choice of
a mate. Yet with that inconsistency of attributes with which
the heathen people commonly
over-complimented their deities,
this blind love, this Cupid, they
figured with a bow and arrows;
and, being sightless, they yet
feigned him to be a notable archer
and an unerring marksman. No
heart was supposed to be proof
against the point of his inevitable
dart. By such incredible fictions
did these poor pagans make a
shift to excuse their vanities, and
to give a sanction to their irregular affections, under the notion
that love was irresistible; whereas,
in a well-regulated mind, these
amorous conceits either find no
place at all, or, having gained a
footing, are easily stifled in tho

beginning by a wise and manly resolution.

This frenzy in the people had long been a source of disquiet to the discreet princess; and many were the conferences she had held with the virtuous prince, her brother, as to the best mode of taking off the minds of the Lycians from this vain superstition. An occasion, furnished by the blind grant of the old duke, their father, seemed now to present itself.

The courtiers then, being assembled to hear the demand which the princess should make, began to conjecture, each one according to the bent of his own disposition, what the thing would be that she should ask for. One said, "Now surely she will ask to have the disposal of the revenues of some wealthy province, to lay them out —as was the manner of Eastern princesses—in costly dresses and jewels becoming a lady of so great expectancies." Another thought that she would seek an extension of power, as women naturally love rule and dominion. But the most part were in hope that she was about to beg the hand of some neighbour prince in marriage, who, by the wealth and contiguity of his dominions, might add strength and safety to the realm of Lycia. But in none of these things was the expectation of these crafty and worldly-minded courtiers gratified; for Hidaspes, first making lowly obeisance to her father, and thanking him on bended knees for so great grace conferred upon her,—according to a plan preconcerted with Leucippus,—made suit as follows:—

"Your loving care of me, O princely father! by which in my tenderest age you made up to me for the loss of a mother at those years when I was scarcely able to comprehend the misfortune, and your bounties to me ever since, have left me nothing to ask for myself, as wanting and desiring nothing. But, for the people whom you govern, I beg and desire a boon. It is known to all nations, that the men of Lycia are noted for a vain and fruitless superstition,—the more hateful as it bears a show of true religion, but is indeed nothing more than a self-pleasing and bold wantonness. Many ages before this, when every man had taken to himself a trade, as hating idleness far worse than death, some one that gave himself to sloth and wine, finding himself by his neighbours rebuked for his unprofitable life, framed to himself a god, whom he pretended to obey in his dishonesty; and, for a name, he called him Cupid. This god of merely man's creating—as the nature of man is ever credulous of any vice which takes part with his dissolute conditions—quickly found followers enough. They multiplied in every age, especially among your Lycians, who to this day remain adorers of this drowsy deity, who certainly was first invented in drink, as sloth and luxury are commonly the first movers in these idle love-passions. This *winged boy*—for so they fancy him

— has his sacrifices, his loose images set up in the land, through all the villages; nay, your own sacred palace is not exempt from them, to the scandal of sound devotion, and dishonour of the true deities, which are only they who give good gifts to man,—as Ceres, who gives us corn; the planter of the olive, Pallas; Neptune, who directs the track of ships over the great ocean, and binds distant lands together in friendly commerce; the inventor of medicine and music, Apollo; and the cloud-compelling Thunderer of Olympus: whereas the gifts of this idle deity—if indeed he have a being at all out of the brain of his frantic worshippers—usually prove destructive and pernicious. My suit, then, is, that this unseemly idol throughout the land be plucked down, and cast into the fire; and that the adoring of the same may be prohibited on pain of death to any of your subjects henceforth found so offending."

Leontius, startled at this unexpected demand from the princess, with tears besought her to ask some wiser thing, and not to bring down upon herself and him the indignation of so great a god.

"There is no such god as you dream of," said then Leucippus boldly, who had hitherto forborne to second the petition of the princess; "but a vain opinion of him has filled the land with love and wantonness. Every young man and maiden, that feel the least desire to one another, dare in no case to suppress it; for they think it to be Cupid's motion, and that he is a god!"

Thus pressed by the solicitations of both his children, and fearing the oath which he had taken, in an evil hour the misgiving father consented; and a proclamation was sent throughout all the provinces for the putting-down of the idol, and suppression of the established Cupid-worship.

Notable, you may be sure, was the stir made in all places among the priests, and among the artificers in gold, in silver, or in marble, who made a gainful trade, either in serving at the altar, or in the manufacture of the images no longer to be tolerated. The cry was clamorous as that at Ephesus when a kindred idol was in danger; for "great had been Cupid of the Lycians." Nevertheless, the power of the duke, backed by the power of his more popular children, prevailed; and the destruction of every vestige of the old religion was but as the work of one day throughout the country.

And now, as the pagan chronicles of Lycia inform us, the displeasure of Cupid went out,—the displeasure of a great god,—flying through all the dukedom, and sowing evils. But upon the first movers of the profanation his angry hand lay heaviest; and there was imposed upon them a strange misery, that all might know that Cupid's revenge was mighty. With his arrows hotter than plagues, or than his own anger, did he fiercely right himself; nor could the prayers of a few concealed worshippers, nor the smoke arising from an altar here and there which had escaped the general overthrow, avert his wrath, or make him to cease from vengeance, until he had made of the once-flourishing country of Lycia a most wretched land. He sent no famines, he let loose no cruel wild beasts among them,—inflictions with one or other of which the rest of the Olympian deities are fabled to have visited the nations under their displeasure,—but took a nearer course of his own; and his invisible arrows went to the *moral heart* of Lycia, infecting and filling court and country with desires of unlawful marriages, unheard-of and monstrous affections, prodigious and misbecoming unions.

The symptoms were first visible in the changed bosom of Hidaspes. This exemplary maiden,—whose cold modesty, almost to a failing, had discouraged the addresses of so many princely suitors that had sought her hand in marriage,—by the venom of this inward pestilence, came on a sudden to cast eyes of affection upon a mean and deformed creature, Zoilus by name, who was a dwarf, and lived about the palace, the common jest of the courtiers. In her besotted eyes he was grown a goodly gentleman; and to her maidens, when any of them reproached him with the defect of his shape in her hearing, she would reply, that "to them, indeed, he might appear defective, and unlike a man, as, indeed, no man was like unto him; for in form and complexion he was beyond painting. He is like," she said, "to nothing that we have seen; yet he doth resemble Apollo, as I have fancied him, when, rising in the east, he bestirs himself, and shakes daylight from his hair." And, overcome with a passion which was heavier than she could bear, she confessed herself a wretched creature, and implored forgiveness of God Cupid, whom she had provoked; and, if possible, that he would grant it to her that she might enjoy her love. Nay, she would court this piece of deformity to his face; and when the wretch, supposing it to be done in mockery, has said that he could wish himself more ill-shaped than he was, so it would contribute to make her grace merry, she would reply, "Oh! think not that I jest; unless it be a jest not to esteem my life in comparison with thine; to hang a thousand kisses in an hour upon those lips; unless it be a jest to vow that I am willing to become your wife, and to take obedience upon me." And by his "own white hand," taking it in hers,—so strong was the delusion, —she besought him to swear to marry her.

The term had not yet expired of the seven days within which the doting duke had sworn to fulfil her will, when, in pursuance of this frenzy, she presented herself before her father, leading in the dwarf by the hand, and, in the face of all the courtiers.

solemnly demanding his hand in marriage. And, when the apeish creature made show of blushing at the unmerited honour, she, to comfort him, bade him not to be ashamed; for, "in her eyes, he was worth a kingdom."

And now, too late, did the fond father repent him of his dotage. But when by no importunity he could prevail upon her to desist from her suit, for his oath's sake he must needs consent to the marriage. But the ceremony was no sooner, to the derision of all present, performed, than, with the just feelings of an outraged parent, he commanded the head of the presumptuous bridegroom to be stricken off, and committed the distracted princess close prisoner to her chamber, where, after many deadly swoonings, with intermingled outcries upon the cruelty of her father, she, in no long time after, died; making ineffectual appeals, to the last, to the mercy of the offended Power,—the Power that had laid its heavy hand upon her, to the bereavement of her good judgment first, and to the extinction of a life that might have proved a blessing to Lycia.

Leontius had scarcely time to be sensible of her danger before a fresh cause for mourning overtook him. His son Leucippus, who had hitherto been a pattern of strict life and modesty, was stricken with a second arrow from the deity, offended for his overturned altars, in which the prince had been a chief instrument. The god caused his heart to fall away, and his crazed fancy to be smitten with the excelling beauty of a wicked widow, by name Bacha. This woman, in the first days of her mourning for her husband, by her dissembling tears and affected coyness, had drawn Leucippus so cunningly into her snares, that, before she would grant him a return of love, she extorted from the easy-hearted prince a contract of marriage, to be fulfilled in the event of his father's death. This guilty intercourse, which they covered with the name of marriage, was not carried with such secrecy but that a rumour of it ran about the palace, and by some officious courtier was brought to the ears of the old duke, who, to satisfy himself of the truth, came hastily to the house of Bacha, where he found his son courting. Taking the prince to task roundly, he sternly asked who that creature was that had bewitched him out of his honour thus. Then Bacha, pretending ignorance of the duke's person, haughtily demanded of Leucippus what saucy old man that was, that without leave had burst into the house of an afflicted widow to hinder her paying her tears (as she pretended) to the dead. Then the duke declaring himself, and threatening her for having corrupted his son, giving her the reproachful terms of witch and sorceress, Leucippus mildly answered, that he "did her wrong." The bad woman, imagining that the prince for very fear would not betray their secret, now conceived a project of monstrous wickedness; which was no less than to ensnare the father with the same arts which had subdued the son, that she might no longer be a concealed wife, nor a princess only under cover, but, by a union with the old man, become at once the true and acknowledged Duchess of Lycia. In a posture of humility, she confessed her ignorance of the duke's quality; but, now she knew it, she besought his pardon for her wild speeches, which proceeded, she said, from a distempered head, which the loss of a dear husband had affected. He might command her life, she told him, which was now of small value to her. The tears which accompanied her words, and her mourning weeds (which, for a blind to the world, she had not yet cast off), heightening her beauty, gave a credence to her protestations of her innocence. But the duke continuing to assail her with reproaches, with a matchless confidence, assuming the air of injured virtue, in a somewhat lofty tone she replied, that though he were her sovereign, to whom in any lawful cause she was bound to submit, yet, if he sought to take away her honour, she stood up to defy him. *That*, she said, was a jewel dearer than any he could give her, which, so long as she should keep, she should esteem herself richer than all the princes of the earth that were without it. If the prince, his son, knew anything to her dishonour, let him tell it. And here she challenged Leucippus before his father to speak the worst of her. If he would, however, sacrifice a woman's character to please an unjust humour of the duke's, she saw no remedy, she said, now *he* was dead (meaning her late husband) that with *his* life would have defended her reputation.

Thus appealed to, Leucippus, who had stood a while astonished at her confident falsehoods, though ignorant of the full drift of them, considering that not the reputation only, but probably the life, of a woman whom he had so loved, and who had made such sacrifices to him of love and beauty, depended upon his absolute concealment of their contract, framed his mouth to a compassionate untruth, and with solemn asseverations confirmed to his father her assurances of her innocence. He denied not that with rich gifts he had assailed her virtue, but had found her relentless to his solicitations; that gold nor greatness had any power over her. Nay, so far he went on, to give force to the protestations of this artful woman, that he confessed to having offered marriage to her, which she, who scorned to listen to any second wedlock, had rejected.

All this while, Leucippus secretly prayed to Heaven to forgive him while he uttered these bold untruths; since it was for the prevention of a greater mischief only, and had no malice in it.

But, warned by the sad sequel which ensued, be thou careful, young reader, how in any case you tell a lie. Lie not, if any man but ask you "how you do," or "what o'clock it is." Be sure you make no false excuse to screen a friend that is most dear to you. Never let the most well intended falsehood escape your lips; for Heaven, which is entirely Truth, will make the seed which you have sown of untruth to yield miseries a thousand-fold upon yours, as it did upon the head of the ill-fated and mistaken Leucippus.

Leontius, finding the assurances of Bacha so confidently seconded by his son, could no longer withhold his belief; and, only forbidding their meeting for the future, took a courteous leave of the lady, presenting her at the same time with a valuable ring, in recompense, as he said, of the injustice which he had done her in his false surmises of her guiltiness. In truth, the surpassing beauty of the lady, with her appearing modesty, had made no less impression upon the heart of the fond old duke than they had awakened in the bosom of his more pardonable son. His first design was to make her his mistress; to the better accomplishing of which, Leucippus was dismissed from the court, under the pretext of some honourable employment abroad. In his absence, Leontius spared no offers to induce her to comply with his purpose. Continually he solicited her with rich offers, with messages, and by personal visits. It

was a ridiculous sight, if it were not rather a sad one, to behold this second and worst dotage, which by Cupid's wrath had fallen upon this fantastical *old new lover*. All his occupation now was in dressing and pranking himself up in youthful attire to please the eyes of his new mistress. His mornings were employed in the devising of trim fashions, in the company of tailors, embroiderers, and feather-dressers. So infatuated was he with these vanities, that, when a servant came and told him that his daughter was dead,—even she whom he had but lately so highly prized,—the words seemed spoken to a deaf person. He either could not or would not understand them; but, like one senseless, fell to babbling about the shape of a new hose and doublet. His crutch, the faithful prop of long aged years, was discarded; and he resumed the youthful fashion of a sword by his side, when his years wanted strength to have drawn it. In this condition of folly, it was no difficult task for the widow, by affected pretences of honour, and arts of amorous denial, to draw in this doting duke to that which she had all along aimed at,—the offer of his crown in marriage. She was now Duchess of Lycia! In her new elevation, the mask was quickly thrown aside, and the impious Bacha appeared in her true qualities. She had never loved the duke, her husband; but had used him as the instrument of her greatness. Taking advantage of his amorous folly, which seemed to gain growth the nearer he approached to his grave, she took upon her the whole rule of Lycia; placing and displacing, at her will, all the great officers of state; and filling the court with creatures of her own, the agents of her guilty pleasures, she removed from the duke's person the oldest and trusticst of his dependants.

Leucippus, who at this juncture was returned from his foreign mission, was met at once with the news of his sister's death and the strange wedlock of the old duke. To the memory of Hidaspes he gave some tears; but these were swiftly swallowed up in his horror and detestation of the conduct of Bacha. In his first fury, he resolved upon a full disclosure of all that had passed between him and his wicked step-mother. Again, he thought, by killing Bacha, to rid the world of a monster. But tenderness for his father recalled him to milder counsels. The fatal secret, nevertheless, sat upon him like lead, while he was determined to confide it to no other. It took his sleep away, and his desire of food; and, if a thought of mirth at any time crossed him, the dreadful truth would recur to check it, as if a messenger should have come to whisper to him of some friend's death. With difficulty he was brought to wish their highnesses faint joy of their marriage; and, at the first sight of Bacha, a friend was fain to hold his wrist hard to prevent him from fainting.

In an interview, which after, at her request, he had with her alone, the bad woman shamed not to take up the subject lightly; to treat as a trifle the marriage vow that had passed between them; and, seeing him sad and silent, to threaten him with the displeasure of the duke, his father, if by words or looks he gave any suspicion to the world of their dangerous secret. "What had happened," she said, "was by no fault of hers. People would have thought her mad if she had refused the duke's offer. She had used no arts to entrap his father. It was Leucippus' own resolute denial of any such thing as a contract having passed between them which had led to the proposal."

The prince, unable to extenuate his share of blame in the calamity, humbly besought her, that "since, by his own great fault, things had been brought to their present pass, she would only live honest for the future, and not abuse the credulous age of the old duke, as he well knew she had the power to do. For himself, seeing that life was no longer desirable to him, if his death was judged by her to be indispensable to her security, she was welcome to lay what trains she pleased to compass it, so long as she would only suffer his father to go to his grave in peace, since *he* had never wronged her."

This temperate appeal was lost upon the heart of Bacha, who from that moment was secretly bent upon effecting the destruction of Leucippus. Her project was, by feeding the ears of the duke with exaggerated praises of his son, to awaken a jealousy in the old man, that she secretly preferred Leucippus. Next, by wilfully insinuating the great popularity of the prince (which was no more, indeed, than the truth) among the Lycians, to instil subtle fears into the duke that his son had laid plots for circumventing his life and throne. By these arts she was working upon the weak mind of the duke almost to distraction, when, at a meeting concocted by herself between the prince and his father, the latter taking Leucippus soundly to task for these alleged treasons, the prince replied only by humbly drawing his sword, with the intention of laying it at his father's feet; and begging him, since he suspected him, to sheathe it in his own bosom, for of his life he had been long weary. Bacha entered at the crisis, and, ere Leucippus could finish his submission, with loud outcries alarmed the courtiers, who, rushing into the presence, found the prince with sword in hand indeed, but with far other intentions than this bad woman imputed to him, plainly accusing him of having drawn it upon his father! Leucippus was quickly disarmed; and the old duke, trembling between fear and age, committed him to close prison, from which, by Bacha's aims, he never should have come out alive but for the interference of the common people, who, loving their prince, and equally detesting Bacha, in a simultaneous mutiny arose, and rescued him from the hands of the officers.

The court was now no longer a place of living for Leucippus; and, hastily thanking his countrymen for his deliverance, which in his heart he rather deprecated than welcomed, as one that wished for death, he took leave of all court hopes, and, abandoning the palace, betook himself to a life of penitence in solitudes.

Not so secretly did he select his place of penance, in a cave among lonely woods and fastnesses, but that his retreat was traced by Bacha, who, baffled in her purpose, raging like some she-wolf, despatched an emissary of her own to destroy him privately.

There was residing at the court of Lycia, at this time, a young maiden, the daughter of Bacha by her first husband, who had hitherto been brought up in the obscurity of a poor country abode with an uncle, but whom Bacha now publicly owned, and had prevailed upon the easy duke to adopt as successor to the throne in wrong of the true heir, his suspected son Leucippus.

This young creature, Urania by name, was as artless and harmless as her mother was crafty and wicked. To the unnatural Bacha she had been an object of neglect and aversion; and for the project of supplanting Leucippus only had she fetched her out of retirement. The bringing-up of

Urania had been among country hinds and lasses: to tend her flocks or superintend her neat dairy had been the extent of her breeding. From her calling, she had contracted a pretty rusticity of dialect, which, among the fine folks of the court, passed for simplicity and folly. She was the unfittest instrument for an ambitious design that could be chosen; for her manners in a palace had a tinge still of her old occupation; and, to her mind, the lowly shepherdess's life was best.

Simplicity is oft a match for prudence: and Urania was not so simple but she understood that she had been sent for to court only in the prince's wrong; and in her heart she was determined to defeat any designs that might be contriving against her brother-in-law. The melancholy bearing of Leucippus had touched her with pity. This wrought in her a kind of love, which, for its object, had no further end than the well-being of the beloved. She looked for no return of it, nor did the possibility of such a blessing in the remotest way occur to her, —so vast a distance she had imaged between her lowly bringing-up and the courtly breeding and graces of Leucippus. Hers was no raging flame, such as had burned destructive in the bosom of poor Hidaspes. Either the vindictive god in mercy had spared this young maiden, or the wrath of the confounding *Cupid* was restrained by a higher Power from discharging the most ma-lignant of his arrows against the peace of so much innocence. Of the extent of her mother's malice she was too guileless to have entertained conjecture; but from hints and whispers, and, above all, from that tender watchfulness with which a true affection like Urania's tends the safety of its object,—fearing even where no cause for fear subsists,—she gathered that some danger was impending over the prince, and with simple heroism resolved to countermine the treason.

It chanced upon a day that Leucippus had been indulging his sad meditations in forests far from human converse, when he was struck with the appearance of a human being, so unusual in that solitude. There stood before him a seeming *youth*, of delicate appearance, clad in coarse and peasantly attire. "He was come," he said, "to seek out the prince, and to be his poor boy and servant, if he would let him."— "Alas! poor youth," replied Leucippus; "why do you follow me, who am as poor as you are?"— "In good faith," was his pretty answer, "I shall be well and rich enough, if you will but love me." And, saying so, he wept. The prince, admiring this strange attachment in a boy, was moved with compassion; and seeing him exhausted, as if with long travel and hunger, invited him in to his poor habitation, setting such refreshments before him as that barren spot afforded. But by no entreaties could he be prevailed upon to take any sustenance; and all that day, and for the two following, he seemed supported only by some gentle flame of love that was within him. He fed only upon the sweet looks and courteous entertainment which he received from Leucippus. Seemingly, he wished to die under the loving eyes of his master. "I cannot eat," he prettily said; "but I shall eat to-morrow."—"You will be dead by that time," replied Leucippus. "I shall be well then," said he; "since you will not love me." Then the prince asking him why he sighed so, "To think," was his innocent reply, "that such a fine man as you should die, and no gay lady love him."—"But you will love me," said Leucippus. "Yes, sure," said he, "till I die; and, when I am in heaven, I shall wish for you." "This is a love," thought the other, "that I never yet heard tell of. But come, thou art sleepy, child: go in, and I will sit with thee." Then, from some words which the poor youth dropped, Leucippus, suspecting that his wits were beginning to ramble, said, "What portends this?"— "I am not sleepy," said the youth; "but you are sad. I would that I could do anything to make you merry! Shall I sing?" But soon, as if recovering strength, "There is one approaching!" he wildly cried out. "Master, look to yourself!"

His words were true: for now entered, with provided weapon, the wicked emissary of Bacha, that we told of; and, directing a mortal thrust at the prince, the supposed boy, with a last effort, interposing his weak body, received it in his bosom, thanking the heavens in death that he had saved "so good a master."

Leucippus, having slain tho villain, was at leisure to discover, in the features of his poor servant, the countenance of his devoted sister-in-law! Through solitary and dangerous ways she had sought him in that disguise; and, finding him, seems to have resolved upon a voluntary death by fasting,—partly that she might die in the presence of her beloved, and partly that she might make known to him in death the love which she wanted boldness to disclose to him while living, but chiefly because she knew that, by her demise, all obstacles would be removed that stood between her prince and his succession to the throne of Lycia.

Leucippus had hardly time to comprehend the strength of love in his Urania, when a trampling of horses resounded through his solitude. It was a party of Lycian horsemen, that had come to seek him, dragging the detested Bacha in their train, who was now to receive the full penalty of her misdeeds. Amidst her frantic fury upon the missing of her daughter, the old duke had suddenly died, not without suspicion of her having administered poison to him. Her punishment was submitted to Leucippus, who was now, with joyful acclaims, saluted as the rightful Duke of Lycia. He, as no way moved with his great wrongs, but considering her simply as the parent of Urania, saluting her only by the title of "Wicked Mother," bade her to live. "That reverend title," he said, and pointed to the bleeding remains of her child, "must be her pardon. He would use no extremity against her, but leave her to Heaven." The hardened mother, not at all relenting at the sad spectacle that lay before her, but making show of dutiful submission to the young duke, and with bended knees approaching him, suddenly with a dagger inflicted a mortal stab upon him; and, with a second stroke stabbing herself, ended both their wretched lives.

Now was the tragedy of Cupid's wrath awfully completed; and, the race of Leontius failing in the deaths of both his children, the chronicle relates that, under their new duke, Ismenus, the offence to the angry Power was expiated; his statues and altars were, with more magnificence than ever, re-edified; and he ceased thenceforth from plaguing the land.

Thus far the pagan historians relate erring. But from this vain idol story a not unprofitable moral may be gathered against the abuse of the natural but dangerous *passion of love*. In the story of Hidaspes, we see the preposterous linking of beauty with deformity; of princely expectancies with mean and low conditions, in the case of the prince, her brother; and of decrepit age with youth, in the ill end of their doting father, Leontius. By their examples we are warned to decline all *unequal and ill-assorted unions*.

THE DEFEAT OF TIME;

OR, A TALE OF THE FAIRIES.

TITANIA and her moonlight elves were assembled under the canopy of a huge oak, that served to shelter them from the moon's radiance, which, being now at her full moon, shot forth intolerable rays,—intolerable, I mean, to the subtile texture of their little shadowy bodies,—but dispensing an agreeable coolness to us grosser mortals. An air of discomfort sate upon the queen and upon her courtiers. Their tiny friskings and gambols were forgot; and even Robin Goodfellow, for the first time in his little airy life, looked grave. For the queen had had melancholy forebodings of late, founded upon an ancient prophecy laid up in the records of Fairyland, that the date of fairy existence should be *then* extinct when men should cease to believe in them. And she knew how that the race of the Nymphs, which were her predecessors, and had been the guardians of the sacred floods, and of the silver fountains, and of the consecrated hills and woods, had utterly disappeared before the chilling touch of man's incredulity; and she sighed bitterly at the approaching fate of herself and of her subjects, which was dependent upon so fickle a lease as the capricious and ever-mutable faith of man. When, as if to realise her fears, a melancholy shape came gliding in, and *that* was—Time, who with his intolerable scythe mows down kings and kingdoms; at whose dread approach the fays huddled together as a flock of timorous sheep; and the most courageous among them crept into acorn-cups, not enduring the sight of that ancientest of monarchs. Titania's first impulse was to wish the presence of her false lord, King Oberon,—who was far away, in the pursuit of a strange beauty, a fay of Indian Land,—that with his good lance and sword, like a faithful knight and husband, he might defend her against Time. But she soon checked that thought as vain; for what could the prowess of the mighty Oberon himself, albeit the stoutest champion in Fairyland, have availed against so huge a giant, whose bald top touched the skies? So, in the mildest tone, she besought the spectre, that in his mercy he would overlook and pass by her small subjects, as too diminutive and powerless to add any worthy trophy to his renown. And she besought him to employ his resistless strength against the ambitious children of men, and to lay waste their aspiring works; to tumble down their towers and turrets, and the Babels of their pride,—fit objects of his devouring scythe,—but to spare her and her harmless race, who had no existence beyond a dream; frail objects of a creed that lived but in the faith of the believer. And with her little arms, as well as she could, she grasped the stern knees of Time; and, waxing speechless with fear, she beckoned to her chief attendants and maids of honour to come forth from their hiding-places, and to plead the plea of the fairies. And one of those small, delicate creatures came forth at her bidding, clad all in white like a chorister, and in a low, melodious tone, 'not louder than the hum of a pretty bee,—when it seems to be demurring whether it shall settle upon this sweet flower or that before it settles,—set forth her humble petition. "We fairies," she said, "are .the most inoffensive race that live, and least deserving to perish. It is we that have the care of all sweet melodies, that no discords may offend the sun, who is the great soul of music. We rouse the lark at morn; and the pretty Echoes, which respond to all the twittering choir, are of our making. Wherefore, great King of Years, as ever you have loved the music which is raining from a morning cloud sent from the messenger of day, the lark, as he mounts to heaven's gate, beyond the ken of mortals; or if ever you have listened with a charmed ear to the night-bird, that—

    "'In the flowery spring,
Amidst the leaves set, makes the thickets
    ring
Of her sour sorrows, sweetened with her
    song—'"

spare our tender tribes, and we will muffle up the sheep-bell for thee, that thy pleasure take no interruption whenever thou shalt listen unto Philomel."

And Time answered, that "he had heard that song too long; and he was even wearied with that ancient strain that recorded the wrong of Tereus. But, if she would know in what music Time delighted, it was, when sleep and darkness lay upon crowded cities, to hark to the midnight chime which is tolling from a hundred clocks, like the last knell over the soul of a dead world; or to the crush of the fall of some age-worn edifice, which is as the voice of himself when he disparteth kingdoms."

A second female fay took up the plea, and said, "We be the handmaids of the Spring, and tend upon the birth of all sweet buds: and the pastoral cowslips are our friends; and the pansies and the violets, like nuns; and the quaking harebell is in our wardship; and the hyacinth, once a fair youth, and dear to Phœbus."

Then Time made answer, in his wrath striking the harmless ground with his hurtful scythe, that "they must not think that he was one that cared for flowers, except to see them wither, and to take her beauty from the rose."

And a third fairy took up the plea, and said, "We are kindly things: and it is we that sit at evening, and shake rich odours from sweet bowers upon discoursing lovers, that seem to each other to be their own sighs; and we keep off the bat and the owl from their privacy, and the ill-boding whistler; and we flit in sweet dreams across the brains of infancy, and conjure up a smile upon its soft lips to beguile the careful mother, while its little soul is fled for a brief minute or two to sport with our youngest fairies."

Then Saturn (which is Time) made answer, that "they should not think that he delighted in tender babes, that had devoured his own, till foolish Rhea cheated him with a stone, which he swallowed, thinking it to be the infant Jupiter." And thereat, in token, he disclosed to view his enormous tooth, in which appeared monstrous dents left by that unnatural meal; and his great throat, that seemed capable of devouring up the earth and all its inhabitants at one meal. "And for lovers," he continued, "my delight is, with a hurrying hand to snatch them away from their love-meetings by stealth at nights; and, in absence, to stand like a motionless statue, or their leaden planet of mishap (whence I had my name), till I make their minutes seem ages."

Next stood up a male fairy, clad all in green, like a forester or one of Robin Hood's mates, and, doffing his tiny cap, said, "We are small foresters, that live in woods, training the young boughs in graceful intricacies, with blue snatches of the sky between: we frame all shady roofs and arches rude; and sometimes, when we are plying our tender hatchets, men say that the tapping woodpecker is nigh. And it is we that scoop the hollow cell of the squirrel, and carve quaint letters upon the rinds of trees, which in sylvan solitudes sweetly recall to the mind of the heat-oppressed swain, ere he lies down to slumber, the name of his fair one, dainty Aminta, gentle Rosalind, or chastest Laura, as it may happen."

Saturn, nothing moved with this courteous address, bade him be gone, or, "if he would be a woodman, to go forth and fell oak for the fairies' coffins which would forthwith be wanting. For himself, he took no delight in haunting the woods, till their golden plumage (the yellow leaves) were beginning to fall, and leave the brown-black limbs bare, like Nature in her skeleton dress."

Then stood up one of those gentle fairies that are good to man, and blushed red as any rose while he told a modest story of one of his own good deeds. "It chanced upon a time," he said, "that while we were looking cowslips in the meads, while yet the dew was hanging on the buds like beads, we found a babe left in its swathing-clothes,—a little sorrowful, deserted thing, begot of love, but begetting no love in others; guiltless of shame, but doomed to shame for its parents' offence in bringing it by indirect courses into the world. It was pity to see the abandoned little orphan left to the world's care by an unnatural mother. How the cold dew kept wetting its childish coats! and its little hair, how it was bedabbled, that was like gossamer! Its pouting mouth, unknowing how to speak, lay half opened like a rose-lipped shell; and its cheek was softer than any peach, upon which the tears, for very roundness, could not long dwell, but fell off, in clearness like pearls,—some on the grass, and some on his little hand; and some haply wandered to the little dimpled well under his mouth, which Love himself seemed to have planned out, but less for tears than for smilings. Pity it was, too, to see how the burning sun had scorched its helpless limbs; for it lay without shade or shelter, or mother's breast, for foul weather or fair. So, having compassion on its sad plight, my fellows and I turned ourselves into grasshoppers, and swarmed about the babe, making such shrill cries as that pretty little chirping creature makes in its mirth, till with our noise we attracted the attention of a passing rustic, a tender-hearted hind, who, wondering at our small but loud concert, strayed aside curiously, and found the babe, where it lay in the remote grass, and, taking it up, lapped it in his russet coat, and bore it to his cottage, where his wife kindly nurtured it till it grew up a goodly personage. How this babe prospered afterwards, let proud London tell. This was that famous Sir Thomas Gresham, who was the chiefest of her merchants, the richest, the wisest.

Witness his many goodly vessels on the Thames, freighted with costly merchandise, jewels from Ind, and pearls for courtly dames, and silks of Samarcand. And witness, more than all, that stately Bourse (or Exchange) which he caused to be built, a mart for merchants from east and west, whose graceful summit still bears, in token of the fairies' favours, his chosen crest, the grasshopper. And, like the grasshopper, may it please you, great king, to suffer us also to live, partakers of the green earth!"

The fairy had scarce ended his plea, when a shrill cry, not unlike the grasshopper's, was heard. Poor Puck—or Robin Goodfellow, as he is sometimes called—had recovered a little from his first fright, and, in one of his mad freaks, had perched upon the beard of old Time, which was flowing, ample, and majestic; and was amusing himself with plucking at a hair, which was indeed so massy, that it seemed to him that he was removing some huge beam of timber, rather than a hair; which Time by some ill chance perceiving, snatched up the impish mischief with his great hand, and asked what it was.

"Alas!" quoth Puck, "a little random elf am I, born in one of Nature's sports; a very weed, created for the simple, sweet enjoyment of myself, but for no other purpose, worth, or need, that ever I could learn. 'Tis I that bob the angler's idle cork, till the patient man is ready to breathe a curse. I steal the morsel from the gossip's fork, or stop the sneezing chanter in mid psalm; and when an infant has been born with hard or homely features, mothers say I changed the child at nurse: but to fulfil any graver purpose I have not wit enough, and hardly the will. I am a pinch of lively dust to frisk upon the wind: a tear would make a puddle of me; and so I tickle myself with the lightest straw, and shun all griefs that might make me stagnant. This is my small philosophy."

Then Time, dropping him on the ground, as a thing too inconsiderable for his vengeance, grasped fast his mighty scythe: and now, not Puck alone, but the whole state of fairies, had gone to inevitable wreck and destruction, had not a timely apparition interposed, at whose boldness Time was astounded; for he came not with the habit or the forces of a deity, who alone might cope with Time, but as a simple mortal, clad as you might see a forester that hunts after wild conies by the cold moonshine; or a stalker of stray deer, stealthy and bold. But by the golden lustre in his eye, and the passionate wanness in his cheek, and by the fair and ample space of his forehead, which seemed a palace framed for the habitation of all glorious thoughts, he knew that this was his great rival, who had power given him to rescue whatsoever victims Time should clutch, and to cause them to live for ever in his immortal verse. And, muttering the name of Shakspeare, Time spread his roc-like wings, and fled the controlling presence; and the liberated court of the fairies, with Titania at their head, flocked around the gentle ghost, giving him thanks, nodding to him, and doing him courtesies, who had crowned them henceforth with a permanent existence, to live in the minds of men, while verse shall have power to charm, or midsummer moons shall brighten.

* * * * *

What particular endearments passed between the fairies and their poet, passes my pencil to delineate; but, if you are curious to be informed, I must refer you, gentle reader, to the "Plea of the Midsummer Fairies," a most agreeable poem lately put forth by my friend Thomas Hood; of the first half of which the above is nothing but a meagre and harsh prose abstract. Farewell!

The words of Mercury are harsh after the songs of Apollo.

A DEATH-BED.

IN A LETTER TO B. H., ESQ.,
OF B——.

I called upon you this morning, and found that you were gone to visit a dying friend. I had been upon a like errand. Poor N. R. has lain dying now for almost a week; such is the penalty we pay for having enjoyed through life a strong constitution. Whether he knew me or not, I know not, or whether he saw me through his poor glazed eyes; but the group I saw about him I shall not forget. Upon the bed, or about it, were assembled his wife, their two daughters, and poor deaf Robert, looking doubly stupified. There they were, and seemed to have been sitting all the week. I could only reach out a hand to Mrs. R. Speaking was impossible in that mute chamber. By this time it must be all over with him. In him I have a loss the world cannot make up. He was my friend, and my father's friend, for all the life that I can remember. I seem to have made foolish friendships since. Those are the friendships, which outlast a second generation. Old as I am getting, in his eyes I was still the child he knew me. To the last he called me Jemmy. I have none to call me Jemmy now. He was the last link that bound me to B——. You are but of yesterday. In him I seem to have lost the old plainness of manners and singleness of heart. Lettered he was not; his reading scarcely exceeded the obituary of the old "Gentleman's Magazine," to which he has never failed of having recourse for these last fifty years. Yet there was the pride of literature about him from that slender perusal; and, moreover, from his office of archive-keeper to your ancient city, in which he must needs pick up some equivocal Latin; which, among his less literary friends, assumed the air of a very pleasant pedantry. Can I forget the erudite look with which, having tried to puzzle out the text of a black-lettered Chaucer in your Corporation Library, to which he was a sort of librarian, he gave it up with this consolatory reflection—"Jemmy," said he, "I do not know what you find in these very old books, but I observe there is a deal of very indifferent spelling in them." His jokes (for he had some) are ended; but they were old perennials, staple, and always as good as new. He had one song, that spake of the "flat bottoms of our foes coming over in darkness," and alluded to a threatened invasion, many years since blown over; this he reserved to be sung on Christmas night, which we always passed with him, and he sang it with the freshness of an impending event. How his eyes would sparkle when he came to the passage:—

> "We'll still make 'em run, and we'll still
> make 'em sweat,
> In spite of the devil and Brussels'
> Gazette!"

What is the "Brussels' Gazette" now? I cry, while I endite these trifles. His poor girls, who are, I believe, compact of solid goodness, will have to receive their afflicted mother at an unsuccessful home in a petty village in ——shire, where for years they have been struggling to raise a girls' school with no effect. Poor deaf Robert (and the less hopeful for being so) is thrown upon a deaf world, without the comfort to his father on his death-bed of knowing him provided for. They are left almost provisionless. Some life assurance there is; but, I fear, not exceeding——. Their hopes must be from your corporation, which their father has served for fifty years. Who or what are your leading members now, I know not. Is there any, to whom, without impertinence, you can represent the true circumstances of the family? You cannot say good enough of poor R. and his poor wife. Oblige me and the dead, if you can.

THE END.